Miracle on Christmas Street

Annie spent most of her childhood with a leg draped over the family rocking chair and a book in her hand. Novels, baking and writing gallons of teenage angst poetry ate up most of her youth. Now, Annie splits her time between corralling her husband into helping her with their cows, begging her bees to show her the honey, reading, audio book binging in the veg patch and spending some very happy hours writing. She has written over twenty category romances for Mills & Boon, Harlequin Romance, one of which won the RoNA Rose Award.

Miracle on Christmas Street

Annie O'Neil

ORION

An Orion paperback

First published in Great Britain in 2020 by Orion Books,
an imprint of The Orion Publishing Group Ltd
Carmelite House, 50 Victoria Embankment,
London EC4Y 0DZ

An Hachette UK company

1 3 5 7 9 10 8 6 4 2

A CIP catalogue record for this book is
available from the British Library.

ISBN (Mass Market Paperback) 978 1 3987 0048 2
ISBN (eBook) 978 1 3987 0049 9

Typeset at The Spartan Press Ltd,
Lymington, Hants

Printed and bound in Great Britain by Clays Ltd,
Elcograf S.p.A.

www.orionbooks.co.uk

This is for Tormod, my very own Kris Kringle.

Black Friday

367 days ago

Jess spied the glowing Santa from across the heaving shop floor. Plastic, cherry-cheeked, his chubby little red-suited body cosily nestled among frosted fronds of fake evergreen, garish holly berries and Day-Glo snowflakes. The wreath screamed holiday kitsch. A glorious combination of the best and worst in Yuletide decor.

It was exactly what she wanted.

Needed? Not so much. But need wasn't what Black Friday shopping was about, was it? In fact, now that she thought about it, squished, as she had been for the past hour in a not entirely friendly queue of shoppers waiting for the security guards to unlock the front doors of Urban Outfitters, greed *crushed* need on days like this. Disheartening? Yes. Something she was going to worry about? Not today. No, today Jess was actively engaging every fibre of her being and, more pressingly, the remains of her dwindling bank account, into making her life look perfect so that, eventually, it would feel perfect. Then, and only then, would the dark suspicion that things had gone completely off track go away.

Who knew a cheese sandwich could wreak so much havoc in a prep-schoolteacher's life?

The increasingly familiar prickling of tears stung at the back of her throat.

Anyway.

She gave the Santa wreath an *I see you* smile.

Did he . . . ? Did Santa just *wink* at her? Well, wasn't this a lovely turn of events? Day-Glo Santa was complicit in her plan to use consumerism to elevate her mood during her enforced absence from work. She locked eyes with him.

Okay, Santa. It's you and me, pal.

Charged with determination and humming 'Have Yourself a Kitschy Little Christmas', Jess began shouldering her way through the crowd of wired shoppers. It was dog eat dog, as if everyone had downed fourteen shots of espresso before the shop doors had opened and then charged in, indiscriminately stuffing their baskets full of on-trend baubles, crocheted 'paper' chains and seasonally accented mini-cactus gardens as if their lives depended upon it. A woman came barrelling past her hauling a gin-filled advent calendar. An eye-wateringly high price tag was swinging from its adorable drawers, no doubt hand-painted by a virginal Laplander under the light of the North Star. The tag told her the calendar was worth her entire month's rent. A princely sum for some airline-sized bottles of gin stuffed into a wooden tree.

Not that she was judging.

Homewares were important. Soft furnishings and just-so knick-knacks had the power to turn a house into a home. She should know. Living in an immaculate testament to charcoal, chrome and glass made her a bit of an expert on what did and didn't work. (#LifeLessonNumberOne:

Don't let your estate-agent boyfriend convince you that living in his company's executive show flat in exchange for discounted rent is a good idea. No knickers hung over the radiator. Ever.)

Two steps forward, one step back. Progress was slow. As pathetic as it seemed, she really, really needed this wreath. It was a symbol. A prize that would remind her that she could and would get her life back under her control. Sure, pinning her entire future on a garish Santa wreath was verging on insane, but crisis points were like that. Sometimes the smallest things made the biggest difference. And in this case, it was one very kitsch Kristopher Kringle.

After a fair amount of shoulder-bashing (there would be bruises) she was finally within grabbing distance. There was only the one wreath left. And it had her name on it.

An immaculately manicured hand appeared in her peripheral vision. There were teensy-tiny, ornately decorated Christmas baubles tastefully dotting each nail. All five of which were reaching for Santa.

N-o-o-o-o-o-o-o-o-o-o-o-o-o-o-o!

Jess stretched forward, intent on getting her own nibbled-to-the-nub fingernails onto Santa first. The second she gained purchase she felt the other woman's hand do the same. She looked up and locked eyes with her opponent.

Oh, great.

She looked exactly like a mum from her school. Ex-school? She'd find out next week once the Head had 'examined the evidence' with the schools' board of governors. Ignoring the churning in her gut, she focused on the task at hand. She could do this. In the teacher's lounge, this type of wife was not-so-quietly referred to as Model Number Two. Model Number One was always a first, and long-term, wife. She was often a judge, hedge-fund manager, or 'kitchen table' gazillionaire who regularly held fundraisers for the rainforest or the tribal peoples of Papua New Guinea. Model Number Two was, more often than not, a second and far more indulged wife. She was almost always married to a dot.com mogul or an ageing rock star. She was generally about half his age (check), had long, ash-blond hair in ripply sheets of pre-Raphaelite perfection (check), wore Lululemon and a knee-length Puffa jacket which swaddled her tiny, perfect, personally trained body straight down to her Alexander McQueen Runway Platform trainers or whatever was *de rigueur* that season (check). This particular variation on Number Two had amazing eyes. Almost unnaturally blue. Azure? Cerulean? Tinted contacts. Had to be. Nothing that perfect was real. The woman's tropical sea-coloured peepers were semi-hooded. A snake about to strike. Her smile, such as it was, was so insincere that there was little doubt it had been stuck in place by her discreet, but highly recommendable facial-contouring specialist. Her eyeshadow and eyeliner were immaculate. Her skin fresh and dewy like a peach. For a moment Jess faltered. Appearances weren't everything. Maybe the smile was actually the strain of a beleaguered stepmother trying to put together a perfect Christmas for her newly inherited family of belligerent tweens.

Jess felt the wreath being tugged away from her. The woman had clearly sensed Jess's momentary lapse in war mode. Right. Screw her and her fictional family. Plastic Santa was hers.

Jess narrowed her eyes. What would she make of this woman if it was parent–teacher conference day?

Number Two looked exactly like the mum who'd insisted Jess be 'sent a strong message' about her failure to maintain control in a school environment. Number Two wouldn't listen to reason. To *facts*. Number Two didn't care that teaching was not only Jess's livelihood, but her vocation, and that being fired would pretty much ruin her life. Jess didn't like Number Two at all. She ground her heels in. Dug deep. And rejoined the battle.

She dropped her gaze to half-mast, blurring the rest of the shop into a fairy-light, tinsel-laced snow-globe of motion as a core-deep determination gripped her very essence. Kitschy Santa was hers. She deserved him. No way was Number Two going to take yet another thing away from her.

'Sorry,' Jess said, grip tightening to white-knuckle level. 'I think I had this first.'

'No, I'm sorry,' the woman said in an adorable Irish accent (because weren't all Irish accents adorable?). 'It's just... it's for my mum. My elderly mum. In a care home. I was pretty sure I spotted it first... if you don't mind.'

Likely story. Her mum couldn't have been older than sixty. Unless she'd given birth when she was fifty. Which meant the likelihood that this woman's mum was mouldering away in a care home was minimal. Sorry, Number Two. Better luck next time!

'I do hate to be contrary,' Jess gave an apologetic shake of the head. 'It's just... my little nephew's in hospital.' Her cheeks pinked. A show of grief, she hoped, rather than her tell. She always blushed when she lied. She neither had a nephew, nor was the imaginary little soul in hospital.

Something hardened in Number Two's eyes. 'What's his name?'

Uhhh . . . 'Tim.'

'Just Tim?' Number Two asked, eyes narrowing further.

What was this? Villanelle Does Christmas?

'Tiny Tim.'

Crap.

'I mean . . . that's his nickname. Because he's little. I'm sure he'll grow out of it. We all are. He's a Green. Like me. Tiny Tim Green.'

'Your nephew is called Tiny Tim.' It wasn't a question. It was an accusation.

'That's right.' Jess readjusted her stance. This was not going to end nicely.

'My mum has early onset dementia.' Number Two countered. 'Has done since she was ten.'

What? No. Surely not. Number Two was a liar, liar pants on fire.

'My nephew doesn't have legs. Or kidneys.'

Number Two's nose crinkled as if she was trying to figure out if that was a thing. It was, but only if you were dead. A wave of uneasiness crashed through the nutmeg latte sloshing around Jess's stomach. Lying about dying children was a sure-fire way to get smote by lightning. Not a wise thing to do seeing as, even though her life was pants, she wanted to live. Doubly bad if Number Two's mum genuinely was grasping at the remains of her memories and a 1950s-style Day-Glo Santa wreath was the only way to relive that one, precious holiday. Again, the scratchy raw tug of tears hit the back of her throat.

Oh, dear God, no. She wasn't actually going to cry, was she? It had been a horrific week. And the weeks to come were bound to be worse, but... she'd found Santa. That meant something, right?

Number Two gave the wreath a tug. She clearly thought she'd won.

Jess tugged back. She didn't want to lose. Or cry. Santa had *winked* at her, for heaven's sake!

Number Two gave it proper yank. So hard Jess lost her footing. Arms windmilling, she slipped on a felt avocado tree decoration and fell backwards crashing straight into the supply of – oh, ouch – Christmas-themed cacti. Had to be. Nothing else would hurt this much. When she eventually stood up, if she ever stood up again, there would be mini cacti attached to her bum, her back, her shoulders. Her not so puffy winter coat was proving to be the perfect cacti pin-cushion. Number Two gave a quick *sorry, not sorry* shrug then disappeared into the crowd. A security guard was approaching. A couple of shoppers were tsking and not-so-silently discussing greed and where it got you.

Suddenly, more than anything, Jess wanted out. Away from strings of chili-pepper lights and beyond-trend Christmas tree ornaments. Away from the bash bash bash of shoppers' shoulders as they barrelled down Oxford Street. Away from all of the London-centric hopes and dreams of being the glitterati's most sought-after prep-school teacher. Clarity came to her as vividly as the un-expected acupuncture session in her posterior. She needed a change. To extract herself from the off-the-barometer expectations of the life she kept telling herself she should be living. There was only one way to do it. She had to

7

remove herself from the whole Darwinian survival thing that existed here. A form of day-to-day life that meant eye contact was dangerous, making new friends was next to impossible and getting a job that paid enough to live in a home where she could hang her knickers out to dry whenever she wanted wasn't laughable. She wanted to be somewhere more... Somewhere where she could storm out of her home and into the next-door neighbour's and demand a cup of tea. Then get it. Somewhere, in short, that wasn't London.

1 December

So this was it. Moving day.

Jess's nerves ratcheted up a notch. The van carrying all of her worldly possessions had just flicked its indicator on as they approached the roundabout at the top of her new high street. It was hard to tell if her body was zinging with happy nerves or oh-no-I've-ruined-everything nerves. She'd been treading a fine line between the two for the past year now. Today she'd find out which would win the battle for supremacy.

The moving van slipped onto the roundabout ahead of her, happily trundling into her new life as if it didn't have a care in the world. She scanned the roundabout. No traffic. She could cut and run. Double back and... go where? Her only choice was the future she'd laid out for herself. New town, new home, new job. It was that or... Or nothing. She flicked on the indicator and made the turn.

Here it was. The heart of Boughton (pronounced 'Bow-town', like a town with a ribbon round it, she was chirpily informed by the estate agent, not 'Buffton'). Her new forever home. Insofar as forever lasted these days. A few streets further along, a 'bijou' semi-detached house was waiting for her, clapping its freshly painted shutters in glee that she was, after extensive dithering, finally going to move in. By herself. To embark on a brand-new life of spinsterhood and woe.

Now, Jess . . . she heard her mother's voice caution.

She regrouped. Of course the rest of her life wouldn't be mired in solitude and despair. It would be filled with joy and discovery. The delight of reclaiming the Jess she once was and prayed she could be again. At least that's what she'd told her parents as they, too, had packed up their bags and set off for their own voyage of discovery. In hindsight, it had been a really dumb thing to say. She should've been honest. She should've told them she was bricking it, and wanted them to be with her as she unpacked her old life into her new one. It had all seemed so achievable a week ago, but now that they were gone? The thought of opening the door to her new house was beginning to develop its own soundtrack and it had lots of minor chords in it.

Her lungs strained against a need for more oxygen. She was going to have a panic attack. No she wasn't. Yes she was. Tennineeightsevensixfivefourthreetwoone . . . annnnnnnd breathe. It was fine. She was fine. She would grow to love her new life exactly the way women grew to love their husbands in an arranged marriage. Especially if the guy was hot.

She forced herself to look around. There was an old-fashioned butcher's, a lovely little bakery, a small cinema that served wine instead of popcorn. What wasn't to love? Three perfect places amid the usual jolly jumble of charity shops, restaurants and newsagents topping and tailing the street. All of which looked . . . different. She squinted, trying to figure out why. It was definitely more twinkly here in Boughton than she remembered. Yes. Something had definitely changed. It was almost seven-thirty which meant it had been pitch black for hours now. Which suggested everything should be shut and shuttered unless...

Did they have late-night shopping in places that weren't London?

She pulled on her brake as the moving van and a Hovis truck played a delicate slow-motion game of inching past one another.

Wait a minute. She got it now. Boughton looked like it had been set-dressed for one of those cheesy Christmas movies.

Though part of her bristled at all the festive, carefree joy, there was another part that softened, loving the twinkly lights and promise of delights yet to come.

The bakery (which had ridiculously moreish cinnamon rolls) had augmented its window display with a huge gingerbread house. The Chinese takeaway (number four on her list of requirements for a new town) had garlanded its steamed-up window with some well-loved tinsel (read: old, but serviceable) and the butcher's had an *Order Now!* sign complete with a row of turkeys doing the cancan. Strung overhead was an abundance of seasonal lights. They weren't as flashy as the ones in London, but something about the understated strands of multicoloured bulbs and long swags of holly-sprigged garlands spoke of a gentler time when Christmas was more about family and less about climbing over complete strangers to get a Black Friday deal at Urban Outfitters.

It should've made her heart sing. To know she was moving to a place that valued the true spirit of the holiday over Day-Glo Santa wreaths. But the simple truth was, she hadn't really got into the Christmas vibe yet. Most years she was all 'Bring on the mistletoe!' This year? Not so much. This year the mistletoe could suck it.

The cinema came into view after she too inched her way past the Hovis truck and its huge picture of an old-fashioned Santa eating a piece of toast. She glanced up at the marquee. It was playing *It's A Wonderful Life*.

Of course it was.

Was it though? Really? Was this her wonderful life?

New house, new job, new haircut, even. They should all be reasons to be absolutely giddy with excitement, but...

She simply didn't know any more. Having had her confidence bodily ripped out of her 367 days ago (yes, she was counting), she wasn't sure whether her favourite holiday was wonderful any more, let alone her entire life. Christmas wasn't about joy and generosity and welcoming people into your heart. Not in London anyway. There it felt like a competition. A time to out-decorate, out-shop, out-photocopy her bum at the best Christmas staff party ever. If she'd been invited to one. Which she hadn't.

She could still try and like the month, she supposed. It wasn't December's fault it was Christmas. December meant winter clothes, which were genuinely her favourite. Her carefully chosen Making A Good First Impression On Moving Day ensemble comprised a jumper with a fox on it, its ears cheekily peeking out from beneath her thick corduroy dungarees, the rolled-up hems of which skidded the tops of her very practical Chelsea boots (complete with white faux-fur lining), a scarlet knit hat with a huge fluffy snowball of a pompom on top, *and* a brand-new set of house keys in the pocket of her I-Practically-Live-In-The-Countryside-But-Not-Really waxed jacket her parents had given her as an early Christmas present because they wouldn't be here for the day itself. Their first apart.

The reality was, this Christmas was one to get through rather than one to be excited for. She had loads of cleaning and organising and unpacking to do and before she knew it, the month would be over, the new year would begin and then she could officially begin to love all the months every bit as much as she knew she was going to love living on Christmas Street.

That's what she'd tell herself anyway.

As she drove past the shop owners turning their open signs to closed, she ran through her Moving Day Plan. Jess loved a plan.

Once she and the movers found her new house, she'd help them carry in her hodgepodge of possessions (half pillaged from her parents, half Ikea.) Helping would not only fill her with endorphins, it would reduce the hourly rate the movers were charging and, with no proper pay cheque coming in until end of January, she was keen to make savings wherever she could. Once the van was unpacked, she would pour the moving lads a celebratory mug of hot chocolate (already in a Thermos on the front passenger seat alongside a cardboard box with three mugs and a few other provisions), after which, she'd give them a jaunty salute and wave them on their merry way, at which juncture – hair freshly tousled, cheeks flushed with exertion – she'd close the door, lean against it and gaze at her new home in delight. The front doorbell would ring. She'd open it only to discover a deeply gorgeous (but not too gorgeous) neighbour standing there. His lightly distressed handyman coveralls would give glimpses of his lean, Diet-Coke-break body as his tool belt shifted sexily along his hips. He'd announce he was a builder by trade (or an artisan craftsman, she dithered on this point). He'd offer to help her put together any Ikea furniture she might have – a desk, a drinks trolley and a bed, which they would save for last. When they finished (merrily sharing life stories minus all of her humiliations of the previous year), the grandmotherly neighbour she imagined living on the other side of her terraced house would appear with a welcome basket filled with baked goods still warm from the oven.

On second thought, she'd scrap Diet-Coke-break neighbour and settle for granny neighbour and her basket of buns. She was woman enough to put her own rivets into her own sockets, or however it was you assembled a bed by numbers. She was a primary schoolteacher, for heaven's sake. She'd once built an entire nativity out of loo rolls and glitter. Surely she could stick a few bits of wood and metal together. Had her self-confidence dropped that low?

Ooo! An Ocado van. Not so 'out in the middle of nowhere' after all. She made a quick mental note to text Amanda, her one remaining teacher friend from London. She could happily assure her she would still have ready access to samphire, golden beetroots and charcoal ginger shots despite the move out of London. Not that she ever bought any of those things when she'd been there, but Amanda had drunkenly insisted, as they'd shared their final farewell bottle of Pinot just under a year ago, that life outside of London would be horrid. Where, she'd asked, would Jess find a cosmo that didn't come in an M&S can?

Good friend that she was, Amanda was still hoping Jess would return. Make a fresh start at another elite school. But... she couldn't. Too much damage had been done.

Besides, Amanda had been wrong about the cosmos. She'd made plenty at her parents' where she'd retreated after her ignominious firing. It had been quite pleasant, in fact. Licking her wounds in close proximity to their drinks cabinet right up until they refused to replace the empty vodka and Cointreau bottles. And then her parents had unexpectedly sold their house after two years of it being on the market and were given their first assignment with Dentists Sans Frontiers (#NotItsRealName). Right about now, they would be slapping on the factor 90, pulling molars and excavating root canals on the Marshall Islands. Which were, if anyone was curious, about as far away from civilisation as could be. Hence the need for free dental care.

They'd said they'd change their plans. Or bring her with them, if she wanted. They were loving and wonderful like that, but in all honesty Jess wanted to be alone. She had wounds that needed tending to. Aspirations to recentre. Her first Christmas alone to get through without wanting to garrotte herself.

She pulled the packet of biscuits she'd been eyeing from the box in the front seat and tore it open. Whoever said a Wagon Wheel didn't make life better hadn't lived.

Jess frowned at her still slightly unfamiliar reflection in the wing mirror. Her last (and only?) act of London daring had been to visit Amanda's stylist and ask for a Claudia Winkleman/Audrey Hepburn-esque fringe. Neither effect had been achieved, but the new fringe gave her something to do with the GHDs her mother had given her when they'd moved to the land of no electricity. Getting the new coif was her way of saying thank you to Amanda for landing her a month's freelance work that would tide her over until her new job began. The gig was for an office supplies company that needed lively blurbs describing the new products in their spring catalogue. There'd be more work if she proved her mettle, and, as her evenings would be free of girlfriend duties now that she was single, fifty shades of paperclips was her destiny.

All of a sudden, as if the journey hadn't been more than the blink of an eye, the moving van pulled over, an arm came out of its window gesturing that she should go ahead, and then, for the first time ever, Jess turned onto Christmas Street as a resident.

A huge white splat crashed against her windscreen.

What the hell?

She yanked the emergency brake because, if she wasn't mistaken, she'd just driven from a clear starry-nighted Britain into a very intense suburban blizzard. She leapt out of the car only to be hit straight in the face with a . . . was that a snowball?

'Sorry!' A male voice called as she blinked away icy fractals of snow. Snow that seemed determined to cling to her hastily applied mascara just in case a freak event occurred and an actual, genuine neighbour popped by to welcome her to the street.

A man came into view as she continued to blink away the snow, failing to slow her hammering heart. She saw his shoes first, trendy trousers second, a very nice quilted jacket third and . . . hmmm . . . He was quite clearly trying not to laugh. 'I'm so, *so* sorry,' he said in a lovely, sing-songy voice that instantly made this peculiar form of welcome not so awful after all. 'We're just...' He swivelled round and put his arms out as if he had just flung open the doors to a magic kingdom and... in a way he had.

It was snowing on Christmas Street. Big huge fluffy flakes of snow floating down from the starry sky above. Ermmm... starry sky? Could it snow when—

Another man ran up – slight, Asian and very beautiful. He slipped his arm round man number one's waist. 'Oh my God, we're so totally sorry.' His eyes flicked to the moving van now idling behind her car. 'Are you the newcomer for number fourteen?'

'Yes?'

Jess actually knew the answer to that, so why had it come out as a question?

'We're Kai and Rex,' the Asian man explained, complete with hand gestures. 'Rex can't throw for toffee. I hope you're all right. We'll send flowers. We own a florist's so don't even try to stop us. Can you get your car down the street? It's all a bit...' He fluttered his hand down the cul-de-sac, which was well lit enough to show the street was entirely covered in snow. Except for the roofs. And some of the gardens. In fact, most of the gardens were bare. Why was it only snowing on the street?

'Hi! Hi, doll. You must be Jess... Green was it?'

A very attractively put-together Australian woman joined their small group. Shiny black hair, evergreen-coloured eyes, and an immaculate Snow White complexion, she looked as though she'd just stepped out of a winter-wear catalogue. The type that made snowball fights look fun rather than the cold, slightly assault-y experience Jess had just had.

The woman put out her hand. 'Drea. Drea Zamboni. I'm at number one.' She pointed at the large brick semi-detached house across the street from where Jess had pulled her car to a halt. A huge snow machine was parked on the pavement in front of the postage-stamp-sized front garden. Enormous plumes of glittering snow were arcing up and over them. Drea put a seasonally manicured hand on Jess's arm. 'I bribed the estate agent to give me your name.' She winked, then gave Jess a smile that some might have interpreted as sinister.

Jess's stomach lurched. This was all a mistake. She should turn around now before discovering the residents of Christmas Street were all vampires or zombies or whatever was worse than vampires or zombies. Wombats? Could wombats be evil? Maybe watching *Game of Thrones* before she'd packed up her laptop hadn't been the best of ideas.

'Kidding.' Drea laughed. 'I didn't bribe him with anything. The man's as loose-lipped as a nun's knickers on Boxing Day.'

Jess opened her mouth to say she was pretty sure that wasn't a saying but Drea was on a roll.

'Sorry about all of the hoo-hah. You're more than welcome to join in. In fact,' she held up a bottle of Australian Chenin blanc and grinned, 'we insist upon it.'

Jess shook her head, not entirely comprehending what was happening on the 'quiet, peaceful cul-de-sac' she'd been promised when she'd signed on the dotted line.

A snow machine, Drea the Australian, Rex and Kai the florists . . . and, further down the street, what appeared to be full-on snowball warfare.

Oh, no. Winter *was* coming.

'C'mon.' Drea's bright green eyes were on Jess as she flicked her hand in a way that indicated the men should turn round and go back to the battleground. Which they did. Who *was* this woman and what power did she wield over the neighbourhood? 'I know it seems a bit mad now, but it's all good fun really.'

'Ermm . . . if you don't mind my asking, what is it, exactly?'

Drea's smile brightened as if she were about to launch into an infomercial. 'It's the first annual Christmas Street Living Advent Calendar.'

Jess's eyebrows went up another notch. 'And that is . . . ?'

'We're Christmas Street, right?'

'Yes . . .' Jess answered slowly, still uncertain as to where this was heading.

'There are twenty-four houses on the street . . .' Drea paused and gave one of those nods that indicated she thought Jess should be catching up about now. When she didn't, Drea spelled it out. 'We were originally going to go for the "put an image up in your front window", but I thought it'd be far more festive if we opened our doors to each other. You know. Like in an actual neighbourhood? Everyone was always asking me if life in Australia was just like *Neighbours*.'

Jess raised her eyebrows. That'd be kind of cool. She glanced around wondering if Susan and Karl were standing by to do triage on the next snowball victim.

Drea snorted. 'It totally isn't, but it's a damn site more neighbourly than it is here, so here's my little stab at bringing some homespun joy to Christmas Street. Right, doll,' her voice shifted to the cheery but strict tone a flight attendant used when they were telling exit-aisle passengers how to pull the doors open and make sure no one wore their stilettos as they slid down the inflatable ramp, 'here's how it's going to work. Each house hosts a little surprise every day until Christmas as if our doors were doors to an actual advent calendar.'

Jess shook her head, still not entirely understanding.

Drea turned Jess towards the cul-de-sac and clicked her thumb against her knuckle as if pressing the button on a PowerPoint presentation control. 'There are twenty-four houses and twenty-four days in the lead-up to Christmas. Each day, the house number corresponding with the day of the month will throw open its doors and give the street a little Yuletide surprise, just like an advent calendar gives you a choccy or a picture of a doll or an artisan vodka, right? Easy-peasy puddin' and pie. We've all got our assignments, so all we have to do now is let the fun begin.'

Jess goldfished for a minute, not entirely sure how to respond. She'd barely said hello to her neighbours in London, let alone thrown open her doors to the entire building. A decade of 'thou shalt not be friendly to thy neighbour' was hard to shake. Especially when this one seemed so full on. Saying that... it did look like everyone was having fun.

Drea continued in her cheery but matter-of-fact way, 'I'm number one, as I said. We've got the snow, of course, to kick things off properly and...' she pointed towards her doorstep where Jess noticed a barbecue smoking away, '...we've got loads of shrimp on the barbie to remind us – *me* – a little bit of home. Christmas is what you grow up with, am I right?'

Jess had grown up with family and mince pies and a

stocking that always had a Chocolate Orange in it. Would she have to give everyone who lived here a Chocolate Orange?

'You're number fourteen, so you've got a couple of weeks to come up with something fun,' Drea said, as if she'd gained access to the Chocolate Orange idea and was dismissing it.

'Two weeks . . .' Jess echoed as she looked round at the street – *her* street – aglow with lights, frosted with snowflakes, filled with people laughing and hurling snowballs at one another. It was then that she felt the first stirrings of the festive magic she thought had died in her last year.

Another snowball hit her. On the knee this time.

Rex shouted, 'Sorry, darling!' He gave Kai a playful wag of the finger. 'Be nice to Jess! Santa's keeping track of all this, you know.'

'Come on, love. Join in. You're part of the street now.' Drea gave her a half hug and lifted up her wine bottle in a toast. 'You're one of us!'

Just as Jess's foot finally hit the first step of her stairs to head up to her as-yet-to-be-put-together bed, the doorbell rang. Her spine went stiff, her shoulders shot up to her ears. Didn't whoever it was know it was time to go to bed now? It'd been a long day. Finishing the packing, watching *Game of Thrones* while she waited for the moving men, loading up the boxes, handing the keys to her parents' house over to the new owners, driving to Boughton, unpacking the van, not to mention burning about a million calories in the snowball fight.

She stopped herself short as the bell sounded again.

She'd wanted this. The whole neighbours-in-and-out-of-each-other's-houses thing. Already it was proving to be a thousand times better than she'd imagined. Not only had she joined in on the snowball fight, so had the van drivers. Then she'd helped build a snowman after enjoying some of Drea's heavenly buttery, garlicky prawns (Aussies knew their way around a prawn), along with a couple of glasses of Christmas cheer. Just to prove she was neighbourly, obviously.

Then, as the families with little ones began shuttling their children off to bed and the empty bottles of Chenin Blanc clanked into the recycling bins, about fifteen people had formed a queue at the back of the van (organised by Drea, surprise surprise) and bish bash bosh – everything she owned in the world was tidily stacked in the sitting room, bar her mattress and its Ikea bedframe, which Kai and Rex had hauled upstairs to her new bedroom. ('Penance, darling. Penance.')

She opened the door, half expecting her imaginary Diet Coke man to be there, screwdriver in one hand, thirst-quenching beverage in another, with an offer to put her bed together.

It was Drea.

'I hope we haven't put you off, darls.' Drea lifted her half-full wine glass in a mini-toast. 'Welcome to the neighbourhood?'

If she'd blinked, Jess would've missed it. But there was a whisper of fragility in the welcome. Just enough to whisk away her initial concern that Drea might be too scary to be friends with.

'Thanks,' Jess said. 'It was great of everyone to help.'

'Really? Because sometimes I know I can be a bit...' Drea made a sound and gesture that meant 'in your face'.

Through it, the fragility Jess had glimpsed was now loud and clear. So much so that Jess was tempted to pull her new neighbour into a hug. A splinter of pain lanced the urge. Interfering had landed her where she was now, so best to keep herself to herself. Her hands anyway.

She opted for the verbal, British version of a hug. 'You all right?'

'Yeah, course, fine. It's just Christmas, isn't it?'

Ermm ... no. That was twenty-four days away.

'I bloody love Christmas,' Drea said, leaning against Jess's doorframe looking out to where the snowman stood on her lawn, head slightly akimbo, carrot nose wilting a bit in the not entirely cold December night air.

'Will you be going home? I mean, back to Australia for it?'

'What? Me? No,' Drea barely gave her a glance, her eyes still fixed on Frosty. 'No, I live here now.'

'Oh, really? Your accent sounds ...' Jess sought the right word '... really fresh.'

Drea laughed. 'Aw look, when you grow up talking a certain way, it's hard to shake it. Anyway. The Brits love it. In my line of work anyway, but no. I'm an Aussie born and bred, but my life is here now. Has been for the past four years. My business is here. My house. Only thing that isn't is my kid.'

Jess's heart squeezed tight as the concern in Drea's eyes turned to pain.

'Oh?' Jess said in lieu of the ream of questions clamouring to be answered.

'He's grown now,' Drea said by way of explanation. 'Twenty-four years old. Works at a law firm. Got his own flat in Melbourne. Tats. Surfboard. Steady relationship.

He's living the dream.' She ended in a whisper, as if living the dream seemed absolutely unimaginable to her.

'Well, if you don't mind me saying, you don't look old enough to have a twenty-four-year-old.' She meant it. Drea looked like she was in her early forties. Tops. And Jess was a good guesser. It was another one of the school-gates games she and the other teachers used to play. The winner got first pick out of the Celebrations box one of the single dads brought once a month as a thank you gift for looking after his children during the day, which was their job, but never mind. Who didn't love a Celebration?

'Teenage bride,' Drea said with a sad smile.

'Really?'

'No,' Drea scoffed, her smile brightening. 'I was up the duff at sixteen, but no way was I going to marry that loser. Anyway, I better let you get up to your beddie-byes. Number two tomorrow.' She pointed her index finger up towards the top of the street, the motion causing her to slosh some of the wine out onto the stoop. 'Whoops! Too much vino for Drea. Right, doll. I'm going to make tracks. I think it's seven-thirty tomorrow. Be there or be square.' She turned two of her fingers into a V, pointed them at her eyes and then at Jess's. 'Welcome to the neighbourhood.'

'Thank you. And thanks for making it so memorable,' Jess said, heartened to realise it had been an amazing way to kickstart her life here.

Drea had already turned, giving a half wave over her shoulder as she stumble-walked diagonally across the street, slipping a bit on some of the snow, shouting out 'Didn't spill a drop!' when she realised Jess was still looking, downed the rest of it in one, then went into her own house.

A few minutes later, having tugged her duvet (still made) out of one of the packing boxes, located a pillow and tucked herself up on the mattress next to the unmade bed frame, Jess realised she was smiling. The day hadn't gone as planned, but it had gone better than she'd expected. Maybe learning to trust her gut again wouldn't be so hard after all.

2 December

Jess thunked her head against the refrigerator door. No milk. No bread. No nothing. Part of the original Moving-in Plan had included whizzing to the shops for a few fresh bits and bobs after the van men had left. Another, more critical part of the plan involved unearthing her cafetière. As things stood, she had three dirty mugs and the dregs of her hot chocolate. Mind you, there still might be a couple of Wagon Wheels.

The doorbell rang.

Seriously? It was what? She glanced at her phone screen: 7 a.m. Why was someone at her door? It was still dark outside.

The whole-doorbell-ringing-and-neighbour-checking-in-on-her thing had been fine last night. Drea was obviously a bit sad and missing her son, which Jess could relate to as she'd spent the last year feeling sad and missing the life she used to have. To the point where it had been a mercy she hadn't had any time to process just how big a change she was making by moving here. But 7 a.m.? Really? She was in her pyjamas. Her fringe was sticking out every which way and, more to the point, she'd not had her all-important first cup of morning coffee.

The bell rang again.

She was tempted to stay hidden in the kitchen. She didn't want to see anyone. Last night had been an anomaly. She needed this one, final month of being a hermit to truly divine whether or not she'd done the right thing.

Once more, the trill of the bell sounded.

Maybe it was the postman. Her parents had said to keep an eye out for a package. She reluctantly padded to the door, her unicorn slippers making scuffing sounds on the Victorian tiling between the kitchen and the front door. Slippers her ex had endlessly mocked her for, to the point she'd put them in storage along with most of the rest of her possessions he'd deemed unsuitable for public viewing, only remembering just how much she'd loved them when she'd properly packed up to leave London. She'd worn them every day since. Her one act of post-relationship How Very Dare You.

There were two shadows behind the stained-glass door panels, which made her pause. Postmen didn't work in pairs, did they? She stared at the door as if it would tell her but became distracted by the stained-glass centrepiece. The oblong design of red, green and gold diamonds running through it had been one of the things that had first attracted her to the house. That, the name of the street and the proximity to the primary academy where she'd be teaching had all been selling points. As had the house at the far end of the cul-de-sac. It was older and larger than the others. Grey slate roof topping warm-butter-and-fawn-coloured bricks. Three square, white sashed windows on top, two on the bottom. A sage-coloured door beneath a small porch roof and chimney pots on either end. There was a white picket fence around some immaculate box hedges, which outlined two perfect squares of dug-over earth. As if it was being prepared for a victory garden. It reminded her a bit of the old Emmerdale farmhouse (her parents had been fans), or somewhere Lizzie Bennet might've lived.

The buzzer went again just as she reached the door. She yanked it open with a not-entirely-charming 'Yes?'

'Hi, darling.' Kai smiled, a swatch of his dark hair falling into his eyes as he wiggled a bottle of milk with a silver top in front of him alongside a Betty's of Harrogate tin with old-fashioned script spelling out the magic word: Coffee. 'We weren't sure if you'd have provisions in yet and, as such, wanted to give you a proper apology for yesterday's snowball assault.'

Rex nodded in agreement. 'Winter weaponry isn't how we usually meet and greet the new neighbours. Can we consider this a do-over?'

Kai didn't wait for her to answer. 'We've put the number of the milk delivery chap on the bottle if you want. Are you more of a tea girl? I can run back and get some if you are.'

Jess grinned, her grumpiness forgotten. 'Coffee's perfect. And please accept my apologies for assaulting you with my gorgeous morning look. Not.' She put her hand on her hip and jutted it to the side, then gave her hair an over-the-shoulder flick as if greeting people in her jim-jams was something she did every day of the week.

Kai made a clucking noise. 'We know we're early and let me assure you, we've seen it all.'

Rex looked at him, eyebrow arched imperiously. 'Have we, now?'

'Course not, darling. It was a jest. But you know better than most that this doesn't happen just by waking up in the morning.' He tipped the milk bottle in the direction of his own face then tilted his chin up so that the porch light bathed him in a warm halogen glow.

Nope. There was nothing Jess could make out that would've indicated he'd spent hours at the dressing table before leaving the house in the morning.

He handed her the milk then put his hand by his face like a fan. 'Shave first. Then a scrub. Eye gel. Moisturiser. Anti-fatigue serum and an SPF. Even in the winter months. Then of course there's the hair routine.'

He looked as though he was about to embark on a detailed explanation of said routine when Rex cut him off. 'Love, we could be here all day. Let's let the poor woman get some coffee into her and keep what remains of the heat inside her house, yeah?'

He held up an insanely beautiful evergreen wreath bedecked with whole pomegranates, dried orange slices and cinnamon sticks. It smelt amazing and looked unbelievable. In London it would've cost well over a hundred pounds. More. She never in her life would've imagined buying one, let alone hanging it on her door (executive living demanded anonymity of front doors). Rex handed it to her, explaining, 'I had to nip into the shop earlier this morning to take a delivery and thought this might add a little boost to the house. Until you get your own Christmas decorations up, obvs.'

Jess's smile faltered. She hadn't so much as opened a box of essentials, let alone thought about getting a Christmas tree. The truth was, she hadn't planned to decorate for the holidays. Last Christmas had been so awful and this one was . . . well . . . she'd kind of wanted to skip over it.

'Don't you like it?' Kai and Rex asked in matching

tones of dismay. Neither of their brows furrowed. Jess hazarded a guess that there was probably a teensy bit of Botox involved in their beauty routines as well.

'Like it?' She finally managed to splutter. 'I love it. Seriously. As you say, it'll really give the place a boost.' It might even let her off the hook for not getting a tree in.

Kai and Rex shared a delighted smile, as if it brought them more joy to give presents than she had in receiving them. She had to admit, having them as neighbours gave her a hit of the warm and fuzzies. She regretted being so grumpy when she'd heard the door go. Which did beg the question . . . were they her Diet-Coke-break men?

'I suppose you can get the estate agents to take this down now,' Rex pointed at the For Sale sign with a bright red Sold banner angled across it.

'Yes, absolutely. It's on the list,' she quipped, not entirely certain she wanted it gone. Not just yet anyway. Even though these guys were great and Drea had put on an incredible advent calendar night, having the For Sale sign outside her house made her feel as if she still had options. She didn't, but the truth was, she felt as though she was masquerading as someone else right now. A confident, happy go-lucky, prawn-eating, snowball-throwing funster. What if they found out who she really was? A shamed teacher banished from a renowned prep school for allegedly harming a child. Would they be so welcoming then? Shutting down the thoughts, she asked, 'Which house do you two live in?'

'We're at number eleven,' Kai said, pointing to a detached house diagonally across from her own, then shifted the wreath up Jess's arm like an enormous bangle before putting the coffee in her free hand. 'You're more than welcome to pop in for anything you need.'

'Outside of business hours,' Rex tacked on, then gave Jess's arm an apologetic squeeze. 'Sorry, love. It's one of the busy seasons at the shop and even though we're always working at this time of year, we're *always* working. We'd better shoot off to furnish the hordes with their boughs of holly and mistletoe – did you need any mistletoe?'

'No,' she answered, a bit too briskly.

Rex, completely unoffended, tapped the side of his nose. 'Well, you know where you can get some if things change.'

'They won't,' she said darkly. Things hadn't exactly ended brilliantly with Martin. And she had quite enough of her own problems to sort out before she began to delve into matters of the heart. Anyway. She gave a stagey shiver. 'Guess I'd better think about keeping some of that heat in.'

They waved an awkward trio of goodbyes, the bonhomie of the gift-giving a bit lost after Jess's terse answers. 'Thanks again!' she shouted after them as they headed down the short path to the pavement. 'See you tonight?'

They half turned, good-natured smiles back in place and nodded. 'Seven-thirty, I think it was.'

'Should I expect igloo-making lessons?' Jess said in a last-ditch attempt to show she was actually fun to be with. 'Reindeer-taming?'

Kai and Rex laughed.

'You can expect something a bit more low-key than Drea's night. She's never been one to opt for subtle,' Kai added in a stage whisper.

They waved, climbed into an immaculate, holly-red

Range Rover and swept off down the street in deep discussion about their day to come, no doubt.

Right! Now that there was coffee and milk in the house, it was time to start tackling the pile of boxes in her lounge.

It was dark again by the time Jess looked out of the lounge window.

Her heart skipped a beat when she saw the street was lit, but empty. Empty save for the small slump of snow where Frosty and his eyes made out of coal had stood a day earlier. Had she missed the advent calendar surprise at number 2? The promise of seeing Kai and Rex so she could show them how she'd hung up their wreath had kept her going throughout the day. She'd also been hoping to soften the edges of her disappointment that her parents hadn't rung – *again* – with a glass of wine and a bit of a natter with Drea. Even if the woman scared her a bit, an entire day of alone time had made her desperate for some company. Right up until they'd left, her parents had been brilliant at keeping her busy. She'd been allowed to sulk and mope for one week and then had been put to work. She had a regular stint on reception at their dental surgery. They'd gently eased her into some online tutoring so she could gain back her confidence in the teaching arena. When another moping session loomed, they'd sent her to the shops for things she was sure they hadn't needed or parked her in front of an onion that needed dicing. Today had been a stark reminder that the only person who could live the rest of her life for her was Jess. She'd had enough of this particular Jess and craved social interaction like air. Even if only for an hour.

She scrabbled around to find her phone among the crumpled-up newspaper she'd used to pack up things back at her parents'. It was six-thirty. Okay. Good. Enough time to have a shower and a sandwich. She mentally ran through the handful of groceries she'd picked up during a quick lunchtime run to the nearby superstore to figure out what she could eat so, if there was wine, it didn't land on an empty stomach. The first thing that sprang to mind, without actually looking, was a big block of cheddar. She could make a cheese-and-crisps sandwich just like her mum used to make her when she was little. Bap, lashings of butter, salt and vinegar crisps atop a thick slab of cheese—

Her stomach churned as the memories flooded back in. She scrunched her eyes tight but could only picture the children's dining hall back at St Benedict's. She opened them again, forcing herself back into the here and now. Ethan was fine. Thank God. And Crispin? Probably lording it about in front of some other poor, unsuspecting art teacher. Little tyrant that he was. Anyway, it wasn't her problem now.

Or was it?

He'd lied and got her fired. Would he do the same again? She'd felt it had been her moral responsibility to let the Head Teacher know the truth, but where had that honesty landed her?

Christmas Street, she sternly reminded herself. Where, hopefully, Santa was keeping tabs on the naughty and nice children so Jess wouldn't ever find herself in such an awful predicament ever again.

She poured her frustration into scrunching some stray newspaper into the one box she hadn't collapsed for her shiny new recycling bin, then stood back in the doorway of the lounge and tried to admire her handiwork.

It looked...

Well...

It looked like someone had been the recipient of her parents' stray furniture and augmented it with the very first sofa she'd laid eyes on eBay. Which was, of course, pretty much what had happened.

It was a bit shocking, really. That she'd cared so little. She was an art teacher: beauty, and being surrounded by it, was her thing. Which was why she'd been tempted to hang Kai and Rex's wreath above the mantelpiece of her small Victorian-style fireplace (currently sporting a finger-painting of a bunny rabbit riding a unicorn she'd been given, framed by a parent and signed by the child, back when she'd held favoured teacher status).

In fairness to the sofa, it was a rather beautiful teal and embodied a yesteryear charm that appealed to her. It was long enough for her to take a nap on (she'd tested it) and deep enough to curl up in and read a book. You could also swirl your finger along the velvety cloth and draw your initials or a heart in it, if you were that way inclined.

On the flip side, it pretty much filled up half of the lounge to the point there was no room for a table on either side of it. It didn't match anything else she had in the room: her dad's old leather wing chair (ripped and in need of recovering), a small bookcase that had so many bumps and nicks that it had passed through the shabby-chic stage and was hurtling towards the leave-it-out-on-the-pavement-for-the-binmen-to-collect stage, and, to remind her of all that had gone before, a small, decorative cactus.

Once she got a few more books on the shelves and maybe threw a blanket or two over the leather chair, it would look fine. Better than fine. It would look homely. A place she'd want to return to at the end of a long day with the students, rather than a storage room for the boxes she had yet to open, including the big box of office supplies she was meant to provide copy for (thanks Amanda!) by the end of the month.

She picked that box up and lugged it into the kitchen, telling herself that what she should feel instead of dispirited was proud. She'd come a long way in a year.

Precisely one year ago, she'd been in tears pretty much all day, every day (and that wasn't just because of the cactus pricks). One week later she'd been jobless. Two weeks after that? Boyfriendless, homeless, aimless. Then a solid year of regrouping at her parents'. It'd taken a fair few ugly cries and a lot of gentle nudging from her mum to even think about online tutoring, let alone doing it, but... she'd got there in the end. Eventually, she'd begun to apply for new jobs at very small, very ordinary-sounding primary schools until, finally, she'd had the confidence to take one at Boughton Primary Academy. It was in a lovely town only an hour down the road from her parents. Not so close they'd think she was clinging, not so far she couldn't make herself a regular feature at their Sunday lunches. They'd gone house-hunting together. Finding the little house on Christmas Street, just a ten-minute walk to her new school, had felt like a sign. As if life was finally aligning in her favour.

Then *Dentists san Frontières* had rung and her parents made the decision to leave. They sold their house. Her mum and dad had said she was more than welcome to join them, but it was pretty clear they were hopeful that she would pull up her socks and get on with the rest of her life. This wasn't, after all, the eighteenth century when she could wander round their house doing useful bits of embroidery and silver polishing until she died of consumption, an unfinished book of poetry by her side. So here she was at the ripe age of thirty-one, trying to make a go of being a grown-up all over again.

An hour later she was all showered and had tidied the crumbs from the Marmite sandwich she'd opted for in the end. Then, before she could talk herself out of it, she pulled on her coat and headed out onto the street.

'Jess!'

She turned at the sound of Drea's unmistakable voice.

Smiling, she eased her way through the smattering of people beginning to gather outside number 2 apart from a pair of children who were trying to build miniature snowmen out of the remains of Frosty.

'Hiya,' Jess said, giving a shy wave to Drea and the couple she was standing with.

'Hi, doll. So glad you could make it.' She planted a kiss on each of Jess's cheeks. 'Looks like we're getting a nice little turnout. I wasn't sure if we'd peaked last night.' Her eyes skidded across the growing crowd as she spoke, but she had her hand on Jess's arm throughout, as if to assure her she was there. 'Right. We'll give everyone a few more minutes before we start, but it's looking good.' She flashed Jess a quick, bright smile. 'Want to meet some more of your neighbours?'

'Yes, that'd be lovely.' Especially now that they weren't hurling snowballs at her.

'Good,' Drea grinned. 'Because I wasn't going to give

you much of a choice in the matter. Now—' She point-edly turned to the couple next to her. They were around her age and were also fairly new on the street. The two young ones playing with the remains of Frosty were theirs and, after a bit of coaxing, also came over to say hello. After about ten more introductions Jess had completely given up on trying to remember anyone's names and figured they would come eventually.

'And tonight, of course, we've got the Sloans at number two. They have triplets, all mad as a box of frogs, but fabulous. Now. Got all that?' Drea asked drily. 'Quiz tomorrow at eight a.m. sharp.' She laughed before Jess could answer. 'Ooo – look, look. I think the show's about to begin.'

Jess turned to number 2, across the road Drea's. From inside, the owners flashed the porch lights.

'Looks like the show's about to begin,' someone said.

'Are they signalling Santa?' An excited child asked, which, of course, made the rest of the children look up at their parents and ask the same.

'I think they want us to quit talking and be quiet,' intoned a man in a business suit who didn't really look as though he was enjoying being out among his neighbours. A woman, presumably his wife, hissed, *shush Giles*, and then turned her attention to number 2's front door, which was now opening. A teenager – tweenager? Hard to tell sometimes – appeared. He was wearing a pair of blinking reindeer antlers, a red nose and a very serious expression. He was holding a huge box wrapped in bright red paper with a big gold ribbon round it and an enormous old bow on top. It screamed Christmas time.

'Hope that's for me and no one else,' a jovial man in a thick parka shouted out.

'Trust you to be the greedy guts, John,' another neighbour called back.

Drea made a sound that shushed the pair of them. Jess hid a smile. She never ever wanted to be on Drea's bad side.

All of a sudden, out from behind the boy marched two more tweenagers in identical costumes followed by their parents. They were all playing kazoos. Was that... was it ... 'Jingle Bells'? Yup. It was definitely 'Jingle Bells'.

As the penny dropped, child number one pulled the lid off the present box, flung it to the side and began working his way through the crowd. There was a kazoo for everyone.

So there was absolutely no doubt as to how the evening was going to progress, Mr Sloan made a hearty ho, ho, ho and called out, 'That's right, everyone. Tonight, coming to you live from Number Two Christmas Street, it's the one and only Carolling Kazoo Choir!'

After some chuckling and groaning and another round of Drea training everyone's attention back to the task at hand, the kazooing began in earnest.

Half an hour later the session wrapped up with a giggle-fuelled round of 'Joy to the World' made even more hilarious by the fact that all of the kazooing was making everyone's nose tickle.

When it was over, as had happened the night before, parents with children shuffled off rather sharpish. Jess could hear a few offers for a drink or cups of tea being bandied about. An acute sense of loneliness swept through her. It was very much a first-day-at-school feeling. The type that made you wish as hard as you could that life could go back to being the way it used to be. Not entirely perfect, but blissfully familiar. She went up on her tiptoes to see if she could spot Kai and Rex when a plastic wine glass appeared in front of her.

Drea.

'Quick one before we turn in?'

Jess smiled and nodded. She'd spent the entire day alone and would most likely do the same again for the next day and the next, so ... she held the glass up while Drea filled it. A few other people reappeared from their houses, picnic wine glasses and screw-top bottles in hand, making jokes about there being no need for ice sleeves for the wine so long as they stayed outdoors.

'This your way of keeping all of the calories burning off before Christmas, Drea?' A woman a couple of doors down did a couple of enthusiastic star jumps then comedically wiped her brow before taking an equally enthusiastic glug of wine.

'Ha, ha,' Drea intoned. She rolled her eyes for Jess's benefit then explained. 'I'm in the fitness industry.'

'Oh?'

Drea waved it off, the miniature Christmas trees on her fingernails catching the street lights as she did. 'Keeps the mortgage paid. So. How do you think you'd do if I gave you a quiz on everyone's names now?'

Jess choked on her wine and laughed. 'I'd fail. Miserably.'

'No worries, doll. You'll get there. It took me ages to meet everyone here, what with the way you Brits prefer hiding behind closed doors.' She smiled at the smattering of people still out on the street. 'This proves my point.'

'What does?'

'That people want to have more of a community feel about where they live. And what better time than Crimbo to kick it off?' She waved a small group of women over. 'C'mon Jess. Let's start again.'

Twenty minutes, a bag of snowflake-shaped pretzels, and another bottle of wine later, Jess had officially committed four people's names to memory: Drea. Kai and Rex. And Martha Snodgrass at number 21, because, seriously, how did you forget that name? She was in her seventies and had had a young lodger for the past six months with whom she was regularly at loggerheads. And from there it got quite fuzzy. There were lots of Emmas and Gemmas, whom the street collectively referred to as the Gem'n'Emms because no one could keep any of them straight. Their husbands were known as the Rob'n'Bobs, even though there was only one of each and one was definitely called Darren. And then there were a truckload of other people she couldn't remember.

She'd get there eventually. Maybe.

'And what about that house?' Jess asked when there was a lull in the conversation. 'Who lives there?'

Everyone's eyes followed Jess's finger down to the end of the street to the large, unlit house down at the end of the street. Number 24. The curtains were drawn tight, making it impossible to detect any signs of life. It was neat and tidy enough. No piles of unattended leaves or dead plants giving it a Norman Bates sort of feel, but ... the way everyone's mood altered from bright and cheery to suspect and withdrawn sent a wriggle of shivers down her spine.

'Oh, that's Mr Winters.' Drea finally broke the silence. 'He's our resident Scrooge.'

Jess was about to say even Scrooge came round in the end, but soon the air was thick with information.

'Keeps to himself, he does.'

'I heard he was racist.'

'Sexist, too.'

'Vegan most likely.'

'Wot? Because he's a racist and a sexist, that makes him a vegan? Where's the logic in that?'

'It's because he was done for murder, wasn't it? He's trying to make amends.'

'No, that's not right. I heard it was white-collar crime and that he's under house arrest. Still got to keep his big house, though, didn't he?'

'That wasn't it at all. They nabbed him for having slaves in his basement. Cook. Cleaner. He had a whole squad of them down there.'

'Oh, stop it the lot of you!' Drea shushed them crossly. 'He's just a sad, lonely old man who doesn't know how to make friends any more, he's been on his own that long. Scrooge. Like I said.'

As a group, eight or so heads turned to stare at Drea. For a moment she looked as though she really cared that there was a sad, lonely man who saw no joy in the world living at the end of their street and then, in the blink of an eye, the compassionate defensiveness was whisked away and replaced by a bright sunshiney smile. 'Right, you lot. It's a school night isn't it? Same time tomorrow?'

'Where are we tomorrow?'

'Number 3.'

A few disaffected murmurs filled the air.

Jess shot a questioning look at Drea.

'Let's just say our hopes aren't high for number 3.' She nodded to number 4, an attractive detached cottage that had a wreath on the door, Christmas tree twinkling away in the window and a tasteful willow weave in the shape of a reindeer 'nibbling' on their front hedge. 'Number four'll be better.'

A collective happy sigh went round the group.

'Chantal's,' A woman said in a hushed tone of reverence.

Drea began collecting bottles, chucking them into the closest recycling bin, pointedly wishing everyone a good night.

'We love Chantal,' a woman told Jess in a way the suggested that she too would soon fall under the mysterious Chantal's spell.

'Why do we love her?' Jess asked.

'She's the reason we're all fat and she's thin and beautiful,' another woman cackled. 'You'll see.'

The group began drifting off to their own homes and, as Drea had been drawn into a conversation with the woman from number 8 about health-and-safety considerations, Jess felt that awkward all-alone feeling creep through her again. Time to go.

When she got back to her house, she frowned at the For Sale sign before her door caught her eye. Her new wreath had slipped and was hanging haphazardly from the knocker. It'd need fixing. Another job. She pulled her keys out of her pocket and went to open the door noticing, as she did, that someone had slipped a tiny bit of mistletoe into the wreath. Against the odds, that warm and fuzzy feeling she'd had the other night returned. Perhaps moving to Christmas Street was the one smart thing she'd done this year.

3 December

'Hello, darling!' Jess's mum waved and her dad lifted up a coconut with a straw stuck in the top.

'*IQKWE!*' Her dad bellowed. 'THAT MEANS HELLO IN MARSHALLESE!'

'Harry, there's no need to shout, she can hear us just fine. YOU CAN HEAR US, CAN'T YOU, DARLING?'

Jess nodded. The video connection was surprisingly good considering they were a gazillion miles away.

'Hi, Mum,' Jess's voice cracked. 'Dad!' A tear plopped onto her cheek.

'Jess, love. What's wrong?'

'Nothing! I – It's good to see you.' An epic under-statement if ever there was one. But as good as it was to see them, it was also difficult. Their tropical shirts, darkening tans and coconut drinks highlighted just how very far away they were and how incredibly alone Jess felt. The advent calendar events had definitely been a nice way to meet her new neighbours, but twenty-two more nights of standing off to the side and then running home before anyone engaged her in conversation wasn't exactly filling up her dance card with a squad of new besties and a glut of Mr Darcys. Not to mention having to come up with something for her own night. Its

44

looming approach genuinely terrified her. An entire street of strangers... judging her. She'd thought of inviting Rex and Kai over for a brainstorming session – Drea was still a bit too intimidating to confess a complete absence of ideas to – but it didn't seem fair to lumber them with her insecurities when they had their shop to run and their own night to host and she hadn't exactly unpacked anything since that first day when she'd opened a whopping three boxes.

'We couldn't miss moving day, could we?' Her mum gave her an expectant smile, clearly hoping Jess would wipe her tears away, unleash a sunshiney smile, then proceed to delight them with tales of how fabulous her new home in her new neighbourhood in the new town where she was meant to be getting on with her new life really was.

Instead, she swept away another few tears and sobbed. 'That was two days ago.'

'What? No. Diane?' Her dad looked at her mum, then at his wrist which, for the first time ever, did not sport a watch.

Jess's mum glared at her husband as if it was his fault. 'Harry. Why aren't we ringing on the right day?'

A back-and-forth volley ensued, her parents trying to pin down exactly who had been in charge of the calendar and time zones and days of the week, to the point Jess instinctively did her teacher's Attention Clap. The magic one that all of the students knew meant she'd be expecting silence in three... two... one...

As if they, too, had been programmed, her parents turned to her, contrite expressions on their faces. 'Sorry, love. We thought we'd got it right. I think we've fallen victim to island time.'

'Already?'

'Oh, love,' Her parents gave a shared sigh of delight. 'It's just so . . . well, the weather's deliciously warm, the people are ever so lovely, and the teeth!' Her mum clapped her hands together and pressed them to her lips. 'Their teeth are wonderful for the most part. Honestly, I think it's largely the Brits here who need help,' she stage whispered. 'Heaven knows who looked after them as children. It certainly wasn't us.'

'Lots to keep you busy, then?' Jess asked, relieved to back on her parents' favourite topic. Gnashers.

'Brits or teeth?'

Jess listened as her mother happily nattered on, her father interjecting every now and again with a factual correction or a bit of a sidebar description. Then they picked up their tablet and took her on a tour of their small but comfortable breeze-block house, which was a short walk from the hospital where they were volunteering. 'It's all right by the sea,' her mother smiled then frowned. 'A lad from one of the NGOs was saying we'd better enjoy it while we could because it'd all be under water soon enough.'

'What? Why?'

'Climate change, darling,' her mother said, tapping the side of her nose. 'It's everywhere.'

Her father yawned, clapping a hand over his face, then gave a sheepish grin. 'Sorry, love. I think it's time we turned in.'

Jess looked at her watch. It was two-thirty her time which meant – 'Is it the middle of the night there?'

Her mother smiled through a yawn of her own. 'We've still got a touch of the jet lag. We go to sleep early, wake up in the middle of the night, have a swim by moonlight, then back to bed.'

Jess forced herself to swallow down another sting of tears. Her parents had changed their lives and were now reaping the rewards. She had to believe that same sparkly-eyed joy would come to her sometime, too. Maybe not in the form of coconut drinks and midnight swims, but it'd be out there. Somewhere.

Either way, her parents were having a whale of a time. Which, of course, they completely deserved. They'd run a busy dental practice for as long as she could remember. They'd given her a lovely upbringing in a lovely village, never wallowing in the fact they'd only had her instead of the 'large unruly brood' she knew they'd wanted. They'd encouraged her to follow her dream of being a teacher rather than push her into joining the family practice. The only time they'd second guessed her decisions was when she'd been offered the job at St Benedict's Preparatory School. Was London the goal or was St Benny's? (Benny's!) Did St Benny's embody the values she embraced? (Of course!) Was she sure working there would make her the teacher she wanted to be? (The *best*!)

It turned out her emphatic answers to the questions had changed. *She* had changed. To the point that her parents, who had already ushered her out into the world as a fledgling adult, had opened their arms and taken her back into their home at her darkest ebb, built her back up, then given her the deposit for her new house which she never, not in a million years, would've been able to

47

afford on her teacher's salary, and ushered her back out the door so she could start her life all over again.

So, if fixing teeth west of the international date line was their jam, they deserved every cracked molar that came their way. Even if it did mean pretending she was looking forward to her first Christmas on her own. Two years ago it wouldn't have mattered quite as much. She'd had a boyfriend, a home, a job in London. She'd been enamoured by how twinkly London became. The presents the parents gave the teachers. The invitations to holidays they received were mad. They included joining a make-up doyenne and her family at their Courchevel chalet for winter half-term, ostensibly as a guest, but really to babysit the children when the parents went out for long boozy lunches. A Russian businessman who seemed to own an entire mountain range with a *dacha* on top. (Snap to the babysitting.) And a film producer who only invited the pretty, unmarried female teachers to 'check out life on the set'. Those were usually politely declined. It was living the dream by proxy. Someone's dream, anyway.

Had loving the trappings of working at St Benny's landed her where she was now? Had it made her take her eye off what was really important: the students? Was that how she'd ended up misjudging the Cheese Sandwich Incident so poorly?

She shoved the thought back into her 'nope, not ready' box and forced herself to smile and wave at her parents as they worked out where the 'end call' button was on their iPad. A few seconds after the screen had faded to black, she heard the metal clank of the post flap.

She jogged to the door, relieved at the distraction from the yawning loneliness she knew would consume her if she let herself dive down the rabbit hole of her past. She missed her parents in a way she'd never missed them before. She owed them a debt of gratitude she knew could only be repaid by pulling herself together and proving to them she had what it took to soldier on.

She picked up the smattering of letters, genuinely delighted to see there were a couple of festive-red envelopes amid the circulars and 'Welcome to BT/British Gas/Scottish Power' bills she'd received so far.

She plopped down cross-legged on the tiled floor and tore the first one open.

It was completely white save for two circles – one black, one red – and a caption that read *Rudolph lets Dasher take the lead in a blizzard.* She laughed, opened it up and glanced to the bottom of the note to see who it was from. Her heart cinched. It was from her mate, Amanda at St Benedict's.

BABES! Wanted to make sure you had something to pop onto that lovely mantelpiece of yours in your fancy new digs. A year on and still missing you dreadfully down here in the big smoke. W(h)ine o'clock continues, but isn't the same without you. Parents are still dreadful. Nativity is even more dreadful (new art teacher isn't a patch on you). Counting down the days until the hols. Hope you're settling in before you start at your new 'real-life' school. Catch up over the Easter break, maybe? An adult playdate? I can bring supplies from Londontown or you can come down and remember what it's like to be rammed into a sardine tin on the way to work. Xoxox Amanda.

Jess conked her head against the wall. She missed Amanda but hearing from her brought back all sorts of squirmy, uncomfortable memories that made her feel exactly as she had when she'd been called into the Head Teacher's office last December. She'd leave responding to the 'playdate' suggestion to another time.

She picked up the next red envelope and slid her finger under the triangle of flap that sealed it. She pulled out the card. It was on lovely unbleached paper and featured a photo of an otter somewhere island-y and some tiny Christmas tree potato stamps round the edges.

She opened the card. Out of the corner of her eye she thought she saw something flutter out, but she couldn't see anything so started to read:

Dear Grandad,

I hope you don't mind me calling you grandad seeing as we've never met, but I was hoping this card could serve as an introduction. My name's Will. I'm one of Robert's boys. Until recently my brother Callum was still in Scotland where, as you probably know, we grew up. I wanted you to know I've moved to Greenleigh, which is only about twenty miles down the road from you. I run a small catering company which is keeping me busy, especially with the holidays on fast approach. I'm not so busy, though, that I wouldn't have time to meet you. Perhaps on Christmas if you're not too busy? I can bring some food over for us to share. I would've gone home, but we've got bookings on every day apart from 'the big one' and, as I said, I'd really like to meet you. I've called the company The

Merry Victualler. We're on all of the usual social media if
you want to look us up.
   I'll leave it there. I thought a letter would be the best
way to introduce myself all things considered.
   Wishing you the very best,
   Will Winters

Winters?

Grandad?

Jess swallowed down a lump of guilt. This obviously
wasn't her letter to read. She flipped the envelope over.

Mr Arnold Winters
24 Christmas Street
Boughton

Crumbs. Not only had she opened and read someone
else's post – an actual crime! – she had opened and read
the post of the sad, lonely possibly racist/sexist/slave-
keeping murderer at the end of the street who had never
met his grandson. She thought of Drea's face when the
rumours had started flying. Had it been protective irritation or actual annoyance? If what people were saying was
true, it was unlikely he'd be throwing a big Christmas
Eve bash. Mind you, who knew what people were saying
behind her back at St Benny's. She resolved to make zero
judgement until she'd met the man herself, which she
would do by hand-delivering the letter to him rather than
cowardly stuffing it back in the post.

She examined the envelope. Luckily she hadn't torn it
open as she had Amanda's card. She went into the kitchen
and opened the box of office supplies she was writing
catalogue copy for and found a little tube of Gorilla Glue.
She applied a generosity of the super glue to the entire

length of the flap, then sealed it. Properly. Waved it in the air to dry it. Rubbed the heel of her palm along it to make extra sure it was closed and appeared to have never, ever been opened by a complete stranger.

She grabbed her jacket from the back of the breakfast bar stool and headed to the door. Her heart leapt into her throat.

There, on the floor, was a business card.

Will Winters

The Merry Victualler
Old-fashioned victuals with a modern twist
Catering for all events

On the back was his phone number, address and email.

That's what must've fallen out of the card when she opened it. She'd been sitting on it or something. She tried to ease her fingernail underneath the seal of the envelope. Nope. No movement. Course not. She'd just used 'Impact Tough™ Formula' on a piece of paper with a glue that guaranteed to dry in ten seconds.

Her tongue went dry as she put the card in her pocket, thinking she'd make up some story about how it had been taped to the outside, then thought better of it because, derrr ... total lie. Will had written the name of his company into the card and maybe, if she was really crafty, she could get Mr Winters to open it while she was there and pretend *he'd* dropped it or, if worst came to worst, slip the card into his mail flap under the cover of night. While wearing a burglar mask. That would never attract anyone's attention. Wearing a ski mask as she capered from lamp post to lamp post of her lovely suburban cul-de-sac. Then she could spend Christmas in prison for two offences. Mail-tampering and whatever dressing as a burglar and posting a business card she'd accidentally stolen was.

Before she could talk herself out of it, envelope in hand, heart pounding, winter coat zipped up to her throat, she left her house and headed down the street.

The sun was already beginning to set – the clear, bright sky darkening to a lovely midnight blue. There was a crisp bite to the air, but not the type of freezing cold that made you hunch your shoulders and look down as if ploughing your way through a blizzard. A handful of wreaths were hanging on a few front doors. A couple of them were as deliciously fancy as hers was, so she was guessing that they, too, had come from Kai and Rex's shop. A few Christmas trees were already blinking away in front windows. Some real, some faux. A couple of houses were definitely competitively decorating. One had gone for the full, garish, cover-every-surface-in-blinking-lights-and-glowing-plastic-Santa/reindeer/snowmen effect, while the other was actually quite magical. It looked like a gingerbread house complete with icing-style 'snow' dripping from the eaves.

There were, of course, some houses that hadn't done anything at all. It was only the third of December and everyone had their own traditions. Jess's family was a First Saturday of December Call to Action kind of home. With just the three of them, everyone's roles were well defined. Jess and her mum called all of the shots and her dad did their bidding right up until Christmas Eve when, after they'd returned from the carols mass at their local church, he got to put his feet up and be pampered with hot toddies, Christmas Eve pyjamas and a new pair of slippers (yup, every year).

A couple of mums with pushchairs were heading down the street towards the primary academy, where she could hear the whoops and calls of children playing outdoors drifting across on a light breeze. It was a quick walk up and around Christmas Street and down the next road. From her bedroom window she could just make out the stone frontage of the building. Apparently there was a cut-through down the bottom of the street near Mr Winters', but not an official one. Either way, it was a route she'd be able to do blindfolded in a few months' time. The mums waved and called out, 'See you tonight.' Which was nice. But awkward. She kind of wanted to sit tonight out. In London people always said, *yeah, yeah see you there,* and then wouldn't show, giving one of a panoply of acceptable excuses (traffic/work/transport). She wasn't sure how that would work here. It would a) be a lie, and b) feel rude. These people didn't know her at all and were making an effort to make her feel welcome. Already she knew that rebuffing their efforts wouldn't sit right.

She arrived in front of number 24 and took a minute to admire it. It was a lovely house. Rectangles of stone. Tiled roof. There was a small covered porch held upright with two slim pillars that, if wrapped in red ribbon, would look like candy canes. Not that she'd gone all 'hey, let's decorate' or anything, it was just... there was something about the house that made her think there weren't any plans to decorate. All of the curtains were shut tight against the day apart from one where – oh! There was a man there. An elderly man who would've looked amazing in period clothing. Jane Austen kind of era. Or Dickens.

Maybe more Dickens because he was quite frowny. Kind of like Clint Eastwood when he played curmudgeonly old men who didn't like any of their neighbours.

She waved and smiled.

His frown deepened.

She held up the envelope.

He yanked the curtains shut.

Jess tried to tell herself that he'd been standing at the window for precisely that very purpose. To close the curtains. But did he have to do it so dramatically?

Her fragile mood morphed into a self-righteous sense of British resolve. She was being neighbourly! Delivering a letter to its rightful owner (after reading the contents, inadvertently stealing the business card then supergluing the whole thing shut again, sure, but . . .).

She went to knock on the door above the very large No Leaflets, No Junk Mail, No Sales People, No Canvassers, No Religious Groups, No Cold Callers sign.

Thorough.

She wasn't any of those things. Just as her hand connected with the door it flew open.

'Can't you read?' Mr Winters demanded, fulfilling the whole crotchety Clint Eastwood role to a tee.

He was immaculately turned out. Clean-shaven. Crisply ironed shirt underneath a grey-on-grey lattice-patterned sweater vest. Precise creases ran down the centre of his trousers. Shoes, not slippers, and shined, no less. His blue eyes were bright and alert and his thick head of white hair was combed with similar precision to his well-ironed clothes. This was not a man biding away his time in an armchair waiting for the Grim Reaper to show up and take him. This was a man with purpose.

'Well?' He demanded again. 'What is it? Can or can't you read?' He tapped a slightly arthritic finger on the sign.

'Yes,' Jess stuttered, completely taken aback at his brusque demeanour. 'I'm not—'

'I don't want your business. Your message of hope. Your offer. I don't do bulk buys, believe in whoever your god is, or Christmas. Is that clear?'

'But I'm—'

'No.'

He slammed the door in her face.

What the actual—?

She'd never had that happen to her before. Had a door slammed right in her face. Couldn't he see she'd been trying to help? Her stiff British resolve didn't know what to do with itself. She felt as bewildered as she had when she'd been called into the Head Teacher's office for assault.

A ringing sound in her ears drowned out all of the street noise. Her skin went prickly and she felt a blast of heat crash through her. No. It was cold. Really cold. Then why was she sweating? Her heart was hammering to the point she struggled to draw a normal breath. This time she was sure she was having a genuine panic attack. Just as she had when the Head had explained to Jess that she would have to take some unpaid time off to consider her behaviour and, of course, be prepared to address the assault charges.

To avoid having a complete meltdown on Mr Winters' porch, she blindly stumbled down the steps and through the small wooden gate and, eyes down, made a beeline for her house, trying and failing to get her breathing under control.

Once there, the tears truly began to fall in a proper ugly cry. She didn't get it. She had been trying to be helpful. To deliver a – oh, bums. The letter was still in her hand. And a bit crinkled now. Why hadn't she just thrust it at him or put it in his letter box?

Because she'd been taken aback, and chances were high that if she had shoved it through the brass letter flap he might've ripped it up without reading it and then poor Will the Merry Victualler would spend the rest of the month being sad because he too had been rejected by the grumpiest grandad in the West.

None of which made her feel any better. Mr Winters' vile behaviour had shot her right back to that place where her childhood bed, a hot-water bottle and endless reruns of *Friends* were the only things that would keep her thoughts from swirling deeper and deeper into the darker recesses of her mind.

She glanced at the clock. It was just past four. The street lights were pinging on, as were the lights on the Christmas tree in the house across the street.

Mirroring Mr Winters' dramatic movements, she yanked her own (newly hung) curtains shut on the world. She'd had enough of today. She'd start again tomorrow. She needed time to find the Jess she thought she knew – and, more importantly, liked – beneath all of this panicky behaviour. No way was she fit to see Mr Winters again today. But she would try tomorrow. She would march down the street and knock on his door and give him the letter because she was a kind person. No matter what the board of governors at St Benedict's thought. The bastards.

A restless nap, three cups of tea and several repeat episodes of *Bake Off* later, the doorbell went.

She reluctantly sloughed her duvet from her shoulders and forced her feet to transport her to the door. Her curtains weren't so foolproof that whoever was knocking wouldn't have seen the flickering light of the television.

She pulled the door open.

Drea. 'Hell's teeth, doll. You look like shit.'

What a charming Australian greeting. Jess shrugged. Whatever. It was probably true. She'd know if she ever found the energy to hang the mirror up above her hall shelf.

'Can I help?' she asked, hoping her tone meant, please go away and leave me alone.

'We're missing you over at number three.' Drea tipped her head towards the house across the street where, yes indeed, there were loads of people. 'We're stringing cranberries and popcorn together.' She peered into Jess's decoration-free lounge. 'Looks like you could do with a few swags on your mantel.

Jess shivered and faked a sneeze. Her red-rimmed-crying eyes could double for winter-cold eyes. 'Sorry. I – I'b dot feeling good.'

Drea backed away. 'Ah, fair enough doll. Soz. I don't do colds.' She pointed at Jess's stairwell. 'You better get yourself into bed.'

Jess faked another sneeze and gave a sorrowful nod of agreement. Yes. She should. And maybe not get up until Christmas was over and the residents of Christmas Street could go back to being like they were in London where it was unheard of to talk to your neighbours unless you really, absolutely needed to. Like, no milk in the house *at all* type of emergency. Murder. That sort of thing. 'Doh-kay.'

Drea blew her an air kiss. 'If you're feeling better tomorrow, be sure to come to number Four. It's a bit earlier. Seven o'clock. Chantal's Christmas biccies. You won't want to miss them. Neck a bottle of Day Nurse if you need to. It'll be worth it. But don't sit next to me if you still have germs.'

'Dank you!' Jess gave her a wave goodbye then, after tidying up the mountain of tissues and tea mugs balanced on the arm of her new sofa, plodded up to her bed reciting the mantra her mother had repeated over and over during those first few months after St Benny's had made it clear they believed an eleven-year-old bully over a thirty-one-year-old teacher.

Tomorrow's a brand-new day.
Tomorrow's a brand-new day.
Tomorrow's a brand-new day.

4 December

'I thought I said I don't want whatever it is you're selling.'

Jess cocked her eyebrow at Mr Winters, a visual distraction so that he wouldn't look at her knees, which were shaking. Yet another not very delightful 'gift' she'd received after the Cheese Sandwich Incident. Physically shaking when she was feeling intimidated. The other was an eye twitch. Things had to be pretty bad for the eye twitch to kick in. You would've thought it'd be the other way round, but go figure. This was how her body was dealing with it. Luckily it was cold so she had an excuse.

Mr Winters was outside his house today. He stood just inside the white picket fence, sweeping his path into even more pristine condition. It matched his exacting hedges, the precision-edged flower beds. The man certainly admired a straight line. Ex-engineer maybe? Architect? Whatever. He was human. And all humans had it in them to be kind. Except for, maybe, axe murderers.

Her mother, who had rung again in the morning full of apologies for the 'calendar snafu', had been right. Today was a brand-new day. One in which she refused to be treated as if she was a bad person when she'd done absolutely nothing wrong.

As if to prove the world was full of nice things, when she'd opened her front door to collect her first-ever milk delivery (in bottles!), she had also found a shoebox filled with strings of popcorn and cranberries along with a note from 'Drea and the Gang' saying they'd missed her and hoped she enjoyed her decorations. She'd hung them along her mantel and surprise, surprise, they did add a cosy touch to her not very lived-in house. A solid reminder that she had moved to this neighbourhood because it felt exactly like that: a neighbourhood. It firmed her resolve not to leave Will and his victuals hanging. Not when she'd been the recipient of such kindness from strangers. Giving the letter to Mr Winters would be paying it forward. As such, she'd forced herself into the shower, brushed her hair into submission, pulled out the straighteners, done some work on her fringe and dressed herself as if she actually cared. Sometimes a girl did have to work on things from the outside to get them to really sink in.

Instead of stuffing the envelope in Mr Winters' hand and running away, she opted for a benign smile. The type she'd give a parent who insisted their child couldn't possibly be disruptive in class when, in actual fact, they were completely and totally disruptive in class.

'I'm not selling anything,' she said, doing her best to channel her inner Drea who would, no doubt, accept absolutely none of this door-slamming guff. 'I'm delivering your post.' Jess held out the card, which she'd ironed because she was still a little bit scared of him.

Mr Winters had on a similar ensemble to yesterday, but today's sweater vest was maroon. Because it was cold, he was also wearing a thick navy parka and a green-and-blue tartan scarf knotted round his neck. It suited him and, against the odds, made his blue eyes seem kinder.

'Right. I see,' he said, eyes on the red envelope. 'Isn't that normally the postman's job?'

She held the letter out to him, positively itching to say it was from his grandson, but, fairly confident he would become apoplectic at the (illegal) invasion of his privacy, she kept that little nugget to herself. She'd figure out a way to get the business card to him. Maybe pop it through his letter box when he went out to the shops. Actually . . . if he opened it right now she could sort of chuck it on the hedge and be all, Oh look! You dropped something. Yes. This was a most excellent plan.

'It was delivered to mine. Accidentally.' She pointed to her house, just a few doors up, then held the envelope out again. 'I'm Jess, by the way. Jess Green.'

He looked at her in a way that suggested he hadn't the foggiest idea why she was introducing herself to him.

'It's just that—' she pointed at the letter in her hand. 'I know your name, you see. Mr Arnold Winters,' she read in a voice that probably would've worked for a town crier but not so much when you were trying to make nice with the street grouch.

He took the letter and stuffed it into his pocket without looking at it.

Wait. What? No. That wasn't the plan. He was meant to open it so she could get the business card to him. Plus, she wanted to watch him read it. Witness him process the fact he had a grandson out there who clearly wanted to mend whatever fences had been broken between him and his son. Will's father. Who she presumed was hundreds of miles away in Scotland. Mr Winters was wearing a tartan scarf. Maybe it'd been a gift his son had given him before whatever happened happened. No wonder poor Mr Winters was so grumpy. He'd not spoken to his son in who knows how many years. Twenty? Twenty-five? That's how old grandsons starting new businesses were, right?

A fresh despair tore at Jess's heart. If she wasn't going to have a merry Christmas *someone* should and suddenly, quite desperately, she wanted that someone to be Mr Winters. Would he even open it? He had to open it. This whole pay-it-forward thing was more complicated when it involved long-lost grandsons and the grandfather in question wasn't fulfilling his role of opening the ruddy card so she could nudge him towards getting in touch.

'Looks like a Christmas card,' she said.

'Hmmm,' he grunted, returning to his handiwork with such exacting care that Jess wondered if he was a British version of Mr Miyagi.

'I've not seen you at any of the advent calendar events. Biscuit decorating tonight. At Chantal's,' she added, because there seemed to be a collective glow of joy whenever her name was mentioned.

Mr Winters didn't respond.

'So...' She said after a few moments of silence, well aware she really was stretching the boundaries of a one-way conversation. 'Got any plans for Christmas?'

He glanced up at her then went back to work. 'Nothing beyond the usual.'

A titbit! She pounced on it.

'Oh? And ... ermm ... what's the usual?'

'Wake up, see the day through, then go to sleep again.'
Ah.

That had roughly been *her* plan. Maybe throw in a few

Celebrations, some cheesy television that would doubtless make her cry, and a ready meal from M&S that at least hinted at a Christmas feast so she could realistically lie to her parents about eating better, but... honestly? Hearing her big Christmas Day plan come from Mr Winters made it sound pretty depressing.

'Not joining anyone for Christmas dinner?'

Again, he gave her one of those hooded, blue-eyed glances of his, clearly irritated by the fact she was still standing there. No. It wasn't irritation. It was pain.

'No.' He turned around, tried to pocket his shears in the same pocket he'd shoved the envelope, couldn't get them in, looked at his pocket, tugged out the envelope, glared at it, then began to walk up the short brick path towards his house.

Desperation to keep him there clawed at her. He was an envelope-opening away from discovering he had a reason to be happy. She simply had to get him to open that ruddy Christmas card. Then he'd know there was no need to spend the holiday alone and at least one of their Christmases wouldn't be sad and lonely.

'What are you putting in the flower beds?' She called out in a last-ditch attempt to get him to stay.

He stopped, looked at the bare earth, the straight line of his shoulders abruptly sagging. When he turned back round he looked as though he'd aged about a hundred years. 'I was thinking of tulips this year, but my knees won't allow for it, so I might just leave it.'

Tulips. The place would look amazing with tulips. Pink, red, candy-striped, whatever. The possibility that he might not have tulips looked as though it was crippling him.

'No! No. You shouldn't leave it. I'll help. My knees work.' She did a peculiar series of squats and lunges to prove to him that, yes indeedy, her knees were in tip-top shape. She hoped he couldn't hear the crunchy noises. It'd been a while since she'd done any form of exercise.

He squinted at her, looked down at one of the patches, then back at her. 'Don't volunteer for something you don't want to do.'

'But I do want to help! Really.' She lowered her pitch down from the upper register she'd been speaking in, looked him straight in the eye and said, 'Really. I do. I'd love to help you plant tulip bulbs.'

He nodded as if he were working out whether or not to accept her offer, then turned around again without saying anything.

Jess stood there a moment, not entirely sure what to do, but Mr Winters had already reached the first step of his porch, making it fairly clear he did not want her help. But he hadn't exactly said no . . .

Before he got to the door, she lowered her voice another octave then said, *à la* the Terminator, 'Okay, Arnold. I'll be back.' Then instantly regretted it. Would he even know who Arnold Schwarzenegger was? Mind you, she'd already done weird calisthenics in front of him and made quite the show of delivering an envelope she should've just put through his letter box like a normal person, so what did it matter if she acted like a nutter?

He nodded, then went inside.

A nod! Success! Now she could help him garden, pretend to find Will's business card, restore harmony to his life and ensure he had the very merriest of Christmases.

*

When the door to number 4 opened, a huge waft of sugar, ginger and spice hit Jess straight in the face. It was bliss. Like entering a North Pole biscuit factory and, from what she could see, it kind of was.

'Hi!' said the pretty mixed-race woman. She had a welcoming smile and a wondrous head of to-die-for hair. She was probably about Jess's age, if that. She had on dark leggings with a snowflake pattern dancing across them, a cherry-red top and a seasonal pinafore complete with dollops of icing and a handprint's worth of glitter. She exuded warmth. 'Come in, please. I'm Chantal and I'm guessing you're Jess from number fourteen?'

Jess nodded and gave a hip height wave. 'Got it in one. I love the pinafore.'

Chantal looked down at it and smiled as if noticing it for the first time. 'Fun, isn't it?'

'Orla Kiely?' Jess guessed.

'Nope. I made it. My auntie sends me the fabric from Nigeria. But I can see where you got the Orla Kiely vibe.' She made an adorable scrunched-nose face. 'Ready to join in the madness?'

She stepped to the side so that Jess could get a full view of the scene.

It looked like a Christmas film set. Trestle tables had taken centre stage in the open-plan lounge all the way through to the kitchen/dining area. They were covered in red and white polka-dotted oilskin cloths and, though she'd arrived at the appointed time, were already teaming with people – old and young. The Gem'n'Emms were there en masse, happily helping their children with errant piping bags, tiny silver and gold sugar beads and, of course, glitter. Heads were bent, concentration was intense, but there was plenty of talking and laughing as people finished decorating a biscuit then showed it to their neighbours before, in quite a few cases, eating their newly crafted piece of edible art.

'Hello, Josh.' Chantal was looking past Jess towards her little brick path that led to the street. 'Zoe! Eli! You ready to decorate some Santas?'

To a chorus of yeses, Jess turned and found herself face to face with an extremely attractive man. He was the right kind of tall (not crick your neck tall, but 'can you reach that tin for little ol' me' tall). Short, neat, dark hair. The greenest eyes Jess had ever seen in her entire life. He was like Jake Gyllenhaal after a proper buff and polish. With stubble.

'Hi.' He put out his hand and gave hers a quick, warm, shake. 'I'm Josh.' He pointed down the street. 'We're number twenty. I warn you now. Don't get your hopes up.'

'Jess. Number fourteen. Snap?'

Why did she keep answering things as questions?

Chantal ushered them all in. As she steered the children towards a couple of empty seats she said to Josh and Jess, 'I'm sure you'll both do something brilliant.' She lowered her voice to a stage whisper, 'Or fear the wrath of Drea.'

'Sorry, what was that?' A familiar Australian voice asked from behind them. When Drea plopped an arm around Jess and Josh's shoulders, Jess instinctively stiffened and forced herself not to wriggle away. 'Good.' Drea grinned. 'You two have finally met.'

They each shot Drea a confused look then Josh gave a cute little shrug, ducked out from under Drea's arm and excused himself. 'Gotta make sure some of that icing ends up on the biscuits, eh? Son? Budge up. Make room for your old dad, eh?'

Drea kept her arm draped around Jess's shoulders as Chantal floated off to get another platter of biscuits from the oven and Josh was consumed in a bustling chorus of Gem'n'Emms calling out 'Hey, Josh!' and 'All right kids?' 'How's all the Christmas preps going? 'Can we get you anything? Glitter?'

'Lovely, isn't he?' Drea said in a low voice.

Jess made an indeterminate noise she hoped meant *yes* and *not really on the market for a boyf.*

'Best eye candy on the street. And single. Well. Widower.'

Jess's hands flew to her heart. 'Oh, God. I'm so sorry. For him, obviously. And the children.'

Drea gave one of her pragmatic 'life's not always a bed of roses, doll face' nods. 'She passed away about a year after the little one was born. Eli. So ... four years back I think? Five? Cervical cancer.'

'That's awful.'

'From all accounts it was.'

'Weren't you here?'

'No. I lived over in Nottingham then.' A tiny muscle flickered at the top of her jawline as if even thinking about Nottingham brought back unwelcome memories.

There was quite clearly a story there. Then again, Jess supposed everyone had a story. Happy. Sad. Mysterious. It wasn't just her and her Cheese Sandwich Incident hiding behind the door of number 14. There were stories everywhere. Even at the beautifully appointed number 24 where poor Mr Winters and his knackered knees were hiding behind tightly closed curtains. Again.

She scanned the sea of faces on the off-chance he'd had a change of heart. Some were becoming a tiny bit more familiar. The Gem'n'Emms, of course. She'd have to be extra diligent with them, figure out who was who as they all had young children who'd no doubt be coming through her classroom over the coming years. Drea. Josh. A new name to add to her list. Who else did she know...?

'Right!' Smiley Drea was back in action. 'Let's get you settled, shall we?'

Before she could protest, Jess was shuttled over to where Josh was overseeing his children. Drea deftly commanded a jolly-looking chap in a set of mechanics overalls to 'find another chair and sharpish, Kev' and before she knew it, Jess was sitting next to Josh with Drea seated across from the pair of them, shooting Jess intense 'get in there' looks.

'Gosh,' Jess said, breaking eye contact with Drea and trying to absorb all of the action playing out along the trestle tables.

'I know, right?' Josh made a comedy face that looked a lot like a man panicking about how on earth he was going to match this evening.

The spread was impressive. Chantal was clearly no stranger to mass catering. There were platters of plain sugar cookies and gingerbread cookies in all sorts of shapes. Stars, reindeer, Santas, trees, presents, snowmen, candy canes. Not to mention tiny mountains of gorgeous little meringue kisses in swirls of red and white that had been scented with peppermint if the fresh wafts of mint were anything to go by. Chantal must've been baking for days.

As if on cue, Chantal appeared and handed Jess three small piping bags with red, green and white frosting in them. 'There're more colours spread out along the table. Glitter, mini-snowflakes, whatever you want. Enjoy.'

Jess was dazzled. 'Is she always this amazing?' she asked Josh.

'This isn't the half of it,' Josh said. 'You should see her stall at the summer fête. Puts Mary Berry to shame. Don't even try to compete. Just enjoy.' He grinned then examined the tray of biscuits in front of them. 'Here you are.' He handed her a sugar cookie in the shape of an angel. 'This looks a suitable one for you to start with.' When their fingers brushed as he handed it to her she blushed.

What a div!

She spent a few pointedly focused minutes giving the angel a white gown, adorning it with green trim, green eyes, a red smile and red hair, before looking up to see if she could locate some glitter. She found hundreds and thousands and used those instead.

'Wow!' Josh called to his children. 'Look at that, Zoe, Eli. Jess has outdone your ol' dad, eh?' Josh showed them his efforts. It was a Santa. Sort of. His belt was wonky. His trousers were green and his beard was blue. It looked exactly like the type of biscuit one of her students would make. She loved it, and the part of her stomach that knew he was single made an out-of-practice flip.

The children laughed at his and oo'ed and ahh'd at hers.

'Yours is perfect,' she said when their eyes met.

'Liar,' he countered.

They shared a smile.

She blushed again. *Idiot!*

'Where'd you learn to decorate so well?'

'I'm an art teacher. Well. Year three teacher now. At the

school. Primary. The one over there.' She pointed in the direction she thought the school might be, willing herself to *stop talking*.

Josh crowed, 'No wonder you're so talented! Lucky us, eh kids? Having the next... ummm... who's a famous artist? Picasso? Manet? Monet?'

She snorted and picked up a star-shaped sugar cookie. It was easier to look at that than Josh because her tummy kept sending out little darts of approval whenever their eyes met. 'I think the chances of out-painting the likes of Monet with icing and hundreds and thousands is relatively slim.'

'I don't know...' He pretending to give her biscuit a proper inspection through a monocle. When he spoke, he sounded as though he'd walked straight out of Buckingham Palace. 'I would say hundreds and thousands lend themselves perfectly to impressionism.'

She contained a laugh and countered in an equally highfalutin voice, 'I think you'll find they're far more suited to pointillism.'

He arched an eyebrow.

She arched one back.

'When you two are done flirting, do you mind if I use one of those piping bags with the white icing?'

They both looked across the table to meet the amused, but expectant expression of a white-haired woman with dark brown eyes, and a slightly sharper look from Drea. Jess was certain Drea had pointed the older woman out the other night. Just as her name was about to leap onto the tip of her tongue, Josh handed her his bag of icing then gave Drea a quick nod Jess couldn't quite read.

''Course, Martha. Forgive me. I've been hogging it.'

71

Martha Snodgrass! Of course. Best name ever.

'Not at all. And I was just teasing,' Martha gave the air between her and Jess a little swipe. 'Martha Snodgrass,' she said with a genteel nod of the head, her hands too occupied with icing to shake.

'Jess Green,' Jess said mimicking the head nod.

'Ah! The new girl. The one at fourteen?'

'That's the one.' Jess smiled, still a bit taken aback at how much people knew about her. She was pretty sure the neighbours flanking her in London *for over a year* hadn't had any idea of her existence.

'If you don't mind my saying, you're a welcome replacement.'

'Oh?' Jess sat up straight. She'd not heard anything about the previous tenants, other than that they were a couple with a second child on the way so wanted to move a bit further out where they could get a larger back garden.

'Music,' Martha intoned. 'They were playing it all the time.'

Josh laughed good-naturedly. 'It wasn't the music you hated, Martha, it was the type of music.'

She gave a tight-lipped nod, adding an expert swirl of icing to the top of her gingerbread Christmas tree as she did. 'Noise pollution is not music,' she said tapping a tiny little gold star into place at the top of the tree.

'I suppose that's true,' Jess said, not really understanding.

When the woman next to Martha distracted her with a question about some miniature snowflakes she wanted to use, Josh leant towards her, the scent of oranges and cloves surrounding her as he did. 'She's got a lodger who's

72

in a band. Tyler. No one knows why she hasn't kicked him out yet.'

Jess gave a non-committal shrug. Maybe Martha was lonely and having someone to complain about was better than having no one there at all. She instantly thought of Mr Winters and wondered if... No. No matchmaking. No interfering with anyone's lives. She'd learnt her lesson. The hard way.

'So what will you be doing for Christmas Day, dear? Any big plans?'

Jess shifted uncomfortably as a few more pairs of eyes turned to her. 'Oh, you know...'

'Hmmm...' said Martha, narrowing her gaze. 'I'm doing a bit of that as well. Would you hand me the hundreds and thousands, please?' Once Jess had passed them over, Martha cleared her throat. 'EmmaGemma,' she said pronouncedly to a couple of the women still waiting to hear Jess's plans, 'could you run me through the recycling bin dates again, please? They keep changing them.'

Jess smiled. Martha had switched the spotlight off her the instant she'd seen Jess's discomfort. She definitely owed her a favour. And also wanted to get out of here before anyone else could ask more questions.

After decorating a handful more cookies, and receiving a discreet invitation from Martha to join her for a sherry during the Queen's speech on Christmas Day, Jess took the opportunity to slip out of her seat when Drea, Josh and his daughter became embroiled in a heated discussion about whether or not a reindeer could also be a unicorn. She thanked Chantal for her incredible evening then, as discreetly as she could, slipped back behind the door of number 14 with a whole new set of considerations to stew over. Her awkwardly flipping stomach had definitely liked Josh. Her flushing cheeks had, too. But she also flushed when she was lying so was she attracted to him or lying to herself about something? Drea's hawk eyes had pinged between the pair of them all night. She'd been quite quiet for Drea, actually. Too quiet. Which made the whole making-new-friends thing a bit more nerve-racking. She saw it all the time in the schoolyard. A lonely, frightened new kid over-keen to make friends with the first child to be nice to them and then, all of the sudden, kablam!, it turned out they'd made a mistake. They should've held out. Waited for someone who may not have seemed the obvious friend choice on the surface but who, in the end, would offer the most rewarding, genuine friendship. Perhaps she was part of some greater ploy of Drea's to take over the whole of Boughton and turn it into Christmasville – a sort of reverse of Potterville. A place where cheer and good tidings were the only things allowed. Which would, of course, mean Jess would have to move because she was really finding it hard to plumb the happy feels these days.

All of which made her think of Mr Winters who, once again, had been a no-show.

People she hadn't ever seen before had come to Chantal's night so if he were to have appeared at any of the nights so far, it would've been hers, but... perhaps he simply didn't like people.

She pressed her face to her front window and stared at the dark house at the end of the street. People who didn't like people didn't let complete strangers help with their tulips. A tiny *ah ha!* moment surfaced. Mr Winters had green fingers. And green-fingered people, no matter how cantankerous on the outside, had to, like the very best chocolates, have gooey insides. Why else would Cadbury have named their big tubs of chocolates Roses? She pulled up a search engine and tapped in a few key words determined to find out exactly which type of rose Mr Winters was, hoping, against hope, that she wasn't kidding herself that his thorny exterior truly did hide a beautiful, yet to be revealed, bloom.

5 December

'Cooooeeeeeee!'
         Drea. Had to be.

'Jess?' There was a knock on the door then a triple ring of the bell. 'Jessica. Open the door. We need to discuss what you're doing on the fourteenth.'

Crumbs. Goosebumps prickled across Jess's skin. She hadn't come up with anything yet. She pulled her feet up onto the sofa and muted the television.

'Jess? I have a plate of biscuits and I am in urgent need of a cup of tea to eat them with,' Drea persisted.

Her mind reeled trying to come up with something. Anything. Well. Not anything. It had to dazzle. Nope. Nothing. She was fresh out of sparkly, knock-your-socks-off-ideas. She squished herself even more tightly into the corner of the sofa.

'Jessica.' Drea laughed and let the mail flap clank into place. 'I can see you. Would you open the bloody door? It's freezing out here.'

Embarrassed, Jess leapt to her feet and pulled open the door. 'Sorry, I—'

'Christ, woman. What's got into you? Do you still have that cold? You seemed all right last night.' She looked around the house. 'Crikey. Please don't tell me you've finished decorating.' She scrunched up her nose as her eyes darted round the place. 'What is it? Some sort of mismatched minimalist look? If so, sorry, doll, epic fail.'

If just about anyone from her old life had made that comment, Jess's hackles would've flown straight up. For some reason, from Drea, it was simply observant. She was right. Jess had done the bare minimum in terms of making her house feel like a home. The estate agent had rung about picking up the For Sale sign earlier. She'd sounded harried, about to head off on a three-week trip somewhere warm and beachy, so Jess had said there was no rush, she'd done it already, they could pick it up in the new year if that suited. A total lie. She hadn't taken it down. She wouldn't, she'd decided. Not until she'd started her new job and made sure she could handle it. That way she'd save the estate agent the trouble of putting up a new one.

Jess ushered Drea in and headed towards the kettle.

Drea followed her with the plate of biscuits. They were clearly from last night and had been decorated by a variety of people, if the craftsmanship was anything to go by.

'Right,' Drea tapped the table with her shiny red fingernail. 'Sit down and talk.'

'I thought you were here to talk to me,' Jess replied, a little more sulkily than a thirty-one-year-old woman should address a new neighbour. Friend? Anyway. She gave her head a shake. 'Sorry. I'm just—'

'Why'd you move here?' Drea cut in.

'I told you, didn't I?'

'No.'

Oh. Perhaps she should've written up a quick little bio and slipped it through everyone's letter box the day she'd moved in. Created a new backstory even. Told everyone she was part of a witness relocation programme. Actually, that would defeat the whole point of being in witness protection. She definitely felt as though she needed a buffer; a cover story for her to live amid this wonderful collection of delightfully normal people going about their day-to-day lives as she tried to get a grip and follow suit.

She looked at Drea's kind, expectant face. Yeah, she was a little bossy, but something instinctively told Jess she was an ally. Perhaps confiding in her would help ease the anxiety gnawing away at her.

The kettle flicked itself off.

'Go on,' Drea nodded towards the counter. 'Make us a cuppa. Builder's for me, please. Then come and sit down and tell Auntie Drea all about it.'

An hour later, Jess felt miles better than she had when she'd woken up. Invigorated even. It could've been the four cookies and two cups of tea she'd consumed, but Drea had a way of putting things into perspective that even her parents hadn't been able to. Although . . . Jess had kind of put the whole St Benny's thing into soft focus. *Time to make a change. Losing perspective on what really mattered. Not in total agreement with the influence parents had over the curriculum.*

Okay fine: she'd lied.

Jess had told Drea she'd had a run-in with a student (true) and the student's parents (true) about a grade (total lie) and that the parents had threatened to sue unless Jess was fired (true) but an alternative arrangement was reached after mediation from another parent on the school board, a judge in real life (a Number One wife), and that Jess had ultimately left of her own free will (partial lie).

'. . . The main point being, if they'd really wanted to sue, they would've,' Drea was saying with a force of conviction that Jess found reassuring. 'They sound rich enough and stupid enough to bowl on in whether or not they should've. Since they didn't? I'm guessing the school advised them on whether or not they had a case. They obviously didn't, so . . . that means you were right all along but they – and by "they" I mean the parents – wanted someone made an example of to appease their egos over the fact that they've spent their lives raising a little shit.'

Jess nodded. That was about the long and short of it, apart from the fact the disagreement hadn't been over Crispin's grades.

As for her? She'd been told she could either leave quietly with a neutral recommendation or leave loudly and be fired for incompetence with no recommendation. They'd known she would choose the former. She was only thirty-one and they knew as well as she did that she had never wanted to do anything but teach.

'People like that make my blood boil,' Drea delicately wiped a crumb away from the corner of her perfectly done-up lips. 'They think it's completely acceptable to cover up the fact they can't raise their own child properly with threats. As if throwing money about will disguise the fact they've raised a heinous little ankle biter.'

'Oh, well . . .' Jess tried to protest but couldn't. Crispin Anand-Haight had been one of her least favourite students. Ever. Over eight years of teaching some two thousand children, so . . . yeah, she pretty much agreed with Drea on this one. 'I just want to draw a line under it, you know? Walk into my new life without anything hanging over me from the old one.'

Drea barked a laugh. 'Good luck with that one, darlin'.' She laughed again, took a sip of tea, choked on it, made a bit of a gagging noise as she tried not to spit her tea out entirely then, eventually, regained her composure only to start laughing again.

It wasn't that funny. Message received, loud and clear. Baggage was baggage, but how could you let go of something that felt as though it had crept into your bones?

'People overcome worse things,' Drea eventually said. 'You'll be fine, doll.'

Jess stopped herself from snapping that having her entire professional reputation falsely besmirched was pretty high up there in the Worst Things That Could Happen list, but took a tactical bite off the gingerbread man instead. It wasn't as if hashing over her past was going to change what had happened.

'What about you?' she asked Drea once she'd finished eating the gingerbread man's head.

'What about me?' Drea's normally confident demeanour stiffened into something a bit closer to defensiveness.

'Why'd you move here? You said you used to live in Nottingham?'

'Oh, yes. Nottingham,' Drea said airily. 'The Melbourne of the Northern Hemisphere.'

Jess's chins doubled in surprise.

'Joke.' Drea took a more thoughtful sip of tea. 'Let's just say, Nottingham was a chapter of my life I could've done without writing.' She picked up a snowflake-shaped biscuit and began to pick off the hundreds and thousands one by one with the tip of her nail, painstakingly lining them up on the kitchen towel Jess had offered in lieu of serviettes.

'So you're from Melbourne?'

Drea nodded.

'When was the last time you were back?'

'Four – five years ago? Not since I moved.' Again, a note of defensiveness covered the response. 'I should've gone back. Not permanently, I'm happy here, but ... I missed a few things with my boy a mother shouldn't.' Another hundred and thousand was removed from the biscuit.

Jess left the next, obvious question unspoken.

'Men,' Drea finally said. '*A* man in the case of Nottingham, but—' she waved her hand in the air between them as if cleaning a slate and starting over. 'It's men who've been at the base of most of my problems.'

Jess stayed silent. It was her best tactic for getting a child to tell the truth, eventually, when they were trying to worm their way out of something with a fib. Not that Drea would be fibbing about anything, but ... who knew?

'What did you think of Josh?' Drea changed the subject, her expression innocent, but her eyes telling another story.

'Nice.' Jess said cautiously. Was she being asked if she fancied him or was Drea making a claim on him? 'He's definitely got the eye-candy thing covered.'

'That he does,' Drea said, eyes dropping back to her biscuit's diminishing amount of hundreds and thousands. 'Do you fancy taking a crack at him?'

'What? Eww! No. I don't want to take a crack at anything.'

Drea rolled her eyes. 'You're a sensitive little bear, aren't you? All I meant was, the man's available, you're a teacher so a shoo-in to get along with his children—'

Jess cut her off. 'Just because I teach children doesn't mean I want to date someone with children.'

Interesting. She hadn't realised that was one of her criteria.

Drea opened her mouth and made a noise as if several sentences were battling to be the first one out of the chute. None of them won.

Jess answered the questions she was pretty sure Drea was trying to ask 'Yes. I do want children of my own one day, but not now. No. I don't want a boyfriend – widowed, single, married, with or without children, hot, ugly, whatever. I want to be on my own. And as for "taking a crack at anyone"?' She faltered. The truth was she was feeling weird about physical contact these days. As if she had some sort of PTSD from the Cheese Sandwich Incident. She could remember her hands on Crispin's arms and then his fist connecting with – *bleurgh*. She didn't want to think about it.

'I'm presuming you have an ex and that he did quite a number on you.'

Jess surprised herself by snorting. Her break-up with Martin had surprisingly little to do with why she was feeling the way she was. 'It's actually a bit weird how little I think of him.'

It was, as well. She'd cared for him. Obviously. Otherwise she wouldn't have been living with him. Had thought she'd loved him, even. They had similar taste in restaurants, box sets, and board games. Not living in one another's pockets, as her parents did, had never been a problem. It was, Jess realised, an easy relationship, but not a very passionate one. The truth was, with their busy, hectic work-based lives, she and Martin barely saw one another except at joint social events, of which there were very few. She was up at five-thirty most mornings, away to school within the hour and not home until seven or eight, when she usually had some marking or preparations for the next day's work. Martin, a city-centric estate agent, had incredibly erratic hours and, as a 'takes contacts to make contacts' kind of guy, was always out meeting and greeting (read: at the pub).

Drea said, 'I like the way he says, "All right, son?"'

Jess blinked, confused. 'Sorry?'

'Josh,' she explained, levering the final hundred and thousand – a red one – off the biscuit. 'Whenever he speaks to Eli, he calls him son. I like it. "Come here, son." "Put that down, son.' '"Good job, son."' She got a faraway look in her eyes, as if she were imagining calling her own son *son*.

'Was your son's father not involved in his life?'

'Nah,' she said with a wave of her hand.

'Are you missing him?'

'Who?'

'Your son,' Jess prompted gently.

Drea's eyes glassed over then she gave her head a short sharp shake. 'Course I do, but he's a man now. Doesn't need his mum micromanaging his life from however many thousands of miles away, does he?'

Jess scrunched up her nose. 'Did you ever do that?'

Drea shook her head then shrugged. 'I was... I – I could've been more consistent with him.'

'How do you mean?'

'I was either all over him for something or telling him to pull his socks up and do whatever it was on his own.

But that was usually because I had a boyfriend and was trying to make him happy.'

Jess shot her a questioning look.

'Most men, in my experience, do not take to another man's sprogs, so . . . I coulda done better.' Drea's nose twitched as if she was fighting some unwelcome tears. She began to tease the hundreds and thousands from yet another biscuit. 'I only kept on at him about the important stuff, though. School. Manners. Responsibility. And he did it. Ploughed through uni and law school without me there nagging him or wrapping him in cotton wool. He's a good kid, even if I do say so myself.'

'What's his name?'

'Spencer.'

The way Drea said it sounded so full of love and longing and regret it made Jess's eyes well up.

'I'd love to meet him one day.'

Drea cleared her throat and finally met Jess's eyes. 'With some luck, you might.'

'Really?' The idea of meeting the male form of Drea was strangely cheering to Jess.

'Yeah. This Christmas. Aww, look. It might not happen, but . . .' She gave her one of those 'I'm going to level with you' looks. 'I sent him a ticket. An airline ticket. To come over. See the new house, meet my new friends.' She gave Jess a pointed smile that instantly deepened the friendship they seemed to be forming.

'Why wouldn't it happen?' Jess asked.

'I send him one every year.'

'*Wow.* That's nice. And . . . ?'

Drea cleared her throat again and put the biscuit down,

pushing the plate away from her as she did. 'He's never come.'

Ah.

'He...' Drea gave the kitchen table a few taps with her fingernails. 'When I left things became quite... complicated between the two of us.'

Jess got up, put the kettle on again and leant on the breakfast bar while Drea continued.

'The truth is, I wasn't the put-together, organised being you see before you when I had Spence. I was a kid, really. My parents kicked me out. They were the country-club type. Not the sort to have a sixteen-year-old debutante daughter wandering round in a family way. There was no way I was going to have the boyfriend involved because he was a right plonker, but it didn't seem to stop me from falling for more of them until I finally got my head screwed on.'

'They kicked you out?' Jess backtracked, completely unable to imagine her parents doing the same. 'What did you do?'

'Only thing I could,' Drea said without a flicker of humour. 'I danced.'

'What?' Jess tried to imagine her in leggings and a sparkly leotard and... actually could.

'Pole-danced, doll. I'd been taking ballet, jazz, modern, the lot right up until I was up the duff. Once I'd had Spence, I put my moves to work on a pole.' Drea tried to imagine men tucking notes into a teenage mother's G-string and shuddered. Drea clocked it and sniffily tacked on, 'I only danced at the no-touch ones with the biggest bouncers and I only did it until I had enough money to do what I really wanted to.'

'Which was?'

'Fitness-based stuff. Exercise.'

Jess shook her head. She wasn't following.

Drea looked over her shoulders as if she were about to disclose an embarrassing secret. 'Have you heard of the Bondi Beach Body?'

Jess nodded. Just about the whole world had heard about it. It had eclipsed Zumba and Soul Cycle and just about every other fitness craze. Amanda did it all the time before work. She called it 'Death by Lunges'. Amanda had great legs.

'That's me,' Drea said.

'What?' Jess nearly spat out her tea. 'You invented it?'

Drea did one of those head-tip to the side moves that said yes, she did, but that she'd earned it. The hard way.

'Wow. That's amazing.'

'Not so much when you consider the bozos I dated along the way. The parenting choices I should've made if I hadn't been so obsessed with finding the right guy. Spence had to handle a lot of growing up stuff on his own. Things he should've had his mum by his side for.' She huffed out an aggrieved sigh and shot Jess a sad smile. 'Story has a happy ending, though. Sort of. I finally ditched the last one two years back. In Nottingham.'

Ah.

'But you haven't been back to Oz?'

Drea dropped her decoration-free biscuit into the bin. 'I think that's enough sharing and caring for today, dollface. All right?

So that was a no, then.

'I'm sure you did a better job than you think you did,' Jess tried to blow a bit more oxygen into the conversation.

'With Spence?' She picked up a star-shaped biscuit. 'Yeah, he's a good lad, all told. Knows right from wrong on the important stuff.' She scrunched up her nose and began flicking hundreds and thousands off of the star. 'I didn't give him the best of examples when it came to relationships.' She finally met Jess's eye. 'I'd love to have gone back, watched him graduate, helped him move into flat, meet his partner, but I didn't earn it. Nor have I earned the right to beg for his forgiveness. It's too much pressure to put on the lad. He's got his ticket. He gets to choose.'

'We all make mistakes.'

'We don't all date blokes who insist upon relocating to another country before your kid leaves uni.'

'I'm sure you had your reasons for agreeing to go. Didn't Barack Obama's mum leave him with his grandparents when she remarried? He turned out all right.'

'She turned out dead,' Drea countered. 'Cancer. Well before he became President.' Drea blinked pointedly, then scrubbed her nails through her hair. 'Look. The point being... I talk a good game about how to be a good person but the truth is, I didn't prioritise the right one. Spencer should've been my number one guy all along.'

'He must know you love him.'

Drea made a strangled noise. 'I'm not so sure about that.'

Jess's heart skipped a beat. One thing she had always been sure of was her parents' love.

'So... when is the ticket good for?' She asked.

'Between now and Christmas.'

Jess gulped. That would be one expensive ticket. Then again, Drea had invented Bondi Beach Body. She could probably afford it. Which did beg the question, why was she living here in this lovely, but not exactly exclusive cul-de-sac.

'Why don't you move back to Australia?' she asked instead. 'You could always live in a different city if you wanted to give him space.'

Drea took a sharp inhalation of breath and shook her head. 'I want Spence to want to come here, you know? By choice. I just want him to know I'm a normal mum now. A normal mum living a normal life.'

And suddenly the living advent calendar made sense. Drea was paying her dues to the Christmas miracle gods to see if she could earn a miracle of her own.

'Well, I will cross absolutely everything I have for you.' Jess held up her fingers and crossed everything she could. All of a sudden her blood ran cold. 'I'm so sorry, Drea. I've got to go.'

'Oh, right.' Drea gave her a dubious look. 'Didn't realise being a sofa limpet was a nine-to-five thing.'

'No, sorry. It's not that. It's . . .' she hesitated. 'It's Mr Winters.'

'What? Number twenty-four?'

'Yup. I told him I'd help him plant tulip bulbs.'

Drea gave her the side eye. 'And how did this arrangement come to pass? '

Jess quickly explained about the Christmas card, accidentally opening it, reading it, feeling hugely guilty and trying to fix it. 'Which, of course, I probably shouldn't have told you either, because now that's two of us who know who shouldn't and Mr Winters is still in the dark.'

'If he hasn't opened the letter.'

'Good point. Although, even if he has opened it, it's

pretty unlikely he'll go on the internet and find Will's catering company. He needs the business card if he is going to get in touch with him.' Jess suddenly felt ill. 'What if the Christmas card has made him even more depressed? Bringing back all of those memories about his son and learning he's had two grandsons all of these years and never known it.'

'You're going to have to fix it, doll.' Drea's tone suggested doing otherwise was completely out of the question. 'If he has a chance to be reunited with family? You've got to make it happen.'

An interesting order coming from someone opting for the 'If You Build It, He Will Come' mode of family issue resolution.

'How?'

'That's your problem, doll.' Drea's expression darkened. 'But if that man does not do something on Christmas Eve for the advent calendar? I will be raging. And I will blame you.' She gave Jess an adorably bright smile. One, Jess now realised, that was the smile of someone who could do a thousand lunges and feel no pain. 'No pressure.'

After Drea left, Jess raced into the shower, dragged a comb through her hair, stuffed an Alice band onto her head because her fringe was definitely not feeling obedient, removed it, put her bobble-topped hat on instead, then raced down the street. She knocked on Mr Winters' door only to be met with a deafening silence. She tried again. Nothing. She peeked into the windows. Nope. No signs of life apart from a large blue-eyed Siamese cat, which gave her a decidedly dismissive flick of the tail before stalking out of the room.

Shoulders slumped and feeling as if she'd let him and

the neighbourhood down, Jess went home, mind spinning with ways to cajole Mr Winters out of his house and, more importantly, how to convince him having the entire neighbourhood over on Christmas Eve would be a good thing.

6 December

6 December
To: WillWinters@TheMerryVictualler.co.uk
From: JessGreen2000@gmail.com
Subject: Your Christmas Card

Dear Mr Winters

Delete delete delete

Dear Will (is it all right if I call you Will?)

Delete delete delete

Dear Will,
Allow me to introduce myself. My name is Jess(ica) Green. I live at number 14 Christmas Street, just down the road from your grandfather, Mr Arnold Winters.

How do I know he is your grandfather, you might be asking yourself. Good question. Well, it's sort of a funny story. The postman accidentally delivered your Christmas card to mine and because I was so excited to have received Christmas cards at my new house, I didn't even bother to check who it was from (or addressed to, obviously) and...

erm . . . I opened it. I'm really, really, really sorry. And then I read it. (Sorry, sorry, sorry times a million, I know it's illegal please don't press charges it was genuinely an honest mistake).

I brought the card to your grandfather straight away, but accidentally managed to superglue the envelope shut without the all-important contact details card. Because your grandfather is a) older than average and b) not entirely keen to increase his social circle from what I can gather, I didn't manage to get your business card to him so I decided I'd write to you instead to see if perhaps you might be able to send him a second Christmas card with a second business card as I would hate for your plan to meet your grandfather to go wrong. I'm so sorry to have created such a mess. I know this is your busy season (great name for the catering company by the way!). Maybe he will need to use your services for Christmas Eve as his house is the final destination for our street's living advent calendar???

Anyway. Sorry. I'm interfering and I have had bad experiences with interfering so I'll just leave it there but if you have any questions or are cross, I understand on both counts.

Yours sincerely

Jess(ica) Green (Number 14 Christmas Street)

'I would say you're a . . . hmmm . . .' Kevin crossed his arms and leant closer in towards Jess. 'You're a tough one.'

Jess bristled and backed up a step. She was feeling decidedly edgy. And it wasn't just because Kev from number 6 was eyeing her up like a prize pony.

Okay. She might be overreacting a little bit to being at the wrong end of his invisible magnifying glass. Kev was perfectly nice, as was his wife, and the actual reason he was peering at her was for his 'what kind of car would you be' party trick. So far he'd handed out three minivans, a Jaguar (Drea), a Porsche, an Aston Martin (Jess's ex would've died to have been told he was one of those), four pastel convertible Volkswagen bugs (the Gem'n'Emms – whose husbands were all primary-coloured Volkswagen camper vans), a Range Rover, a Bugatti, whatever that was (it drew whistles of admiration from most of the men anyway) and, for Martha Snodgrass, an old-fashioned Land Rover. Everyone hid titters or rolled their eyes as she crabbed something about practicality and reliability being preferable to carbon-fibre showpieces, *particularly* as there was no *radio* inside a proper Land Rover with which to blare *poor excuses of music*. She'd finished with a pointed look at Tyler, her lodger, who was too busy enjoying his miniature DeLorean to notice.

Either way, Kevin was taking ages to figure out what kind of car she was like and having everyone's eyes trained on her was making her feel anxious. As if she was transparent and they could all see her flaws. Her heartache. The anxiety she'd been battling for over a year. The scarlet FAIL that had so nearly besmirched her teaching record.

Drea (and Jess's mum, if she were here) would be telling her to buck up. That she was stronger than this. It was her choice what face she decided to show the world. A positive confident one, or the quivering wreck that had emerged after being browbeaten by a pair of over-privileged parents whose son wouldn't survive a second in the real world. That, or he'd become prime minister. It was fifty-fifty on that one.

Out here in front of all of her new neighbours, she'd

love to have that bright can-do attitude. A Teflon exterior. People's opinions bouncing off her. But at home behind her curtains? She was definitely an anxious mess. Especially since, once again, her day had been a bit of a dud.

Though she had refreshed her email enough times to wear out the return key, Will Winters had not written back to her. He was most likely talking to the police and preparing some sort of restraining order or invasion-of-privacy charges.

She'd tried a second time to make good on her offer to lend her bendy knees to Mr Winters so that he could get his tulip bulbs in, but he'd not answered the door again. She'd even done a slow 'walk by' this evening on the off-chance he'd be coming out to join them. But there was no sign of the Siamese cat, the curtains were drawn and not even a hint of lamplight round the edges. The house was big enough that he could be sitting in a room round the back. There was a large stone slab path that presumably led round to the back garden, but adding trespassing to her list of criminal activities probably wasn't the best of ideas. As such, she'd pretended she was on a perfectly innocent stroll. When she saw Rex and Kai coming out of their house, she waved and joined them as they all headed to number 6. Rex and Kai already had their cars. Kai was a little red Corvette and was thrilled. Rex had one of those big 1950s trucks like they had in films like *The Bridges of Madison County*, but this one had miniature milk churns filled with flowers in it. He, too, was delighted. Now it was just Jess. The cheese stands alone, she thought glumly, shifting again, trying to adopt a pose that was less deer in headlights and more, check it out, no one can slap a label on me.

'Get on with it, Kev!' Someone shouted from the back of the crowd. 'It's bloody freezing out here.'

'I've got to go out in half an hour, Kev. Can you speed this up a bit? Oop, mind yourself love, it's a bit slippy there.'

'All right, all right,' Kev pressed his hands in a 'simmer-down folks' gesture. 'Just want to get this last one right.'

'Anyone know if they're gritting the roads? I need to get to the shops.'

'Kev! Freezing my bloody tits off 'ere, mate. Get on with it.'

Kevin from number 6 was a mechanic. He was also an avid toy car collector. As such, his contribution to the advent calendar was a toy car for everyone followed by a race on a glow-in-the-dark ramp he'd set up. It began at the apex of his hedge which was nearly two metres tall and ended at the kerb on the other side of the street. His wife was telling anyone who'd listen that if they wanted more than one car just to say because she'd had more than enough of Kev's 'precious cars' clogging up her shelving units. 'He'd have us all sleeping in the loft if he could,' she was telling someone as they all waited for Kev to decide what kind of car Jess was.

Finally, after what felt like an eternity Kev reached out to the portion of his collection he'd displayed with pride on a card table he'd set up an hour earlier, and plucked a racing-green Mini Cooper from the collection. A little swirl of warmth wrapped round her heart. She'd always liked Mini Coopers. Never in a million years would her life in London have afforded her one, but maybe . . . maybe if she set up a special savings account—

She dismissed the thought. Things don't make life

better. Happiness and confidence and kindness make life better.

Kev held up a rather bland-looking Rover alongside the Mini. Her spirits plummeted. He squinted at Jess, then smiled and handed her the Mini Cooper.

A collective sigh of relief went round the crowd.

Jess smiled at the car, stupidly happy that Kev chose it in the end. A sign, perhaps, that things might be taking a turn for the better? She'd put it on her mantelpiece as a symbol of hope when she got home.

'Right then, Kev,' the neighbour with a previous engagement briskly rubbed his hands together then gave them a loud clap. 'What do you want us to do? Chuck them on the ramp and see how we go?'

Kevin's face filled with horror. He began an exceedingly detailed plan as to how he'd classed the cars and how the races needed to be broken down by model and make when Drea cut in and instructed him, 'Just tell three people to bring their cars up, the winners will then race one another in groups of three and so on until we have a single winner. Right?'

Jess hid a giggle behind her mittened hands. She could easily picture Drea getting the entire street to do press-ups and star jumps if she wanted to. Little wonder they'd all been hurling snowballs at each other on the day she'd arrived. Little wonder, she thought a bit more sadly, that her son saw her in a different light.

Kevin nodded obediently and called out three names.

His wife applauded her and asked Drea if she could come over next time she needed Kevin to do some housework.

'You got it, doll,' Drea winked. 'Now let's get crackin', eh?'

Once the races were under way, Drea worked her way through the crowd with her winning Jaguar and handed Jess a reusable water bottle. 'Stunning Picpoul in there, if you fancy something to take the edge off. I've disguised it so people don't think I'm a complete lush.' She shot Jess a wicked smile then gazed out at the crowd as a queen might survey her people. Grandly.

Jess took a sip of the wine and agreed, it was a nice one. Another little sliver of something lodged inside Jess's chest, the part that was intimidated by Drea, slipped away into the night. She was a really kind woman. Organising the neighbourhood for the living advent calendar. Fostering a sense of togetherness even if it came with little squabbles and – they all clapped as an exuberant five-year-old happy danced at his family's success on the race track – the triumphs. Peering through mail flaps when a neighbour couldn't find it in her to get out of her jim-jams and onto the business of actually doing something to feel proud of. Which made her remember . . .

'Drea?' She handed her back the water bottle.

'Yeah, doll?'

'I noticed Mr Winters hasn't come to any of the events.'

'He's probably hiding from you,' Drea shot back without bothering to look at her.

'What? Why? What makes you think that?' Jess asked, horrified.

'He did it to me when I first moved in.'

'Why?'

She flicked her hand dismissively. 'I wanted a Christmas tree.'

'What? Why did you go there?'

Drea nodded towards Mr Winters' house. 'It used to be the farmhouse for an old Christmas tree farm. Either he sold the land or whoever owned it sold the land and I got it into my head that he had a little Christmas tree farm back there.'

They both looked to the end of the street where there was a small woodland beyond which were a string of playing fields that joined up the primary and secondary schools beyond them.

'Does he?'

Drea shook her head. 'No. Bloody nice back garden, though. The man's got a gift.'

'Not for the gab,' Jess said sadly, accepting another sip of icy-cold wine from Drea's water bottle. Another cheer went up from the crowd. It made her heart constrict that Mr Winters wasn't out here, enjoying the fun. Even Mrs Snodgrass, who clearly liked playing the role of Resident Curmudgeon, was made up at her recent win (she'd taken out one of the Gem'n'Emms and Josh who was wearing a bobbing pair of reindeer antlers). Surely, a man who had no family and no friends that she could see would enjoy the comfort of a neighbourhood gathering. Being old and alone had to be scary enough, but being old and alone at Christmas when he had the chance to be looked after by his grandson...

A thought occurred to her. Maybe he *had* got in touch. Perhaps that's why he wasn't here. He'd looked up Will's company and had driven to meet him. Her stomach went all squidgy at the thought of the two of them sharing mince pies and mulled wine. No. He shouldn't drink and drive. Especially not this time of year. She reimagined the scenario. Mince pies and hot chocolate? Maybe. Or what if… oh, no she didn't like the direction this was going. What if Mr Winters had got in touch, but had hunted Will down at one of his events and started shouting at him about whatever it was that had transpired between him and his son all of those years ago? Accused him of meddling. Interfering where he should've left well enough alone.

The squidginess turned hard and cold. This was all Jess's fault. If she'd kept the Christmas card, Mr Winters would be none the wiser. Then he'd be home and safe and yanking his curtain shut like normal.

Just then a car pulled into the cul-de-sac. It headed straight down the road and pulled to a halt at the edge of the crowd, at which point the driver – Jess couldn't see as she was on the far side of the crowd – pressed his horn. Again and again and again.

People scrambled out of the way amid a flurry of 'Hold your horses' and 'Cool your jets, mate' and 'Bloody impatient old buggers.' A child began to cry. Unexpectedly, the car lurched forward with a heavy screech of shifting gears. Parents grabbed children into their arms and hurled abuse at the driver. Kevin dove to pull his card table full of miniatures out of the way, while a handful of others quickly took up the ramp and track the cars had just been racing down.

When the car passed by Jess, she felt the blood drain from her face. It was Mr Winters. He looked as pale as she felt. He also looked frightened and angry. His hands were wrapped round the steering wheel of his sturdy-looking Volvo estate, his eyes trained on his house at the end of the street. He drove slowly and steadily, the car bumping up onto the short drive that sat alongside his front garden. He parked the car then disappeared out of sight on the path that led round to the back of the house.

Jess didn't blame him. If he was as shaken up as she felt, she would've wanted to run away and hide as well.

'The man's a bloody menace!' someone shouted.

'I think a couple of us should go down and have a word.'

'Don't send anyone nice.'

'No way are we going to his on Christmas Eve.'

'Can you imagine the type of party he'd throw?'

'Probably puts arsenic in his eggnog. Kill the lot of us.'

'Bloody shambles. Couldn't he see there were children? He could've seriously hurt someone!'

'It's like that man in . . . where was it? California? Mixed up the brake and gas pedals, didn't he? Killed hundreds.'

'No, it was less than that.'

'Whatever. People died.'

The street fell silent.

Then, as if the matter had been settled, one of the Gem'n'Emms scooped a toddler up onto her hip, grabbed another child by the hand and turned to Drea. 'You need to uninvite him. I do not want that man anywhere near my children.'

Drea gave her a look that would've silenced the meanest of despots. 'This is a street-wide advent calendar.'

Emma or Gemma huffed. 'He's not exactly the community type, Drea. Why don't you throw the Christmas Eve party? All of this is your fault anyway.'

'My fault?' Drea repeated, her words edged with ice.

'Well, it was your idea,' faltered the Gem'n'Emm. 'It's just . . . we all thought this was going to be a bit of fun but it takes up time no one has, especially at this time of year when there's the children's nativities and school plays and end-of-term concerts, not to mention all of the things they're doing down the church—'

'Fine.' Drea repeated in the same neutral but tiny bit scary tone. 'Call it off.'

People exchanged nervous glances. A few muttered *what's going on*s rose from the crowd as everyone came together in the centre of the street.

'No. Now that's not—' Emma or Gemma threw an anxious glance at a man, presumably her husband, who obediently came and stood beside her, 'I didn't mean call the whole thing off.' She gave a nervous giggle, echoed in different pitches by the other Gem'n'Emms.

'No, seriously. Don't worry about it.' Drea said, now speaking as casually as if she were telling someone not to worry about returning a book they'd borrowed three years ago. 'If it's that much trouble, especially at this very, very special time of year featuring harmony and forgiveness, forget about it.'

'No!' Emma or Gemma protested. 'I – we – we like it.'

'But not if a sad, lonely old man who couldn't get to his house because we were in the middle of the street takes part? Is that the condition? Is that how you want this to play out?'

Emma or Gemma threw a nervous look over her shoulder. 'No, I, uhhh—'

Drea pounced. 'Right! Good. So we're all back on board. See you all tomorrow at number seven.'

Again, there were a few indecipherable mutterings, but no one contradicted Drea's announcement that things would carry on as planned.

As everyone headed back to their homes or huddled in small groups on the pavement, Drea pulled Jess to the side. 'I need you to back me up on this.'

'Sorry?'

'About old man Winters.'

They both looked down at the end of the street. Mr Winters' house was still pitch-black save ... oh ... there *was* a light on, just visible through the stained-glass window above his door.

'Let's have a coffee *mañana* and come up with a plan. Unless you're busy,' Drea added.

The way she tacked on the last bit made Jess bristle. She had things to do. Descriptions of pushpins to write. Boxes of books she'd read when she was twelve to unpack. An Ikea bed frame to assemble.

'Ten's fine.'

'Good.' Drea flashed her a proper warm smile. 'Thanks, doll. It's good having an ally in all of this.'

Aww. That was nice.

They shared a smile.

'Who is it tomorrow?' Jess asked after refusing another sip of Drea's wine.

Drea rolled her eyes. 'The hippies.'

They both looked over to number 7. There was nothing that screamed hippy about the first in a line of three row houses. The wreath on their door looked homemade and their recycling bins were full. Was that the tell?

'Is it a bad thing that they're hippies?'

'Not if you like flax seed and patchouli,' Drea intoned. 'They'll probably smudge us all then give us homemade fat balls for the birds and lecture us on climate change.'

As if on cue, a middle-aged woman with a mix of

brown and grey hair woven into a wiry plait that circled her head like a ... well ... not a halo exactly, appeared before them in a waft of patchouli and sage. She was wearing a thick wool jacket with the distinct mustiness of the men's section of a charity shop and sturdy boots that looked as if they'd been cobbled by a hobbit. She handed them each a piece of paper.

Drea looked at it then asked, 'Why are you letting me know about last year's climate change march?'

'Oops, sorry,' the woman chirped, suddenly all smiles. 'I was reusing old fliers so as not to waste.' She flipped Drea's paper round to the other side where there was a handwritten note.

Drea gave it a quick scan. 'Clothes trade?'

'Exactly,' the woman said.

'You want me to bring clothes I don't want out onto the street for a big jumble sale?'

'No.' Hippy Woman frowned in a way that suggested she was used to being misunderstood but didn't understand why. 'It's a trade.'

'You want me to trade?'

'Yes.' Hippy Woman put her smile back on. 'We're on our third year of not buying new clothes.'

'Great.' Drea smiled at her. 'So what's that got to do with the advent calendar?'

'You know what they say,' Hippy Woman said as if the answer was hanging right there in the frosty air between them.

'No,' Drea said. 'I don't.'

'Waste not want not?' Jess suggested.

Hippy Woman gave her a kindly, but very patronising

pat on the arm. 'Everything in excess is opposed to nature.'

Drea made a dismissive noise. 'How about this instead? Moderation is a fatal thing. Nothing succeeds like excess.'

'Well!' Hippy Woman said through gritted teeth, her tone falsely bright. 'If that means you're volunteering to bring lots of things to give away, I'm sure everyone will be thrilled. You've always had such ... interesting ... taste in clothes.'

Drea didn't even bother to mute her laugh as the woman walked away. 'Poor thing. Her husband made her stop colouring her hair years back. I think letting the grey grow in has given her a martyr complex. Anyway, love,' she briskly continued. 'I've gotta dash. I have a conference call with the team back in Oz. Be good and I'll see you tomorrow, yeah?'

Without waiting for a reply she waved goodbye over her shoulder and headed down the street to her house. Jess turned to her own house, her gaze catching on an upstairs window at Mr Winters' as she did. He was there, looking out onto the increasingly empty street, but was far away enough that it was impossible to read his expression. She waved. He pulled the curtains shut. She knew the feeling. Letting anyone beyond her parents know how broken she'd felt over the past year had been terrifying. Even that had been a level of raw that had frightened her. She couldn't bear the thought of Mr Winters alone in that big house. No childhood bedroom to hide away in. No mum and dad to bring him hot chocolate or Wagon Wheels. She knew she couldn't be that sort of replacement. The family kind. But she could find a way to assure him he wasn't alone. Amanda used to call it Jess's teaching

Super Power. Divining which children were the gregarious ones, the shy ones, the bullies. Shifting the balance of the class so that they all knew where they stood: equally, together. There were no favourites in her class, but there were children who needed extra coaxing, extra assurance that they had been seen.

If she could do that. Tap back into that super power, she knew that first day at Boughton Primary Academy would be a doddle.

The light disappeared behind the curtain. Jess gave it a nod. 'It's okay, Mr Winters', she thought. 'I see you. You are not alone.'

7 December

Jess did a final spell check and sent off the document. Her freelance copywriting gig wouldn't make her a millionaire, but it, and her new project of luring Mr Winters out into the world, stopped her from obsessing about whether or not she would still have that old 'Jess Green sparkle' when she began her now job. Describing paperclips and report folders to wondrous effect would also enable her to buy a hugely calorific meal for one on Christmas Day. Not that she'd googled her options even remotely obsessively when she'd woken up in the middle of the night wondering if 'being a Mini' meant she'd be alone for the rest of her entire life (a new panic she'd added to her ever-growing list).

Mercifully, the internet had reliably informed her that there was a veritable cornucopia of ways to delight her palate should she choose to gorge herself silly on seasonal fare. M&S had a ready meal for one – turkey, spuds, sprouts, the works. If she felt like pushing the boat out but did not actually know what any of the ingredients were, Waitrose had a Heston Turkey Dinner featuring a quail with gold leaf, goji berries and something else beginning with 'g' she wasn't entirely sure was a food group. Lidl had a frozen chicken dinner that included a rather succinct square of chocolate cake. In the end, all of the googling had made her really sad. There were so many choices of meals for one. Which meant there would be countless people eating Christmas dinner on their own. All of which was making her lean towards buying a pizza and all three of her favourite flavours of ice cream and considering Christmas a do-over for next year.

Before turning her laptop off, she refreshed her email (again), then checked the junk mail (again), only to determine that no, she still hadn't missed a return email from Will Winters. Which surely meant – not that she was catastrophising or anything – that Will was definitely in the process of putting out a restraining order on her and had very likely cautioned his grandfather never to speak to her again. Which made her really, really sad.

Sure Mr Winters was grumpy. And last night had definitely not thrown the best of lights on him as a lovely neighbour or his ability to drive, but . . .

Underneath it? She thought she saw what Drea saw. Sadness. The type that permeated your cell structure. Shaded the way you saw the world. The type of sadness she'd felt when she'd been accused of hurting a child when, in actual fact, she'd been trying to help one. A fresh, dynamic energy gripped her nervous system.

As soon as Drea came over, the two of them were going to plant Arnold Winters' tulip bulbs. Whether or not they had his permission. Sometimes people were so sad they didn't know what they wanted. He knew he wanted tulips, but for some ridiculous reason, was denying himself the pleasure.

A text pinged through from Drea. She was still on her

conference call. Couldn't get out of it. Wouldn't be able to make their rendezvous. Soz doll face. Catch up laters?

Jess's spirits plummeted. She'd been looking forward to going to Mr Winters'.

So . . . what was stopping her? She didn't need a safety buddy. She'd spoken to him on her own before. She could do it again.

A determination she hadn't felt in ages gripped her.

She bundled the office supplies she'd finished into the 'done' box, pleased to see it filling up. So far she'd ticked off the super glue (easy to laud the merits of), three different styles of mini-staplers, ten different varieties of stapler-taker-outers (#NotTheirRealName) and all of the Easter-themed office supplies. Who knew bunny-shaped Post-its could be so alluring?

Focusing on all of the fluffy-chick-topped pens, coloured egg stationery and miniature bunny fairy lights (so cute!) had been a nice distraction from all of the other things she didn't want to think about, but every time she finished, real life was still there, staring her in the face. Until now. This was the first time a real-life idea gave her back that bouncy feeling she used to feel every day heading off to St Benedict's.

Not only would she get some tulip bulbs and bring them to Mr Winters, she would get him a wreath. Kai and Rex's wreath was the one thing guaranteed to make her smile every day and not just because it was gorgeous, but because it had been a gift from strangers. Strangers who had hit her in the face with a snowball, true. But then she was a stranger who had opened Mr Winters' post, so . . . kind of the same thing?

Twenty minutes later she was parked up just off the

high street and working her way past festive window displays towards Berry's Blooms. Every single shopfront was wreathed in lights or baubles or swags of evergreen or all three. A stark reminder that she still hadn't done anything at her own home. She was bringing some Christmas cheer to someone else so hopefully that would even things out.

She kept her eyes peeled for the archway that led to the courtyard where their shop was. Apparently, it had been a jam factory back in the day. When her eyes caught on the old-fashioned sign hanging proud of the archway, her breath caught in her throat. It was surrounded by a wreath made entirely of pineapples and plums. It looked amazing. And then she saw the archway. It was covered in a panoply of dried fruits and holly and mistletoe just begging everyone who passed through it to take a selfie. Which she did. She'd send it to her parents to prove she was having a wonderful time and not remotely considering whether she should sell her new house and quit her new job before she'd had a chance to get attached to either of them. When she turned the corner into the courtyard, her heart skipped a beat. Rather than the garish displays some of the stores had opted for, Rex and Kai had decorated not only their shop, but the entire courtyard to look like a magical winter woodland. The brick walls were hidden beneath beautifully decorated Christmas trees. Each tree was bedecked with a delicate whorl of fairy lights, giving teasing glimpses of a rich array of frosted pine cones, beautiful wooden ornaments, oranges studded with cloves and, yes, pomegranates held in place by a criss-cross of green velvet ribbons. The smattering of benches that were dappled about the courtyard were covered in thick sheepskin rugs and small fire-pits with Swedish logs crackled away in front of them. Strings of delicate lights in the shape of stars were hung like bunting above her. A man in a thick wooden hat was honest-to-goodness roasting chestnuts over an open fire at the far end of the courtyard. It was like stepping into a Dickens storybook with set dressing by Selfridges. Amazing.

'Jess! Darling!' Rex grabbed her into a tight hug. 'What brings you to our little corner of the world?'

'I . . .' she stared at him half speechless. 'You're an artist. A botanical artist!' She finally managed.

He laughed. 'No, that's Kai, love. It's in the genes. I'm the business end of Berry Blooms. Kai's the one who makes all of the magic. You should see what that man can do with a pomelo!' He gave her a very saucy wink, hooked his hand into her arm then turned her round to their shop which was, unsurprisingly, dazzlingly wonderful. Not only did they offer an array of seasonal delights, they also had a wall filled with beautiful hand-tied bouquets, chunky candles, Christmas cacti (she winced), and . . . ooh . . . a DIY section.

'Want to make something?' Rex asked, clocking her smile.

She grinned. 'I'd like to make a wreath. Can we do that?'

'Course you can love. But . . .' He hesitated then called towards an open doorway at the back of the shop. 'Kai-Kai!'

Kai came bounding out, a thick green cotton apron with leather shoulder straps covering another stylish winter ensemble (dark corduroy slimline trousers, turtleneck jumper – black, to match his eyes and insanely long lashes, and a Burberry gilet). He looked like a rock star.

'Hey, honey bun!' He threw his arms wide open, a pair of clippers in one hand, a long reel of silver ribbon in the other.

After they hugged he stood back and gave her a quick pursed-lip inspection. 'Why are we here? Let Uncle Kai have a guess...' His eyes flicked to Rex's then back to Jess's. 'Oh, no.' He put down the things in his hand on the worktable beside him and gave her an apologetic smile. 'Sorry. If you want to make a wreath, it's a no.'

Jess's smile faltered.

'Oh, c'mon, love. Don't be sad. It's only because—' He gave a quick look over his shoulder. 'Keep a secret? It's going to be our thing.'

'Thing?'

'For the advent-calendar night. We're going to borrow Chantal's trestle tables and set up wreath-making supplies for everyone. And don't even try to tell me half the houses already have one, because, hello! There are never enough wreaths. Am I right?' He didn't wait for an answer. Clearly, he was right. 'Was it for you, sugar bean? The wreath?'

'No. I was going to do one for Mr Winters.'

Another look was exchanged between Kai and Rex. This one was not quite so jolly.

'Mr Winters of number twenty-four, Mr Winters?'

'That's the one!' Jess had aimed for chipper but had ended up sounding more 'please let that be okay' anxious. 'It's just... I know last night was mad and he almost ran over some people, but he didn't and he obviously didn't *mean* to—'

'You sure about that?' Rex intoned.

'Seriously.' Jess needed them to understand how sad Mr

Winters was, but without betraying the secret grandson she wasn't meant to know about. 'He's just... he's...'

'An old git with too much time on his hands to be pleasant?' offered Rex.

'Now, honey, don't be mean,' said Kai, though the sides of his lips were twitching.

'It was tulips I was hoping to get for him, actually.'

Rex rolled his eyes. 'Of course he'd want something out of season.'

Jess gritted her teeth. Why were they so prepared to make unkind assumptions about him? From what she'd gathered, no one knew his real story, so why leap to all of these mean conclusions?

'Do you have tulip bulbs?' She asked when they failed to say anything. 'It was bulbs he was after, not the blooms.'

'Yes,' Rex said with a nod. 'Course we do, love. Sorry. We've just had a couple of run-ins with Mr Winters in the past and whilst we like to consider ourselves good neighbours, he's the sort that can make it tough.'

'Why?— Did you have run-ins?'

The two shared a look, this one potent with sadness.

'We used to walk our dog, Alexa, along the cut-through by his house...' Kai's breath hitched and Rex took over.

'Alexa may have, once or twice, accidentally chased Mr Winters' cat up a tree. Or two. Possibly.'

'I didn't know you two had a dog.'

Again, that grief-charged energy surged through the shop.

'We used to, darling,' Rex said softly. 'She took her journey to the Rainbow Bridge at the beginning of the year. This'll be our first Christmas without her.'

A lump formed in Jess's throat as Rex and Kai's hands sought each other's for a reassuring squeeze. They had obviously adored her.

Unable to come up with anything healing to say that wasn't geared for the under-tens, Jess asked, 'Was she named after the Amazon virtual assistant?'

Both of their lips thinned. Rex gave a little eye roll. 'No, darling. Alexa *Chung*.'

Ah. Of course.

She thunked her forehead then asked, more gently, 'And . . . have you thought of getting another dog?'

'Too soon. Too soon!' Kai squeaked, turning away to dig a handkerchief out of his pocket.

Rex's face creased as much as it could but Jess thought she saw a hint of something that suggested he wouldn't mind getting a new dog. He threw a quick glance at Kai's back and mouthed, 'It's been awful.'

When Kai turned back round he had pinned on one of those cheerful in the face of adversity faces. 'Now, we were on the topic of Mr Winters. Any particular reason you're feeling the need to buy him tulip bulbs?'

'I think he's lonely.'

'Sweetie.' Kai gave her arm a squeeze. 'I can see what you're doing, but we've lived on the street for years now and he's always been the same. You're trying to soften the heart of the ice king.'

'Ice melts,' Jess said. In her inside voice. In her outside voice she said, 'So . . . tulip bulbs?'

Their shop turned out to be a bit of a Tardis. Through yet another archway there was a covered open-air area with all sorts of potted plants, miniature potted Christmas trees – both plain and decorated ('some folk simply don't have the time or imagination, love, so we do it for them').

'We've not got the daff bulbs anymore. It's always best to get those in by September at the latest.'

'She doesn't need a lecture, darling. She needs bulbs.' Rex said, giving his husband's shoulders a light rub.

'Any idea what colour scheme he's going for this year?' Kai asked in a more conciliatory tone.

Mr Winters did colour schemes? Interesting. 'What did he do last year?'

Kai and Rex stared at one another as if they were each a Magic 8 ball and then, at the same time said, 'Blue.'

Jess's eyebrows raised. Blue. Like his mood, no doubt. 'What colours do you have?' She asked.

Fifteen minutes later she had a carrier bag full of earth-scented bulbs waiting to be tucked into the soil in front of Mr Winters' house. First step of her mission: complete.

'Look.' Drea pointed towards the hedge where Josh's children were currently dressing him up in a tiara and a set of fairy wings. 'Lovely, isn't it?'

'Yes,' Jess sighed. 'He is.'

'Someone's got a cru-ush,' Drea teased.

'No, someone doesn't,' Jess snorted. Lying. But also, not lying. Having Josh as a neighbour was kind of like school drop-off had been back when St Benny's had had the privilege of schooling the Beckhams' youngest children. All of the female teachers had enjoyed drooling over David, but were perfectly happy in the knowledge he would never be theirs. She felt the same about Josh. Lovely eye candy. No need to find out the calorie count or, more to the point, who would claw her eyes out if she stepped onto hallowed ground.

'Whatever you want to tell yourself, doll,' Drea shrugged, returning to her 'work' at one of three clothes racks the Hippies had set out on their freshly dug-out driveway that would be replanted, they told everyone, with the choicest of pollinators ('Every bit of green matters!'). From the looks of things, everyone on the street had had a massive clear-out and already several families had headed back home with (reusable) shopping bags full of other people's treasures.

'This would suit you, Jess.' Drea lifted a barely there red dress from the clothes rack. It was beautiful. Delicate gossamer-thin fabric that wafted in the breeze. It looked expensive. It also looked as though it belonged on a perfect body in a fancy restaurant.

Drea wiggled it in front of her face. 'Bet Josh would like you in this.'

Jess crinkled her nose. She was not thinking about completely gorgeous Josh and was definitely not think-ing about being wined and dined. 'I don't really think it screams primary schoolteacher.'

'Oh, c'mon,' Drea gently elbowed her. 'It's free.'

'It looks like something I would have to bring to an-other clothes exchange in a year.' Jess laughed, trying to get Drea to put it back on the rack.

'What? You hate it?'

'No!' Jess back-pedalled, suddenly a little nervous the dress had been donated by Drea. 'It's great, it's just... not me.'

Drea held it up in front of Jess, gave her an intense inspection then conceded. 'Yeah, you're right. You're more of a floral maxi-dress girl.' She hung it back on the rack with a huff.

'Was it yours?'

'Yeah,' Drea admitted, shifting the clothes along the rack with a practised glance, move on, glance, move on. 'It was part of the Old Drea ensemble.'

Jess gave her a curious side-eye. 'Meaning?'

Drea gave a flick of the hand. 'It didn't spark joy. Time to be clutter-cleared.' She held out a dress that would've left very little to the imagination if actual mortals could've squeezed into it. 'I used to wear this kind of nonsense back when I was dating.'

'You gave up dating?'

'I gave up *men*,' Drea said dramatically. Although, pretty much everything Drea said sounded dramatic, as if she travelled with a personal soundtrack to accompany her every move. Right now, Jess imagined, some soft music harking back to days gone by would begin as Drea looked up, eyes lit by the explosion of lights coming from the house across the street where the Christmas electricity bill was bound to be a shocker. Drea's perfectly curled lashes might bead up with a few tears, threatening but not daring to trickle down her proud cheeks.

And then she began to cackle like a banshee. 'Aw, look. It's a bullshit line I use to try and convince myself I'm perfectly happy without a man in my bed. I'm not. I love them. I love sex. I love cooking for them. I love being pampered by them. I have a weakness for them. One I need to conquer.' Her smile faltered.

Jess adopted a nonchalant air. 'Maybe there's a Men-a-holics Anonymous you could attend.'

'Yeah, doll. They're called women's refuges.'

The light mood evaporated.

'You weren't— He didn't— Was there—?'

Drea continued to shift hanger after hanger along the rack, the scritch-scritch sound adding a sharper edge to her expression. She looked up and gave Jess her trademark everything's fine smile. 'What've you got planned for your night? Something spectacular?'

'That's umm . . . yeah, I'm keeping that a surprise.' She managed, still trying to equate the strong, amazing woman in front of her with someone who'd be subject to domestic abuse. Drea didn't seem the type. Then again, Jess wasn't the type to hurt a child, so . . . She tried to shrug it off.

'And by "surprise" you mean you don't know yet,' Drea asked with a roll of her now completely dry eyes.

'Yes,' Jess admitted with a sheepish grin. 'Forgive me?'

'As long as you pull the cat out of the bag on the night.'

'Consider it done.' They gave each other a fist bump, the solidarity of the moment feeling a bit more powerful than your everyday fist bump.

'Hey, Jess! Drea.' Kai catwalked up to them with a boa round his neck. 'Like my new evening wear?'

'Hell's teeth, man.' Drea took it off his neck and swirled the thick, frothy concoction round her own neck. 'Ostrich feathers. I knew it.' She nestled into it then ran it out the length of her arms as if she were no stranger to the boa and what to do with it. 'Who the hell is giving this away? It's the real deal.'

Jess stroked it, as did Rex. They both made *mmm, soft* noises as a rather intense 'possession is nine-tenths of the law' discussion broke out between Kai and Drea.

'How'd you go with your tulip bulbs down the road?'

Rex asked, his head tipping slightly towards Mr Winters' dimly lit home.

'Oh, that. Well ...'

It had been a nightmare, basically. She'd knocked on his door, which Mr Winters had promptly opened, glared at her, then barked, 'Why the hell won't you leave me alone like a normal person?' Then he'd slammed the door shut. She'd run home, furious, and would have stayed at home tonight eating her body weight in ice cream if Drea hadn't come by an hour earlier and shouted into her post flap, 'Little pig, little pig, let me come in!' She'd only left when she'd extracted a promise to see Jess here, at the Hippies', at seven sharp.

'Sorry, love.' Rex gave her a sympathetic half hug. 'The man is determined not to be friendly. Just leave him as he is. It's how he likes it.'

'Maybe you're right.'

'I am right,' Rex said, seriously this time. 'He doesn't like interference. Not with the postman, not with neighbours, no family that I've ever seen. The man is an island and likes it that way.'

The word 'interference' stung sharper than it should have.

It's what Crispin's mother had said. That Jess had been interfering in a matter that had had nothing to do with her.

A child who suffered severe dairy allergies about to get a cheese sandwich in the face was very much something to do with her. At least ... she'd thought so at the time. She'd gone back and forth over it so many times, it was difficult to know any more.

'It's sad, I know,' Rex said, both of them turning to

look at the dark house with a tiny bit of light peeking through one of the downstairs windows. 'Some people are beyond help.'

'Maybe I'll just leave the bulbs at his front door.'

'Maybe you should plant them in your own garden,' Rex said firmly.

Defeated by the fear of creating more trouble than good, Jess reluctantly nodded. Maybe Mr Winters would see the flowers and reach out to her in the spring. And maybe pigs would fly down Christmas Street with a sleigh full of chocolate reindeer.

She looked to the top of the street. No pigs.

She tuned back into Kai and Drea, who were nailing down a fifty-fifty shared ownership deal with the boa, and whoever found out who the original owner was got to wear it on New Year's Eve. They shook on it and grinned.

At least someone was leaving happy.

7 December
22:17
To: JessGreen2000@gmail.com
From: WillWinters@TheMerryVictualler.co.uk
Subject: RE: Your Christmas Card

Dear Jess(ica),
Sorry for not writing back sooner. I've been neck deep in a mince-pie production line of one, a hellish occurrence which need never be revisited.

Thank you so much for getting my misdirected card to my grandfather.
Grandfather.
It feels peculiar calling him that as I've never met him.

And even though it is a bit strange that you read the letter, I'm also a wee bit grateful. Gratitude from a Scottish male is a rare thing to encounter, so... behold. We're used to beating our chests and proclaiming ourselves entirely self-sufficient, but the truth is I can't speak to anyone in my own family about it because of history. Stuffing things in closets and never mentioning them again is our family's modus operandi.

The actual truth, as we're sharing, is that I'm not surprised the letter never reached him. Everything's a bit of a mess. Catering college doesn't prepare us fledgling chefs for much beyond perfect vol-au-vents and a sure-fire way to save a hollandaise. As such, I'm newly single, in a new town, in a new country, all of which makes me a bit of a Billy No-Mates during a season that is specifically geared towards togetherness. I know. Boo hoo. Poor me. It's not as if anyone made me move here or forced me to work every hour God sent driving my poor girlfriend to distraction, but now that I'm on me tod, I hadn't realised how alone I am down here.

The type of alone that gives you enough time to realise how all of that work and no play setting up my company definitely made Will a dull boy. Hence, wanting to meet and make room in my life for my grandfather. To get some balance. Not that I'm managing all that brilliantly on that front as it is officially the silly season for caterers, but I've got my eye on a storefront premises that would really change the business into something viable. If I get through all of my Christmas bookings intact, I can afford it as well as some staff to get that old work–life balance back in play. Tomorrow's a brand-new day, right?

Anyway. I'm rambling. Feel free to delete, ignore, totally

eradicate this from your mind. I'll get another card to him. I'd hand-deliver it, but for my sins, am serving mini-cranberry and Stilton tarts and baby blinis straight through to Christmas Eve. Among other things. They aren't the only things I can cook. Strewth. I really am rambling. You have my full permission to delete immediately.

Yours etc. etc.

Will Winters

8 December

To: WillWinters@TheMerryVictualler.co.uk
From: JessGreen2000@gmail.com
Subject: RE: RE: Your Christmas Card

Dear Will
Phew! So relieved.

Delete delete delete

Dear Will –
I did delete your message and then I undeleted it. LOL

Delete delete delete

Dear Will,
I'm so happy to have heard from you. There's something about your grandfather that makes me want to bring a smile to his grumpy old face. Which, I'm guessing, is a bit wrinklier than your face and possibly your father's?

Delete delete delete

Your computer will turn off in 60 seconds unless...

'What on God's green earth are you doing?'

Jess screamed and dropped her trowel.

Mr Winters stormed down his porch, in so far as his knees would allow him, and lurched to a halt, looming over the patch of rather beautifully tilled earth in front of his house where Jess was kneeling. 'I repeat. What exactly do you think you're doing?'

'Planting tulip bulbs?' She held up a net bag full of bulbs. It turned out planting tulip bulbs in December during a cold snap wasn't the zippiest of jobs. Her plans had been to whizz in, dig a few holes, stuff the bulbs in, then run back home and wait until spring for the magic to happen. 'I was hoping it would be a nice surprise,' she tacked on because, obviously, there were evil tulip-bulb planters out there.

Mr Winters glowered at her, which weirdly made her want to giggle. Glowering was something that usually happened in the middle-grade books she assigned her students. It was one of those words she always had to demonstrate to define. The children would always laugh at her grumpy face which was why, she supposed, she had a Pavlovian response to someone doing it to her.

'You think it's funny do you? Trespassing in someone's garden? Putting bulbs in the ground when you've been given no permission whatsoever to touch what wasn't yours?'

'No.' She really didn't. Especially now that he'd put it that way.

His cat appeared out of nowhere and gave her a haughty look as if doubling down on the disdain the pair of them clearly shared for her.

If central nervous systems could get the shakes, hers was getting a bad case of them. 'I'm really sorry.'

She pushed herself up, not even bothering to swipe at the frozen granules of earth stuck to her knees. She took a step back, feeling too close to the anger radiating from Mr Winters. The back of her knees hit the hedge, causing her to lose her balance. Rather than lurch forward into Mr Winters she did a weird step, trip and fall manoeuvre that landed her in a rather impressive backbend over the picket fence.

'Umm...' She said in a high-pitched voice. 'I'm a little bit stuck here.'

'Well, what do you want me to do about it?' Mr Winters groused out of sight. All she could see was the upside-down view of someone taking out their recycling bin, glancing down their way, then scuttling back into their house.

So much for love thy neighbour.

'Help me?' If she let herself go she would collapse into his hedge and, very likely, cause more damage than she already had. Not an option. If she had done any of Drea's Bondi Beach Body videos she'd have some core body strength with which to pull herself back up to standing. Which she hadn't. So, that idea was a non-starter. If she was a former member of Cirque du Soleil she'd be able to do a nifty walkover, stand up smiling on the other side of the fence, offer him a bow of apology then run home as fast as she could and never show her face at this end of Christmas Street ever again. Damn her parents for being nice enough for her not to want to run away to the circus as a child!

'C'mon then, lass.'

A large wrinkly hand appeared in front of her face. As doddery as he was on his knees, Mr Winters wasn't exactly a frail old man, so Jess braced one hand firmly on the ground then accepted the proffered one with another. Trying to take as much of her own weight as she could, she managed a very ungainly return to being vertical and found herself awfully close to Mr Winters. Nose-to-nose close. From this angle, he wasn't nearly as scary. Maybe it was because, for this nanosecond in time, he looked genuinely concerned.

His eyes were really lovely. So blue! They looked young. And annoyed. Apparently the nanosecond of compassion was over.

He backed up as she was still wedged against the hedge. She squatted down and began to collect up the netted bags of bulbs and her trowel (an opulently floral-patterned tool that came from the genre of gardening tools that looked as though they shouldn't actually ever be dirty, but Amanda had given it to her as a way to 'ease into country life' so she'd kept it). 'Sorry. I thought I was helping, but I clearly over-reached.'

'Helping? Spying more like.'

'*What?*'

'Oh, I know what you're all saying. That I tried to run the lot of you down the other night.'

She tried not to squirm. Some people were saying that. But just as many weren't.

'Not at all,' she insisted as solidly as she could. 'I told them you'd been surprised by everyone being in the street and that your foot must've slipped but that there was no way you would've intentionally hurt anyone.' Well. Drea had. She'd just stood there. But she'd been close to Drea when she'd said it. Had she nodded? She hoped she'd nodded.

He grunted.

She almost grunted back. Not a very nice thank you for standing next to the person who'd defended his honour. Whatever. Fine.

She began pawing at the earth where she was pretty sure she'd planted a bulb.

'I thought I told you to stop that nonsense!'

She gave him what she hoped was an enough-already look. 'I'm getting the bulbs out, aren't I?'

Mercifully, she found the bulb and showed it to him.

His frown deepened. 'You planted it upside down.'

'What? No.' She looked at the bulb. 'How do you even know?'

He reached out and took the bulb from her. Pointing at the fat flat-bottomed end he said, 'The roots come out here, the stem comes out here.'

'Oh.' She should know that sort of thing. 'My bad.'

'I don't know what that means,' he retorted with a supercilious air.

She shot him a glare then began pawing away at the earth, fingernails ripping to shreds, intent on digging out the other three *erroneously* planted tulip bulbs. 'It means, I was trying to *help*. I was *trying* to do a *nice* thing. Trying to be neighbourly.' She gave herself a slightly too-hard punch in the chest then jabbed her trowel in his direction. 'Unlike you, who don't seem to want any neighbours anywhere near you. But maybe that's why you live in this big old house at the end of the street so you can glare at everyone and send them packing before they even attempt to do something kind!'

She stood up with a proper harrumph and glared at him.

He glared back and snarled, 'I could teach you how, if you like.'

'Teach me what?' she asked, hoping her tone made it crystal clear she didn't want to be taught anything. Least of all by this living breathing pile of stroppiness.

'To plant tulip bulbs. Properly.' His eyes were glued to hers and she could see little huffs of breath coming out of his nose like a moose preparing to go into battle. Or perhaps a reindeer, given the season.

'That would be nice,' she snapped back.

His eyes dropped to her hand. 'That's a ridiculous trowel.'

'My trowel was *gift*. From a *friend*. A friend who was trying to do something *nice*,' Jess ground out realising, as she did, that this whole sparring thing was actually rather fun. And, as Mr Winters had yet to depart, perhaps he was enjoying it, too.

His eyes flashed with something she couldn't put her finger on. 'Your friend could do with a lesson in pragmatism.'

Jess's mood took another turn. He could insult her all he wanted. She was, after all, trespassing on his property and planting upside-down tulip bulbs into his beautifully prepared flower bed. But trash-talk the one friend who'd all but moved her into her flat and let her ugly cry whenever she'd wanted for the entire two weeks she'd been suspended from St Benny's? No way, pal. This time, he'd crossed a line.

In a voice she barely recognised she said, 'My friend lives in a London flat with no garden, subsequently making it *im*practical to own a trowel, so I'm going to give her kudos for even knowing what one is.'

Ha. There. Put that in your pipe and smoke it, Mr Arnold Winters.

He narrowed his gaze, chin tilted up so that he was literally looking down his nose at her then turned and walked round the side of the house.

Well, this was awkward.

She stood there swinging her arms round her like a scarecrow caught in a cross wind. What was one to do in this scenario? Take the opportunity to flee and pretend this never happened? Or stick around to see if he really meant it about teaching her how to plant bulbs.

She tried to imagine how she would feel if she woke up to discover someone rooting around in her flower garden. Which, when she put it that way, sounded really invasive.

Okay. Fair enough. He had a right to be cross. She'd give it five minutes. Five minutes of looking like a div in Mr Winters' garden. Then, at least, she'd have something to report back to Will when she finally got her act together and wrote to him. It was why she'd come down in the first place. She'd tried to write him the perfect 'yes, please stay in touch' email that subtly but not too intrusively gave her an in for finding out the mystery behind the falling out between Mr Winters and his son. Not that it was any of her business, but he was her neighbour and he seemed more sad than unkind, particularly when you caught him off guard as she had. Or maybe she was just trying to right a wrong that was completely out of her control just to prove to herself she had the power to do something good.

'Here.'

Mr Winters was back. He handed her a huge pair of gardening gloves. 'For the cold.'

'Oh. Thank you.'

He grunted.

She put them on, gave them a clap. He pointed at the patch and she knelt down again.

They'd clearly used up all of their words in their narky exchange. Fair enough. She wasn't feeling all that chatty either. There was also the lurking danger she'd give away the fact she knew about Will. If this was actually a truce, it'd be a shame to ruin it straight away. She was pretty sure once he found out she'd read his mail tensions would flare up again, but maybe by then they would've established a friendship and he'd forgive her.

Maybe.

Once he'd ascertained and approved of her colour scheme (dark purples, rich pinks and a smattering of ivories) he taught her how to throw them out so they would grow in natural-looking droves rather than look as if they were lined up at a horse guards parade (his words, not hers). He spoke in a soft Yorkshire accent (now that he wasn't so busy being gruff) and kept disappearing behind his house and returning with all sorts of different gadgets. He had not one, but two different types of bulb planters (standing and hand-held). He had a dibbler. Which was difficult not to giggle over, but proved very effective once she finally got the 'in, left, right' wriggle manoeuvre down to Mr Winters' satisfaction.

'You certainly know a lot about planting bulbs,' she said.

'Always keep your brain ticking over with something new,' he countered, tapping the side of his head with a gloved hand. 'Once that stops, you'll know you're ready to meet your maker.'

As a teacher she couldn't really argue, although . . . try telling that to the Head Teacher at St Benny's. A woman so mired in tradition it was a wonder she didn't reek of mothballs. On the plus side, it was good to know Mr Winters wasn't ready to shuffle off his mortal coil. Sure, he was a bit scratchy on the outside, but something told her that if you hung around for a while and weren't into hugging, there was a loyal, kind man buried somewhere in there.

Once they'd got all of the bulbs in – which, done properly, took about an hour – she was feeling warm, satisfied and just a little bit smug because they'd actually spent a companionable period of time together. It would be nice to report back to Will that his grandfather was both a good teacher and gruffly delightful.

'Oof!' She said, giving her brow a fake swipe. 'I could do with a big mug of hot chocolate about now.'

Mr Winters' less-than-charming demeanour flickered back to life. 'I've not got anything like that in the house.'

She swotted at the air between them and once again stood up, this time wiping her knees clean and picking up the empty net bags that had held the bulbs. 'Don't worry. I won't impose myself on you any longer than necessary.'

Something briefly shadowed his features that looked an awful lot like disappointment.

Her heart crumpled in on itself. She opened her mouth, about to say she'd happily impose herself on him anytime he liked, when the loud squeal of an electric guitar streaked through the air.

Number 21.

Tyler. Had to be.

His features reassembled themselves into the short-tempered sourpuss she'd first met. Speaking of which . . . she looked round and saw Mr Winters' cat preening itself on the porch.

'What's her name?' she asked, trying to put a bit of their fragile comradery back on the table.

'*His*,' Mr Winters corrected. 'Mr Perkins.'

'That's an unusual name.' Jess waited for an explanation.

With a shake of the head, he muttered something along the lines of keeping her eye out in the spring. She should be expecting returns on her work late March or early April, weather depending, and then, tools in hand, he disappeared round the back of the house with an air of finality.

Now it was her turn to feel disappointed. Though the morning had begun with a fight – well, a bickering session – it had been strangely satisfying. It was how she used to feel as a teenager when her parents would plead with her to clean her messy room. She'd always stropped off and then, sulkily, complied with their wishes, only to prance down the stairs a few hours later desperate to show off her new 'show room'. She snorted. Little wonder she'd ended up with an estate agent.

It struck her how little she thought of Martin and the life they'd once sort of kind of shared. Perhaps the relationship had been as superficial as the show flat they'd lived in. Looked great, but none of it had been made to last.

She left Mr Winters' garden, careful to close the white picket fence behind her. Not quite ready to go home, she decided to walk the entire loop of the street. Up the far side across from hers then back down to her lovely red door, behind which she knew three sets of pastel highlighters were waiting to be matched to their perfect adjectives alongside a whole heap of other office supplies. And, of course, there was the unfinished email to Will.

It was interesting going up the street knowing she'd be getting more than a glimpse into her neighbours' lives over the coming days. Much like the homemade advent calendars her parents used to put together for her, the Christmas Street residents had been far more generous and thoughtful than anyone at the high-tech high-rise where she used to live.

And, of course, there were the unexpected dividends to showing up, standing on the edge of the crowd and feeling a bit of a berk. Already, she was fairly certain she'd found a friend in Drea. The Gem'n'Emms were nice, even if she still felt a bit wary round them as their small children would all be trooping through her classroom one day (if she didn't bottle it and book a ticket to join her parents in the tropics and teach coconut-shell art). Kev the mechanic was handy to know as she was driving her mother's hand-me-down car, given to her with a warning that its lifespan might not be all that long if it wasn't properly looked after. Rex and Kai were totally fabulous. She was outside their house right now and it looked beautiful. Surprise, surprise. It was one of the few detached houses on the street. It was situated a bit further back than some of the other homes, giving it a larger front garden than most. As lovers of plants and beauty, she supposed she shouldn't have been surprised they'd opted for more garden over a driveway as a few of the other homes had (apart from the Hippies, obvs). They had put a huge, thick swag of evergreen all round their front door woven with tiny little fairy lights. The maroon door had a beautiful swag of winterberry branches tied off with a velvet ribbon in a deep forest green. In the centre of their garden was a beautifully swirled boxwood hedge that had a gorgeous whorl of cherry-sized lights twirling round it.

Further up the street, the guitar music blasted even louder. The triple-glazing the previous tenants of her house had put in must work wonders if the music had been blaring like this every day. She hoped Mrs Snodgrass had hearing aids she could turn off at these moments.

When Jess reached number 21, she glanced through the window to see Mrs Snodgrass marching into her lounge with an upside-down broom in her hand and a look like thunder on her face. She gave the ceiling a few solid thumps.

The music abruptly stopped and she heard a shouted, 'Sorry, Martha!' A minute later it started up again at a lower volume.

Jess gave a little shudder on behalf of Mrs Snodgrass. Poor woman. She must really need the money to keep him round. It made her realise how truly fortunate she was to have had her life collapse into a million pieces in front of parents able to help her pour the foundation for a new one. The deposit had been a godsend. She made a little note to try and ring them again. Island time was clearly getting the better of the pair of them as they kept missing one another.

She should also, she supposed, get in touch with Amanda. She'd leapt to her friend's defence so quickly this morning because she was actually feeling guilty.

Amanda kept leaving her WhatsApp voice messages with increasingly pleading messages to ring her. She had news, apparently. News Jess was sure she didn't want to hear if it couldn't be relayed in a text. It would either be about Martin (who lived near-ish Amanda and attended a weekly quiz night at the same pub albeit, with different teams) or St Benny's. Even thinking about either of them made her skin all clammy. So calling up a friend from her old life to hear about the two boys (one little, one not so little) who'd sent her running for the hills? Nah. She could give that a miss. She'd send her a WhatsApp today. Say she'd been really busy with the street advent-calendar thing and the copywriting work. Which was a little bit true. She was hardly going to tell her she'd also been busy emptying multiple tubs of ice cream while staring at her sparsely decorated house wondering if it would ever feel like home. She may have sunk low. But not that low. Yet.

8 December
21:19
To: WillWinters@TheMerryVictualler.co.uk
From: JessGreen2000@gmail.com
Subject: RE: RE: Your Christmas Card

Dear Will,
Thank you for your email about my email. I am so relieved I didn't upset you by the accidental opening and reading (*cringe!*) of your Christmas card. Nice charity, by the way. Do you always support Scottish wildlife or was it just a lucky dip on the cool cards front?

Anyhow, just wanted to let you know that through a weird set of circumstances I ended up spending my morning learning the fine art of tulip-bulb planting from your grandfather. The man knows his way round a dibbler!

I hope your next card gets delivered and rest assured I am triple-checking every envelope before I open it now, so if it arrives here again, it will stay firmly closed!

Now that you've made me hungry for mini-blinis and miniature Stilton and cranberry tarts (it was cranberry, right?), I might have to take a little trip to M&S to get myself some seasonal canapés for supper.

All the best x Jess(ica) at number 14

9 December

To: JessGreen2000@gmail.com
From: WillWinters@TheMerryVictualler.co.uk
Subject: NOOOOOOOO!!!!!!!!!!!!!

Dear Jess(ica) at number 14,
STEP AWAY FROM THE STORE-BOUGHT CANAPÉS!!!!!
  Actually, that's not entirely fair. Some of the things out
there are great and, the Scots in me must point out, a
bargain. Besides, who can resist a lovely lump of cheddar
skewered to some tinned pineapple? Not me. Appreciate
my snobbery comes from the completely biased perspective
of a trendy skinny-jeans-wearing desperado, slaving away
to make his mark on the catering world with his genuine
belief in the merits of local, seasonal produce. Mind you, my
love of mini-Welsh rarebits on parsnip crisps doesn't stop
customers from ordering cream cheese and smoked salmon
blinis, or me making them, but at least I can ensure the
salmon are ethically sourced Scottish fish from family-based
businesses and that the blinis are made from locally grown
and ground flour.
  Crumbs.

I'm preaching aren't I? Used to drive my ex nuts. Suffice it to say I've learned a few valuable lessons along the way. Still learning. Always keep your brain ticking over with something new as my father says. Once that stops, you'll know you're ready to meet your maker.

Utterly loving the image of Grandad – Grampa? I have no idea what to call him. Sir??? – tutoring you on the ways and means of properly planting a tulip bulb. I suppose it shouldn't surprise me to hear it, as my father is equally exacting. The apple might have rolled far away from the tree, but it sounds as though it fell close in the beginning. Or is that me grasping at straws? Speaking of straws, I've got about a million cheese straws to make before tomorrow's extravaganza. It's a Freemason's lunch I am just a little bit scared of. Will they try to lure me into their fold or sacrifice me as an offering to whatever it is Masons believe in? Commerce, I think. D'oh! Missed a trick. I should've put all of the spoon dishes into mini Mason jars. *Idiot.*

Right. Sorry. Must shoot off. Thanks again for keeping me updated on my grandfather's shenanigans (such as they are). I expect the tulip display will be wonderful if my own father's green thumb is anything to go by. Oh! Speaking of which, the Scottish charity is from the island my parents are wardens of. It's a wee isle up at the tip-top of the Orkneys where they moved after my brother and I left uni and were no longer, and I quote, 'bleeding them dry'. They wander round making sure sheep stay on the right side of stone dykes that insist upon falling down every time the wind huffs a breath of air. They also do plant surveys and count birds. Don't ask how. I have no idea. It's my parents' version of payback, I suppose. Dad worked for BP for a gazillion years but has always been a nature nut, so I suppose buying his cards is my way of offering my own pitiable payback for a nice childhood (minus the grandad, but that, as you know, is another story).

Better shoot off now, or I'm in danger of spilling my entire life story. If you have any more encounters with my grandfather/grampa/gramps, do let me know. It's like getting clues to a Christmas present you never knew you wanted.

Best – Will

*

'See you soon, darling!' Jess's mum and dad were waving at her. 'And do keep your eye out for the Parcel Force man. He—'

'Or *she*,' her mother butted in.

'—*Santa*,' her father intoned, 'will be bringing you something in time for Crimbo.' They blew some kisses then said a few words she couldn't understand so it must've been in Marshallese. That, or her parents had hit the coconut rum a bit early.

She turned off the app and stared at her blank laptop screen, not quite ready to write back to Will or record a message for her parents. They'd finally figured out how to send video messages via Marco Polo and had taken to doing that instead of trying to connect for actual phone calls. Generators/time zones/island life all seemed to be playing havoc with her parents' previously predictable routines. Not that she was resentful. Having wallowed in her sorrows beneath her unicorn-and-rainbow-covered duvet in her childhood room for the past year, it was high time she learned to stand on her own two feet. Like Will Winters seemed to be doing. He was working his socks off, from the sounds of things. Maybe she should volunteer to drape some ribbons of salmon onto bits of toast—

She pulled herself up short. That would be creepy. She had interfered enough already. The fact Will was so open and seemed quite happy to share all sorts of personal details she couldn't imagine telling a stranger was a bit weird, but... maybe, as he was working so hard and had had a bad break-up and his childhood duvet was as out of reach as hers was... maybe she was all he had until he connected with his grandfather. Poor Will. He deserved his grandfather. Just as Mr Winters deserved a grandson.

A quickfire rat-a-tat-tat sounded on the front door.

Jess yelped.

'Open up, buttercup!' Drea called through the mail flap.

Crikey. The woman certainly knew how to get a girl's attention. Jess pressed her hands to her chest, trying to get her heart to slow down as the mail flap clanked back into place. Relieved not to be in her pyjamas for once, she opened the door with a smile and invited her in.

'Here you are, doll.' Drea handed her a candy-striped takeaway coffee cup that, even from a distance, sent out delicious wafts of cinnamon and nutmeg. 'Something to give you a bit of zip so you can finally start putting some personal touches on this blank slate of yours.'

Jess looked behind her at the hallway leading to the kitchen. White walls. White doors. Beige runner carpet lining the white stairs that led to more... white. Anyone could live here. Or no one.

Which made her heart sink.

Drea was right. It was time to do something to make the house look lived in. Beyond, of course, her fabulous teal-coloured velvet sofa. That said, the thought of personalising her home still made her squirmy. As if making an interior decor statement would define who she was from now until the end of time. And the truth was, she didn't really know who she was right now, let alone the Jess she wanted to be. Apart from confident. And happy. And a teacher.

Okay. Those were some good building blocks.

'Hello! Earth to Jess!'

She blinked her focus back on to Drea who was waving a hand in her face. 'What's it going to be?'

'What do you mean?'

Drea's eyes went wide with disbelief that they weren't both riding the same train of thought. 'Tick tock, doll face. You've only got five days until it's your night and from what I can gather, most of the nights are going to be relatively shit until we get to yours. It's your chance to make a proper impression on the street.'

'Kai and Rex won't have a shi—' Jess stopped herself from giving away the secret.

'Awww, look at you not wanting to swear. You really are a primary schoolteacher aren't you?' Drea, not one to wait for answers, made a concessionary noise, then said, 'Fair enough. But whatever they do will be tasteful and tasteful doesn't always mean fun, am I right?'

'Does every night need to be fun?'

This time Drea really did look at her as if she'd gone round the twist. 'I am not even going to dignify that with an answer.' She nodded at Jess's drink. 'Go on. Drink up then it's confession time. Tell your Auntie Dré-Dré what you're going to do.'

Jess laughed. 'Are you sure you don't want to come in?'

'Positive. I've got loads of paperwork screaming to be finished, but until I know what you're doing I won't be able to focus.'

Jess was pretty sure Drea could do whatever she put her mind to and that this was her form of dithering. She had half a mind to ask her if she'd heard from her son yet, but remembering how sad Drea had looked when she'd spoken about him before, decided to keep schtum. 'I told you. It's a secret.'

'Yeah. Right.' Drea gave a this is clearly hopeless shrug and half turned to go. 'I'll see you tonight, yeah? Gin at the bin? I'll bring gin if you bring the tonic.'

'Bin night again?' Jess scratched her head. In London they stuffed everything into one bag and put it down a chute to a big monster bin no matter what the day of the week.

'Brown ones today.'

'What are those for?'

Drea fixed her with a despairing look. 'Doll. They're for your garden rubbish. It's obviously not the time of year for heaps of debris, but I doubt the lot who were in before you would've done much of a clear out, lazy sods that they were.' She looked at Jess, waiting for some sort of report. None was forthcoming. It was so dark most of the time and her energy hadn't exactly been zinging off the charts... 'Please tell me you've been in your garden.'

'Errr...'

'Oh, for the love of Pete, woman!' Drea suddenly looked deadly serious. It was kind of scary. 'All of that business that happened down in London? It's over now. You're going to have to find a way to pick yourself up and move past it. You're the one in charge of your destiny. No one else. Moping around is not going to change what happened in the past. Doing something about the future – *your* future – will. You got me?'

Jess nodded, her heart too lodged in her throat to speak. Even though she hadn't told Drea the full story, the advice still hit home.

'Enjoy your coffee,' Drea called out as she made her trademark exit of walking, talking and throwing a backwards wiggly-fingered wave over her shoulder.

When she'd gone, Jess slumped to the floor, her back against the closed door, and stared at her blank canvas of a hallway. It matched her blank canvas of a lounge (minus the sofa and popcorn and cranberry strands), the blank canvas of a kitchen, the bare bedrooms where, yes, her bed was still unassembled, and the tiny south-facing room nestled next to the guest room. When she'd first seen the place, she'd imagined turning it into a tiny art studio. A place to rekindle her love of doing quirky takes on classic paintings. Years of doing art with children had pulled her in other directions and, as she'd been unable to hang up anything in the flats she'd lived in with Martin, putting her own creative touch on things had slipped off the radar. Which, now that she thought of it, was a real shame. She'd loved getting lost in a painting. She was no Michelangelo, but she was a pretty good mimic. The thrill she got when she was crafting something out of a few random squirts of colour was exactly what had propelled her to become a teacher. It was exhilarating. Seeing something completely blank – like a canvas, or a corner of notebook paper – become something entirely different.

When she'd been at uni doing her art degree, she used to trawl the charity shops for gilt-edged picture frames.

The real deals were insanely expensive, but as she was painting fake art, putting it in faux frames seemed rather fitting. Fruity forgeries, her father used to call them. When they'd packed up their house, her parents had offered her a couple of the paintings that had been hanging in their lounge. One was an iconic image of Henry VIII with his face replaced by the plump Labrador retriever they'd had when she was a girl. The other was a painting of the Queen in hunting clothes, looking through a pair of binoculars, only her head was replaced by a deer's. Her parents, devoted royalists to the core, adored it and insisted the Queen would too if she were to ever see it. Jess had dithered about taking them, ultimately deciding she'd best leave her previous ambitions where they were. In the past.

Which begged the question, why had the little room held so much appeal for her? She'd not even so much as opened the door to it yet. Her parents had insisted she pack her old easel and a few other art supplies, but they remained in boxes in the small boot room in the back. Maybe...

She took a swig of her coffee. It was really good. And exactly what she'd wanted without even knowing it. How did Drea do that? How did Drea know a lot of things? Like the fact that banging on her door every morning and making her account for herself was something Jess had begun to look forward to.

You're the one in charge of your destiny.

Drea was right. Sitting around moping was only making her more depressed. Was that what she wanted for herself? Her future students? A gloomy thirty-something has-been who'd given the best of herself to London's most privileged students only to be sent packing?

No. She wanted to give them someone brighter, better. Someone who knew you didn't need *things* to be happy. You needed... her enthusiasm wavered... what was it you needed to be happy? She looked down at the coffee cup in her hand, its spicy scent still sending tendrils of holiday spirit into the air.

You needed coffee.

You needed neighbours who cared enough to be cross with you.

She thought of her morning out in the cold with Mr Winters.

Sometimes you needed a crabby neighbour who needed to be led out of his own part of the doldrums. And a secret grandson waiting in the wings to bring even more cheer.

Right. It was action time. Destiny? Jess Green was on her way.

A proper crowd was gathering outside number 9 Christmas Street. It was a good twenty minutes past the hour and there were still no lights on at the house. Or, as someone had sniggered earlier, not a creature was stirring, not even a mouse, then rattled a bin which made all of the Gem'n'Emms scream. The intrigue of what awaited them was creating quite the buzz. All of the other surprises hadn't really had huge reveals apart from the kazoo choir, so people were beginning to bandy about guesses as to what it could be.

'Who lives here again?'

Jess turned at the sound of Josh's voice, which was

surprisingly close to her ear. She'd thought they were more at the wave-at-one-another-from-a-distance kind of friendly, rather than whisper in one another's ear friendly. Interesting. And also a little bit sexy. She turned towards him as if magnetised, her nose drawn towards that magical nook between his chin and shoulder that smelt of oranges and sugar and . . . Almost a second too late, she forced herself back onto her heels and adopted a nonchalant air, hoping it would cover the ohmygodyousmellsogood feelings she was experiencing.

She shrugged. 'I'm probably not the best person to ask.' She nodded over to where Drea was actively charming (read: browbeating) another neighbour into telling her what their plans were for their night.

Jess felt something at her knee. She looked down, expecting a child. Ah. Now she knew why Josh was so close. A Bernese mountain dog had him on the end of her short lead and someone in front of her was dangling the remains of a sausage roll in their hand. She knelt down so that she was face to face with the pooch. She was gorgeous. Dark brown eyes. Light brown eyebrows. A perfect swoosh of white arrowing up and over her forehead towards her inky black back.

'Jess, meet Audrey.'

'Audrey?' Jess looked up at Josh and once again felt that tingle of connection as their eyes met.

'My wife – umm—' He looked away from Jess and at the dog. 'We named her after Audrey Hepburn.'

His wife. Yes. Of course. The reason the whole entire street was vigilantly protective of him. That and his gorgeousness. Poor Josh. And, screw your head on, Jess! Fancying him was ridiculous. He was a) obviously still mourning the loss of his wife, because that's how it worked when you had small children, right? and b) he was too old for her. He was early forties, maybe? So ... not ancient, but still ... More to the point: c) she didn't want a boyfriend. Especially not one who was totally gorgeous, the entire street adored, and smelt of sugar cookies even when there weren't sugar cookies around. And oranges. Did she mention the oranges?

There was also that little niggle of something she couldn't quite pin down that made her think Josh wasn't really the direction she should be looking if, perchance, a complete miracle occurred and she were to ever consider dating someone ever again. The dog, however? The dog she could love in the here and now. She glanced around all of the legs to see if she could catch a glimpse of Zoe and Eli and saw them chasing after one of the Sloan triplets who, kazoo in hand, was taking on the role of the Pied Piper of Christmas Street.

Audrey licked her face as if to redirect Jess's attention back to her.

Jess nestled into the dog's thick fur coat. 'You're certainly gorgeous enough to be a film star. Mmm ... Dog smell. I miss dog smell.'

'Don't they have dogs in London?'

Jess stood and gave him her most serious expression. 'Handbag only. And heavily perfumed. It's the law.'

Josh forced his features into a sombre expression. 'Shame. Audrey would take quite the handbag.'

'That she would.'

'What're you two looking so serious about. This is a party!'

Drea wriggled between them, her hands finding

purchase on their shoulders so she could give them each a short, sharp, spine-jarring shake. 'This better be one helluva reveal.'

Just then a car appeared at the top of the street. It worked its way down and slipped into a spot a couple of doors up from where the crowd had gathered outside number 9. A harried-looking woman ran out of the car. She was wearing a nurse's uniform beneath a winter coat that had seen better days. She was holding a couple of plastic boxes in her hands. She ran into her house (number 9) without looking at anyone. About a minute later the front porch light flicked on. She came out with a small, collapsible card table with the boxes on it. She flicked the lids open, taped a piece of paper to the front of the table then shouted, 'Sorry. I'm needed at work. Sorry, sorry.' Then she jumped back into her car and disappeared down the street.

Everyone looked at each other bewildered.

'"Take One and Merry Christmas",' someone read.

Drea, who Jess would've expected to deliver quite the commentary, remained silent. For about five seconds. And then she began clapping. 'Let's hear it for Katie Ash, everyone! A devoted nurse using her break to give us all a mince pie. Sets an example, doesn't it?'

They all agreed. Yes. It did set an example.

Drea's response really touched Jess. She'd had glimpses that this ballsy woman had quite the soft spot, but this showed a level of compassion she'd not yet given her credit for.

As they formed an orderly queue and each took a pie, Drea insisted they leave a few for Katie to enjoy when she returned home. She also clocked Drea putting her bottle of gin on the note and, with a pen she'd dug out of her pocket, scribbled 'for laters' with an arrow. 'That's all right, doll, isn't it?' she asked when she noticed Jess looking.

'Absolutely,' Jess said.

'Right!' Drea gave her hands a clap then settled her gaze on Josh. 'Only a week or so to come up with something amazing. Hope you're preparing to dazzle.'

'Wouldn't dream of anything less.'

They held one another's gazes confusingly long enough for Jess to feel like a third wheel, then Josh threw her a little 'help me' glance. A glance he was well aware Drea could see.

'Don't you worry, Joshy.' Drea laughed, 'I have faith in you.'

'That's what scares me,' Josh grinned.

Drea smiled back, a mysterious Cheshire Cat grin playing upon her lips. 'That's what scares us all, Josh. Having faith in something we know nothing about.'

And with that, she lifted up her mince pie in a toast, and popped the entire thing into her mouth.

10 December

The clink-clank of the post flap pulled Jess out of her office-supplies reverie.

She cocked her ear and listened for Drea's *coooeee*.

It didn't come.

Strange. Maybe she had called out and Jess had been too absorbed in her work to hear.

Unlikely. Drea could command a crowd of three hundred to do burpees as easily as Jess drew breath. And push-pins weren't that interesting.

Jess stretched, then began to put away the day's office supplies she'd been writing up. Today's copywriting had been twenty parts wistful to five parts embittered. A journey through the chalk, crayon and felt-tip pens she probably wouldn't have for the little ones any more now that she wasn't teaching London's most privileged children. Which made her cross. Having access to all of these amazing art supplies made the world of difference to a child.

She checked herself.

It was down to the teacher to make the most of what they had and despite everything the Cheese Sandwich Incident had stripped away from her, it hadn't taken away her imagination. It was a bit dusty, sure. But it was still there. All she had to do was find a way to fire it back up again.

It occurred to her that the clink-clank had possibly been the postman. Her eyes flicked up to the clock. Yup. It was past noon. Definitely the postman.

She went out into the hall and saw a small pile of post, mostly circulars and catalogues, but a couple of envelopes that looked personal. Mistaken deliveries, most likely. Apart from Amanda and her parents, few people knew she was here.

She picked up the post and carefully went through it, not wanting to rip open another card meant for another neighbour.

The two cards – one in a red envelope and one in silver – were both for her.

There was also a large A4 letter embossed with an all-too familiar letterhead. St Benedict's.

All of her hard-won calm vanished in an instant. What did they want? And why were they writing to her now? Hadn't they made it more than clear a year ago that they wanted her out of their school and away from the children? A low-grade buzzing began in her brain while a myriad of reasons – all of them apocalyptic – whirred through Jess's mind as she tried to figure out why on earth someone from St Benedict's would be writing to her. And how did they even know she lived here? The only forwarding address she'd had since Martin and she had gone their separate ways was her parents. She checked the envelope again. Ah. It was forwarded from her parents' who'd had everything redirected to her while they were abroad.

She put it to the back of the pile and looked, instead,

at the first of the two seasonal envelopes. The penmanship was in a vaguely familiar hand. Her heart did a little leap up and over the disquiet she'd just been feeling.

It was from Will Winters. To her.

She opened it up and grinned. The front of the card had an image of a Highland cow overlooking a snowy landscape, its horns decorated with fairy lights. She laughed.

Inside, the message was short and sweet (mostly sweet). It thanked her for getting his card to his grandfather and wished her a Merry Christmas. There was also an offer to make her a meal once the madness of Christmas was over. He had made a decision not to do New Year's Eve parties, so perhaps a New Year's Day brunch?

What a result! She was a horrible cook, so dining on a young-buck chef's cuisine sounded a great way to welcome in the new year. Particularly as she was still undecided about pizza or the M&S Christmas ready meal for one on the Big Day. Perhaps the temptation of a bit of hollandaise sauce would be just the thing to bring an actual smile to Mr Winters' face. That, and the discovery of a grandson.

Smiling, she opened the other card which was also written in a familiar hand. Very familiar.

Her heart plummeted.

It was from Martin.

How did he know she was here? She checked the envelope. Nope. Not forwarded. It was addressed properly. Number 14 Christmas Street. He must've wheeled it out of Amanda. What the man lacked in sensitivity he made up for in charm.

While things hadn't ended horribly – they'd trotted out the usual placations: 'natural crossroads', 'long distance is tough', 'better now than once we'd let things go too far' – it hadn't been brilliant. He'd said some things that would stay with her forever. Shards of criticism that lodged too easily in her already-fragile confidence. Criticism that had made her wonder if he'd ever been in love with her at all and, to be honest, vice versa. He'd told her she'd been weak. Not stood her ground. That Crispin was obviously a spoilt, little tyrant. Then, in the same breath he'd said she should've sucked up the criticism and stayed at St Benny's. If she had ever brought him to the extracurricular activities teachers sometimes invited their other halves to, he could've made a killing. To which she'd retorted if she'd known the whole purpose of her professional life was to find him new clients, she would've become a waitress at Stringfellows or wherever it was Russian oligarchs hung out while their bodyguards were picking up their children from school. Besides, she'd sniped, he was never around for her extracurriculars because he was too bloody busy scampering around London finding clients himself; he'd taken particular objection to the word scampering. And then they'd split up. Once they'd made their decision, it was as if a line had been drawn. She'd not really wondered what he'd been up to, presuming he was busy enjoying 'not being reined in by someone else's schedule'. He'd not once called to check in on her at her parents', though she knew he knew she'd been at her absolute lowest. Amanda, who saw him at the quiz night once a week, said she'd been dropping in the odd bit of information about Jess despite her plea to just leave it. She didn't want Martin to know she'd once made and eaten an entire tray of Creme

Egg brownies in one sitting. (Don't judge. She'd needed the tryptophan). In fact, she didn't want Martin to know anything. She added the request to her mental list of things she needed to tell Amanda when she finally got a grip and rang her back.

She slipped the card from the envelope. Trendy. Stylish. She flipped it over. Yup. It was a work one. The message inside was short and written in the distant, sparing way one might write to a spinster aunt. He hoped she was well and that life was being kind to her and that her Christmas would be a merry one. He supposed she already knew, but he was off to the Maldives for the hols and would be moving into a flat near Wimbledon in the New Year. All the best, Martin.

She thought about binning it and pretending it didn't exist in the same way Martin had shrugged and said 'Don't worry about it. It'll blow over' when she'd come home in tears that fateful day at work. But it was hard to ignore the fact that he was going on the holiday they'd once talked about enjoying together. And moving – permanently from the sounds of it – to a part of London she'd always liked and that had been closer to St Benny's than Battersea where they'd moved from show home to show home. And, more to the point, weird that he thought she would already know about it. Was this a sign he'd always thought her world revolved around him and not the other way round? A very likely option. He often said things just because he thought he should rather than because he meant them. A salesman through and through.

She tried to picture herself on the beach with Martin. Clinking cocktail glasses with him. Asking him to put sun cream on her shoulders before they turned pink. She couldn't.

Then she tried the same with a flat in Wimbledon, ultimately failing to marry the ultra-modern styles he'd preferred to the decidedly homelier style she leant towards. Hmmm . . . breaking up had definitely been the right thing to do. Even so, how very dare he go on their holiday? She doubted he was going on his own, which made the fact he was telling her doubly irritating. There were any number of azure seas with immaculate beaches to visit. Why couldn't he go to one of them? Too high off the endorphins of meeting a stylish female estate agent who felt belongings were passé and found personal touches gauche, no doubt. A match made in heaven.

She debated about putting the card next to Amanda's on her mantelpiece but decided against it. It would only bring bad memories. Taking a page out of Drea's 'choose your own destiny' book, she popped it into the recycling bin, fairly confident the lack of a return address meant Martin wasn't expecting a card in return.

Which raised the question, *why send a card at all?*

She stared long and hard at the envelope from St Benny's – typed, so indecipherable as to who the sender was – then stuffed it in a kitchen drawer that was well on its way to becoming 'the drawer with all of the random stuff in it'.

Feeling decidedly less chipper than she had been ten minutes earlier, she forced herself to think of the first thing that made her happy.

10 December
13:01

To: WillWinters@TheMerryVictualler.co.uk
From: JessGreen2000@gmail.com
Subject: RE: NOOOOOOOOOOOOOOOO!

Dear Will

Ha! Don't be dismayed, but my refrigerator is a showcase for everything you probably loathe. Pre-made this. Ready meal that. Mini mac-and-cheese balls. Honey-glazed sausage party packets and, just to make sure I had some veg, I dunked carrots into my melted Camembert last night. Yes, I ate the whole thing myself and yes, that was dinner. (I'm relying on the hard labour I did at your grandfather's a couple of days back as the excuse I need for the calorific intake.) Dessert was a horrendous mince pie at the street's advent calendar. (Now I feel mean. It was amazing the poor woman at number 9 managed to do anything at all. She's an NHS nurse, bless her cotton socks.).

    I received your card today. Love the fairy-light cow horns! I am returning the kindness in a paltry way via this email. I'm a bit bah-humbug this year apart from the mini mac-and-cheese balls, LOL. I've decided not to send out cards (bad year, long story, probably a bit like your break-up but with a job loss, relocation and a few dark nights of the soul in which to re-examine my moral compass. Definitely looking forward to the New Year! Hmmm... Looks like you're not the only one who pours their heart out to a stranger. Although, now that I've had a Christmas card from you, does that change things? Are we friends now? Confidants? Weird question. Forget I asked. As you may or may not know, writing all of this in parentheses makes it invisible).

Your card was a nice antidote to the other bits of post I received: a mysterious Christmas card from my ex. Mysterious because he told me he was going on his hols to the Maldives and would then be buying a flat in Wimbledon. This from a man who claimed it would take an act of God to cleave him away from London during the holidays and a second, more impressive act, to get him to ever buy a flat. (He wanted his first buy to be a mansion in Notting Hill.) There was also a letter I don't have the guts to open from my old job. (Definitely not a Christmas card.)

Anyway... I should let you go, seeing as you're the busy one. I don't start my new job until the 9th of Jan and am finding the free time a bit weird. You'd think I'd take up knitting or stamp collecting, but they don't appeal. If you're cool with it, I'll take up spying. Wish me luck as I slip on my mac and scuttle from bin to bin on a quest to see if your grandad's put your card on his mantelpiece (assuming he has one as there are not one, but two chimney pots coming from his house). (And I'm kidding. I would never spy.)

Best – Jess x

10 December
13:17
To: JessGreen2000@gmail.com
From: WillWinters@TheMerryVictualler.co.uk
Subject: RE: NOOOOOOOO!!!!!!!!!!!!!

Jess – you have my blessing on the spying front so long as it doesn't veer into creepy. More later. Forgive rudeness. Vol au vents call! Wx

'Oops! Easy there.'

Jess's feet ice skated in different directions as she flailed then grabbed hold of the first thing she could. Something rock solid. She lurched into an upright position only to bash straight into Josh's chest. *Crumbnations.* The man was a wall of muscle. She looked up into his handsome face as she received another waft of oranges and sugar cookies, hoping he missed her face's inevitable shift into swoony soft focus. He could be a body double for ... hmmm ... someone deeply gorgeous. No. He was his own variety of gorgeous. And his own variety of Do Not Go There Jess He is a Dating Mirage. Someone she thought she wanted, but didn't really because of that itsy bitsy niggle she couldn't define or shake.

'Thanks.' She gently extracted herself from his hold. 'Icy.' She pointed to the ground as if he needed to know where the ice was that had made her slip. God. No wonder Martin had wanted someone more with it. Not that he'd put it that way when he'd felt obliged to explain to her exactly why he didn't think staying together would be a good idea, but it was clear he would've been much happier with a city mouse to her always slightly off-kilter country one.

'Definitely. They need to get the gritting machine down here. Same thing probably happened to Mr Winters when his car skidded towards everyone.'

Jess thunked her forehead with the heel of her hand. 'That's it! His car skidded on black ice! I *knew* he wouldn't have done anything like that on purpose.'

They looked down at the end of the street towards Mr Winters' house. It was dark, curtains drawn. As usual. She had passed by earlier in the day on a faux 'checking out everyone's Christmas decorations' walk. Even though it had been late afternoon and there had been lights on in his lounge, it was difficult to see in as his house was set up higher than the rest of the houses on the street, as if putting in all of these newer builds had pushed his house up and out of the way of the hustle bustle of the world moving on as he stayed in his cocoon. Then Mr Perkins had jumped into the window ledge and given her the evils so she'd moved on.

'Any clue what you're going to do for the advent calendar?' Josh asked, eyes still on Mr Winters' house.

'Nope. You?'

'*Nada.*' He gave her a cheeky sidelong look. He began to hum a song from *Sweeney Todd*, which . . . double swoon! The man knew musical theatre. He was, without a doubt, the Hugh Jackman of Christmas Street. But younger. And a widow. And, yes, still off limits. 'Drea's going to turn us into mincemeat if we don't dazzle.'

'Yes, Drea will,' said Drea, along with her signature move of whipping an arm round each of their necks and pulling them into a weird and slightly strangley sports hug. She released them and shot them each a look. 'What are we staring at?'

'Number twenty-four.'

Drea made a frustrated noise. 'He's still not got back to me, the old goat.'

Jess stiffened protectively then remembered Drea was as defensive about Mr Winters as she was. 'Maybe he likes to play his cards close to his chest.'

'Yes, dear.' Drea rolled her eyes and then, to Josh,

said, 'You can see why our darling Jess here is a primary schoolteacher, can't you?'

'Oh, yes, that's right!' Josh pushed aside a tousle of chestnut waves, the bulk of it flopping back onto his forehead. 'I forgot you might be looking after my little monsters. What year are you teaching?'

Drea gave Jess a not so subtle, 'get in there girl' look.

Not being the biggest fan of 'little monsters', Jess still managed a smile because she knew Zoe and Eli were perfectly nice children. 'Year three. Plus I'm the art co-ordinator for all of the years, so I imagine I'll be meeting most of the children.'

'Wait a minute!' He mimicked her head-thunking gesture. 'You're the replacement for Mrs Jameson.'

'That's right.' They'd only met briefly, but she'd seemed lovely. An early-forty-something woman who'd said she'd always wanted to retrain as a garden designer so she thought she'd better get to it before old age set in.

'Shame how things ended.'

Jess's stomach scrunched up in sync with her forehead. 'How do you mean?'

Had she been fired, too? Accused of assault?

'Well...' Josh explained in a voice you used to say someone had got cancer or something equally awful. 'That her husband got transferred to Canada.'

Errr... 'And why is this bad? Do they not have gardens to design in Canada?'

Josh did one of those laugh-huffs things that produced a little cloud between them. 'No. Not that. It's that all of the children absolutely adored her. I don't think I've ever known a teacher to be so loved. The other teachers loved her. The students. The parents. The local council

considered putting up a plaque, but as she's still living...'
Josh gave a shrug that indicated a statue in the centre of
town probably wouldn't have been enough. 'We all dug
deep for her leaving day. Got her some lovely pressies. And
the tears! You've never seen so many bereft children...'

Jess began to tune out, mostly because her brain was
buzzing with fear. Replacing the most popular teacher
ever? How was she going to fill those shoes? She looked
down at her faux fur-lined boots and silently asked them,
How? *How*?

'Anyway,' Josh was concluding. 'You'll be fine. I'm sure
they'll adjust in time.'

Drea tucked her arm into Jess's and turned her away
from Josh with a whispered 'You're gaping, doll face.'

They were now facing number 10. It was a single family
home – as large as the semi-detached ones flanking it –
with a small lawn and a drive leading up to a red garage
door. The porch lights flashed.

'It's Morse code!' Kev the mechanic shouted out.

'Do you think they've been taken hostage?' One of the
Gem'n'Emms giggled.

'Who lives there?' Jess asked Drea.

'The Nishios.'

She tried to place the name for a minute then asked,
'Is that a Japanese surname?'

'Yeah. They've been to a few of the nights. Hiro – the
husband – moved over to teach at the uni on some sort
of exchange, ended up meeting his English rose and ba-
da-bing, ba-da-boom, four children later and here they
are in the heart of British suburbia.'

A teacher. Like her. Who had found love, marriage and
not one but four baby carriages. Jess's heart constricted

with longing that she'd find the same level of fulfilment one day. Maybe not in the form of four baby carriages, but... The burst of joy she used to get each morning when the school bell rang and the students began to fill her classroom would be a good start. If, of course, the students ever recovered from the loss of the beyond-perfect Mrs Jameson.

'What does he teach?' she forced herself to ask.

Drea shrugged. 'Classics, I think. English literature. The pair of them. They're always off to the Brontë's house or some Jane Austen festival or another. Love their cosplay, they do.'

Jess smiled. They sounded like a great couple. And she was a sucker for a feisty heroine in a bonnet. Maybe if Will Winters taught her how to cook something beyond microwaved scrambled eggs on toast, she could invite them over for dinner one night. 'Any idea what they're going to do?'

'Not a clue – oh, look. The front blinds are opening. Are those... is he doing that by remote control?'

It looked like it. A hush came over the crowd as the automatic blinds lifted to reveal the Nishio family in a perfect Victorian Christmas tableau. There were *ooos* and *ahhhhs* and then applause. The attention to detail was amazing.

They had a beautifully decorated Christmas tree complete with real candles on its perfectly aligned branches. Mrs Nishio, a tall redhead with rosy cheeks, was wearing a plum-coloured dress that looked as if it could've walked straight off the set of *A Christmas Carol*. She stood at one end of an old oak dining table upon which lay an incredible Christmas meal. A large ham, some sort of moulded pudding, a platter of roast potatoes. The works. Mr Nishio, a portly gentleman discreetly pocketing a remote control, was holding a carving knife above a beautifully roasted goose that still had curls of steam rising from it.

The two youngest children, girls, probably around six or seven, were wearing exquisite, matching velvet dresses in a deep green.

'They're twins,' Drea said, pointing to the little girls. 'Scrumptious little munchkins aren't they?'

They were. They were also perfectly still. One of them was mischievously holding a coin above a Christmas pudding while the other sat on a rocking horse and was holding a cat that clearly hadn't been briefed on the 'do not move' edict.

One of the older boys was poised as if pulling a chair out for his mother, while the other boy was holding an immaculately wrapped Christmas present to his ear as if he were shaking it for clues.

And then the blind began to close.

'Is that it?'

'Looks like it.'

'Aren't they going to hand out sarnies or anything? Some of those roasties?' Kev gave his tummy a solid pat only to get an elbow in the ribs from his wife along with a reminder that they had a perfectly serviceable tea waiting for them at home.

A few of the children squatted down to see what remained of the tableau and then, as the blind reached the bottom of the window, the cat ran along the sill with a goose leg in its mouth.

Drea began another round of applause. 'Bloody

marvellous. Sets a high bar for the rest of you lot, doesn't it? Kai? Rex? You two ready for tomorrow night?'

'Absolutely, Drea. Wouldn't want to let the street down, would we?'

'Better not,' she said warningly, and then laughed her disarmingly cheery laugh.

'Oh!' Kai went up on his tiptoes and whispered something into Rex's ear. They conferred a moment between them then Kai made a ding-ding-ding sound as if he were putting a knife to the side of a crystal glass. 'As you're all here, we were wondering if you wouldn't mind tomorrow night's session being a little earlier?'

There were a few shouts indicating most people thought it was all right.

'Excellent. As it's Saturday, we thought we'd leave the evening to everyone to enjoy whatever Christmas parties they have lined up.'

'Too bloody right!' Shouted someone.

'Mark!' remonstrated one of the Gem'n'Emms. 'Language.'

Rex shushed the crowd and instructed, 'We're going to be outside for about an hour, so wear warm clothes.'

'What time?'

'Five o'clock.'

There were a handful of 'we'll have to delay/push forward the children's tea' comments bandied about, but ultimately everyone agreed that five was fine, *despite* the adjustments and yes, everyone was sensible, they'd all wear their warm clothes and couldn't wait to see what tomorrow's surprise was. And then, as if a switch had been flicked, the street emptied until it was just Drea and Jess.

They stared at one another a moment. Then giggled.

Drea flicked her thumb towards number 1. 'There's a bottle of rosé in there with our names on it. And some pasta if you aren't a fussy eater.'

'Sounds perfect.' Jess said, glad for a reason not to go back to her house. She'd felt funny there ever since she got the post. Kryptonite in the form of an embossed envelope stuffed into a kitchen drawer. Kryptonite that made naming the house she had yet to call home even more difficult.

11 December

There was some sort of strange chirruping next to Jess's head. Strange, because the noise very distinctly sounded like a frog. It was pitch-black. She tentatively put her hand out. Hmmm. Nothing around her felt like her bed (still unmade).

The chirruping began afresh. Eventually, through the fug of what had been a rather comatose sleep, Jess realised it was her phone. She batted around for it only to hear it fall off the cushy thing she was lying on that must be a sofa. She followed suit. Why did her head hurt so much? She hadn't remembered being in a fight last night.

She heard a power shower kick into action above her.

She didn't have a power shower. Why was she on the floor beside a sofa that wasn't— Ohh.

She was at Drea's. They had drunk wine last night. Lots of wine. More than one bottle anyway. There may have been pasta. There may also have been lots of YouTubing Drea in her new-millennium, big-haired, animal-print unitard heyday. She was Australia's Jane Fonda. The UK's... umm... Davina? But better. Step-aerobics. Jazzercize. Thighmasters. She was spectacular. Drea had either taught it, championed it or worn the outfit. She had entire Pinterest pages devoted to her.

Early on, she'd rejected the soft-lit studio workout video aesthetic. The type that always had a pair of mauve armchairs, geometric-patterned carpets and huge potted artificial plants that culminated in the set looking more like a dentist's waiting room than a living room which she presumed the producers had been aiming for. She'd started her own type of work out. The Bondi Beach Body. It had taken her a while to 'get her claws into the business', but she'd done it and made it accessible to everyone. You could wear whatever you wanted, do it wherever you wanted, and, depending upon if you ever actually did the workouts, 'your body and booty were well on their way to being beach-tastic' – a tagline Jess had made her repeat again and again with Jess trying, and failing, to mimic her Aussie accent until they'd both dissolved in hysterics.

There had even been one point, after Drea had said she could come over on Christmas Day if her son didn't show, when they had exchanged very slurry and very impassioned, 'I love you—' 'No! *Listen.* I love *you*'s.'

#Embarrassing.

Jess's head made a crinkling sound. Why was her head crinkling? She gingerly touched it to see if it had turned into something breakable. It appeared she was wearing a paper crown. Why was she – ohhhh.

They'd broken into Drea's supply of Christmas crackers (lush, proper crackers with prizes you would actually use, like miniature screwdrivers for glasses, and bottle stops which, on reflection, they should have used). They'd pulled out the party hats and sung a bit of off-key 'All By Myself' after Drea had confessed she didn't think her son was going to come. 'He's not mentioned it once. Not. A. Peep.'

'What are you doing on the floor?'

Jess lurched up realising a bit too late that there was a trickle of drool on her cheek. She batted her fringe away, as if that would help her overall aesthetic, and offered Drea what she hoped was a smile.

'Why are you on the floor?' Drea repeated, giving her a little nudge with the toe of her trainer.

'Are you going for a run?'

Drea looked at her ensemble, a rather fabulous Lululemon winter athleisurewear ensemble – solids on top, discreet camo-patterned leggings on the bottom – then back at Jess. 'Cold shower and a run followed by a hot shower's the only way to get the booze out of the system, isn't it?' She fixed Jess with a stern look. 'You're a bad influence. C'mon. Get up. I'll make you a coffee before I go – unless you want to come with me?'

One rocket-fuel shot of espresso later, Jess refused a second invitation to 'crank out a few miles', preferring to take her walk of shame under cover of darkness. A shower, some sort of actual planning for the advent calendar and one-upping the saintly Mrs Jameson were on today's list of things to do. That. Or a nap.

Jess bolted up from the sofa.

She did a quick check. Yes. It was hers this time. No drool. Her eyes flicked to her phone. Three o'clock. A whole day wasted. Avoided, more like. Getting yet another text from Amanda saying they MUST TALK AND SOON had solved the chirping phone mystery but had also thrown her hackles up. The Amanda she knew would always tell her what was going on rather than tease out the details. She was not a secret keeper. In fairness,

Jess could've just rung her as requested and put an end to it, but the fact Amanda's texts and messages flanked the arrival of the letter from St Benny's was suspicious. It led her to the conclusion she feared most. The school and/or Crispin's parents had definitely decided to sue her. No doubt a thick missive from Pinstriped, Buttonholed & Privileged law firm would be arriving in today's post.

The doorbell rang followed by a knock and not so much as a whisper of a *coooeee*. Not Drea, then. Thankfully, Jess's drapes were closed, so whoever it was wouldn't know she was napping away her life. After a quick squat and check in the hall mirror (still leaning against the wall waiting to be hung up), she confirmed that her fringe was only partially skew-wiff and that her face's cushion creases weren't too obvious, she opened the door feigning a brightness she wasn't feeling.

'Hi, darling, hi. All right?'

It was Kai and Rex, looking immaculately put together as usual. Kai leant in for his customary cheek kisses.

'Mmm. You smell good,' Jess said.

'Myrrh and tonka bean. You like?'

'Sounds seasonal.'

Rex leant in for his kisses with another waft of something delicious. 'I'm frankincense and bergamot.'

Jess nodded her approval and drew in a few little extra wisps of fragrance in the way a chef might cup a hand and move the scent of his wine reduction towards him. 'Scents of the three kings I take it? Have you arrived with . . . erm . . . gold?'

Kai indulged her with a laugh then shook his head no. 'Just two queens hoping for a favour.'

They both looked so expectant and delighted at

whatever it was they were going to ask, Jess felt a sudden rush of excitement light her up. 'Oh my God, you got a puppy and you want me to babysit?'

Kai's face fell and Rex gave his head a confused little shake. 'No, love, sorry.'

'No, I'm sorry,' she fell over herself apologising. 'I don't know what made me think—' She stopped herself before she dug her hole any deeper and said, 'Anything. I will do anything to help.'

'Don't be so quick to say yes, love. You don't know what it is we're after.'

It was a good point. If she'd stopped and thought before she'd done what she had at St Benedict's, she might be packing her bikini and factor 50 for a couple of cocktail-soaked weeks in the Maldives right now. After, of course, having attending Ethan's funeral. She shoved the thought away. Ethan hadn't died. That was the main thing.

'Okay. I take it back then.' She said, jauntily jiggling her eyebrows so they'd know she was kidding.

'Please don't,' Kai put his hands in prayer position, looking a bit like the puppy dog he claimed he didn't want. 'We need someone who's good at dealing with the unruly masses. And by unruly masses, we mean everyone who lives on Christmas Street.'

'Why?'

'For the wreath-making session.'

She frowned. They were the experts. 'Why do you need my help?'

'Because we don't want them to be ugly.'

She looked from Rex to Kai and back again. 'And you need my help as an ugly-wreath monitor?'

'Not exactly.'

Two hours later Jess was feeling much more in her element than she had anticipated. She liked big happy groups of people trying to create things and had, with each hot glue-gunned addition to a wreath, felt a bit of that buzz she got from a really good teaching session. She hadn't instantly slipped into Mrs Jameson's Best Teacher Ever shoes. Yet. But she did feel as if these were little baby steps in the right direction.

An added bonus came in the form of a hall pass on the awkward chitchat sessions Drea kept strong-arming her into with Josh and his kids. She was hopping from family to family, sticking a finger on a bow here, twisting a bit of wire over a pomegranate there, teasing cloves into clementines, quite certain she'd return home smelling like a bowl of Christmas potpourri – which, all things considered, wasn't a bad personal scent.

Kai and Rex were decked out in utterly sumptuous king outfits (beautiful silk head-wraps and gorgeous jewel-coloured robes) while she'd been stuck with a tea towel, a fake beard and one of Rex's old dressing gowns (it was actually quite a lovely dressing gown and she had on three layers of clothes underneath which made her look more Michelin man than wise man, but pragmatics of warmth definitely pipped fashion to the post on this frosty night).

What made the night even better was that everyone *loved* Rex and Kai's idea: make a wreath as a gift to pay forward.

They had borrowed Chantal's trestle tables, and had set them out under the street lights at the end of the cul-de-sac as they didn't have a drive of their own. There were heaps of folding chairs or, for those who preferred standing, space to stand at the tables. They also had a hotplate with a huge jam pan full of mulled wine and a platter of very swish mince pies ('We have a trade for goods deal with the local bakery. They get a wreath, we get a bounty of pies.') Mr Winters had yet to appear, but Jess could see there was light coming from around the curtains in his sitting room.

The tables were a hive of activity. Instructions were given as to how to bend pine fronds round the circular frames, or tie tight, substantial bows if a swag was preferred. There were mountains of 'individual touches' to choose from. Cranberries, holly berries, goji berries (no, not really, but there was something else... bay? Juniper!) There were long skeins of ribbon, bowls of dried oranges, platters of pomegranates and a mini-mountain of Brussels sprouts 'which looked much more seasonal on the star-shaped frame if anyone was up to it'. It was fabulous watching everyone's brows furrow with intense concentration, their decision to use this bow or that, one piece of fruit or another every bit as important as cookie-decorating day had been when it came to hundreds and thousands or edible silver balls. Speaking of which, Chantal – Jess was completely unsurprised to see – was making *the* most fabulous wreath she'd ever laid eyes on, apart, of course, from Rex and Kai's wondrous creations.

'Jess?'

An elegantly gloved hand beckoned her from the far end of one of the trestle tables. It, and the rest of the fur-coated arm, belonged to Mrs Snodgrass. She was looking incredibly stylish tonight. In place of her usual ensemble of a practical wool pantsuit and sensible all-seasons coat most likely purchased in the 1970s, Martha, along with her slim-fit leather gloves, was wearing the type of fur hat that was generally seen on a Bond girl. A Bond girl wearing a matching coat that went all the way down to her ankles while skiing down Mont Blanc ahead of a pack of machine-gun-wielding baddies. Martha had on the matching coat minus the skis. *Ooh la la!*

'Yes, Martha?'

'It's Mrs Snodgrass, dear, unless told otherwise.' She was instantly corrected.

'Yes, Mrs Snodgrass.' Jess said contritely.

'Please, dear, *do* call me Martha,' Mrs Snodgrass said with a smile. 'Now. If I want to get these holly berries to look as if they've been Jack Frosted what do I do?'

Jess talked her through how to use the artificial snow can and then, when they'd decided Martha's arthritic fingers weren't quite up to the task, she did it for her. As she was handing it back she saw Martha try to cover a yawn with an embroidered handkerchief she had clutched in her hand.

'Late night?' Jess asked.

'They're all late nights,' she groused.

'What do you mean?'

Martha glanced down the table to where Tyler was playing a Jimi Hendrix-style air guitar version of 'Silent Night' for some of the children.

'When he plays something tolerable, he's actually very talented,' Martha snipped.

'I'm guessing he doesn't choose tolerable all that often?'

'Try never.'

'You should give him a warning, Martha,' piped in a neighbour Jess hadn't yet met. The nurse maybe? 'Get someone else in. I'm always happy to ring the police for you. Say he's a public nuisance or whatever.'

'Oh, we've been through all that,' Martha swotted away the suggestion then pointed to a thick roll of red ribbon. 'What do you think to fashioning me a big bow, Jess? Would that be all right?'

'Course it would,' Jess said, smiling because she was getting the impression Mrs Snodgrass enjoying complaining about Tyler as much as Tyler enjoyed shredding guitar solos.

She pulled out a long stretch of ribbon and got to work. She was enjoying the hands-on work more than she'd thought. It was a lot like being back at St Benny's but without the rules and regulations, or the compulsion to keep glitter off the children's eye-wateringly expensive uniforms (a snip, really, when put up against the school fees). It was, in fact, a bit how she'd imagined life would be when she'd bought the house on Christmas Street to teach at a normal school in a normal town with normal children. In other words, it was fun. When Kai and Rex had first asked her to help, she'd felt herself put on the brakes just as she had when her parents had suggested easing back into teaching via online tutorials. But, as with her parents suggestion, the reality was proving exactly the medicine she needed to remind herself just how much she enjoyed teaching. And, of course, messing about with loads of free art supplies.

She handed the completed bow back to Martha for inspection. 'I love your outfit.'

'Oh, this?' Martha pressed her gloved hands to the fluffy collar framing her delicate jawline. 'I hadn't even remembered having it and the other day when I was clearing out, I unearthed it and thought... why not?'

'Why not indeed?' Rex came up to join them, a big box of silver and gold pine cones resting on his hip. 'It's fabulous. And you look fabulous in it. Whose is it?'

'Mine,' Martha pressed her fingers a bit possessively into the fluffy fur. 'It was a gift.'

'I meant the designer, Martha. That's not an off-the-rack jobbie.'

Martha brightened then softened as if remembering the moment she'd first seen it. 'Dior, darling,' she said in a husky, late-night radio voice none of them had heard from her.

Rex whistled. 'Nice gift.'

Martha shrugged. 'The Seventies were a different era. Especially in Soho.'

'Oh, it was from a Londoner, then, was it?'

'No...' her voice trailed off then, in a whisper added, 'A Parisian.'

'Ooo err, missus. Look at you and your Parisian lover.'

'He wasn't a lover,' Martha arched an imperious eyebrow, then shaded her eyes against the streetlight as she intoned, 'He was a fan.'

'Of...?' Rex put down the box and squatted down so Martha didn't have to strain to look up at him.

She squidged her features as if deciding whether or not to say, then rather primly admitted, 'My singing.'

'Martha, you dark horse, you.' Rex scanned the crowd. 'Tyler, have you heard this!' He stood back up and beckoned for Tyler to come over.

Martha's features quickly turned sour. 'Stop that. It's

my business and I'd like to keep it that way, thank you very much.'

Jess gave her arm a squeeze but Martha shook her off and stood, wavering a bit to get her balance as she did.

'That's enough, Rex. Thank you for a lovely evening. Now goodnight.'

She walked off without a backwards glance, leaving them all a bit flabbergasted.

'I didn't mean to—' Rex began.

'Course you didn't,' Jess assured him. No one knew why Martha had had the abrupt about-face. She looked down at the table. 'Oh! She left her wreath, should I go after her?'

'We were making them for others, weren't we?'

'Do you know who she was making it for?'

'Josh,' said a couple of people, as if they'd timed it.

'She usually does stuff for Josh,' said another as a someone else announced, 'But I was doing mine for Josh.'

'Really? No. I was, too.'

'Sugar,' said another.

There was giggling and some huffs of disappointment. It appeared the whole of Christmas Street had been making their wreaths for Josh.

'Josh?' Rex called down to the far end of the table where Josh, his children and their Bernese mountain dog were trying to wrangle a couple of tangerines onto a wire wreath frame. 'Do you need a wreath?'

He barked a laugh. 'God, no. We've got one on the front door, the back door, the gate. The mums at school have been ever so generous.'

A few discomfited glances were exchanged.

Jess threw a look at the house behind her. 'What if we gave it to Mr Winters?'

The table fell silent. Then:

'Oh, I don't know if he'd like that.'

'He never really does anything for the holidays.'

'He does flowers in the spring,' she pointed out.

'Spring isn't exactly a holiday is it, Jess?'

''Spose not, but—'

'But nothing. It's not like he's out here making one for you, is it?'

'He's going to be doing something on December the twenty-fourth,' an Australian voice cut through the chatter.

An awkward silence hummed along the table.

'Go on, Jess. You give it to him if you like,' Drea said. 'I'm sure Martha wouldn't mind.'

In one weighted move, Jess felt everyone's eyes land on her. It made her skin crawl. Exactly the way it had after she'd shouted at Crispin, 'Don't. You. *Dare*!'

She'd made a call.

It had gone wrong.

More so than any other gut reaction she'd had in her life.

She glanced at Rex to try and gauge what he thought.

'It's up to you, love. None of us has developed a rapport with him.'

'He almost ran over my *child*,' gritted one of the Gem'n'Emms.

'That was an accident,' someone said, not sounding entirely convinced.

'Was it? Was it *really*?' she replied.

Kai bounded up and pointedly put a portable speaker

on the middle of the table. He cupped his hands to his mouth and called out a bright *woo hoo!* for everyone's attention. 'How about we top up our mulled wines and have a go at our own version of "Do They Know It's Christmas"?'

Shoulders lowered, tensions eased and soon everyone was singing with gusto. Tyler climbed up onto the middle of one of the tables and added a passionate air-guitar performance to the mix. Laughter and music filled the street again.

A loud, reverberant door slam silenced everything bar the tinny sound of Boy George.

'Turn that bloody racket off!'

It was Mr Winters.

Jess's heart sank.

The song came to an end.

Without waiting for a response, he turned round and stomped back into his house.

12 December

Jess knew she was walking on thin ice. And she wasn't just talking figuratively. Overnight, as if the chilly atmosphere between the residents of Christmas Street and Mr Winters had transferred across to Mother Nature, the street had been covered in a sheen of slippery hoar frost. Pretty, but potentially harmful.

Though the thin wintry light of day had only just appeared, Jess had been up for hours. Her gut was telling her one thing, but her need to steer clear of trouble was saying another. After lots of soul-searching and two enormous mugs of hot chocolate, she'd finished off Mrs Snodgrass's wreath, hooked it round her arm and headed off with her heart on her sleeve to ask Martha if she could give it to Mr Winters.

Mr Winters was unhappy for a reason. Martha had become very cross, very quickly for a reason. The same way Jess went silent with internal despair every time someone asked her how excited she was to try and fill Mrs Jameson's shoes come the start of the winter term.

Carefully making her way down the street, she headed towards number 21.

A car began to crawl past her then stopped. The darkened window of the family-style SUV came down. It was a Gem'n'Emm. 'All right, Jess? On your way to the cut through to church?'

Jess froze, desperately wishing she could hide behind the wreath slung on her arm. She was hardly going to say she was on a UN peace mission to get a wreath on Mr Winters' door given last night's debacle. She'd heard a clutch of Gem'n'Emms vow to boycott Mr Winters' evening even if he did shock the street by doing an event on Christmas Eve. Poisoned mince pies, most likely, one of them had not so quietly whispered.

She shook her head. 'No, just out for a stroll.'

The Gem'n' Emm's eyes dipped down to the wreath then back up again.

'Oh, shame. We were going to offer you a ride. Have a proper chat.'

'Sorry.' Jess was pretty sure the proper chat was going to include persuasive arguments to join the party line in How To Feel About Mr Winters. If there was one thing she definitely didn't like, it was being told how to feel about people when her gut was guiding her elsewhere. Although... her gut had led her up the Swanee before. No. It hadn't. She had to believe she was right. That *this* was right. Otherwise, the entire foundation of who she was might as well crumble up and disappear.

'They've got a lovely children's mass next weekend,' the Gem'n'Emm said. Pointedly. 'Mrs Jameson used to help out. A real inspiration she was.'

After Jess gave a non-committal, high-pitched *Ooh, that sounds nice*, the Gem'n'Emm sniffed and added, 'If you're interested, that is. I know the school's C of E, so I just assumed—' She stopped abruptly, as if Jesus had whispered a reminder to her that he welcomed everyone into his fold, even the ones who didn't go to church every Sunday, then stuck her palms by her face and wiggled them jazz-hands style. 'Nativity. Carols. The lot. Easy enough to cram you in back with the kiddies!' Her expression accordioned into one of deep concern. 'Drea says you're on your own for the holidays. We're happy to take you under our wing. Unless, of course, you have other plans?'

This last question came out as more of an accusation than an invitation.

Jess forced herself to smile. Gem'n'Emm was trying to be nice in the best way she knew how. It wasn't her fault Jess had absolutely nothing to do on her favourite holiday ever.

Two years ago today she would've known exactly how the holidays would play out. The actual break would be at her parents. Martin would be invited and decline. Her parents would tell her she looked too thin and too tired, ply her with food and tiptoe round while she napped. After supper there'd be a round robin with the remote as to who got to pick the evening Christmas film. (Jess, Netflix Holiday Princess movies; her dad, one of the Die Hard films, didn't matter which one; and her mum, *It's a Wonderful Life*, no substitutes. They all adored *Elf, Miracle on 34th Street* and *Love Actually* in equal measure.) There would be long country walks with her family and their friends, drinks at her Uncle Colin's for punch, even though every year they vowed never to go back because of the evil hangovers the day after, but they always did. In between all of this Jess did a lot of googling, trying to decide what she should spend her Christmas money from the parents at St Benny's on. The year before had been a doozy. Three hundred quid in John Lewis vouchers, four Jo Malone candles, a bouquet-a-month subscription and the inevitable invitation to 'tutor' one family's children at their chalet. She'd said no because those kind of invitations gave her the willies. As if one day, rather than ask for a false set of marks, the parents would ask her to murder a nanny who'd been shagging an errant husband, or give her passport to an illegal maid they'd been holding hostage for several years because no one ironed a shirt collar like she did. Yet another skew on her world view that had landed her here, very solidly, in the centre of reality, which was precisely where she wanted to be. None of which was helping her find a tactful way to dodge the invitation.

'Jess?' Gem'n'Emm's children had rolled down their window and were peering at her as if they, too, needed to know what her holiday plans were. 'We can throw in dinner with the kids if you're interested. We always have tacos before the service, don't we kids?'

'Tacos!' They echoed and clapped. 'Yum!'

Jess did love a good taco. She wasn't so sure about being counted as one of the children seeing as she was an adult woman, but she had also absolutely adored this time of year. Especially the bits that involved children. Right up until she was fired then forced to sit through the nativity, the carols, the thanks to the parents for all of their contributions with special helpings of gratitude to the Anand-Haight family for being so generous . . . *all things considered.* (They'd paid for a trained donkey to walk in and out of the school's chapel with a rather thrilled-looking 'Mary' riding side-saddle – with a helmet on beneath her white shawl because Crispin's parents, above anything, knew health and safety was paramount when it came to children.)

'Shall we leave you to mull it over?' The Gem'n'Emm asked.

'Yes, thanks,' Jess smiled apologetically, waving mechanically as they slid up their windows and rolled off down the road towards the church, where Jess could hear a peel of bells beginning.

It was a nice invitation. A lovely one, in fact. Exactly the sort of invitation she would've offered to someone new and alone on her street if she had a happy family all primed for the holidays. In fact, Jess found herself spoilt for choice. There was Drea's invitation to join her (if her son didn't show), Kev's invitation to join him and his family for their annual deep-fried turkey and Mrs Snodgrass's invitation to join her for a small tipple during the Queen's speech. Each of the offers had made her heart pound with gratitude that the street she'd chosen to live on was filled with people who were so kind.

She would say no, of course. To all of them. Accepting the invitations would involve actual talking, unlike the advent-calendar events which involved little more than chit-chat. There would also be wine. And questions. Talking, wine and questions would inevitably lead to pouring her guts out. The whole gory story. And she wasn't about to fall into that particular rabbit hole again. Not unless . . . And there she went, straight back down to the *what if* tug and pull of what would've happened if only she'd minded her own business.

She was so lost in her thoughts it was a bit of a shock to find herself staring at Martha putting a box outside her front door.

'All right there, dear?' Martha asked when she saw Jess.

'Yes, sorry, I—' she went to hold up the wreath but before she could explain her mission Martha interrupted her.

'I think I owe you an apology, Jess. For being snippy.'

'You weren't—'

'Yes, I was. I've lived in the same skin for well over seventy years now and I know when I'm snippy and when I'm not. I was snippy and I didn't much like it.'

'Oh, well . . . you don't have to apologise.'

'No, dear. You're wrong. I do. It's the people round us who look after us, and I was rude.'

Jess wanted to contradict her again, but thought better of it. Martha had been round the block a few more times than she had and, as she said, knew herself better than anyone else did. Jess looked down at the cardboard box and saw a couple of feathers peeking out. Feathers that looked an awful lot like the feathers on Kai and Drea's shared boa.

Martha caught her looking. 'Nothing to see here, dear.'

'Oh, I beg to differ,' Jess said, already preparing to race across to Drea's and tell her she might not have to share after all. 'This looks remarkably like a boa we saw only recently.'

'No, that one was ostrich. This is—' Martha stopped, pressed her lips tightly together and shook her head. 'Oh, you're good. A real Angela Lansbury, aren't you?'

Jess gave her one of those *maybe, maybe not* smiles she hoped looked slightly mysterious and twinkly-eyed. She'd quite happily become the neighbourhood detective if it was going to be this fun.

Martha threw up her hands, exasperated. 'All right,

fine. *Yes*. It was me who donated the boa. I thought I couldn't let the other one go, but on reflection it turned out I could. I can let it all go.'

'What? What do you mean?'

She pointed a semi-gnarled finger towards the box. 'The coat and hat are in there, too. Ridiculous for me to have pulled them out of the mothballs and even more ridiculous to have thought I could relive my glory days.'

'Glory days?'

Martha's mood shifted from cantankerous to forlorn. She gave Jess a kindly but sad smile along with an arm pat. 'You'll find out one day when you're old and grey, dear. I'm sorry to say it, but all of you young people will soon come to realise life is full of dreams you have to let go.'

A crashing sound came from indoors. Startled, Martha lost her footing. Jess lurched forward to steady her, inadvertently swinging the wreath at the door and knocking it wide open. There, at the foot of the stairs, lay Tyler, sprawled in a skinny-jeaned, spider-legged mess.

'Oh, dear. Tyler!' Martha's hands flew to her cheeks. Before she could get to him, he popped up and grinned.

'Not to worry, Mrs S. My bad for not looking.' He looked round him and then pointed at a couple of boxes that he'd clearly tripped over. 'Oh, ho. What's in here? Has Santa come early?'

Mrs Snodgrass tsked. 'I was trying to get them out to the car before you came down, but with all of the old aches and pains . . .'

Tyler was by her side in an instant, guiding her to a comfortable-looking armchair of the very well-loved variety. A cat was lounging across the top of it and quickly shifted into Martha's lap when she was settled.

'You mad old woman.' Tyler tutted, not unlike an old woman himself. 'What have I told you about lifting heavy things on your own? I'm the one who should be doing that, not you.'

Jess, still standing in the doorway, felt her heart squeeze tight. It was easy to see why Martha didn't kick Tyler out. He was doting on her as if she were his own flesh and blood. Tough on the outside, soft on the inside, the pair of them.

'Are you planning on spending my entire heating budget today, dear?' Martha asked, eyebrow cocked, an imperious expression playing upon her features as she gave her feline a long stroke upon its back. Jess pulled the door shut, wreath still on her arm, errand incomplete, feeling every bit an idiot.

'Put yourself on the *other* side of the door, dear!' Martha shouted through the closed door.

Tyler pulled it open for her. 'That's her version of an invitation. Jess, was it?' He shut the door behind her once she had walked in and put out a hand for her to shake. 'Tyler Butterfield.'

'Nice to meet you.'

'Same. Now!' He rubbed his hands together. 'What have we here?' He went to pick up one of the boxes.

'Mind yourself, young man, they're heavy.'

Tyler grunted as he picked one up. 'What on earth have you got in here?'

'Nothing that would interest you,' Martha snipped, her regal expression shadowing.

Tyler opened the box.

'Tyler!'

'Vinyl!' He cried over Martha's admonition, putting the box on the coffee table and kneeling in front of it. 'Martha Snodgrass, you sly old dog, you.'

'Don't you call me a dog, Tyler Butterfield. You know very well I'm a cat person through and through. Now close that box up and carry it out to the car, please.'

'Not if you're giving them away.' Tyler said without a hint of apology. 'I'll have them. Have you seen these?' He held up an album for Jess. 'John Coltrane. The Bird. Ella Fitzgerald. Hell's teeth, Martha. You had some good taste in music.'

'Language, Tyler. And I think you'll find I *have* good taste in music. I'm not dead yet.'

He grinned up at Jess. 'I'm banking on her outliving me.' He held up another album for Martha to see. 'Who's this? Marti Morgan?'

There was a beautiful woman on the cover. A beautiful woman wearing a thick, opulent fur coat walking out of a club called Ronnie Scott's. If Jess remembered correctly, it was London's premiere jazz venue right in the heart of Soho. A rush of adrenalin shot through her. The beautiful woman was wearing the same opulent fur coat Martha had been wearing last night.

'Is that you, Martha?' Jess asked.

The shadows fell again. Darker this time. Jess felt as though she was witnessing something very, very private. Her stomach churned with discomfort. Maybe staying out on the porch had been the better option.

'Put that away, Tyler,' Martha instructed. 'I want it in the tip.'

Her tone was so sharp that both he and Jess looked

away. Abruptly, Tyler jumped up and ran up the stairs. There was some shuffling around, a loud thump, a few curse words and then he thundered back down the stairs with a record deck under one arm and a portable speaker in his hand. He rustled round behind the sofa, plugged it all in, unsheathed the album, put it on the record deck and smiled at Martha.

'Let's have a listen.'

'No.'

'I'm overruling you.' He put the needle onto the record.

Martha lurched forward then back into the worn cushions of her armchair, her eyes closing in resignation. She pressed her fingers to her forehead, as if fighting a migraine, as the first pure notes of a female voice emerged from the whirring of the needle circling the vinyl.

'Martha,' Tyler sat back on his heels after they'd listened for several spellbound minutes. 'You're a fucking legend.'

'*Language*,' Martha cautioned, eyes still closed, but . . . if Jess wasn't mistaken . . . the tiniest hint of a smile?

An hour, a cup of tea and a much more relaxed atmosphere later, Jess waved goodbye to the pair, securing a promise to see them later that night for the advent event at number 12. 'Any idea what the two of you are doing?'

Martha shook her head. 'Not given it a moment's thought, dear. I was planning on playing the too-old-to-tango card and insisting Tyler do something.'

'Thanks for the heads up on that, *Marti*,' Tyler intoned with a *this should be a laugh* snort.

'You two should do a duet,' Jess suggested, pointing at the record, instantly wishing she'd kept her mouth shut when Martha shot her a cease-and-desist look.

'Not a word about this to anyone,' she warned.

Jess 'locked' her lips and threw away the key. 'Not a word. And you're sure you're happy for me to give this to Mr Winters?' She lifted up the wreath so that her face was in the middle of it.

'More than.' Martha said, her wrinkly fingers giving Jess's arm a conciliatory squeeze. 'And while you're there, do me a favour, will you?'

'Absolutely.'

'Tell him I'm tired of being the only old codger out there every night freezing myself to the bone.' Despite the stern expression, there was a twinkle in her eye.

On impulse Jess leant forward and gave her leathery cheek a kiss. This was what Christmas was about. Being nice to people even if they were extra grumpy. 'It would be my pleasure.'

Ten minutes later, Jess found herself nose to nose with Mr Winters growling, 'Well, a very, merry, Christmas to you too, Mr Scrooge.'

Mr Winters slammed his door in her face. Which was fair enough, given that she'd just lobbed quite the number of unseasonal insults in his direction.

Barely restraining herself from throwing Martha's lovely wreath at his door, Jess whirled about, stomped down the steps, slammed through the picket-fence gate, whirled around again, glared at the house, trying to plumb a lucid thought from the deafening roar of blood in her head, and finally came up with a question: What could she do to make the grumpiest man on the cul-de-sac even grumpier?

She came up with an answer.

And then she did it.

13 December

13 December
23:57
To: WillWinters@TheMerryVictualler.co.uk
From: JessGreen2000@gmail.com
Subject: Update from Christmas Street

Dear Will,

I hope your life isn't too overrun by vol-au-vents and mini-turkey-drumsticks (is that a thing or is it all Henry VIII-style sizes???) I'm guessing I haven't heard from you because you're insanely busy. The penultimate weekend before Christmas must be mad.

Just a little update for you. We had a wreath-making day outside your grandfather's a couple of nights back that ended up in a bit of a holiday sing-song which, I'm sorry to report, upset your grandfather (the volume must've been messing with his quiet evening in). Anyway, I saw him yesterday after one of the street's other residents, Martha Snodgrass (who turns out to have a secret past as a jazz singer!!!), kindly gifted the wreath she made. It's now hung on his outside gate. Have you seen the house? It has a genuine picket fence. I love a picket fence. And with Martha's wreath on it, it gives the house a little splash

189

of festive cheer. As do... erm... the other twelve or so wreaths flanking it.

The truth is, he and I had a teensy tiny run-in over the wreath (well, Christmas in general). After a rather lively exchange, he may have slammed the door in my face. I didn't take this very well and might have accidentally-on-purpose asked all of my neighbours who were awake at ten last night to let me hang their wreaths on his fence in protest. He's a bit Christmas resistant, but, in fairness, so am I, so not judging!! Much.

In fact, it's my turn to do the advent calendar tomorrow (twenty-four hours and counting). I have zero idea what to do. Sunday night's was good. Pin the nose on Rudolph with mulled wine (you drank wine then pinned the nose unless, of course, you were a kid, in which case it was red cordial). Tonight's was weird. Maybe it's because they're number 13, I don't know, but... When we arrived we were all handed something. A broom, a dusting cloth, the hoover. And elves' hats. Then we were all set to work to make up 'Santa's Magic Wonderland'. And by Santa's Magic Wonderland, what my neighbours actually meant was: clean their house and set it up for Christmas with them supervising. (Note to self: never accept a dinner invitation to number 13. Could end up making it myself!)

Do you even know what I'm talking about? I'd never heard of a living advent calendar before I moved here. Basically, it involves turning our street, which has twenty-four houses, into a living advent calendar. First night snowball fights, second kazoo carolling etc., etc. My idea of a total nightmare as I'd vowed not to do Christmas this year. Yes, I could hide in my house like your grandfather does, but, I will reluctantly admit, some of the nights have

been fun and as a newbie on the street who is becoming
a bit close to morphing into a hermit, decorating sugar
cookies and making wreaths is as good a way as any to get
to know thy neighbour. Did I mention I have NO idea what
to do? None. Nada. Nul. This head is bereft of any creativity.

Sorry. You're getting a bit of a stream of consciousness
here. (My neighbour/new friend/enabler Drea had a hip flask
of rum she was freely sharing and I'm doing that whole
'write drunk, edit sober' thing that I'm not sure is genuine
advice.)

Oh, who am I kidding? I'm totally in a bad mood. I
was happy on Sunday (reference: discovery of elderly
neighbour's secret past as jazz singer) and then, when I
went to see your grandad (can I call him grandad? Pops?
No. He's not a pops) he was all gruff-response this and
take-your-business-elsewhere-young-lady that and I was
trying so hard to be cheerful and not tell him I know all
about you (well, a little bit about you). He kept rebuffing my
efforts to help him be cheery. Because we should all try
and be cheery, right? 'Tis the season and all that. And then
when he slammed the door in my face. It flipped me back
to a place that, I'll be honest, I revisit a bit too frequently.

Shall I tell you about it? (#SpoilerAlert: you may
want to cut and run at this point). I'll tell you about it.
(#LastAndFinalWarning) One year, three weeks and about...
six hours ago??? my whole life changed because of a
cheese sandwich. (Brie and cranberry, if you must know).
At this point, you may be asking yourself, how could a
cheese sandwich strip someone of their creativity, compel
them to move and make them scream at an old man that
he wouldn't know Christmas cheer if it bit him on the nose?
(Apologies. I was filtering earlier.)

Well, lemme tell ya. (Get a snack. You'll need it).

Thirteen months ago (there it is again! Unlucky thirteen) I was an art teacher at a fancy-schmancy prep school in London. St Benedict's. I absolutely loved it. We had all the resources a teacher (and a child) could ever dream of. Beautiful grounds. Amazing buildings. Unbelievable perks if the parents liked you. If you haven't heard of it, think... Eton for the offspring of rock stars/oligarchs/make-up empresses. You get the idea. Anyone whose children require security teams or unironically ask after the seasonal smoothie bar for elevenses.

So. One seemingly regular day I was on dining-hall duty. (Yes, we were normal enough to do that.) We all took turns. You wander around making sure the children are being charming to one another. Lifting their pinkies aloft when sipping their tea. (Kidding. That last part was a total lie). It was my turn. One minute I was wandering round, happy as a lark, the next minute? Slow-motion horror show. Crispy Banana-Hate (name changed for child-protection laws), aged thirteen and the only offspring of our richest parents, had been merrily eating his lunch, or so I thought, when all of the sudden he was up and out of his seat and on the brink of hurling his focaccia, brie and cranberry sandwich (I know... I know) at a fourth-year student called Ethan. Ethan is small and nerdy. Nose always in a book. If his parents weren't loaded, his glasses would regularly have tape on them because he was always tripping over something or getting accidentally-on-purpose knocked around by the older kids. He's not the type of kid to stand up for himself, or the type to garner friends to do it for him. He's a little sweetie if you take the time to get to know him. And smart. And totally allergic to dairy. The type of allergic that means he will literally die if it touches him. Like the peanut people.

So I did what I thought anyone would do. I grabbed Crispy's shoulders and whirled him round so that he wouldn't hit Ethan with the brie. This is where it all gets a bit fuzzy/dark/totally why I warned you to stop reading. Crispy punched me in the stomach. So hard I lost my balance. I fought to regain my footing, but in so doing, inadvertently brushed Crispy's face with one of my hands. He told the Head Teacher I assaulted him. I didn't, of course, but as I was being escorted from the school premises later that afternoon he was standing in a window and I saw scratch marks. He must've done it to himself. It's the only way I can imagine he got them. (This is all totally difficult and unbelievably humiliating to admit, which is probably why I'm telling you, a person I've never met and probably never will meet, but you do good email and send lovely Christmas cards so thank you very much, I hope you don't regret it now. If you're even still reading. Hello?) Anyway. Surprise, surprise. I was suspended. Investigations were launched. Reports were filed. Ethan, god bless him and his little argyle cotton socks transferred to a smaller, more 'diet-sensitive' school (read: epi-pens on tap). His parents had said I'd done the right thing; but they were taking their school fees elsewhere, so who was going to listen to them, right? I was then informed I had a choice. To be sued by the Banana-Hates or quietly leave the school with a neutral reference.

Shit. Just realised I used Ethan's real name. Please wipe it from your mind. And in-box. My bad.

My boyfriend at the time (who dumped me shortly afterwards), saw the bruises but refused to believe a kid could've done it. Well. Let me assure you, this particular thirteen-year-old is a black belt in discreet, nasty, injuries. Just like Nicole Kidman's husband was in that mini-series Reese Witherspoon made. Did you see it? Probably not. Anyway, by the time they let me back in the school, the bruises had faded and I hadn't taken any pictures so there was no evidence and everyone was looking at me like I was evil and I couldn't bear it because I love teaching those little fuckers. I mean darlings. Most of them are darlings. They're all kids, you know? Products of the world around them. Crispy? Devil's spawn. But – long story short – this is me trying to pull myself back together after quite the breakdown. I start teaching again at a small primary academy in January. I'm scared shitless. I've also found out I'm replacing the most deeply loved teacher in the world. Universe. Bigger. Whatever galaxies black holes lead to. Ones with even better teachers? Point being, I don't want to let the children down, but I'm finding it hard to trust myself any more. I mean, who offers a charming older gentleman a wreath only to turn into a psycho when he says no? Do normal people ask the rest of the neighbourhood to hang their Christmas wreaths on sad lonely old men's (lovely) picket fences just because they're not down with the Yule? No. I've gone mental. I'm sorry. I should apologise to your grandfather, but . . . it's insanely late. He's probably in bed and waking him up to offer him an apology for something he might not even know I've done is immensely stupid. Gah!!! I have no clue what I'm going to do tomorrow when the neighbourhood turns up expecting holiday cheer. Maybe they won't. Maybe they're all calling each other wondering whether or not I'm an axe murderer. Say the word and I'll take them down.

Best, Jess(ica) Green

14 December

The trouble with pressing send on an email was, once you'd done it? It was impossible to retrieve. It was also impossible to go to sleep afterwards. Jess had actively considered sneaking out in the middle of the night to take all of the wreaths down but each time she psyched herself up she'd heard a car, or caught a light flicking on in a window, or had fallen into a listless half-sleep only to dream of being chased by a zombie Santa. Waking up wasn't much better.

Pouring her entire life story out to a stranger who was the grandson of the grumpy old man whose house she'd just Christmas punk'd definitely fell into the realms of Very Bad Ideas.

Jess grappled about on the floor for her phone: 5 a.m. Better than three, when she'd last looked. She rolled off her mattress (bed frame still unmade) and into a cross-legged position by the window. What had she been thinking? Spilling her guts to Will like that?

She could blame the rum, but it really was time to start owning her behaviour. It was a lecture she'd delivered to Amanda more than once when her friend had mooched into work with another tale of 'accidentally having one too many' and snogging someone she'd now have to shake off because, of course, she'd stupidly given him all of her social-media links. Amanda was over-friendly like that. She also always blamed the booze. Jess knew doing the same would be falling into the same dangerous trap she'd been cornered in by Crispin. Last night had been the shameful denouement of yet more 'it's you not me' behaviour that she decried in others. It was time to wrap up all of this 'woe is me, it wasn't my fault' attitude she'd been wearing like a unicorn onesie that absolved her from any wrong-doing. She hadn't hit Crispin. Not even close. But had she fought her corner? No. Not even close. She feebly shook her fist in the air then watched as it flopped back down onto her flannel pyjamas. The ones with the holly berries on them. She'd dug them out of a box last night to see if they'd give her any inspiration about what she could do today when the entire neighbourhood showed up expecting to be dazzled with holiday cheer. Or – the chilling thought that had kept her up half the night dropped a few more degrees – not only would they not show up, they'd send a representative who would hand over a petition signed by everyone demanding that she move. Move and hand in her notice at the academy before she'd even started. Mrs Jameson never would've done a thing like that, they'd say. Torture an old man with symbols of peace and joy. Speaking of which . . . she tiptoed over to her window and stuck her head out, squinting through the grainy light of the street lamps. Yup. They were still there. In fact, she could be wrong, but there appeared to be a few more. He must not have gone out yesterday. That, or he thought leaving them up was the easiest way to get Jess 'and her ilk', as he'd referred to the rest of the neighbours, to leave him alone.

Right. She owed Mr Winters an apology. The type of

epic apology that would also convince him to take part in the advent calendar so that Drea didn't kill her when/ if her son arrived for his much-anticipated visit. Mrs Jameson could have done it. Not that she would've hung an excess of wreaths on his fence in the first place, but... her teaching baton had been handed to Jess and she was going to run with it. In a bit.

She would have coffee, wait for the sun to rise, then go over, offer him her deepest apologies for being a bully, collect each of the wreaths and give them back to their rightful owners, explaining to everyone how she had been wrong to get everyone to help her gang up on him. No way was she going to start the school term being the mad teacher who did the Christmas version of egging the neighbourhood Grinch's front door. She'd made a call and had got it wrong. Very wrong. And she was the only one who could put it right. By throwing herself at Mr Winters' mercy, theoretically, he'd forgive her and come up with an amazing plan to be part of the Christmas Street festivities, and all would be right in the world again. But first... coffee. And, as she was trying to be brave, a look at her emails.

14 December
03:37
To: JessGreen2000@gmail.com
From: WillWinters@TheMerryVictualler.co.uk
Subject: RE: Update from Christmas Street

Dear Jess –
By all means, leave them up! Sounds like he could do with the Christmas cheer. If he takes them down then, at

the very least, you will know you were right and he'll have got some exercise which, at his age, is probably never a bad thing. They're easy access and not too heavy, right? Nothing made out of antlers, I presume? (Antler wreaths are strangely popular on the Orkneys).

Sorry for such a short note. As you rightly guessed, it's completely mental right now. That school where you were sounds like a higher level of funky, and by funky I mean... not the soul-brother kind. You're well shot of them. So-called 'ordinary' people are brilliant and, in my estimation, not ordinary at all. Will send longer email once I manage to uncurl my fingers. Note to self: Never agree to wrap 500 angels on horseback (figs with prosciutto) for an osteopathy/chiropractor's regional holiday party. (And no, the irony is not lost on me.)

Regards xW

Coffee consumed, winter coat on, Jess did a couple of star jumps before opening the door to leave – only to find herself face to face with Drea. A distinctly unhappy-looking Drea.

'Hi?'

'I was feeling extra Christmassy when I woke up this morning.'

'Oh?' Umm... Drea looked like Drea... but didn't sound like Drea. 'That's good. Weren't you away?'

'Yes,' Drea said in a polite tone intimating Jess was a simpleton. 'I was at a fitness conference. A conference devoted to nourishing good health. Or, put more season-ally, bringing those around us tidings of comfort and joy.' There was an unsettling pressure on the last word, as if that Christmas joy she had just topped up had now dissipated.

'When did you get back?' Jess asked, wondering if Drea's cars was one of the ones that had stopped her from running down the street and taking down all of the wreaths at 3AM.

'Late last night,' Drea said, still speaking in that weird possessed-by-an-over-polite-demon voice. 'I slept well, woke up happy. Took a shower using some lovely seasonal gel. I put my hair up with a red scrunchy, I even considered putting on a ridiculous Christmas jumper in advance of my new friend Jessica's advent-calendar evening.'

'Oh? That should be ... erm ...' Jess wasn't quite sure what it should be as Drea continued.

'I put on my lovely winter coat, came out of my front door and thought what a lovely street I live on. A street where everyone cares and shares with one another.'

Uh-oh. The knots in Jess's stomach tightened.

'A place where we all gather together to make wreaths, not for ourselves, but for one another.'

Yup. This was definitely heading where she'd hoped it wouldn't.

'So I was about to get in my car to run a few errands, my heart filled with nothing but holiday cheer when what to my wondering eyes should appear?'

Jess was relatively sure it wasn't a sleigh. Or eight tiny reindeer.

'I— Drea, I was just on my way to fix—'

Drea cut her off, now openly blazing with anger. 'I don't want to hear it. What I *do* want to know,' she said making decisive little nicks in the space between them with her fingernails, 'is if you remember that this whole advent-calendar thing was meant to be *fun*. Right? Fun. It was meant to bring us together as a *community*, not as a mob. We want people to be happy to live here. Not ringing up their estate agents asking after safer neighbour-hoods.'

'I know... I... Did he call the police?' She scanned the street.

Clearly unconcerned if Jess was arrested, Drea folded her arms across her chest and asked, 'Do you know what advent means?'

A horror gripped Jess by the throat as her mind went blank. She should. She didn't. She couldn't under Drea's displeased glare.

'It means, doll face, glorious and joyful anticipation of the arrival of the chosen son. Which, for me, this year, means *my* son.' She made an ah-ah noise as Jess tried to apologise. 'Did you know there are four symbols for advent?'

Jess shook her head. No, she didn't.

Drea held up a solitary finger, then three more as she pelleted Jess with the answers to the rhetorical question, 'Peace. Love. Joy. Hope. *Hope*, Jessica Green. I was hoping you were going to be a lovely addition to this neighbour-hood. Not someone intent on sabotaging my efforts to make this a kind and desirable place to live. A place my son might want to visit his mother. A place he would then return to. Not somewhere *Daily Mail* reporters stalk to highlight Christmas ASBOs in action.'

Again Jess tried to apologise, her stomach a mess of fear that paparazzi were hiding in her hedge recording every word of this one-sided exchange. Her eyes snagged on her For Sale sign. That Sold sticker would be coming off soon, then.

'Drea, I honestly didn't—'

Drea held up her hand, her body already half turning towards the street. 'I've got work today, doll face, but let it be known, I am disappointed in you. By the time we gather here tonight? I want you to have fixed it.'

Jess tried to swallow and couldn't. Disappointment was a thousand times worse than fury. Any child with a conscience knew that. On top of which, Drea was right. Her response to Mr Winters' refusal of the wreath was over the top. She'd have to fix this. No matter what.

As Drea stalked off down the street, Jess resolved to give her the best Christmas ever. Even if it killed her.

As Drea roared away in her throaty sports car, Jess pulled up her proverbial socks. She owed someone an apology.

Mr Winters took his time answering the door. No doubt, the first painful phase of a lengthy penance Jess would have to pay for being so horrid. But she'd pay it. If it meant planting tulip bulbs until the end of time, she'd do it.

When he opened the door, instead of immediately slamming it in her face as he should have, he took a step back as if preparing to invite her in.

Unexpected.

The eloquent apology she'd been rehearsing flew out of her head. In its place came a series of staccato blurts. 'Good morning. Hello. Chilly out. Umm . . . quick question. Have you seen your front fence?'

He nodded sombrely. 'I have.'

In a rush she promised to take all of the wreaths down, especially the one with battery-operated stormtroopers, because it didn't represent what a wreath should represent, which was life. Eternal life. Did he know that? She hadn't until just now when she'd looked it up. Kind of like the symbols of advent. Did he know those? She rattled them off – peacelovehopejoy – then began a painfully detailed apology. She didn't know what had come over her, she'd had a very bad year, it had made her do strange things and this was the worst thing of all because she thought he was lovely, *really* lovely, and that she had, in her own backwards incredibly stupid way, been trying to inject a bit of holiday cheer into his life because to her he seemed sad not angry as a lot of people thought and she couldn't bear it that he was sad because she knew how powerfully debilitating being sad could be.

At this point he held up a hand. Possibly because she had started poking herself on the chest with her index finger with such force it had given her the hiccoughs, all of which made the apology sound even weirder.

'Leave them, lass.'

'What? Absolutely not. I'll take them down.'

'Honestly. Leave them as they are.' He gave a wry little chuckle. 'It reminds me of something my Anne would've done.'

Jess quirked her head to the side. 'Anne?'

'My wife,' he said. 'My late wife,' he added much more soberly and then as if that were the gateway towards a new phase in their relationship, he opened up one of his broad hands and ushered her in, 'Come in, lass, out of the cold.'

A few minutes later Jess was ensconced in a lovely, if slightly worn, armchair across from a crackling fire and being handed a perfectly brewed cup of tea, with another apology that he had no hot chocolate in the house. Once he'd put his own cup on a side table, Mr Winters sat down heavily in his armchair and gave his knees a rub. Mr Perkins was sitting on a nearby faded pouffe keeping his steely gaze on Jess as if to say, *I see you. Make no false moves.*

'I think I owe you an explanation,' Mr Winters said after taking a sip of his tea.

Jess began to protest, but Mr Winters spoke over her.

'You're right. I am sad. The type of sad you can't erase no matter how many wreaths are hung upon your gate.'

Jess swallowed.

As if he'd made a deal with himself that he had to explain, he continued in a mechanical tone, 'Thirty-five years ago, my Anne had a bit of a headache. A cold, actually. Or so she thought. It was enough for her to want to lie down anyway.'

Jess took a sip of tea, not even flinching as the hot liquid scalded the back of her throat.

'It was about two o'clock in the afternoon and our son, Robert, rang all the way from Edinburgh where he was at university. Caught her just before she'd gone upstairs.' His index finger traced the journey his wife would've taken from the foot of the stairs to an old avocado-coloured rotary dial telephone on a table just inside the sitting room where they were sat.

When he spoke again, he sounded as if he was reading a timeline he'd been over and over and still had yet to make sense of.

'He had a word with his mum and was concerned enough about her cold – she was never ill, you see – to ask her to put me on the line. He thought I should bring her to the GP's. Anne was against it. Said she was needed a short rest was all. Robert disagreed. I disagreed with Robert; I said his mother knew best and I would respect her wishes.'

He stopped, took a sip of tea, and looked at the cat, who promptly came over and sat by his foot as if he knew Mr Winters needed some solidarity, but not so much that it would make his emotions spill up and over into the room.

'When I went to check on her an hour or so later, she was very still. Too still.' He frowned at his tea. 'She'd died. Right there in her sleep. A diabetic coma, said the coroner.' He looked up at Jess, his blue eyes filled with disbelief. 'She'd never had a diagnosis like that. Diabetes. She'd never even liked sweets.'

Jess felt as though her heart was cracking in two. Of all of the scenarios she'd tried to imagine that would have caused a thirty-five-year rift between father and son, this was not one of them.

She put her cup down on a doily, her hands shaking. Poor Mr Winters. Poor Mrs Winters. And Robert. And Will. How awful for all of them.

'Robert's not spoken to me since. Well. Not since the funeral. And I've not found a way to shake the feeling that he'd been right all along. I should've taken her to the GP as he advised. It was all my fault. She'd be right here if I'd listened to my son.'

Jess shook her head, no, it wasn't his fault, surely he had to know that; but before she could find the best way to say the words he clearly needed to hear he gave his head a few of those nod/shake things that meant they were done now. 'Anyway, Anne would've done something similar to what you did if I'd been gruff with her about something meant to be nice. Hung up wreaths or planted tulip bulbs upside down, so . . . you leave them right where they are, Jessica.' His eyes caught hers again to stem any more apologies. 'I may be sad, but this has made me think perhaps it's time to find a way to live with it. Not let it define me quite so much as I have done.'

She could relate to that. The Cheese Sandwich Incident would never go away, but she had to find a way not to let it shadow the rest of her life.

As if sensing yet another change in mood, Mr Perkins deftly jumped up and onto Mr Winters' lap and curled up in a tight, protective ball. Absently, Mr Winters began to stroke him, his thoughts clearly drifting back to a time and place Jess could never access.

She thanked him for the tea and put on her coat because it was pretty clear he'd maxed out his sharing time.

Her heart ached for him. She said goodbye, assuring him, once again, that she wouldn't touch the wreaths, nor would she let anyone else. Between his house and her own, Jess's resolve grew. She would make Mr Winters' and Drea's – screw it – the whole of Christmas Street's Christmas the very best Christmas ever. And not just to one up Mrs Jameson. It was to mark a change. Prove she could learn from and live with the mistakes she'd made.

'Smells nice,' Drea said accusingly when Jess opened the door to her brisk rat-a-tat-tat knock.

'Thanks?'

'They're still there,' Drea glowered.

Jess bowed her head. 'I know. I did go down there.'

Drea arched a perfectly shaped eyebrow. 'And...?'

'I apologised. I said I'd take them down and he said not to.'

Drea's brow furrowed. 'He did?'

Jess nodded. It wasn't her story to share so she said what Mr Winters had instructed her to tell everyone. 'He says thank you for the wreaths, it was a kind gesture.'

'Seriously?' Drea looked shocked, then suspicious. 'What else did he say?'

'Not much.' Jess put on her best poker face. 'Aren't you going to ask what we're doing tonight?'

It was six-thirty. Half an hour earlier than the time she'd put out on the WhatsApp 'Christmas Street Advent Calendar' chat Drea had created a week or so back when people kept randomly turning up wondering when things would kick off. Not that Jess ever looked at it. She had largely relied on Drea and the good old-fashioned technique of looking out her window to figure out when kick-off time began.

Drea made a noise. She was still clearly trying to work out what had gone down at Mr Winters'. 'Go on then,' she finally said. 'Show us what you've got planned.' Jess stood to the side and held out her hand game-show hostess style, anxiously awaiting Drea's reaction.

'It's a Christmas tree,' she finally explained.

'I can see that,' Drea said dryly, her eyes inching round the Christmas tree Jess had painted onto the big white expanse of wall between her living room and kitchen.

Jess was actually quite proud of it. She'd been pressed for time so hadn't done all of the detailing she would've liked, but the lush boughs had the odd squirrel painted in. A few pine cones. A robin. She jogged over to the sofa where she'd put the stencils. 'So, the idea is that everyone paints an ornament to represent their house. I've got number stencils here...' She held them up. They'd been part of this week's office supplies and had given her the idea in the first place. 'Emoji stencils, flower stencils, some Christmas-themed ones... and they paint it on. I counted the boughs and everything. Enough for everyone.'

Drea made a scrunchy face then gave a fatigued sigh. 'Well, at least you didn't go all out on dazzling folk, all things considered.'

Now it was Jess's turn to have a scrunchy face. 'What do you mean "all things considered"?'

The truth was, she had gone all out. For her anyway. She'd borrowed Kai and Rex's jam pan so that she could make several litres of steaming hot chocolate. She'd used her mum's old stock pot to make as many litres again of *glühwein*, both of which were burbling away on the stovetop waiting to be ladled into the lovely recyclable cups she'd bought at considerably more expense that she had spare right now. She'd also gone to the local bakery and bought piles of thumbprint cookies, gorgeously moreish biscuits with a dollop of red jam or minty green frosting in the centre.

Drea fished into her pocket, pulled out her phone and held it in front of Jess. 'Haven't you read the thread?

'What thread?'

'The Christmas Street thread,' Drea said impatiently, thumbing through a few messages then holding the phone out to Jess.

Ah. It was the night of the school play. *Peter Pan*, apparently. One of the Gem'n'Emms' sons had the lead role and as such ... there was apology after apology after apology.

An unexpected wash of relief eased the tension she hadn't realised she'd been holding in her shoulders. Although, it did mean her plan to fill Drea with Christmas cheer was going to fail. She chewed on her lip wondering if she could hire in a few people to liven the place up.

'Sorry, doll face.' Drea gave her arm a squeeze, misreading her disappointed expression. 'Sorry for-being a bitch earlier. I've just got a lot riding on this advent lark, you know?'

'No,' Jess insisted. 'It's me who should be apologising to you.'

Drea pushed out her lips as if she were thinking on it. 'Go on then.'

'What? Apologise?'

'Yeah.' She looked happier now, so Jess fell over herself in the same halting way she had to Arnold until Drea started cackling and gave Jess's cheek a pinch and a pat, both of which kind of hurt. 'That's good. Consider yourself forgiven. For now.' She threw a look over her shoulder towards the empty street. 'A few people might show up. Is your new bestie coming?'

'Who?'

'Arnold Winters.'

'Oh! Yes. No. I mean ... he said he might.'

'Seriously?' Drea looked genuinely gobsmacked. 'I was kidding.'

'So was I when I invited him to come along, I mean – he is obviously welcome, but what with his attendance track record and everything ...' She waved her hands between them. 'Anyway, he said he might come.'

'Did he say it in the way most British people say it?'

Jess gave her a sidelong look. 'What way is that?'

'All sincere and yeah, yeah, absolutely, and then not show up?'

Jess shook off her initial defensive response and thought about it. It was, after all, a go-to response in London. No. No, he had seemed genuine enough. 'I think he might?'

Drea narrowed her eyes as a spy might at the apex of an interrogation to find out exactly where the stolen thermonuclear missiles that could destroy the world were hidden. 'What exactly happened between you two?'

Jess's tummy went all squirmy. It really wasn't her place to tell. 'I apologised and before I could get through it all he said not to worry about it.'

'Hellooooooo!' Rex's voice rang out from Jess's gate. 'We're ready to be dazzled!' Kai bounced in alongside him and started doling out cheek kisses under a fresh sprig of mistletoe.

And then, before Jess knew it, her evening was under way.

About a dozen people came in the end, which, considering the size of her house, Kev's capacity for *glühwein* and the fact she'd painted the tree in her not exactly enormous corridor, was probably a good thing. Despite an underlying fear she was being ghosted by all of her future pupil's parents for being vile to poor Mr Winters, everyone seemed to genuinely believe they were at the school play, which, judging by the amount of minivans pulling back into the cul-de-sac around the time people were leaving . . . it did appear to be the case. And, despite the non-appearance of Mr Winters, the night had been fun. The tree looked great.

Kai and Rex's decoration was their house number with climber roses twined round it. Drea used a surfer stencil with the surfer holding a huge number one. Kev, surprise surprise, had drawn a racing car with his house number on the door. Martha had come along, no Tyler ('band practice or some such'). She'd painted a Victrola and had grown a bit rosy-cheeked after accepting a cup of *glühwein* from Kev as he called out last orders. The couple at number 13 who had had them clean up their house had done a bicycle. Apparently they were triathletes and that was why they never got any housework done. ('Too much training, love. Too much training.') The handful of other neighbours had painted a dog, a golden pear, a rocking horse; and Katie, the lovely nurse from across the way, had rushed in, spray-painted in a stencil of some ice skates, and had grown a bit misty as she told them how she'd been a figure skater as a girl, but an injury early on had forced her to explore 'other options'. Jess had insisted she take two cups of takeaway hot chocolate before she rushed off to start an overnight shift. She seemed really nice and really tired. Jess hoped they'd be friends one day. No Josh, but it wasn't as if adding a new crush to her list of things to do would help her clutter-clear her problem shelf. Speaking of which, she stuck her head out the door and looked down the street again. Nope. No Mr Winters.

She lifted her hand to her mouth and then forced herself to lower it. Over the course of the evening, she'd reduced her newly grown nails to nubs again in her effort to refrain from running down the street and offering him an arm to lean on for the short walk down to hers. Drea, to her credit, didn't say anything, but after everyone had left and Drea had helped her sweep up the kitchen and tidy away all of the paint and stencils, she had stepped outside Jess's house, made a pointed look down towards Mr Winters' then said, 'It's an English thing.'

'*I'm* English,' Jess reminded her.

Drea laughed. 'Yeah, but . . . you know what, doll? I'm glad you and he made peace. Hopefully it means the old bugger'll pull something out of the bag in ten days' time.'

'Ten days?' Jess's stomach lurched. 'Is it that soon?'

'Yup!' Drea tapped her watch. 'And counting.' Her voice was weighted with a host of unspoken expectation. In ten days' time her son would or wouldn't have taken up her offer. In ten days' time, Mr Winters would or wouldn't delight the neighbourhood as a month's worth of advent evenings drew to an apex. In ten days' time, the tone of Christmas proper would be set, for better or for worse.

Half an hour later, tucked up in bed with her laptop, Jess's finger hovered above the send key. To email or not to email. That was the question.

Don't ask, don't get, she decided and jabbed the button, almost seeing the short, heartfelt missive wing its way to Melbourne where it would, with any luck, be instantly opened by Drea's son. There was only one Spencer Zamboni in the whole of Australia according to Google. The whole of the world, actually. And Jess was going to do her damnedest to make sure he was right here on Christmas Street in ten days' time.

15 December

'Oh, you're there! How wonderful!'

Jess's mum clinked her coconut cup to her father's then towards the laptop camera, her cheeks already a tell-tale pink. Looked like someone was enjoying her sundowners.

'We thought we'd take the risk and see if you were home,' her father said after a gulp of his own drink.

'Yay!' Jess cheered half-heartedly. She waved her hands around pompom-style then lifted up her over-sized coffee mug to air clink with her parents' cocktails. This while tugging her hoodie over her shoulders to make it look as though she was actually dressed for the day rather than still wearing her jim-jams as the non-existent sun hit the yardarm. 'How's it going in the tropics?'

'Oh, Jessica. I had *such* an interesting compacted molar today,' her mother began. Jess half listened, took a bite of white toast off-camera (white food was forbidden in her parents' home ... cavity monsters), then doodled a snowman with rabbit ears, only to realise when she looked up again that they were looking at her expectantly.

'Oh, dear,' her mum put down her coconut cup, worry creasing her forehead. 'You're not regretting things, are you, Jess? Being on your own over the holidays?'

She swotted her husband's arm. 'Harry! I told you we should've stayed. Look at her. She's gaunt with sorrow.'

'Mum,' Jess tried to interrupt. 'I'm not—'

'Absolutely dreadful,' her mother persisted, her nose looming as she leant in to examine Jess on their laptop screen. 'Are you taking your vitamins? You could need some D supplements.'

Jess pulled a face. No she didn't. She'd not strictly showered or done anything to her face yet, but 'gaunt with sorrow'? Frustration, more like. She'd been working herself up to head back to Mr Winters'. Though they'd spoken quite a lot yesterday, she felt their talk needed a follow-up if she was going to convince him to do something special on Christmas Eve.

'She does look a bit peaky.' Her father was saying as he, too, leant towards the camera, the lens fish-bowling his face.

'Jess…' her father put on his gentle voice. The one he used when he thought she was snarling at him because she was suffering from *women's troubles*, 'Would you like to come out and join us? It's not too late, you know. The flights only go on a Tuesday and a Friday and it'll probably cost double, but the offer still stands.'

'I'll bet they'd love some assistance down at the local school.' Her mother butted in. 'Plus there are some *wonderful* young people out here. Quite a few single men, in fact. Why, just the other day I did a periodontal—'

Jess began waving her hands. 'Nope! No, thank you. Please do not finish that sentence. I do not want you to be my overseas Match.com, thank you very much.'

'Jess, love. We're trying to help—'

'Setting me up with a man who lives in the Marshall

213

Islands and is suffering from periodontal disease is not helping.'

'Well, it looks like someone woke up on the wrong side of the bed,' her mum sniffed.

'I'm fine. Honestly, I just...' She was trying to get her life back on track and it turned out moving somewhere wasn't quite the escape from all of her dark thoughts that she'd hoped it would be. Turns out they'd come with her. As Mr Winters' had suggested, it was figuring out who was in charge that was the challenge. The problems or the problem solver.

'Coooeeee!' The mail flap clanked open. 'Jess?'

'Sorry, guys. I've got to go.' Jess blew them a kiss and promised to call them again soon.

'Drea.' She pulled open the door with a slightly exasperated smile. 'What can I do for you?'

'Crikey.' Drea pretended to shield herself from a horrific sight. 'Who dragged you through a hedge this morning?'

Jess did not dignify this with an answer.

'Are you going to offer me a cup of coffee?' Drea asked.

Jess wheeled round and headed back to the kitchen to fill up the kettle. Everyone was bossy today. *Date this person. Take those vitamins. Comb your hair.*

'I'll take that as a yes,' Drea shouted after her, before letting herself in and taking up her usual post at the breakfast bar. After the kettle had boiled and Jess had spooned some coffee into the cafetière, Drea asked, 'What's got into you?'

'Nothing.'

'Liar.'

'So?'

'I've got problems of my own.'

'So?' Jess repeated, a bit less combatively than the first time.

'You're supposed to help me.'

She slammed the press down on the cafetière, splashing herself with hot coffee in the process. 'Bums! Ouch. Why am I the one who's supposed to help?'

Drea's quarrelsome expression faltered. 'Because you're my friend.'

Guilt, gratitude and about nine hundred other feelings flooded Jess's heart. Drea considered them friends. She grabbed a J-cloth from the sink and began wiping. Now that she properly thought about it, Drea had single-handedly made moving to Christmas Street about a billion times more welcoming than it could've been. Without Drea, there was a very distinct possibility Jess would've sat in her little house describing non-essential office supplies without exchanging so much as a 'hello, how are you?' to a single neighbour.

She selected a mug that had a unicorn with hearts on it as a means of silent apology, filled it with coffee and handed it to her. 'Milk?'

'Just a splash.' Drea said, clearly still miffed as she patted her perfect derriere. 'Lactose calories always land here.'

'Interesting. Where do the chocolate cake calories land?'

'Nowhere,' Drea riposted with a smug smile. 'I don't eat chocolate cake, do I?'

'Oh, Little Miss Perfect, aren't you?' Jess teased.

Drea's smile dropped away.

'What? Did I say something wrong?'

'No.'

She clearly had.

'My son says that sometimes.' Drea said after a sip of coffee. '"We can't all be Little Miss Perfect like you,"' she mimicked.

'It's good to strive for things,' Jess said, trying to be supportive while silently panicking about the email she'd sent last night and had yet to have a response to. 'I don't know anyone else who could've pulled off the Christmas Street advent calendar apart from you.'

Drea scowled at her coffee. 'You know as well as I do that "pulling it off" mostly entails pushing people into a corner so that they have to do my bidding.'

'No. That's not true,' Jess protested. Well. Maybe it was a little, but once people had realised how fun it was, almost everyone had begun to look forward to it. She added. 'It's been a real success so far.'

Drea rolled her eyes and they both fell into a weighted silence.

Looks like they were both battling demons today. Seeing her parents – tanned, smiling, really enjoying the fruits of everything they'd worked for all their lives – had made her happy, but also . . . it made her feel like she was at the beginning of such a long road. As if the eight years at St Benny's had only been a dress rehearsal for her real life and now that she'd seen some of the pitfalls and danger zones, she was starting all over again. From scratch. Not entirely sure she wouldn't be doing the same again in another eight years.

Jess took a sip of her coffee then, after the silence had become too pronounced, asked, 'So . . . what's up?'

'I don't think Spencer's coming.'

A slew of colourful language exploded in her head. Was

this because of her email? She forced herself to squeak, 'What makes you say that?'

'Aww, nothing in particular, but when we had our Skype call today—'

'Wait. You Skype?'

Drea looked at her as if she were two sandwiches short of a picnic. 'Yeah. I speak to him every Tuesday.'

'I thought you said you didn't speak.'

'We do, but business only, so I don't count it. Mother–son moments over spreadsheets aren't filled with warm fuzzies.' When Jess sent her an *I don't understand* look, she explained, 'He handles all of the legal bumph for Bondi Beach Body. Profits, contracts, licenses. Everything that goes into his trust.'

The way Drea said it was so forlorn, so hungry for something more than a weekly exchange of facts and figures, that it made Jess's heart strain at the seams.

She scrambled for something to say. 'That's a nice thing to do. Making a trust for him.'

Drea flicked her hand in the air. 'He doesn't care about the money. Bloody bugger wants the trust to go towards something else.'

'Like what?'

Drea's gaze darkened, her manicured finger tracing round and round the top of her coffee mug, then looked up to meet Jess's eyes. 'He wants to start a domestic abuse safety and recovery house.'

Jess blinked a few times, the fleeting conversation they'd had about women's refuges leaping to the fore. 'And is there any reason you wouldn't want him to do this?'

Drea's eyes flared hot and bright. 'He wants to put my name on it.'

Oh. Well. That was complicated.

Jess took a sip of her coffee.

Drea huffed out an exasperated sigh. 'I will say this once, then we will never speak of it again. Clear?'

Jess nodded, her hands tightening round her mug.

'Spence's dad was gone before our relationship had the chance to develop into anything good, bad or otherwise. It was a while before I bagged another bloke, but something about my parent's insisting I'd never find a man as a single mum made me determined to prove them wrong. The next chap was ... shall we say ... more complicated. Or classic. Depends upon the angle. Wooed me, told me having a kid was no problem. Promised to take care of us, love us forever, yadda yadda yadda, and then boom! One day I did or said something wrong and—' She punched her fist out close enough to make Jess flinch. 'I got my act together. Left. Swore it would never happen again. Went back. And then it happened again. I left again. Found another bloke. And another. There wasn't always violence, but there was always something. Too tight, too loose, too controlling, too blasé. I was a dark-haired Goldilocks desperate to find my Mr Just Right. When I moved to the UK with Brett – the one from Nottingham – and he turned out to be a proper tosspot, I gave up. No more men.'

'So ... why didn't you move back to Melbourne?'

'Too late.'

'Too late for what?'

'Spence had already drawn his line in the sand. Told me I had chosen blokes over being a mum long before I boarded the plane and—' Her eyes brimmed with tears which she quickly shook away. 'Anyway. You know the rest.'

'Building the refuge with his trust fund sounds a lot like an olive branch to me,' Jess said.

'He wants to make an example of me.' Drea made a guttural sound at the back of her throat.

'It sounds like he's proud of you,' Jess said. 'For finding the strength to walk away.'

'It's my bloody business, isn't it?' Drea snarled. 'Why the hell would I want people to know my shame? It's humiliating. The last thing I ever, *ever* want to do, is advertise the fact that through all of my 'you have control of your own destiny' wank in my videos, the truth was, I was the weak one. I not only allowed a man to hit me, but I'd stayed after he'd done it.'

And there it was. Drea's secret.

As if a tap had been opened inside of her, Jess fully absorbed the fact that all of the loneliness she'd felt while enduring her own shameful secret had been, not for nothing, but . . . Well. She wasn't alone. Not in the slightest. Everyone had a secret. Broken dreams like Katie the nurse who'd hoped to win an Olympic medal one day only to have to realign her goals. Martha Snodgrass's past as a fur-coat-wearing jazz singer now tucked away out of sight. Drea's abuse. The wrongful accusation that changed Jess's life forever. Mr Winters' rage and unspoken anguish over his wife's senseless death. Everyone was carrying around something in their heart that could, if they let it, make them look as if they'd been dragged through a hedge. Drea had burpeed her way out of her pain. Mr Winters had closed the door on his. Jess? She wasn't quite sure what she was doing. Trying to move away from it?

Well, that turned out to be impossible. But what she

could do was own it, and make sure she was opening her heart to others as she did.

'Come here, woman,' Jess walked round to the other side of the breakfast bar and pulled her friend into a hug. Drea resisted at first and then, as if her life depended upon it, hugged Jess with a fierceness that was almost frightening.

After securing a promise to meet later that night in advance of the advent event at number 15, Drea left, Jess pulled on her bobble hat, then tugged on her coat and headed to Mr Winters'.

'Thanks for inviting me in. I didn't mean to take up much of your time.'

'It's all right, lass. It's nice to make a proper pot of tea every now and again.'

'It's really nice,' Jess took another sip of the aromatic liquid as proof that she meant it.

'Lapsang souchong,' said Mr Winters. 'It was Anne's favourite.'

'Wow!' Jess smiled, impressed. 'Your wife knew how to spot a trend.'

Mr Winters forehead crinkled. 'We first had it in China. Years back, of course.' He gave a soft laugh. 'Anne liked it so much she brought a kilo of it home with her. Couldn't find it anywhere in the UK back then. Not in these parts anyway. It was—' he did a little mental arithmetic '—1979.'

'You went to China in 1979?'

He nodded. 'We used to go all over. Brazil. Australia. Madagascar. Never took a business trip without her, up until the children arrived, and even then...' He drifted off, eyes dropping to his teacup as if it might hold the remains of his sentence.

'Did the children come, too?' Jess prompted.

He shook his head. 'No, Anne was with them most of the time, but her parents had come to stay so she could take the trip to China with me. It had been our anniversary, you see.' Again, his eyes dropped to his teacup.

'And what was it you did, exactly? That took you to all of these places?'

'Oh, I don't think you'll find it very glamorous,' he said with a wave of his hand.

'I teach children how to manhandle crayons,' she laughed. 'I'm sure whatever it is you did – or do – will sound glamorous.'

'Don't you make fun of yourself. Teachers are some of the most valuable members of society we have. Anne often spoke of training as a teacher.'

Jess smiled her thanks. Based on his age, she was guessing he and Anne were married back in the 1960s. When children came along, women had often stopped work, unlike in her own parents' 1980s marriage when 'having it all' was the goal. There could've been another reason of course, but she didn't want to pry too much. Either way, she liked how he was speaking about Anne so freely. It had to be difficult. Or, perhaps, a long-awaited joy. His son and he had fallen out thirty-five long years ago. Longer than Jess had been alive. She couldn't imagine not being able to talk about someone she loved as much as he clearly had loved Anne. Decades of silence because of guilt over something that ultimately he never could have known.

'I designed and sold vending machines,' Mr Winters said, giving the teapot a swirl then offering Jess a top-up.

Jessica laughed, delighted. 'Seriously? How cool is that?'

Mr Winters pulled a face. 'Cool? I don't know if I would've put it that way, although . . .' A soft smile teased away the frown lines. 'My boy Robert used to love it.'

'Oh?' Jess said, desperate to ask a million questions about Robert and whether or not Mr Winters was interested in extending an olive branch to him via Will or any other way. In fact, she would've loved to ask a million questions about his entire life, but, as she did with the children at school, she let her silence do the talking.

After the teacups had been refilled and the tea tasted and nodded over, Mr Winters said, 'Did you know there's a vending machine in China now designed specifically to sell live hairy crabs?'

She grinned. 'I didn't even know there were live hairy crabs to vend!'

'Oh, you'd be surprised at the things that end up for sale in a specially designed machine. Pizza, burritos, mashed potatoes, cars. All sorts. You need to think outside the box to put it *in* the box, as it were.'

The pride with which he made the statement made Jess smile. She imagined him saying it to his son and then, had he had the chance, his grandson. A scratchy tickling began at the back of her throat. Before it could gain purchase she cleared it and asked, 'What was your favourite place? To visit.'

'Scotland,' he replied without hesitation.

'Really? Wow. I would've thought with all of your travels you would've—'

'No,' he cut her off with a shake of the head, his eyes taking on a distant faraway look. 'We travelled so much throughout the year, Anne always liked to stay here in the UK when it came to taking Robert on holiday.'

'And is that why he lives there now, do you think?'

Jess clapped her hand to her mouth. She hadn't meant to say anything about him at all let alone the fact she knew he lived in Scotland.

Mr Winters eyed her silently for a moment then said, 'Will mentioned he'd been in touch to thank you for forwarding on the letter to me. In his card.' He nodded towards the window ledge where, sure enough, there was a card with a Highland cow draped in Christmas lights.

'He did?' she squeaked.

'Aye, he did.'

'And . . . have you been in touch with him at all? Will?'

Arnold shook his head in the negative. Jess's heart sank. That was a shame. If his emails were anything to go by, Will seemed a really positive, amazing young man. A grandson anyone could be proud of. 'Were you planning on it? Getting in touch?' Already she could picture Will rustling round this big old country-style kitchen, putting together an elaborate, but not highfalutin, Christmas meal for the two of them.

'I don't think so,' Mr Winters said.

'Why not?'

'Would you?' Mr Winters asked, that familiar edge of rancour cutting his words more crisply as he delivered them. 'If you were in my shoes?'

Jess chewed on the inside of her cheek. It was a fair question. She hadn't rung Amanda yet. Not because she was scared of her friend, it was more . . . she was scared of facing the past she used to have. She'd been so swept up in the culture of being a St Benny's teacher, there was a part of her that wondered if she'd deserved it. Not the punch, obviously, because no one deserves to be punched in the stomach, but... maybe she'd lost sight of what really mattered.

The thought scraped uncomfortably across her conscience. Ethan had mattered. His life had mattered. Still did. Which made her blurt, 'It might turn out all right.'

Mr Winters' leather shoes scraped across the linoleum flooring as he crossed his arms defensively over his chest. 'Tell me, lass. How would you explain to the grandson you'd never met that the reason his father, my son, has not spoken to me in thirty-five years, is because I killed his grandmother? I killed the most beautiful, patient, kind, loving woman the world has ever known, and you think my grandson would be impressed by that?'

'No! I mean, you didn't kill her. The diabetes did.' Jess protested.

'In Robert's eyes, that's precisely what I did.'

'But you weren't to know. It's awful, yes, but none of you knew she had diabetes, let alone the signs to look out for if she was going into a coma.'

Mr Winters gave a violent shudder, as if hearing the word afresh was akin to hearing them the very first time. 'I knew she wasn't feeling well.'

'You said you'd take her to the GP. She didn't want to go.'

'I should've insisted.'

'Why? She would've insisted otherwise,' Jess leant forward, forearms on the thick wooden kitchen table between them.

He tipped his head back and forth in a way that suggested he had been over this sticking point a million times before.

The pain in his face was palpable. Jess could hardly bear it. How he'd lived with this burden of guilt for so long and remained even remotely human was beyond her.

'It wasn't your fault,' she said.

'Try telling that to Robert.'

'Maybe he knows.' Jess shrugged.

Arnold gave her a sharp look.

'Why else would Will have reached out to you? Maybe his father – Robert – expressed some remorse about what had happened between the two of you, but doesn't know how to make the first move?'

'That's his move to make,' Mr Winters said stubbornly.

Jess was guessing the same stubbornness was why his son hadn't got in touch. That, or what Will had said was true. That Robert never spoke about Mr Winters and it was purely out of personal interest that Will had sought him out.

Jess gave the inside of her cheek another chew. Now that Arnold knew she knew about Will, there had to be a way to bring them together. She'd ask Drea, but given her track record in the complicated-relations-with-offspring department, she would probably suggest a free airline ticket and a don't-hold-your-breath policy.

Jess closed her eyes, picturing the disappointment and pain Drea had shown when she thought her son wouldn't come. She and Arnold were such good people. And they clearly loved their children. They deserved happiness. Especially at Christmas when all of life's darker moments seemed to grow darker still, attached to some people like unwelcome lead weights. Surely the fact that Drea had finally spoken about her past, and that Mr Winters had mysteriously opened up to her, meant something.

Mr Winters rapped his knuckles on the table and stood up. 'Right, young lady. I'd best let you get on with your day.'

She rose, not needing more of a cue to wrap up the 'feelings' talk. 'Thanks for the tea.' She brought her mug to the sink and washed it. 'So, ummm … do you want me to do anything?'

'What do you mean?'

'You know … it's coming up to your night for the advent calendar and you obviously missed mine when I was planning on giving you some tips or maybe having a little brainstorm, but I'd be more than happy to—'

'No, no. That's not for me, duck. It's all right for you to keep the wreaths up on the fence, but that'll be the end of my part in all of this, all right?'

He gave her a look so final, all of the lightness she'd been feeling turned dark. 'Will you come to any of the events? I hear it's dreidel lessons at the Goldsteins' tonight.'

He scrunched his nose up as if trying to remember what a dreidel was, then shook his head again. 'No. Not for me. I'll keep myself to myself, ta.'

Jess knew better than to push it. She pulled her coat off the back of the kitchen chair she'd been sitting in and stuffed her arms into the sleeves. Mr Winters stood behind her and helped shift it properly into place. Once again the idea of him meeting Martha Snodgrass came to mind. She was just about to pass on the 'old farts freezing their bums off' comment but could tell from the fatigue hitting his features that Mr Winters had had enough for the day.

'Well, thank you for the tea,' she gave him a wave.

'Thank you for the company,' he said, opening then shutting the door behind her.

Jess headed back to hers not knowing whether to feel elated or gutted. Maybe that was life, really. Part happy, part sad, and it was up to you to find a way to live with both. She turned and looked at his house, the wreaths, hung a bit higgledy-piggledy, looked like a smiley face with the lights on in the two downstairs windows as they were now.

Perhaps she needed to take a page out of his late wife's book. Meddle with mirth. Bombard him with kindness and maybe one day, he'd find a way to reach out to his grandson and then, perhaps, his son.

16 December

To: WillWinters@TheMerryVictualler.co.uk
From: JessGreen2000@gmail.com
Subject: More news from Christmas Street

Hey Will!
Jess(ica) here.

I went onto your Insta site and OMG. Your food looks AMAZING! I have no idea what took me so long, but now that I know The Merry Victualler is utterly scrumdiddlyumptious, I plan to be an online devotee and, hopefully, take you up on that brunch offer one day. I'd offer to cook for you, but not entirely sure burnt toast and beans straight from a tin would be your jam.

I hope you're managing to uncurl your fingers and find some life time in among all of the devils on horseback and shrimp in mink. I'm going to have to tell my neighbour Martha about that one. She is a jazz singer wrapped in mink. Langoustine, pancetta and date purée? I think Oliver Twist put it best: Please, sir! I want some more. That goat's cheese cake with red onion jam? #DiedAndGoneToHeaven. Who would've known to put all of that together? You, I guess. Why aren't there any pictures of you on Insta or your website? Camera shy or are you maintaining a 'man behind the curtain' mystique?

Anyway... not to take up too much of your time, I was trying to think of a discreet way to tell you I have had not one, but two proper sit downs with your grandfather, and I couldn't come up with one. So... I have had not one but two proper sit downs with your grandfather. He also knows I know about you and that you know about me. He... he's got his reasons for not writing back. I don't necessarily agree with them, but I think, when you have the time, you should hear what happened between him and your father from the horse's mouth, as it were.

There. That's my interfering ways all wrapped up for the day. T-minus ten days and counting. Then you're a free agent until... do Merry Victuallers cater for... ummm... epiphany? We three kings of Vietnamese spring rolls? (You can see why I wasn't drawn to the profession...)

Hope you're all right. Best xo Jess(ica)

'Cold enough for you?' Drea asked.

Jess grinned and held up the hairdryer attached to an extension lead and blew some hot air at Drea's face. 'Better?'

'Much,' Drea said dryly.

Somehow they'd ended up furthest away from the two heat lamps Maurice Headley, next door at number 16, had set up outside his garage where, once again, everyone was working away on Chantal's folding tables.

Maurice was the street's resident beekeeper. He had two hives in his back garden and an unbelievably tidy set of equipment in his garage, and tended a few more hives down the road in someone's apple orchard. He had planned on teaching everyone the fine art of mead making, but as Drea had suggested it wasn't an entirely child-friendly activity, he'd opted to teach them how to roll beeswax candles. Apparently, it was so easy, they'd been assured by Maurice, that they should each have a set of perfectly rolled candles within five minutes, pending, of course, waiting their turn to soften the wax with the handful of hairdryers Maurice had borrowed from the Gem'n'Emms.

Drea had been a bit more subdued than normal. Jess didn't want to press, but was pretty sure it was about Spencer. She sent another silent prayer to the sky that he had seen her email and was making all of the necessary arrangements.

To try and elicit a smile from Drea, Jess held her sheet of red dyed wax up to her nose and inhaled. 'Mmm... this smells so good.'

Drea arched a brow then said in a low voice, 'Not as good as the man sitting next to you. *Again.*' Her eyes flicked to Josh who was laughing at one of the Gem'n'Emms' retelling of last year's nativity when the two children playing the donkey had inadvertently performed the magician's trick of splitting into two then coming back together again. Josh leant back as he roared with appreciative laughter, just close enough for Jess to take a discreet sniff. Mmm...

Realising she'd been caught in the act, she threw Drea a look she hoped said, 'it's not what you're thinking'. It wasn't her fault she loved that tangy combo of citrus and sugar.

Drea tried to get Josh's attention when Martha, who

was sitting on his other side, snagged it first. She claimed her arthritis wouldn't allow for her to roll the candle as tightly as Maurice had instructed. Jess smirked. If anyone was pouring on the feminine charms, it was definitely Martha who, Jess was pleased to see, was wearing her fur coat again.

Drea nudged Jess in the ribs hard enough to send her off balance so that her shoulder bashed into Josh's.

'Sorry,' she and Josh said together, eyes meeting as they did.

My goodness he was lovely. Were all widowers this lovely?

'How's your candle-making going?' he asked.

'I don't think this was quite what Maurice had in mind.' Jess held up the results of her efforts, taking a quick glance towards the end of the table where Maurice was showing Josh's children how to hold the blow dryer to the sheet of candle wax then roll it . . . one, two, three . . . up into a perfect candle. Show-off.

Josh held up his candle. The top of it drooped so that the whole thing was more wonky candy-cane-shaped than candle-shaped. Jess laughed. 'Looks like neither of us will be getting jobs at the candle factory anytime soon.' As she spoke, her own candle wilted into the same forlorn shape. They both began giggling, shoulders shaking, shifting against the other. Little waves of sparkle dust lit up her chest as the giggles died out and their eye contact intensified.

'Well, would you look at that,' Drea said pronouncedly, nodding at the pair of them holding their candles side by side. 'A match made in heaven.'

Jess snorted in a vain attempt to pretend she hadn't just had a miniature gymnastics team doing backflips in her tummy. She liked Josh, but she was pretty sure it was the same kind of crush she'd had on film stars. Fun, but nothing to consider seriously.

Josh laughed, leaning a bit further into her space. 'Let's see how you went, Drea.'

Drea, to Jess's astonishment, flushed and swept her candle into the basket Maurice had asked everyone to put any failed efforts into so that he could melt the wax down and make fresh sheets. 'Crafts aren't really my bag. Right!' She clapped her hands together. 'For those of you who have been too busy showing off your skills, hot chocolates are still available in the garage courtesy of Mrs H who's manning the camp stove. I think we can all agree the Headleys have done a great job tonight, yeah? Some of us proved more adept than others,' she said with a pointed look at Jess. 'Let's have a round of applause for the man who has brought a little light into all of our lives. Maurice?' She smirked at Jess again as everyone applauded, then when the clapping died down she continued, 'And now, if I'm not mistaken, I think Gemmmmaaaaa . . . Lloyd, Gemma Lloyd from number seventeen has an announcement about her night tomorrow, am I right?'

She scanned the table until they hit on one of the Gem'n'Emms who was waving a mittened hand in the air and nodding that yes, that was right, she had an announcement. Her ash-blonde bob was peeking out of a red knit hat with a glittering silver pompom on top and, Jess was impressed to see, her two red candles were done perfectly, as were her two children's and her husband's. Her heart constricted. They looked like the picture-perfect family. She wondered if she'd have that with someone one day.

'Shall I get you a hot chocolate?'

Jess looked up at Josh and smiled. Yes. She would like a hot chocolate.

Drea whooped. 'Make that two, Joshy, yeah? And I'd like extra marshmallows on mine as you're asking. Fat free,' She tacked on amid a series of shushes from the other end of the table where Gemma had started speaking in her soft, kitten-like voice. Drea glared at Jess as if she'd been the one talking then pointed her fingers at her eyes then at Gemma. Jess rolled her eyes and did as she was told. Drea would make a brilliant primary schoolteacher.

'. . . so if you have something that you don't want but would make a lovely gift for someone else—' Gemma was saying.

'Does this have to be a Secret Santa gift from last year? Because I usually get rid of those sharpish.'

More shushes went round the tables.

'It can be anything you think the recipient will enjoy just so long as you don't spend any money on it.' Gemma talk-whispered.

Josh returned with the hot chocolates. You couldn't see the liquid in Drea's for all of the marshmallows in it. She giggled coquettishly as he handed it to her. Their eyes caught and held as Drea's fingers brushed against Josh's during the cup transfer.

Oh, hel-*lo*, thought Jess. The chocolate wasn't the only thing that was steamy tonight. Drea caught her looking and threw a *What're you looking at* glare in her direction then pretended to be really interested in the hat Gemma was walking round the table for people to draw names from.

'Oh, hell's teeth,' Kev moaned as he read his name.

'Who did you get?' His wife asked.

'You're not supposed to say,' someone shouted. 'It's a *secret* Santa?'

'What if the person I drew is never in a million years going to come along?' Kev asked.

Everyone came to the same conclusion as one, eyes swivelling towards Mr Winters' house where, Jess was quietly pleased to see, a light was on in the living-room window silhouetting Mr Perkins. Still no Christmas tree, but ... the man did have a dozen-plus wreaths hanging on his fence.

'I bet he'll come,' she said before she thought better of it.

All of the eyes swivelled to her. 'I mean, you know, he's cool with the wreaths and everything, so ... maybe he'll come?' The solitary sip of hot chocolate she'd managed to take sloshed from one side of her belly to the other.

'I don't fancy my chances,' said Kev.

'What about the person who he's supposed to give a gift for. How's that going to work if he isn't even here?'

'Katie's not here either.' Drea crisply informed them all. 'She's on shift at the hospital so I said I'd bring her name to her, which, of course, sets a precedent. I'm sure Jess here, our Number Twenty-four Ambassador, will be more than happy to bring Mr Winters' name to him. Won't you Jess?'

Everyone's eyes were on her. In the way a jury looks at the condemned. Accusatorily.

She glanced at Drea who, Jess realised, suddenly looked quite strained round the eyes. Adopting Drea's own signature move, Jess whacked an arm round her and gave her a half hug as she addressed the crowd. 'I'm more than happy to drop off a name to him and, if he's feeling shy,

I'll pick up and bring his gift along tomorrow night. Is that cool with everyone?' She didn't care if it was or wasn't cool. Nobody was going to bully Mr Winters or Drea. Not on her watch. Especially not at Christmas.

'The man's not shy, he's an ogre.'

'How do you know? Have you ever spoken to him? Heard his life story?' Drea shook her shoulders out of Jess's hold, gave everyone a serious look, then took a long draft of her hot chocolate, which would've made the moment completely intense if a wodge of marshmallow hadn't stuck to the end of her nose. It was, however, serious enough for no one to laugh.

Jess jumped in again, 'If you don't want to give him a gift, Kev, I'll take his name and you can take another.'

A few seconds of awkward silence ticked past.

'Oh, for crying out loud,' Martha finally said. 'Hand it to me, Kevin. I'll give the poor old doddery fool a gift since you lot are so useless.'

'No,' Kev protested, holding the piece of paper close. 'I drew it. I'll do it. I won't have anyone saying Kevin Strong's a bad neighbour.'

'No one's saying that, Kev,' his wife said, picking up her candles as if preparing to go. 'They're saying *he's* not a good neighbour.'

'Keep's himself to himself,' one of the Rob'n'Bobs contributed in a way that implied he thought that was a good thing.

'Love, that's what they say about serial killers.' His wife closed her eyes and pursed her lips with a little *I despair* noise.

Martha held out her leather-gloved hand. 'Give it to me, Kevin. Take another.'

Kevin did as he was told.

When the basket made its way round to Jess she took one for herself and one for Mr Winters, making a point of saying as much, then putting the folded-up piece of paper in her pocket. She made a note in her phone calendar to remind herself to bring it over to him in the morning, along with a gift he could give the person as she really didn't have a clue whether or not he'd actually participate.

When everyone had their name, Drea looked spent, so Jess took over strongly encouraging a few dads to help pack up the tables and troop them back over to Chantal's in exchange for some Christmas-themed cupcakes she just happened to have spare after whipping up a batch that afternoon. Drea wandered distractedly back home, marshmallow still on her nose and Josh, now holding four perfect candles and his two wonky ones, waved goodbye with a hopeful, 'See you tomorrow?' before Jess, too, called it a night. When she got home she checked her emails. One from Amanda demanding a phone call. Hmmm... her eyes flicked to kitchen drawer where the letter from St Benny's still sat, unopened.

She'd call her. When she was ready, she'd call her.

16 December
13:17
To: JessGreen2000@gmail.com
From: WillWinters@TheMerryVictualler.co.uk
Subject: RE: More news from Christmas Street

Dear Jess(ica)
Wow. I just... wow. You've been busy. Life as a private eye definitely suits you.

236

I don't even know what to say. I'd love to see him. Meet him. Hear his story. Be the grandson he's never had. Saying that, I'm stupidly busy, but seriously – if you say the word, I'll find a way to carve out some time to come before the New Year. I've learnt the hard way that being there when it counts is a lot more important than showing up when it suits. Saying that – I don't want to pounce now if the iron's too hot. Is that a thing? Maybe there is no perfect time.

Here's my gut spill: my relationship basically broke down because I was a selfish workaholic who thought his business was more important than his personal business. I might have painted a picture of me, the young buck caterer, trying to go where no caterer had gone before, but the truth is, I thought I was going to marry her. That we'd get the house, the kids, the labradoodle. But I kept changing the goalposts. I wanted to move to a town where I could afford to set up. I wanted to hit a certain level of revenue. Then I wanted to upgrade the level of clients. Then I wanted to upgrade premises and so it went.

She was my business partner, my life partner, my sous chef, and she left me. It was entirely my fault. Which is why I gave her everything (sold the house we'd just bought, the car we'd just leased, the deposit on the puppy we'd earmarked for Christmas... did you know a dog is for life and not just for Christmas?) So that was last Christmas. This year has been spent solely on the business and trying to get my finances back in order, but somewhere along the way I realised life on my own is damn-fucking-lonely and I'd love meet my grandad. Put some good into the world after having sucked the life out of someone else's. (The ex is engaged to someone else, by the way. He works nine-to-five, takes her on city breaks and, yes, they got the puppy. It's adorable.)

I'm not telling you this to be all woe is me. I'm telling you so that you understand why I want to meet him and why I'm also shit-scared of letting someone else down, but your email reminded me that this isn't about me. It's about him and it sounds like the old fellow needs someone in his life to help look after him. I'm so glad he has you and, as soon as I get these last few jobs out of the way, he'll have me, too. I owe you a debt of gratitude. And one of my crab sandwiches. They're killer, even if I say so myself.

All of which is to say, don't be so hard on yourself about what happened back in London. Start paying attention to all of the amazing things you have done. The good karma you've put back into the world and will do again. Yeah. You got fired. But you picked yourself up and got a new job. A new house. In a new town. How many people do you know have the strength after they've been kicked down to get back up and do that? Not many. You've done well, so pat yourself on the back from me. And, when we eventually meet, which we will, I will definitely give you some cooking lessons including a foolproof reason to get those beans OUT of the tin and heated before you eat them. (Hint: BACON).

Best xxWill

17 December

'Jeeeeeessssss!'

Amanda's voice went up and down an octave as if she were waving a hand in front of Jess's face trying to get her to pop out of a daydream.

'*Call me.*'

Jess involuntarily flinched. It was the way Amanda said '*Now*' when she'd had enough of a child who wouldn't take their seat in class. One part firm and fair to two parts 'you've entered the realms of unreasonable and *there will be* consequences'.

She frowned at the phone and clicked the message off before Amanda had finished. She'd sounded ... well ... slightly uncomfortable. As if she was trying too hard to be chirpy. It was the kind of tone someone uses if they know bad news is looming. When she'd been at her parents', she'd felt able to take and return some of Amanda's calls because she knew a cuddle from her dad or a sweet cup of tea from her mum was always available to her afterwards if she needed it. It wasn't as if they were exactly harrowing affairs. Mostly the calls involved Amanda telling her how vile the Head was being, silly stories of the students, gossip about the Numbers Ones and Twos (mostly Twos) and a very tactical avoidance of all things

Crispin Anand-Haight. As time passed, though, the distance between the calls grew, along with Jess's reduced tolerance to hearing stories about the life she used to lead that, between the lines, she could tell Amanda still very clearly loved living. (She'd gone to Courchevel, St Moritz and Aspen last year. *Oh, Jess. I'm sooooo fat on all of that après-ski cake!*)

With the St Benny's letter sitting in her drawer, no parents to whimper to and Amanda sounding less Amanda-ish, Jess wasn't sure her emotional self-care toolbox was up to a post-phone call fix-it job. She was still too raw about the past and too nervous about her future: a lovely little primary academy, in a lovely town where absolutely everyone would, eventually, know everything about you. It was, of course, the last part that was scariest.

She glanced out the window. The For Sale sign was lit by a stray ray of sun. She wasn't quite ready to take it down yet, but, increasingly, even thinking about taking off the Sold banner made her heart sink. She was beginning to like it here. She knew she hadn't exactly been living here properly yet. The piles of unpacked boxes and the mattress on her bedroom floor were testament to that, but already she felt as though she had an arsenal of friends to call on, if she needed to. Bonkers Drea who needed support as much as she gave it. The Gem'n'Emms and all of their ash-blonde efficiency. Kev, who, last time he'd been by, had offered to look under her car's bonnet because he'd noticed a peculiar sound the last time she'd gone out to the shops. He'd offered the same service just yesterday to the Nishios who had taken him up on the offer and pronounced him 'quite the mechanic'. Martha for ... ermm ... Seventies fashion advice and, of course, Mr Winters.

Speaking of whom ...

The arched eyebrow and thinned lips were more amused than annoyed when Arnold opened his door.

'Morning,' Jess chirped.

Mr Winters nodded in response. Not the friendliest of greetings, but nor was he slamming the door in her face. She wasn't always in the mood for company but, thanks to Drea's regular visits to her house, she was learning that sometimes you didn't know you wanted company until it was there, smiling at you. Besides. She was on a mission. They were going to brainstorm ideas for Christmas Eve.

Jess held out a small folded piece of paper. 'Here.'

'What's that then?'

'Your Secret Santa.'

He tried handing it back to her.

Jess tucked her hands into her pockets. 'You know what a Secret Santa is, right?'

He nodded but said nothing.

'Cool. I'll pick it up, or you up, at seven?'

'I'm not going out today,' he grumbled.

'Even better,' Jess cranked up the power of her *you can do this* smile. Even the most stubborn children found this particular smile hard to resist. 'The gifts are meant to be something from home that you don't want. Like ...' Her mind reeled as she tried to think of something quick and easy to wrap up. '... some seeds or something from your greenhouse? A gift someone gave you that wasn't quite right. Some bric-a-brac?'

'Bric-a-brac,' he repeated.

241

'Yeah, you know, like doilies or—'

'I know what bric-a-brac is, duck. I just don't see why giving something I don't want any more to someone else would bring any sort of Christmas cheer.'

Jess pulled her coat zip up and down for a minute trying to come up with something inspirational to say about one person's junk being another person's treasure. 'Maybe I should come in. You don't want to lose any more heat, do you? I know there's a senior discount and everything but you don't really want to contribute to... ermm... global-warming?'

Nice one, Jess. Good way to remind the poor man not only that he's old, but that his generation ruined the planet.

'Look,' he finally said, not moving an inch. 'I know what you're doing and believe it or not, I appreciate it.' Jess's smile barely gained purchase before he continued, '... *but* the truth is, I'm finding all of this...' he waved his hand between the pair of them, '... this interaction business is a bit too much.'

'Oh. Gosh. I'm sorry,' Jess said, her cheeks colouring with shame.

Mr Winters shifted, as uncomfortable with this conversation as she was. 'You're trying to do a good thing. I shouldn't have been so bloody rude when you first started coming by. Habit, I guess. Keeping people at arm's length.'

Thirty-five years was a long time to keep people at bay. No wonder he was out of practice at letting them in.

Jess looked to the porch floor, then back up into Mr Winters' clear blue eyes. 'Weren't there neighbours or friends who helped after, you know, Anne passed?'

'After Anne died, you mean,' he quietly corrected. He

thought a moment, then said, 'I suppose there might have been. I have vague memories of Robert and me being given all sorts of stews and casseroles and the like, but once he'd gone back to Scotland...' He stopped and ran a hand through his thick white hair. 'I was so angry and busy trying not to lose my job I guess I didn't notice who did what.'

'Who were you angry with?'

'Myself, mostly,' he admitted. 'Though I probably didn't see it that way at the time. I didn't want folk to have to try to be nice to the demon who'd taken away the loveliest woman this town had ever known.'

'It wasn't your fault!' Unable to stop herself, Jess reached out and gave Mr Winters' arm a squeeze. How awful for him to have to live with all of this anguish. A self-imposed torment that didn't seem to have faded through the years. He looked down at her hand. She put it back into her pocket, fighting the prickling of tears, but stayed quiet as he continued.

'Once Robert and I had our disagreement after the funeral I suppose I felt as though I didn't deserve to be on the receiving end of anyone's kindnesses.'

He said it matter of factly. No self-pity. It was simply the way things were. He'd made a call and it had been the wrong one. His son had never spoken to him again and he'd lived the past thirty-five years punishing himself for something he simply couldn't have known.

Jess thought of her own behaviour in the aftermath of the Cheese Sandwich Incident. There had been a lot of lying in bed. Much chocolate consumption. An abundance of *O woe is me*. But eventually, through the loving support of her parents and her bone-deep passion for teaching, she'd pulled herself out of that murky wallow and was, with plenty of wobbles, trying to start over.

But starting over was something Mr Winters didn't seem to have done. It must be so painful for him. Living in that house with all of those memories. 'Why didn't you move?' she asked.

'How else would Robert know where to find me?' he said with a sharp look, visibly shocked there was even a need to ask.

Jess's hands flew to her heart. All of these years, he'd held out hope. And yet . . . now that Will had reached out to him, he was too frightened to meet. Her chest strained with pain for him, then, as if a dam burst, vowed to reunite them.

'Why don't you write to Will? Ring him?'

Mr Winters shook his head. 'I don't know. I'm not sure opening up old wounds is such a good idea.'

'From where I'm standing? It seems like you never let them close. And,' she quickly added before he could interject, 'for what it's worth, I don't think you've deserved to be in pain this long. I know I never met her, but from the way you talk about her, I don't think Anne would've liked you to put yourself through this.'

He blinked a few times, as if trying to digest the notion that his late wife could absolve him of the guilt he felt, then shook his head. 'That's kind of you, but there's nowt you can do about it when the one thing you want is the one thing you can never have.'

His words sank straight to the bottom of her gut.

Of course his pain was different to hers. She could still teach. Sure, it'd be scary and she'd probably wobble, more than once, but she had the option to try again. Try to be better, stronger, more resilient. Because the truth was, no matter how far away she moved from London, there would be more Crispin Anand-Haights, and there would also be as many Ethans and all of those other glorious children who made teaching such a brilliant job. And Mr Winters was right. There would never be another Anne Winters. But there was a Will Winters...

And where there was a Will...

'Arnold ... can I invite myself in for a cup of tea?'

He frowned at her then stood back from the door. 'Go on then. As you say, climate change...'

17 December
15:17
To: WillWinters@TheMerryVictualler.co.uk
From: JessGreen2000@gmail.com
Subject: RE: RE: More News From Christmas Street

Hey Will –
I hope you got my last email in response to yours.
Sometimes I worry they disappear into the ether never to return. It sounds like life has turned you into one of those rarefied creatures: the self-aware male. Long may you flourish and teach your wise ways to those who follow in your path! (And by the way? Those scallop-pops look AMAZING! Can we learn to make those?).

Now. To the point.

I know it's crazy late notice, but you know how you said you'd try to make room for your grandfather before the holidays if it was in any way possible? I think now might be the time.

So, if you're free tonight, here's my idea...

'Bloody hell it's cold.'

'Kevin! Language. There're children here.'

'Not my children—'

'Shush.'

Mr Winters gave Jess a sidelong look. She gave him her best stab at a smile through her wince. Not exactly the most community-minded chatter to happen upon, but they were here and that was what mattered.

'Anyone tell Emma that it's sub-zero out here?'

'I've got a chicken that needs taking out of the oven.'

'This is Gemma's not Emma's night.'

'Which one?'

'Gemma! There's only one of them.'

'Really?'

Mr Winters sent Jess an inquisitive look. Jess could only shrug. The Gemma–Emma conundrum might remain one of life's eternal mysteries.

'Hey, doll. Nice night for it, yeah?'

Drea sounded casual. Too casual. Jess fell into exactly the same mode because standing here next to Mr Winters was a bit weird. 'Hey! Hi, Drea. You've met Mr Winters, right? Arnold, this is Drea Zamboni. Down at number one?'

Mr Winters held out a gloved hand and gave Drea's a solid shake. 'Yes, she's . . . we've . . .'

'I've hounded the poor man with flyers galore over the years, haven't I, Mr Winters? You're a tough old boot. Ignored every one of them. Good on ya.'

He gave her a half smile, clearly unsure if it was a compliment or not.

'Those your gifts?'

Jess and Mr Winters looked down at their hands. Jess

held a small wrapped box and Mr Winters had a much larger wooden one with a solitary red ribbon round it.

'You're meant to put them there on the table Gem's set up on the drive, yeah?' Drea pointed them towards the table which was, of course, where most people's attention was focused, waiting for the event to begin.

Mr Winters took a step backwards.

'Here, mate. I'll take it.' Drea didn't wait for an answer, just lifted the box out of his arms with a light 'Oof!', marched through the crowd and plonked it on the table. 'Now that's what I call a present,' she said, nodding at the wooden box. A brave statement considering she didn't have the slightest clue what was in it. Jess followed in her wake, popped her gift on the table then scuttled back to Mr Winters' side, shifting from foot to foot more out of nervousness than cold, although it was definitely one of those 'blow your breath into smoke rings' sorts of nights.

The dulcet tones of Cliff Richard began wafting from the house along with the arrival of Gemma in a slightly too saucy to be appropriate Mrs Claus outfit.

A couple of the Rob'n'Bobs wolf-whistled and were promptly shushed by their wives and the protective glare of Gemma's husband, who was behind her wearing a snug-fitting elf costume. Their children, two adorable little platinum-blond boys, were also wearing elf costumes but theirs looked tailor-made. It was clear to see where the money went in their home, which, all things considered, made Jess's heart go a bit gooey. *Awww.* Families. They could be messy sometimes but they could also be great. Which reminded her ... She did a quick scan of the crowd for a young version of Mr Winters. She hadn't heard back from Will and really doubted he'd make it, but it'd be so nice for Arnold if he did show up. And she had to admit, she wondered if the real-life Will was like email Will, who she had grown rather fond of. But mostly, Jess wanted Mr Winters to have something and someone to look forward to instead of facing yet another year of loneliness and self-recrimination. Her eyes lit on and caught with Josh's. He raised his eyebrows and did the guy chin-tilt thing. She smiled and flushed, which was stupid because she seriously did not imagine any sort of future between them.

Drea nudged her in the ribs, making her flush even deeper.

What on earth was she doing being all flirty with a parent dad? She knew, having witnessed it on multiple occasions at St Benny's, that flirting with a parent dad, particularly the widowed parent dad the entire street was insanely protective of, was class-A stupid.

Everyone fell silent, straining to hear Gemma's tiny, whispery voice, as she rang a bell and said, 'Ohmygoodness, that must've been an angel getting its wings!'

'What?'

'It's from *It's a Wonderful Life* – remember?'

'Clarence?'

'They all get wings. With the bell. But yes, Clarence does, too.'

The person with the chicken in the oven brought it up again with a muttered *chop chop* and Gemma, who was clearly immensely shy, flushed crimson. Her husband protectively waded into the breach and began handing out presents. There was a lot of collective laughing and ribbing as joke gifts were opened and presented to the group. At one point some headlights flashed onto the street. Jess went up on tiptoe to see who it was, but the car did a three-point turn and was gone before she could see.

Kev got a litre of car oil.

Katie the nurse got a taped-up box of the Operation board game.

Rex and Kai got a candle in rainbow stripes that they lavished praise on before yawning and making a quick exit. (*Work! It's a madhouse!*)

Drea got a mini-loudspeaker that changed her voice into Minnie Mouse and the Terminator. Someone made Gemma do it which, of course, got a huge laugh. Jess turned to gauge Arnold's reaction. His features looked tight and anxious, as if he wanted the whole thing over and done with. She gave his arm a pat and said, 'Our turn soon. It's going in order of the houses.' He gave her a thin-lipped nod.

The triathletes got a packet of Dettol easy-wipes to which they said, ha-ha very funny, then tried to book everyone in for next year.

The chicken roaster received an I ♥ My Neighbour mug before bowing out of proceedings because the chicken was calling.

Jess received a bag of carrots 'for the reindeer' from one of the Gem'n'Emms with an apologetic, 'Sorry. We don't know you well enough to give you something stupid.'

The comment stung a little, but Jess reminded herself that it was, of course, true. Drea suggested she juice the carrots with ginger and then throw in some tequila if it was after five.

Josh was the recipient of Mr Winters' present. He

looked really touched when he opened up the wooden wine box to discover it was filled with pre-planted daffodil bulbs and would need little attention beyond some watering in order to flourish.

'Just, you know, make sure the soil doesn't go dry,' Mr Winters said.

'That's . . .' Josh cleared his throat. 'They were Claire's favourites.'

'I know they were, lad.'

Everyone grew still. Claire was Josh's wife.

Mr Winters nodded and something passed between the two men that only those who have loved and lost could share. A common understanding.

Martha received a dual foot massager which Tyler took great delight in. 'You and me, Mazza! How about a nice night in front of *Mastermind* and we can hit all of those pressure points, eh?' She rolled her eyes at him, but Jess could see she was amused.

Finally it was Mr Winters' turn.

Everyone knew Martha had taken his name, so the group's attention pinged between the pair of them as if they were watching the final at Wimbledon.

Clearly uncomfortable in the limelight he fumbled with the square thin package. He pulled the shiny red paper off it and revealed an album. 'Marti Morgan,' he said, brow furrowing.

'It may not be your style of music, but apart from Tyler the mix-master here, I thought you might be the only one old enough to have an actual record player.' She smiled at Mr Winters. 'If it's not your style of music, there are plenty more where that came from. You're more than welcome to come over, have a cup of tea and see what you think.'

Tyler nodded along enthusiastically as if, he too, had been part of this plan. 'I'll drive you if the walk's too far.'

Mr Winters' harrumphed. Martha lived two doors up from him. 'I may be old and feeble, young man, but not that old and that feeble.' He gave Martha a quick nod. Her offer had been acknowledged and possibly accepted.

Gemma whispered her thanks to everyone but said she'd probably better get in as she couldn't feel her fingers or toes anymore. Everyone quickly followed suit and, despite some grumbling that he didn't need a nursemaid, not yet anyway, Jess and Drea walked Mr Winters home, not so subtly reminding him about the Christmas piñata at number 18 the next night at six.

'Nice job, Jess,' Drea said once Mr Winters was safely indoors.

'For what?'

'Getting the tortoise out of his shell.'

Jess felt the warmth of the compliment hit her insides. 'Any word from Spencer?' she asked a bit too innocently.

'Nah,' Drea gave a brusque shake of her head. 'But it's meeting day next Tuesday. Pretty much the last day he can get on a flight and still make it for Christmas, so... we'll see.'

They arrived outside of Jess's house. She gave Drea a quick, tight hug then crossed all of her fingers. 'I'll stay like this until tomorrow.'

Drea huffed out a laugh and then softened. 'Thanks, doll. It's nice having someone on side.'

And that was it, wasn't it, Jess thought as she shut the

door behind her, grinned at her painted Christmas tree, then headed for her nightly hot chocolate fix. Knowing someone was out there, on your side. It was what had thrown her so off-kilter when the Cheese Sandwich Incident had gone down. The people she'd thought would be there for her – the Head Teacher, her boyfriend, the other teachers – hadn't been. And even though Amanda had handed her tissues and poured her glass upon glass of Pinot, she'd not stood up for Jess. Nor had she demanded a meeting with the Head to say she knew Crispin had a tendency to bully the other children. That he manipulated situations to make himself the victor, regardless of what had happened. It explained why taking her calls was so hard. She felt betrayed.

A ping sounded from her laptop.

17 December
20:43
To: JessGreen2000@gmail.com
From: WillWinters@TheMerryVictualler.co.uk
Subject: RE: RE: RE: More News From Christmas Street

Dear Jess(ica)
MEA CULPA!!!! I was literally on my way there. I was at the actual entrance to Christmas Street when I got a call from the fire brigade. The fire alarms had gone off at the catering kitchen. Idiot me left a batch of mince pies in the oven and . . . incineration. Luckily not too much damage, but it meant I couldn't come along and meet Grandad and you when I really was hoping to.

Flat out until the big day, but please keep trying. I know it isn't your responsibility to keep me in touch with Grandad (that feels right... so I think I'll go with that), but the efforts you're making mean a lot. Scallop-pops are insanely easy. They're on the list.

    Wx

18 December

Jess opened the box, gasped, then teared up.

'What? You all right?' Drea peered over the top of the box then at Jess's face as she swiped a couple of tears off her cheeks. 'Nope. Don't get it. You're going to have to explain.'

Coloured pens. Pencils. A jumbo crayon box with an insane two hundred and eighty-eight crayons within its beautiful cardboard boundaries. Glitter. A ridiculous amount of glitter. Pasta shapes. Wooden spoons. Pipe cleaners. The lot.

Her parents had outdone themselves, and it wasn't even Christmas yet. The box had arrived with a big: OPEN <u>BEFORE</u> CHRISTMAS penned in her father's assured block handwriting and, of course, his signature smiley face complete with a perfect set of teeth.

'It's from my parents,' she said.

'Is this traditional? Kiddy crafts for their grown-up daughter?'

'They're not so much for me,' her voice caught in her throat again. 'They're for the kids.'

'What? They don't have supplies at the school?'

'No, they do, but . . .' She made a scrunchy face and shook her head, finding it impossible to explain how Jess's parents knew she adored watching a child's eyes light on an array of art supplies and then get to work. It was one of the best feelings ever. Seeing that spark of delight. Of possibility. This was her parents' way of saying, 'We know you've been struggling, but think of all of the joy that is waiting for you.'

She thought about the Instamatic camera and handful of film boxes she'd wrapped and tucked into one of her mother's walking boots for their Christmas present and suddenly wished she'd given them something more personal. Something to show how deeply she appreciated all they'd done for her this last year. It couldn't have been easy. Putting back together the puddle of tears that had poured into their house a year ago. At this stage in life, she was meant to be looking after them, or, at the very least, *herself*. They were perfectly capable of looking after themselves. Thousands of miles away on a lump of coral and sand with nothing but periodontitis and overbites to bring them joy . . .

She looked round the kitchen, still only semi-functional. She'd gently refused her mum's archaic mixer and whizzer and deep-fat fryer, wanting to take her time to properly set up her home, her way.

She'd been here nearly three weeks now and, apart from having wrapped up the office supplies descriptions and bagging a failsafe stapler, had she done that? Begun to make her mark?

White walls. Bog-standard kitchen table and chairs. White plates. Deciding what impression she'd wanted to make with her dinnerware hadn't seemed important back when she'd stood in the middle of Ikea feeling friendless and not very hungry.

There was the Christmas tree in the hallway that never failed to make her grin, but would she want it to be Christmas all year long? Or, more pressingly, would she be painting over it for new owners if she bottled it when the school year began? As if on cue a family walked past the front window, two of the children singing an off-key rendition of 'Rudolph the Red-Nosed Reindeer' in between wondering why the 'new lady' hadn't taken her For Sale sign down.

Drea picked up the card resting on top of the package. 'May I?'

'Please,' Jess sniffled, not knowing whether to busy herself making a fresh cafetière of coffee or to indulge in a little boo-hoo, even though Drea would tell her to pull her socks up because there were worse things in the world than having parents who sent incredible gifts and renewed offers to be flown to the tropics. And, of course, she would be right. It was a big juicy loving gift, whereas what Drea was going through with her son was mired in complicated emotions and tricky visits to the past and, from the looks of it, no visits in the future.

Jess knew beyond a shadow of a doubt she could and would see her parents again, and when she did? It'd be comfortable and loving and full of laughter and, most probably, vegetable crisps.

Drea had a weekly half-hour conversation about spreadsheets. Her heart squeezed tight for her friend. She wished she could do something guaranteed to convince Spencer to come. Should she send another email? Ring him? Do a video recording round the neighbourhood showing him how incredible his mum was, detailing how welcoming she'd been to Jess from day one (snowball fights aside) and, most importantly, how very, very much she clearly adored him.

'Aww, that's nice, doll.' Drea put the card up on the counter and gave it a little pat. 'They're obviously worried about you.'

'What? No. They're just . . .' Were they? She genuinely doubted they would've gone to the Marshall Islands if they'd thought she wasn't up to looking after herself. They were only looking after their little girl. Which made her teary all over again.

Drea handed her a menthol tissue then rearranged the card, featuring a Santa Claus in a Hawaiian shirt and shorts, so that it faced Jess. 'This is what parents do when they're worried. They interfere. You'll learn one day.' She got a mischievous look on her face. 'When Josh and Jess are sitting on a tree, k-i-s-s-i-n-g.'

'Ha! As if.' She swatted away the notion. Letting something build that wasn't really there was silly. 'I don't fancy Josh, I fancy the *idea* of Josh and that is totally different. Anyway,' she wiggled her fingers in front of Drea's smirk then pointed at the box of art supplies. 'This isn't interfering, it's – it's love.'

'You say tom-ay-to, I say they're exactly the same thing. From Spencer's point of view, anyway.'

Jess couldn't think of a counter-argument for that. Not something wonderful and wise that the Dalai Lama or Michelle Obama would say, anyway. She wondered if that was what had happened between Mr Winters and his son. Polarised perspectives. Mr Winters had been trying to be respectful of his wife's wishes to have a nap while his son saw it as neglect.

One man's trash; another man's treasure.

One boy's brie and cranberry leftovers; another boy's kryptonite.

Maybe that's what life was. A huge series of misunderstandings that people who cared for one another spent a lifetime trying to unravel.

Her eyes dipped to the drawer where the letter still sat, unopened, and she took a sip of coffee as Drea did the same, each of them slipping into silent reflection.

'Do you think the Winter Warlock will be coming along tonight?' Drea eventually asked, breaking the thoughtful silence.

'Who?'

'Arnold,' Drea said in an Arnold Schwarzenegger voice.

'Oh, yes. No. Maybe?' Jess shrugged. She wasn't really sure. 'We could go round and get him.'

'That is the correct answer. I'll pick you up,' Drea said, taking a last sip of her coffee and dipping her free hand into Jess's art supplies. She brandished a hot pink marker pen then popped it into her pocket with a toothy grin. 'Right! That's me prepared for another day of inspiring the masses to get off their—' She grinned and let Jess silently fill in the blank as she showed herself out.

Jess picked up the box of art supplies, her smile widening. It might not be the perfect Christmas, but maybe it wouldn't be one to wish away. Not just yet anyway.

Though a light was on in the front room, there was no answer at the door.

'Maybe he's powdering his nose,' Jess said.

'Doubt it,' Drea sniffed, pointing towards the far end of the street where the crowd was gathering and, from the sound of electric guitar blaring, Tyler was mid-rehearsal. 'It's too loud for him. He's probably hiding.'

Jess peered down the street towards the growing number of neighbours milling outside number 18, the men watching and offering advice as a couple of dads tried to set up a rather enormous triangle frame on the square of front lawn.

'What's that for?' Jess asked.

'The Grinch piñata.' Drea said as if it were completely obvious.

'They're doing a Grinch piñata?'

Drea shrugged. 'That, or they're preparing for a public hanging. How's your conscience?'

Jess snorted – awkwardly – and gave Mr Winters' doorbell one last *brrrring*.

'Nope. Not here,' Drea concluded for the pair of them.

Jess craned round to see if she could catch a glimpse of something, anything to assure her he was all right. They'd opened up a lot of old baggage over the past couple of days and she was frightened it might be too overwhelming for him. He didn't seem the type to do anything rash, but as happy a time of year as it was, for some people it was a time of year that drained away any tidings of comfort of joy.

She was just about to knock again when Drea took a step down and lurched, hands spread wide trying to catch hold of something. Jess grabbed her arm, holding her steady until she righted herself.

'*Strewth*!' Drea grumbled with a glare at the steps. 'The frost must be turning to ice already. If the ruddy council would ever grit the street it'd be a bloody Christmas miracle.'

Mr Perkins appeared in the window, gave her a haughty look, then stalked off. If something really bad had happened to Mr Winters, Jess was sure he would create a proper ruckus, so taking that and Drea's pointed tapping on her Apple watch as a cue, they left.

They walked down the street, careful not to lose their balance on the slippery bits, Drea kvetching about the two blinking street lights that never seemed to wholly commit to being on. Drea had, Jess had noticed, become increasingly cranky the closer it got to her Tuesday meeting with her son. From the outside, it seemed as though Drea and her son both wanted a reconciliation, but each on their own terms. In Jess's experience that simply wasn't possible.

They arrived at the edge of the crowd, were offered a handful of snowflake-shaped pretzels and, much to their surprise, saw Martha at the far side of the garden in deep conversation with none other than Mr Winters.

'Well, well, well, my little chickadee,' Drea rubbed her hands together. 'Shall we go earwig?'

Jess shushed Drea, ever so pleased to see Mr Winters chatting, not entirely comfortably, but chatting nonetheless. 'Let's let them carry on without us, yeah?'

'All right, ladies?'

Drea and Jess turned as one to find Josh long-armed at the end of Audrey's lead as his two children, dressed as superheroes, ran towards the centre of the circle where most of the children were gathering.

'Josh, hi. Hi, doll. Howzit? Your turn soon, yeah?'

Jess knelt and gave Audrey a cuddle while Drea pressed Josh for details on his night. For some reason she always felt doubly ridiculous talking to Josh when Drea was watching, so the dog cuddle was just fine.

'All right everyone!' The Rob'n'Bob gave his hands a brisk clap and rub. 'Are you ready to get your piñata on?'

The children whooped and cheered and Kev asked why they'd made the piñata look like him. Everyone laughed as they gathered round the frame, which now sported at its centre a huge Grinch piñata, filled with Celebrations *and* Quality Street if the rumour mill was anything to go by.

'Get out yer insulin shots!' laughed Katie the nurse.

The Rob'n'Bob lifted up a huge bowl of clementines. 'We're all over health and safety at this house,' he crowed.

Jess's eyes flicked to Mr Winters.

He was midway to lifting his hot chocolate to his lips. He stopped, looked at the mixture, then discreetly tipped it into the hedge.

If Jess had been anywhere near him, she would've given him a hug. If he'd let her. They'd made quite a lot of progress over the past week, but she was pretty sure they weren't quite ready to hug it all out.

'Right!' A cricket bat was handed to Josh's daughter Zoe, who looked completely adorable in her Wonder Woman get up complete with Elsa gloves and cape. She was blindfolded and had a few semi-successful whacks at the piñata. Jess clapped and laughed, turning just in time to catch the interesting sight of Drea watching Josh, not Zoe. Drea gave her a sharp *What?* look then pinned an avidly interested expression on the next child as the blindfold was tied on.

'Where's Ruby?'

Heads swivelled round as everyone tried to find the last child to have a turn at the now very dishevelled-looking piñata before matters were turned over to Tyler, who had turned up flushed from an hour's worth of 'rocking out, man'.

A little girl dressed as an angel was spotted playing an invisible game of hopscotch on the street with a couple of other girls down near where Mr Winters was standing. He, Jess had surreptitiously noticed, had been inching his way out of the heart of the crowd and towards an easy escape route.

Several calls chimed together to call Ruby, who turned, made a sharp swivel and ran in Mr Winters' direction. One minute she was running. The next she was being held millimetres from the ground by the scruff of her neck. Mr Winters dragged her upright, halo and wings askew. Ruby made a horrifying choking noise, looked up at Mr Winters, then let out an ear-piercing scream.

There was a terrifying silence and then chaos reigned.

Ruby's mother swooped in and grabbed her daughter.

'What the bloody hell do you think you're doing?' shouted a father. Presumably Ruby's.

Jess's heart pounded in her chest as she fought to be heard above the clamour.

Accusations rained down on Mr Winters, who looked smaller and smaller as the words pummelled him.

'She slipped!' Jess said, not sure if anyone heard her or not. 'He was trying to help.'

'What do you have against children anyway?'

'No one's ever done you harm!'

'What a nasty man.'

'He was helping her!' Jess tried to shout louder, to no avail.

'Not a nice bone in his body.'

'We're definitely not going to his on the twenty-fourth. *If* he even bothers.'

'That piñata should've been Mr Winters not Scrooge.'

'HE WAS TRYING TO HELP HER!' Jess bellowed, unable to bear it, or Mr Winters' heartbreaking expression anymore.

All eyes turned to Jess.

An all-consuming fear shunted through her. The parents' expressions, all accusatory, looked so familiar and yet ... completely different. The same as the St Benedict's board of governors had looked when, for the first time in eight years, she'd met them as a defendant rather than a champion of the children they'd all committed to care for and protect.

'She's right. Jess is right,' Josh stepped up alongside Jess. He gave her and then Mr Winters a quick, supportive nod. His brow furrowing as he assured everyone, 'He was helping her. I saw it all clearly. Ruby, love?' Josh gave the now tear-streaked little girl a gentle smile. 'Did you slip when you were running up the pavement?'

Ruby looked at her mother and father for support. Both of her parents looked increasingly uncomfortable. Jess's whole body was shaking with nervous energy.

'You don't have to answer, sweetie,' her mum said.

Mr Winters began to head towards his house, hands stuffed in his coat pockets, shoulders looking frail, hunched against the cold. Jess felt torn. Should she run after Mr Winters or stand up to the crowd here who had got the incident so very wrong?

Her father, who clearly wanted some resolution, persisted, 'Ruby, love? Did the man hurt you or help you?'

Ruby threw a panicked look towards Mr Winters,

tears trickling down her cheeks then whispered, 'Helped,' before burying her face in her mother's shoulder.

A series of *Oh, well, he should've said*s surfaced amid a smattering of, *It's not like he's the friendliest of chaps, is it?* and *How were we to know he was helping?*

'Maybe we should apologise?' Jess suggested.

'To who?' One of the Gem'n'Emms asked.

'Mr Winters,' Josh and Jess said as one.

Drea threw in a 'There's no "I" in team' comment that didn't quite hit the mark, but Jess gave both her and Josh grateful smiles. It felt amazing having backup. She hoped Mr Winters saw it like that. She'd never felt more alone than when she'd faced the 'firing squad' at St Benny's. Amanda had sworn she would speak to the Head on her behalf but when pressed, had bowed out, saying as she hadn't been in the dining hall it might not do her any good, so she'd better not. Martin hadn't been any better. He'd pretended to care for about half a second and then flipped teams saying wouldn't she be better making nice with Crispin's parents seeing as they were insanely loaded? As if the whole reason she'd become a teacher was to hobnob with the haves of the world in the hopes her estate-agent boyfriend could bag a few sales. Jess ached to run after Mr Winters and tell him she knew exactly how he felt but her feet seemed to be cemented to the ground.

'Hey! Arnold, hang on a tick.' Josh jogged down to where Mr Winters was carefully making his way along the pavement, already halfway down the street.

They all watched as the two men shared a quiet word. At one point, Josh put his hand on Mr Winters' shoulder and, Jess was pleased to see, it wasn't shaken off. Their conversation seemed to reach an end when Arnold turned to look back up the street. His face bore the saddest expression of resignation Jess thought she'd ever seen. As if he had known all along that coming out would lead to something like this. *Point made*, he seemed to be saying. And, even more gutting, *You win.*

The evening dismantled fairly sharpish. After the Rob'n'Bobs failed to crack open the Grinch, Mrs Nishio took over. She gave the piñata a surprisingly solid thwack. '"What are men to rocks and mountains?"' she said with wink to her husband as the children fell upon the shiny wrapped chocolates like wolves. Then everyone disappeared into their houses along with reminders that it was Christmas Jenga the next day so be sure to bring pocket warmers because everyone would need fully functioning fingers.

Josh sent his children back to the house with Audrey and, as he watched them disappear up his drive, asked Jess and Drea who had stood together, watching silently as the festivities dissolved, if they fancied coming to his for Sunday lunch. 'Nothing posh,' Josh said apologetically. 'But the children and I make a mean batch of Yorkshire puddings.'

'I love Yorkshire puddings,' Jess patted her belly, suddenly hungrier than she had been in weeks.

Drea gave Jess a polite smile, then, to Josh a sincere, 'May I bring anything? Veg? Pudding?'

Jess squinted at her. Who stole Drea and replaced her with Little Miss Happy Homemaker?

Josh shook his head, no. 'We've got a routine. If it's cool, we'll stick with it, but . . .' his eyes glinted as his smile broadened. 'A nice bottle of that Picpoul you had the other night wouldn't go amiss. I never drink when it's just the kids and me, so...' His gaze drifted to Jess, whose cheeks instantly pinked.

'I'll bring some, too. Wine. For drinking.' She blithered a few more things before looking at her empty wrist and exclaiming, 'Oh, gosh! Is that the time! I think my parents are ringing me. Better get back.'

'Your parents in the Marshall Islands where it's six in the morning?' Drea asked, her lips twitching with amusement.

'Yes. Early risers. Always have been!'

Jess ran into her house and slumped against the door. She had about sixteen hours to learn how to be in Josh's presence and behave like a normal human. She squatted down and stared at herself in the as-yet-to-be-hung mirror. Her cheeks were flaming. It was going to be a long night.

18 December
20:42
To: WillWinters@TheMerryVictualler.co.uk
From: JessGreen2000@gmail.com
Subject: Bleurghhhhh

Hey Will –
Disaster. Your grandad came out tonight to one of the Christmas events which was amazing. And then he was helping this little girl who slipped, but to some of the parents it looked like he wasn't helping and there were some not very nice things bandied about which made your grandad run for the hills (well, his house, but you know what I mean).

Just thought you should know. It was really awful. It made me feel exactly the way I did when the board of governors said it was 'indecipherable' as to whether or not I had genuinely been trying to help Ethan or if I was trying to hurt Crispy, so I can't even imagine how it made your grandfather feel. Especially after what he went through with your gran.

Anyway. Sorry to dump this on you, just thought you should know. Tomorrow night's Christmas Jenga, whatever that is, at number 19, but I doubt Arnold will be making a showing.

I'll pop in on him, but if there's any way you could show up, maybe that would redress the balance??????

Best x J(ess)

19 December

19 December
03:07
To: JessGreen2000@gmail.com
From: WillWinters@TheMerryVictualler.co.uk
Subject: RE: Bleurghhhhh

Jessica –
Sorry. I missed something here. What exactly did my
grandfather go through with my grandmother?
    Late night. Sorry to be rushed. Christmas market in
Harrogate tomorrow, then the final push until Christmas Day.
Once all the invoices are in I can officially call the premises
of The Merry Victualler mine.

19 December
08:08
To: WillWinters@TheMerryVictualler.co.uk
From: JessGreen2000@gmail.com
Subject: Sorrysorrysorrysorrysorry

Hey Will –
Ummm ... I shouldn't have said that. If I had a sword I'd fall
on it right now. It really is his story to tell and as it's family

stuff and I don't know what your father's told you and, obviously, I haven't heard his side of the story which I'm guessing you have (??), I haven't said anything. Obviously. Until last night when I said something.

#NotEntirelySureWhatToDoNow

xJ

19 December
08:10
To: JessGreen2000@gmail.com
From: WillWinters@TheMerryVictualler.co.uk
Subject: RE: Sorrysorrysorrysorrysorry

You could start by telling me what he told you.

W

Apologies for any typos. Email written in haste on iPhone

19 December
08:17
To: WillWinters@TheMerryVictualler.co.uk
From: JessGreen2000@gmail.com
Subject: RE: RE: Sorrysorrysorrysorrysorry

Hey Will –
I guess it's ridiculous to try and extract a pinkie promise from you that you won't tell him that I told you, but... it is your family's history, so... here goes.

Thirty-five years ago when your father was away studying in Scotland, your grandmother had what she thought was a cold...

'Open up, Buttercup!'

Jess ran down the stairs, towel still whorled round her wet hair, and pulled open the door. 'Wow. You scrub up nice.'

Drea struck a pose. Jess whistled, then shivered, quickly ushering Drea in out of the mid-winter drizzle. She looked amazing. Her hair, outfit and make-up were immaculate. The overall effect was effortless beauty. A style Jess had achieved a solitary time when Martin had invited her to a swanky do hosted by a modelling agency who booked short-term lets from his company. She'd booked the longest appointment she could at a MAC store and then tried not to blink or smile for the next few hours. It had been hell.

Drea, who clearly did not suffer from Jess's problems with clumpy mascara, wayward eyeliner and streaky blusher, struck a new pose in the doorframe to Jess's lounge. 'Catalogue chic, or ... wistful yet aspirational perfume?'

'Both,' said Jess noting the almost imperceptible veneer of fragility cloaking Drea's need for feedback. 'You look like Angelina Jolie but healthier.'

Drea fuzzed her lips, but Jess could tell she was pleased. She scanned Jess's hastily pulled together ensemble. Chunky knit cotton jumper. Teal. Winter-green corduroy skirt with appliqué flowers. Thick woolly tights. Purple. Fly boots, soooo comfortable but not even close to being FMBs. Not that she wanted that to be what her outfit said when she and Drea showed up at Josh's. Did she? No. Maybe? With Drea looking all fabulous and Sunday-lunch glam, she felt more mousey school teacher than fun, thirty-something, singleton neighbour. Oh, God. Now she was having an identity crisis on top of it all.

'Why are you running so late?' Drea asked, crossing to the painted Christmas tree and scanning through the 'decorations'.

Jess climbed a stair or two, huffing out a dramatic sigh. 'Mr Winters.'

'What? You've been down to his?'

'No.'

Drea made a 'so why are you telling me this' face.

'I told Will about him.'

'Will the secret grandson?'

'The one and only.'

'I thought the secret grandson already knew about him.'

'He did – *does*. But he didn't know why Mr Winters hadn't spoken to his dad in thirty-five years.'

Drea went hawk-eyed. 'And you do?'

Jess touched her trembling hand to the towel round her head. 'Umm. Why don't you pour yourself a pre-lunch wine? It's in the fridge. I just need a couple minutes to dry my hair.'

'Oh no you don't, young lady.'

'Yes,' Jess took a pointed look at her watch, then flicked her thumb in the direction of Josh's. 'I really do.'

'No,' Drea morphed into Maleficent before her eyes. 'You really don't. You're going to sit down on the toilet and I'm going to do your hair for you while you tell Auntie Dré-Dré all about it. If something needs fixing before December the twenty-fourth on the off-chance my little boy shows up, I'm going to fix it. Or, more accurately, you are. Understand this...' Her green eyes flashed as she hit the first step of the stairs. 'Nothing is going to eff-up my son's Christmas. So come Christmas Eve? I want this street *blazing* with holiday cheer. Got it?'

Jess swallowed. She got it, but how was she going to achieve it?

Drea, it turned out, would be such an asset at Guantanamo or wherever it was spies extracted state secrets these days. Jess told her everything. From the suspected cold to the fight after the funeral to the thirty-five-year cold war, the family Robert had raised in Scotland, the grandson who, despite having never met him, seemed to think there might be some possibility of peace. Peace and support Mr Winters so desperately needed, especially after last night's debacle.

Though part of her felt awful for blabbing, another part was relieved that someone else knew Mr Winters wasn't being a grumpy old man just for the fun of it. He was experiencing genuine, bone-deep pain and, much like the way she'd felt over the past year, couldn't see a way out of it.

'Do you think Will might make more of an effort to get in touch now that he knows?' Jess asked, scalp tingling as Drea whorled a brush through her fringe one last time, stood back, and examined her handiwork with a frown, her gaze dipping to Jess's.

'Don't know. What sort of bloke do you think he is? This . . . Will.'

'Nice,' she said, feeling as though the word didn't quite cover it. It was hard to say without having met the man. On paper, and on email, he seemed really kind. Genuinely kind, in fact. He was obviously hard-working, had been through some tough times emotionally, but had come out the other side stronger and more aware of how his behaviour affected others and how he wanted to treat those around him in future. He wanted to develop a relationship with his grandfather, which suggested strong family bonds meant a lot to him. And, apart from this morning's exchange, there was something easy-going about him that made Jess feel extra-comfortable spilling her guts to him and, from all accounts, vice versa. The past few weeks had felt, in a weird way, as if they'd been on a long-haul flight together. Happily buckled up, side by side, instinctively knowing they shared one of those rare, instant connections that made it easy to tell one another their life stories ten thousand feet above the rest of the world.

'C'mon,' Drea said, clearly not expecting a long-winded answer. 'Get up. We're late.'

After a quick glance in the mirror and a tight, fierce thank you hug for getting her errant fringe to look even a fraction like Claudia Winkleman's, the pair of them collected their bottles of wine and, in Drea's case, a box of chocolates 'for the kiddos', and headed to Josh's.

Three hours later, Jess was riding quite the food-and-wine buzz. Or maybe – and she was only admitting this silently, cautiously and a little bit wishfully – maybe she was riding a 'feels good to be part of something bigger than herself' buzz.

Josh's house was bustling. Before they'd even entered, it hummed with happy noises, all cosy looking and inviting, with steamed-up windows and awash with amazing smells. Inside, stacks of school uniforms were draped on one end of the sofa, half of which had been dismantled into a fort where Eli had been teaching Audrey how to read. Zoe was wearing an oversized adult's t-shirt as a dress – her mum's, maybe? It must've been from her hen do – unless 'Before she says "I Do", let's have a Drink or Two' referred to squash. There were tumbles of children's books and stacks of paperwork Josh hastily tidied on top of the laptop he swooped off the dining table along with the iron. He put it, a basket overflowing with Lego, and an extremely impressive dressing-up box, made out of an actual steamer trunk with a sticker on it for Timbuctoo, by the stairs.

Josh had also, it turned out, totally lied about his cooking. He claimed their delicious meal was simply a case of reading the recipe, but the man clearly knew his way round a roast chicken. And the yorkies! Double yum. Josh was clearly loving 'grown-up' time, but had a great way of engaging his children in actual conversations rather than the list of instructions so many parents counted as 'active parenting'.

Drea had kept conversation flowing like a normal human. There was job talk (Josh was head of IT at the university where the Nishios taught); shared angst over Christmas shopping (painful for Eli but in Zoe's case anything with a unicorn or glitter usually worked); bills (never-ending, but things could be worse. They counted themselves lucky.) All this while Jess and the children spent the bulk of the meal, including the demolition of Drea's unbelievably delicious White Forest roulade, speculating about Santa, how busy he was, whether or not he liked houses with more or less decorations outside, whether having a very skinny chimney was a genuine problem come Christmas Eve, and also what Jess's plans were at the primary academy for making sure they got chocolate cake more often. With hundreds and thousands. Apparently this was a big discussion point among the five- to eight-year-olds. Zoe had also talked her through why their kitchen counters had an abundance of casserole dishes with Post-its on them. Apparently, even though Josh had thought he'd made it clear he was good with making dinner for the children after his wife had passed, many of the neighbours had built making 'just a little something for him and the children' into their routines. As such there was Monday cottage pie from the Nishios; Wednesday was usually some sort of veggie pasta bake or lasagne from one of the Gem'n'Emms and so on. Josh actually knew all of their names and surnames *and* the Rob'n'Bob's names. Completely impressive and yes, she'd asked for a cheat sheet because the first day of school was going to be totally embarrassing if she couldn't name one of them.

Having eaten her body weight in some of everything – roasties, chicken, honey-roasted carrots and three Yorkshire puds – and not strictly refusing each time Josh refilled her wine glass, unlike Drea who demurely slid her hand across the top of her glass (weird and totally unlike Drea), Jess was now paying the price for her gluttony. Propped up against the side of the sofa, she was on childcare duty after Drea airily announced, 'the adults would see to the cleaning up while Jess did her 'thing with the kiddies'.

'I think you should wear this,' Zoe announced, handing Jess a conical princess hat with a gorgeous swish of diaphanous fabric speckled with sparkly bits.

Eli was currently draped in a Darth Vader costume

with an Olaf head perched atop his own. His eyes, visible through Olaf's mouth, were glued on the television as the chaos of *Home Alone* played out for the gazillionth time across the UK, the rest of him moving as and when Zoe changed her mind about what she wanted him to wear. He was very amenable, Eli. She suspected Zoe would dress him up for their night, tomorrow, when they'd decided that the evening's entertainment would be a Best-Dressed Holiday Pet show. If no pets were available, it was agreed a stuffed animal could stand in, but not stuffed spiders, because stuffed spiders weren't Christmassy even if they had on red hats. (Zoe was a stickler for details.)

'What about Audrey? Do you want to show me what she's going to wear?' Jess tried not to slur. Or yawn. She was very sleepy and super comfy. Maybe she could ease on down to a casual horizontal position and have a teensy tiny . . . A large furry nose presented itself in front of her then gave her cheek a lick. 'Hello, Audrey.'

Zoe plopped herself down in Jess's lap and took the Bernese's face in her hands. 'She always looks good in red,' she said after a minute's consideration. Zoe clambered out of Jess's lap then lifted a few things out of the dress-up box, swiftly rejecting one thing after another until eventually settling upon a Wonder Woman headband, a Princess Leia arm cuff and a Red Riding Hood cloak. 'Okay. Sit there and put your arm around Audrey,' she instructed Jess.

Eli was rearranged so that he was lying like a sultan on the sofa above Jess. Zoe climbed back into Jess's lap and struck a thoughtful pose while Audrey opted to parade back and forth, clearly enamoured with her new get up.

'Daddy! Daddy! Bring your camera.'

When Josh came into the lounge, his face went through a kaleidoscope of expressions. Amused. Delighted. Happy. Sad.

The sadness hit Jess right in the solar plexus. Had his wife been a fan of dress-up and Jess an unwitting usurper of the role? Claire's photo was hanging in a couple of places round the house and, when Zoe had insisted on giving her a full tour, she'd seen specially framed photos next to each of the children's beds. She looked energetic, pretty and very much in love with her family. She exuded the special 'Top Mum' glow she and Amanda used to pray for when the next round of students and parents arrived at the school gate. The type of women who simply . . . were. No airs, no graces, just kindness. Usually a bit hassled, because what parent wasn't, but always laughing and giving a 'what can you do?' shrug when their child threw up on their shoes. Exactly the sort of woman Jess would've been proud to call a friend.

'Daddy, take a picture,' Zoe demanded. 'We'll leave it for Santa with his carrots.'

Drea appeared behind Josh, her own features going through an entirely different kaleidoscope of expressions. Surprise, yearning, and something that looked so much like hope Jess didn't quite know how to respond. Audrey plonked herself down across Jess's shins and Josh scooped his phone off the hall table and was telling them all to smile, but Jess couldn't keep her eyes off Drea. She looked as if big knots of longing and despair were tangling up in her chest and making it difficult for her to breathe. As if this were a moment of family life she'd always imagined having and never would. Jess made a silent note to play dress-up with Drea next time they hit the Picpoul. It wouldn't be quite the same, but...

'Everybody say cheese!' Josh instructed.

After a few more poses, Audrey started to paw off her mask, was wearing her cape like a bib and had somehow lost her arm cuff. Zoe tried to get Eli to change his costume, but he wouldn't because he wanted to see *Home Alone* Kevin receive his room service, which prompted him to ask his father if he could get room service for his breakfast in the morning.

'Right! I think we'd better get ourselves rugged up for Christmas Jenga, yeah? Get our winter gear on?' Drea clapped her hands and smiled, very clearly back to being Drea again.

Everyone obeyed her efficient instructions and in a matter of minutes the lounge was tidied up, they'd all put on weather-appropriate clothing, had bundled all of the To Be Returned casseroles into their arms and had even printed out Best-Dressed Pet Show Holiday Bonanza flyers, before bundling out of the door and heading next door. Drea, Jess decided, was the world's eighth natural wonder.

'Well that was a disaster,' Drea tugged off her coat and plopped it on the banister as Jess hadn't yet hung up the coat hooks she'd yet to buy. 'Who paints their Jenga set red and green then stacks the wet blocks on top of one another to dry?'

Jess shrugged. She didn't think it was worth being quite as annoyed about it as Drea was. It'd actually been kind of funny. Besides, the weather was so horrible it had probably been just as well that they'd couldn't play.

The neighbours who hadn't been able to jam themselves into the Cummings' garage had all worried aloud about head colds, in particular Martha who, even under cover, had sneezed and yawned quite a lot, explaining that if *someone* hadn't been playing their *godawful* so-called music *half the night* she might've got some proper sleep. Just a few minutes in, they had all headed home, hands stuffed with flyers and ideas being shared about how to best dress their pet for the next night's fashion parade. All, of course, except for Mr Winters, who hadn't come, and Kai and Rex, who had refused a flyer and had walked home silently, hand in hand. She suspected they might sit tomorrow night out.

'Wine,' Drea commanded as if number 19's failure to make their night a success had been a personal slight.

Jess flicked the kettle on for herself. She had entered that awful 'hangover while still awake' phase of the evening and thought hair-of-the-dogging it probably wasn't for the best. Keen to not let Drea's spirits sag too low this close to the month's big event, Jess poured her a glass of wine and said, 'I suppose you could look at it from another angle.'

'And what angle would that be, exactly?' snapped Drea, accepting the glass of wine then grandly swooping it out as she answered the question herself, 'Destroying Christmas in advance so that the real day seems better? Not the best of tactics.'

'No. I didn't meant that, it's ... maybe everyone could do with a day off.'

'What's that supposed to mean?' Drea shot daggers at her.

'Nothing. I just mean ... you know?'

'No, Miss Clever Clogs.' Drea pushed herself up to a haughty Queen of England pose. 'I'm afraid you're going to have to spell it out for me.'

'It's just a busy time of year and adding in this extra business—'

'Oh, sorry,' Drea fixed Jess with an entirely unapologetic stare. 'I didn't realise I was adding to everyone's stresses and strains. Next year I'll just keep myself to myself, shall I?' Her eyes were blazing with fury.

Jess sucked her lips into her mouth and ground her teeth down along them while she did a quick backwards count from ten. She didn't want to bicker and she certainly didn't want Drea to think everything she'd done for the living advent calendar was an irritation. It had been the total opposite. She forced her brain to regroup and turn her feedback into parent–teacher conference mode: focus on the positive, and find silver linings in the negatives.

'I think the advent calendar is one of the best things that's ever happened to me.'

Drea scoffed, took another gulp of wine then, eyebrows templing said, 'Really?'

'Yeah. Really. I can't think of any better way to have met all of my neighbours. I mean, look.' She pointed towards her hallway where her tree and all of its individually painted ornaments stood as testament to the fact she was well and truly part of the neighbourhood. 'I wouldn't have a tree if it wasn't for you.'

Drea made a vaguely mollified sound.

'Or known that boas were made of ostrich feathers. Or learned how to make wreaths or how to plant tulips.' As she spoke, Jess began to realise just how true it all was. The advent nights had well and truly made her feel part of something wonderful. Everyone may have started out being dubious, but nineteen days in, it was clear participation had gone far beyond token shows of being neighbourly. She was just about to say as much when Drea cut her off.

'Speaking of tulips, how's your work going with Mr Winters?'

Jess glanced at her phone. Still no email. The nervous thoughts she'd been keeping at bay – partly in thanks to the free-flowing wine but also due to having such a lovely, silly, family-based day – all flooded back into play.

'I think I may have ruined Mr Winters' life,' Jess moaned, conking her head on the breakfast bar.

'At least he's only got a few more years left to live,' Drea said. 'I ruined my son's life and he's got yonks yet to rub it in.'

'Awww . . . c'mon. It isn't that bad between you, is it?'

Drea's face screwed up tight, her thumbs pressing into her eye sockets as if to will something else to come to mind other than all the mistakes she'd made. 'No. No, doll, but it certainly could be better.' She traced her finger along the top of the half-empty wine glass. 'When you need to live on opposite sides of the world to keep the peace . . .'

'My parents are on the other side of the world,' Jess said, hoping that would help.

Drea raised her wine glass up in a toast. 'They would've happily brought you with them, and that, my dear, is the difference. I ran away from my boy. From the past he wanted me to confront. And I'm paying for it. Every. Single. Day.'

Jess dumped her tea down the sink and pulled out the fancy canister of hot chocolate her parents had tucked in among all of the art supplies. 'Should we have some of this, cuddle up on the sofa and talk it out?'

Drea blinked a few rapid, perfectly mascaraed blinks then said, 'Aww, doll face. That'd be lovely. And I'll plait your hair after, yeah?' Then she cackled like a hyena and necked the rest of her wine.

An hour deep into the second Bridget Jones and her third set of plaits, Jess made two pre-New Year's resolutions. One? Never to let Drea plait her hair again unless she needed a facelift. Two? Make Christmas as perfect for Drea as Drea was trying to make it for everyone else.

20 December

Jess was running on nervous energy. She'd refreshed her laptop about twenty times in a row, even taking the time to unplug and restart it to see if somehow her or Will's email had been caught between the wall socket and the computer. Then she did the same set of IT forensics for Spencer's email. She even did a burpee when she caught a glimpse of Drea running by on what she presumed was a detoxifying morning run, hoping it would add to the aura of good vibes she was trying to build around the next few days.

The laptop flickered back to life. Jess jabbed at the mail icon.

Nothing.

Why hadn't either of them written back?

Something. Anything! Even an angry email railing against meddling neighbours interfering where they shouldn't have. Would an angry email stop her? Maybe this was lesson she couldn't learn. Standing by and doing nothing simply wasn't in her genetic make-up.

Although, she'd done nothing when Josh had suggested she join him and the children on a visit to a nearby stately home that was putting on a Winter Wonderland. Even though it had been utterly lovely lounging around his house and playing with his children, she still wasn't entirely sure she wanted to be nudged in the direction Drea was obviously nudging her. Into Josh's arms.

It wasn't anything against Josh. Quite the opposite, in fact. He was completely lovely, as were his children, and, of course, there was the blushing-whenever-she-was-in-his-presence thing; but despite all that, or perhaps *because* of all that, she felt as though she really needed to stand on her own two feet for a while now that her parents weren't propping her up any longer. Or Amanda. Or Drea, for that matter. The cool big sister she'd never had. It was time for Jess to be like Adele. Maybe not so much the make-a-platinum-album-based-on-her-embittered-experiences-at-an-over-priced-elitist-prep-school/break-up/job-search Adele (Never mind, I'll fail . . . a childlike youuuuu . . . no more playground time or Oxbridge hopes for yooooooooooUUUU). No, it was more figuring out exactly who she was and who she wanted to be before she tried to mould herself into someone else's life.

A lightbulb in her head lit up. Maybe that was the problem. She'd been square-peg/round-holing it in London. Trying to jam herself into a lifestyle that wasn't her own. Like the time when Amanda had forced her to go shopping at Harvey Nichols. She'd insisted they try on clothes on the designer floor even though Jess would never in a million years be able to afford them and, more to the point, would feel uncomfortable and anxious in them. Terrified she'd jam the zipper or snag a row of thousand-pound sequins or any number of things she bet Amanda, or Drea, for that matter, wouldn't have thought about twice. Funny, actually. That Drea lived on this quiet little street in, well, not so much the middle of nowhere ... but she was a woman who had the means to live anywhere and yet she didn't. Was Drea after what most of the people on Christmas Street were aiming for when they'd happily slapped a SOLD banner across their own For Sale signs? A bit of normalcy? A quiet-ish life on a lovely street without too much fuss and bother? Neighbours who cared enough to build you into their casserole rota?

Her mobile rang.

She grabbed it and was nanoseconds away from pressing the answer icon when she saw who it was. Amanda.

She stared at the phone, frozen with indecision. She couldn't silence it because everyone under the age of fifty knew two rings and an abrupt stop meant you'd been dismissed. She couldn't answer it because, well, she was scared. And yet ... wasn't this part of standing on her own two feet? Facing her past so she could embark on her future, a bit battle-scarred, but stronger. More confident. Happier in her own skin?

The doorbell rang.

No follow-up command to open the door.

Not Drea, then.

She stuck her head out into the hallway, phone still ringing in her hand. There was one tall shadow and two smaller shadows. She grinned. She was literally being saved by the bell. She stuffed the phone in the kitchen drawer along with the unopened St Benny's envelope, then jogged over to open the door.

As expected, it was Josh, Zoe and Eli. As was also to be expected, she blushed when Josh flashed her that crooked smile of his. He had freckles that ran across his nose. Had she noticed that before? The freckles? They hinted at the boy he'd once been and spoke to the man he had become, despite the heartache he'd been through. A man who had borne the deepest of sorrows but found the strength to face his future with a smile. She definitely needed to take a page out of Josh's book.

'Here,' he said, handing her a small stack of post.

'Oh! Do you have a new job?'

'Yes,' he gave his chest a proud thump as the children giggled and pointed at the postman who was heading up the street. 'Postman Josh at your service.'

'Daddy, you'll have to change your name to Pat if you really want a job,' Zoe said as if he was the silliest daddy ever.

'Are they all called Pat?' Eli asked, making Jess love him a little bit more. He was the type of kid who would be able to draw an entire imaginary kingdom on the tip of an intergalactic iceberg but would struggle with choosing whether to spell *through* or *threw*. She couldn't wait to be part of his education. It'd be fun watching both of them grow. Which was both heartening and a little bit freaky.

'Jessica,' Josh said with unexpected gravity.

'Yes, Joshua?' She asked, slightly mimicking his tone, but not entirely sure if he was being play serious or actually serious.

'We need your help.'

She looked down at Zoe and Eli, who both nodded. Yes. It was true. Her help was required.

The whole keeping-her-blushes-under-control was blown to smithereens when Josh grabbed hold of Jess's hands between his mittened ones and went all puppy-dog-eyed on her. 'Please, Jessica Green,' he began as her breath caught in her throat. 'Please, will you do us the honour of being one of the judges of the Christmas Street Best-Dressed Pet Parade?'

Ah.

She sucked in a sharp breath. Most of the families on Christmas Street who owned a pet also had children who went to the academy. Did she want to be doling out red and blue ribbons, currying favour and disdain before her first day?

Her eyes snagged on a dark-green van slowly working its way down the street. The driver, a dark-haired chap, was looking away from her, the van slowing, presumably to read the numbers, then slipping from view as Josh repositioned himself into the centre of her eyeline.

She thought back to the lecture she'd just given herself about Josh and being a grown-up and standing on her own two feet. She would literally be grading these families' children in a few weeks' time. Surely she could handle a cute pets parade where, hopefully, everyone was a winner?

She gently extracted her hands from his and gave him her best imperious look. 'Yes. Yes I will,' she nodded and then made a wait-a-minute face.

'I sense a condition coming,' Josh said, his smile wavering as he threw a 'c'mon, help your ol' pops out here' look to his children. Good grief, the man was adorable.

'You have sensed correctly,' she parried, a little crackle of electricity zipping through her as their eyes met again.

'You can wear the princess hat again if you like,' Zoe said, her face a picture of solemnity.

'I'll let you into my fort,' offered Eli.

'Those are both very generous offers,' Jess thanked them, her eyes darting down to the end of the street towards a certain picket fence. 'I think one judge is not a great idea and was wondering...'

Josh pulled a face. 'Really?'

He'd clearly read her mind. 'I think it might be nice.'

'Or a nightmare. I mean, he's a nice-enough bloke and all, but... I'm not sure some of the other parents are in agreement.'

'Well, then,' Jess said with her best Mary Poppins voice. 'We'll just have to get them to see things our way.'

In all honesty, she couldn't see Mr Winters agreeing to be a judge, but if she'd ruined his chances of having a grandson, she was going to give him the next best thing: a stand-in granddaughter. And even though she didn't have tonnes of experience in this department she was pretty sure granddaughters backed up their grandfathers. Especially when the chips were down.

'So...' Jess said. 'Mr Winters as a judge? What do we think?'

'In our house we tend to do things by vote.' Josh said. 'Kids? What do we think? Do we ask Mr Winters to judge alongside Jess and Drea?'

'You've asked Drea?'

Josh squinted at her.

Oh, God. Had she just sounded jealous? He was looking at her funny. Yup. She'd sounded jealous. How embarrassing. Of course they'd ask Drea. Drea was great at everything and the living advent calendar was her idea and she tidied up before leaving people's houses, not made bigger messes by playing dress-up. And Jess's yes had come with a condition. She bet Drea's hadn't. She

288

would've said, 'Sure thing, Josh-a-roo,' then bounced off for another fortifying run. Jess saw Mr Winters' front door open. She saw an opportunity and took it.

'Looks like Christmas has come early for someone,' Jess said, a bit breathless from having hotfooted it down the street, losing her balance only a couple of times as she skidded on the morning frost pockets that seemed a staple on the pavement these days.

Mr Winters looked down at the box in his hands. It was about the size of a large meat pie, wrapped with old-fashioned butcher's paper and bedecked with a simple red and white striped ribbon. Did someone send him a pie? Jess remembered how Martha seemed to take a special interest in Mr Winters' welfare. Perhaps she'd taken a shine to him. There weren't any postmarks or anything.

'I didn't order anything.' He looked confused, as if this had never happened to him before. Receiving without first giving something.

'Is there a return address or a card?'

He handed her the package, almost as if he was frightened of it. Jess gave it a once-over. Nope. There was nothing. It had obviously been hand-delivered.

She thought back to the green van that had been on the street a bit earlier. She hadn't noticed it leaving, but . . . 'Did someone ring the bell and give this to you?'

'They rang the bell,' Mr Winters confirmed, 'but there was no one here when I got to the door. Too slow, I guess.'

Hmmm. Delivery people were insanely busy this time of year, but a sprig of hope bloomed in Jess's chest. She wondered . . . maybe . . .

Mr Winters gave a little shudder as a gust of wind hit the pair of them. The weather had definitely taken a turn for the worse these past couple of days.

'Shall we open it inside?'

Mr Winters looked at the package as if it could, very possibly, contain a bomb.

'I'll open it here,' she decided for the pair of them. When she unwrapped the package she beamed, her chest flooding with relief.

'Here,' she held out the box of handmade mince pies, each with a different design on top – a snowflake, tiny little bells, a star. 'These are from your grandson.'

Mr Winters wasn't one for big shows of emotion, but the news hit him as hard as if Jess had actually pushed him. She reached out to steady him and, again, taking matters into her own hands, announced she would be making them both a cup of tea and they would eat a mince pie together before she left him on his own to digest the news.

'Can you get drunk from a mince pie?' Jess giggled a few minutes later, mug of tea in one hand, pie in the other, icing sugar, no doubt, on her nose. 'This one definitely has rum in it.'

'This one's not, but it's got something else in it.' Mr Winters held it out for Jess to see.

'Cranberries,' she said. 'Looks good.'

''Tis.' Mr Winters eyed the pie and then gave it a nod as a stockman might a prize bull.

The moment caught Jess in the throat. This was a handmade mince pie from his grandson. The grandson he never knew he had and still had yet to meet.

It was completely delicious and, so easy to tell, made with love.

They were all gorgeous. There were about four dozen in total. Cranberry, rum, traditional, and one that was stuffed with blackcurrants and apple.

It was a shame Will — if indeed it had been Will in the van — hadn't stayed to see this moment himself, but perhaps Mr Winters had been slow in getting to the door and Will had an event to get back to. Or maybe, like his grandfather, he too was shy about meeting him, and doing it in little increments was his way of building up to the big moment.

Whichever, it meant that even though he knew the truth about what had happened between his father and grandfather, he wasn't holding him accountable for it. There was the distinct possibility he was holding Jess accountable for it because a) he knew her address and b) she'd been standing in the doorway when he'd driven by. But . . . c) Josh and the children had been there. Maybe he'd thought they were an item? Which really shouldn't have made a difference because it wasn't as if she and Will were an item, they were more . . . modern-day pen pals who'd hit a little bump in the communications road. And she was very likely almost a decade older than him. Maybe she'd send him a note. Let him know his mince pies were amazing and that Mr Winters had been deeply touched by the gesture.

After a few more minutes of companionable munching and chatting about the weather, and the icy roads, and general curiosity as to why Will thought Mr Winters might want four dozen mince pies, Jess eased the idea of being a judge for the Christmas Pet Show into conversation.

The old familiar bristling resurfaced. 'No. I'm afraid not, lass. Not something I'm up to.'

'I think it would be a really great thing to do, you know, in creating stronger community relations.'

They both made faces. Why was she sounding like a politician canvassing for a vote? Because, in a way, she was. 'Look,' she laid her cards on the table, 'if I write to Will and say you received the mince pies and thought they were excellent, would you pretend to be a judge for me?'

'Eh?'

'Just stand next to me. Nod. Point. Agree with everything Drea says because she's going to be the one calling the shots anyway, and in exchange, I'll send Will an email and let him know you thought his gesture was really kind.'

Mr Winters' nose twitched. Just a smidge. But enough to tell Jess if she gave him just enough breathing room he'd say . . .

'Yes.'

'This should totally be on YouTube,' Drea said, pointing at a teenager still trying to get his pet hamster to sit in the car Kev had given his father a couple of weeks back as he tugged it along by a red ribbon.

Jess laughed. It was hilarious. Even if it was ruddy freezing.

There were far more pets on Christmas Street than any of them had imagined. It was going to be impossible to pick an overall winner, which was why, in the end, when Mr Winters had said there was no chance he could pick a winner and suggested that they make up some sort of prize for everyone, they had decided to do exactly that.

Kai, who had surprised Jess by showing up, had quickly done up a dozen-odd bows; and Rex, who had spent the bulk of the evening cuddling the collected canines, had hot-glued little white circles with silver backing onto the centre of them, then had written the pet's names in a florid script. (Drea had insisted everyone register their pet and sign a disclaimer as, yet again, the gritting trucks had failed to arrive before sundown.)

Now, as it was prize-giving time, Drea, Jess and Mr Winters were all standing behind his picket fence as the participants, willing or otherwise, did a final parade round the arc in front of his house that served as a perfect 'show ground' for the parade. Everyone could see. Everyone who wanted to participate could. And Mr Winters had a bit of added security by being behind his picket fence so any slipping children would be their parents' responsibility. So far so good.

The prizes – handed out along with mince pies Mr Winters gruffly informed everyone were from his grandson – went down a storm and, unlike yesterday when a general crankiness had reigned, the neighbours all left with proper smiles on their faces. The hamster won Top Gear Pet (an inspired idea from Mr Winters). One of the Gem'n'Emms' cats won Best Mrs Claus. The Nishios' schnauzer (unseen by many before now) won Best Elf. And the list went on right up to Audrey, the evening's Red-Carpet Ready Christmas Canine. She was sporting a rather glamorous ensemble including Kai and Drea's boa – a moment filled with ooos and ahhhs and one solitary cry of dismay (Martha) as the boa trailed behind the

Bernese mountain dog like a street duster. Zoe – who was wearing her own version of a red-carpet outfit in the form of a little mermaid bodice, a Princess Anna cape and the Wonder Woman headband – did not stop smiling, and when Josh lifted her up on his shoulders kept shouting, 'Christmas Street is the best place in the world!'

Even Mr Winters managed a smile at this one, quickly hidden behind his thick tartan scarf.

Kai, clearly strained from spending an evening smiling at all of the pets and their owners, made a quiet signal to Rex and slipped away.

Her heart ached for him. It was a shame he didn't want a new dog as Rex so clearly did, but, as she was learning, everyone had their own journey through the fug of grief and it wasn't anyone's place to pass judgement.

She refocused on the happy crowd in front of Mr Winters' place, showing one another their ribbons and catching up on last-minute plans for the holidays.

'Gorgeous,' Jess grinned.

'Yes,' Drea whispered. 'He is.'

Jess quirked her head to the side. 'Are you taking about the hamster?'

Drea gave her a confused look then popped on her trademark smile, gave her cheek a lipsticky kiss then said, 'I'm offski, doll face. Conference call tomorrow.'

Jess watched her go, hoping against hope Spencer would appear on Drea's screen with a suitcase by his side and a promise to see his mother on Christmas Eve.

'Jessica?' Mr Winters pulled his coat a bit more snugly round him. 'You won't forget to ask your screen to send a message to Will, will you?'

Ask her screen? Oh!

"Course. I'll email him first thing.'

'Good,' Mr Winters gave the type of nod she imagined he'd given at work when someone had presented him with a job well done.

She gave him a little salute. 'I'll report back tomorrow.'

He nodded. 'You do that.'

'Okay.' She couldn't stop grinning. She loved that he had helped tonight. 'I'm going now.'

'Very good then.'

'Night.'

'Jess?'

'Yes?'

'Go home.'

'Okay.' A few steps beyond the picket fence she couldn't resist whirling round and using her Terminator voice, 'I'll be back.'

He was already climbing the steps towards an expectant Mr Perkins, but when he got to the top, Arnold waved and, as he shut the door, she could see that he, too, was smiling.

21 December

Jess woke with a sense of anticipation buzzing through her, which was strange, as her daily list of things to do (get up, make coffee, twiddle thumbs and contemplate future) had been roughly the same since she'd moved in. Bar, of course, the initial flurry of describing office supplies, the daily anticipation of the advent-calendar reveal and the late morning *coooeee!* through her post flap which had, sadly, been waning in frequency the closer to Christmas they were. She spooned coffee into the glass beaker wondering what her life would be like once she was teaching again. Better? More stressful? Humdrum?

As she poured her first cup of coffee, her laptop jangled with a Skype call.

'Hey, Mum! Hi, Dad.' She peered at them. Something was off. 'Are you... are you two all right?'

'Yes, sorry, darling. We're both a bit puffed is all.'

'Why?'

Her parents looked at one another to see who would explain.

'We've been learning to climb coconut trees,' her mother finally said holding up her hands, which were wrapped in white gauze bar the fingertips. 'The traditional way.'

'Why?'

'We wanted to help hang up the fairy lights. You know how they...' Her father made a swirling gesture which, surprisingly, made sense. Her father gave a happy little grin then began asking Jess about her day, the house and how settling in was going; and before long they were making promises to set their alarms so that they had calls on both Christmas Eve and Christmas morning. So they could open and eat their chocolate oranges together (her parents had put one of those in the art box as well) and then on Christmas morning 'exchange' proper gifts, even though Jess had insisted the deposit on the house counted as a proper gift for, like, the next thirty years.

After Jess had extracted a promise from them that they'd limit their holiday decor to trees no higher than six feet, the call ended. Jess opened up the mail app and, once again, was disappointed to see there was nothing from Will or Spencer. There was an email version of the St Benedict's Christmas card, which included a note explaining how they'd gone paper-free to contribute to the environment and had made a donation to Childline – which was so two-faced it made her want to throw up in her mouth. It was also suspicious, because she definitely hadn't received one last year. How had she hopped back onto their Christmas list?

Whatever. That was then and right now she needed to make good on her promise to Mr Winters.

21 December
11:32
To: WillWinters@TheMerryVictualler.co.uk
From: JessGreen2000@gmail.com
Subject: PIES!!!!!!

Dear Will,

It's Jess(ica) here.

I just wanted to let you know that your amazingly delicious (dare I say... scrumptious) mince pies were received at your grandfather's.

Lucky me, I happened to be passing by. Was that you in the green van? I don't know if you noticed, but I was standing in the doorway talking to another neighbour.

Erm... awkward pause... I am hoping your kind gesture was a way of letting Mr Winters know you know what's going on and still want to get in touch but that you're busy right now. I haven't told him I told you about, you know, everything, but the man's not daft. He knows we email one another because he is the one who suggested I 'ask my screen' aka – my laptop – to send you a note to tell you he liked the pies.

I know it's crazy time for you so I won't take too much of your time, but I thought you should know he shared some of the pies (definitely not all because, yes, they're good enough to hoard) with the street when he served as a judge on the Christmas Street Pet Parade last night. Tonight's at number 21 (obvs). It's Martha Snodgrass who is, give or take a decade, somewhere around your grandfather's age. I have no idea what she's going to do. Lecture us on seasonal noise pollution or give us all a boa-wearing lesson (slightly long story). Watch. This. Space.

I hope you don't hate these updates. I just... you seem so nice and your grandfather is obviously so sad and it's been great seeing him start to peek out of his tortoise shell a little bit and I bet he would do it even more if/when you actually come by and meet him, so... I'll leave it there?

All the best – Jess(ica) x

'Get your glad rags on, girl!'

Drea opened the bottle of champagne she was holding with a sword. An actual sword.

'What on earth are you doing?'

Drea sucked a bit of the foam from her hand then beamed as she expertly slid the sword into a sheath hanging from her hip. 'Celebrating.'

'Oh?'

'Spencer.' Drea said, her grin pretty much hitting ear to ear. 'He's coming. Christmas Eve, the little devil.'

'Oh, Drea!' Jess did a happy dance that was also a little bit for herself. 'I'm absolutely thrilled for you. That's brilliant news.'

'It is, isn't it,' Drea beamed, then frowned. 'Why aren't you running off to fetch champagne glasses, doll? The evening is ripe for excitement.'

Martha Snodgrass wasn't as full of *joie de vivre* as Drea was by the time the bulk of the neighbourhood had gathered outside her house, the children off in a group competing to blow the best cold breath 'smoke' ring. She looked nervous, a bit snappy about people sticking to the paved areas and away from her tied-up rose bushes but, Jess was pleased to see, she was looking fabulous and warm in her fur coat and hat.

'This is going to be short and sweet,' announced Martha in her usual straightforward way. 'Some of us aren't so great with all of this standing around we've been required to do of an evening.' She shot Drea a little 'that means you' glare then rang her actual, genuine bell on the side of the small porch.

Tyler appeared from behind her, like a matador

brandishing his cape, only it was a guitar and, a bit more clunkily, a speaker. He shoved a big wedge of hair back from his pale face, sat on the speaker after unpocketing a microphone he'd handed to Martha, who said 'Hello' into it then instantly apologised to everyone for the volume. He gave the guitar a rather alarming torrent of distorted cranks and squeals. Jess wasn't entirely sure if they were meant to like it; and from the looks on everyone else's faces, nor were they. Several of the smaller children clamped their little mittened hands to their ears.

'Tyler,' Martha snapped, then, more genteelly into the microphone, 'Now, if you'll all just quiet down, we can get this over and done with.'

'Hear, hear. I've got a shepherd's pie in the oven, so let's get this moving.'

'Do you think it's going to snow? It's cold enough—'

'It's cold enough for you to stop talking.'

'Shhhhhh!!!!'

'Ladies and gentleman, I'd like to welcome you to Marti Morgan and Tyler Butterfield's Christmas Street Holiday Blues Club.'

Everyone perked up and, more to the point, buttoned up.

The voice that had come out of the microphone wasn't at all old ladyish. It was rich and confident and extra comfortable with being centre-stage – every eye in the house was on her. Martha, or rather Marti, shot Tyler one of her imperious looks complete with arched eyebrow, and then she winked. 'That's better,' she said to her spellbound audience. 'I always preferred to hear a pin drop before the music began.'

Jess gave Drea an open-jawed look, then Mr Winters,

but neither of them were looking at her. They were staring at Martha and her fur coat and the boa she was tangling her daringly coloured nails through. Her entire aura exuded glamour. Showbiz Martha, it turned out, was quite the looker when she put a mind to it.

After Tyler gave the guitar an initial, more familiar strum, and one of the Gem'n'Emms began handing round little tealights in jam jars, Jess felt everyone's shoulders begin to relax. Tyler made an impish face, held his hand above the guitar fretboard, twirled a pick through his other fingers, then began to play an absolutely beautiful, slow and luxurious version of 'Silent Night'.

Collectively the group leant in and then ... oh, and then ... Martha began to sing.

Marti Morgan was a legend. Her voice danced and played along with Tyler's sometimes cheeky, sometimes haunting spin on the classic carol. She soared up and down the octaves as easily as a child swept down a slide then ran back up again for more. Joyously. With complete and utter commitment.

And then it began to snow.

The moment could not have been more magical. The night wasn't at all like it had been for poor homeless Mary and Joseph seeking, then ultimately, finding shelter in a manger in Bethlehem and arriving just in the nick of time to give birth to Jesus, but this felt a similar type of magic. A rare moment of beauty that bound everyone together for a singular, never to be repeated, moment in time.

And then, just like that, as the last notes of both Martha's voice and the guitar hung in the air then faded into the darkness, it was over.

'Right you lot, mind the roses as you go,' Martha instructed, her gimlet eyes pinned to the small crowd that had managed to jam themselves onto her flagstone path.

Taylor started playing 'Let It Snow' as everyone applauded Martha, expressed amazement that they had such a star in their midst, and, much more congenially than when they had arrived, wished one another a good evening and exchanged promises to see one another the next night even though, yes, they were all busy and up to their eyeballs with things to do. It was special, they all agreed, very special to live on a street where they could come together and share a bit of themselves and, yes, surprise one another.

Mr Winters made a quick farewell to Jess, but did, she was pleased to see, make sure he caught Martha's eye to send her a wave of thanks and a finger touched to his nose as if confirming that she was every bit as good as the album she'd given him. Drea gave Jess a hug and sighed and kept saying, 'Isn't life wonderful?' As if her news about her son's impending visit had actually changed the hue of the world from grey to glistening. It probably had. What a difference a phone call could make.

Which did make Jess wonder... was it time to call Amanda?

Tonight proved that things weren't always as they seemed. Martha wasn't a cranky old woman who hated noise pollution; Mr Winters wasn't a grumpy serial killer. Nor was anyone else many of the other things people purported them to be excepting, perhaps, the hippies, who genuinely did leave clouds of patchouli and sage in their wake.

All of which could mean that Amanda was genuinely calling to say hello.

So why the hell not. She'd ring her. She felt confident enough about where she was to tell Amanda about her new life and her new future.

Moving to Christmas Street was probably the best decision she'd made since she'd left St Benedict's. She grinned, watching as hugs were exchanged. Reminders to put out the paper bins and not the bottle bins were called out. A promise to get a long-awaited bit of Tupperware back to its rightful owner was made. Drea was extracting time and any 'incidentals' from the couple at number 22. Ordinary exchanges that somehow, amid the light snowfall and the lingering beauty of Martha and Tyler's song, seemed extraordinary.

Jess looked down at the tea light flickering away in the small jam jar she'd been given. People were setting them in a little row at the edge of Martha's porch, so she did the same. A tiny bit of limelight for the star in their midst as everyone made their way back to their own lives. Their secrets, hopes and dreams feeling just a bit warmer, a bit happier and, with any luck, a bit more peaceful.

Jess pulled the phone back from her ear and stared at it.

That was weird. The ringtone wasn't like a normal one. It had the click and whirr of a foreign—

'Hello? Jess?' Amanda sounded tinny, a little bit sleepy, and horrified. Someone yawned. A familiar male voice could be heard in the background asking who was on the phone. Amanda shushed him, making the mistake of using Martin's name as she did.

Martin was with Amanda.

Martin was supposed to be in the Maldives.

Jess felt a chill run through her.

Martin and Amanda were on her holiday in the Maldives.

'Hey! Jess. So good to hear from you, babes. All right?'

Jess's stomach churned and for some weird reason she felt as if her nostrils were being stuffed with the scent of suntan oil and sour cocktails.

She was tempted to hang up. A far more satisfying thing to do if she'd had Mr Winter's old-fashioned handset that you could actually bash down onto the receiver. But... something else compelled her to stay on the line.

Perhaps it was the stick-to-it-iveness her teachers had remarked on in her own school reports. An inability to leave jobs half-finished, no matter how many others would have walked away.

She thought back to all of the times she and Amanda had drunkenly made up school reports for one another. Amanda had actually spat out her wine when, after a particularly voracious week of hitting the Tinder scene, Jess had come out with, *Amanda shows great potential for tactical awareness and possesses an excellent ability to play well with others.*

'Jess?' Amanda prompted.

'Sorry, still here,' Jess said, keeping her voice as steady as she could. 'Umm... how're the Maldives?'

'Oh, Jess.' Amanda's voice sounded scratchy. 'I tried getting in touch before to tell you everything.'

Jess nodded, forgetting it probably would've been more useful to respond verbally.

Jessica tends to withdraw in times of stress when reaching out might prove more beneficial.

It was true. Amanda had tried to get in touch. Several times. Would knowing in advance have made it better? Easier? Finding out that her best friend from London, her supposed comrade in arms, was on her dream holiday with her ex-boyfriend and, from the looks of it, moving into the flat Martin swore he would never settle for? She wondered what types of throw cushions they would bicker over. Whether or not Martin would agree to a casually draped throw on one end of the sofa. Jess had regularly pleaded for one, making the case that watching *Game of Thrones* without a blanket to hand was just about impossible. Seeing as they were on holiday in the tropics together after what could have only been a few months – weeks? – together, time in which they'd fallen in love and bought a flat, perhaps they were in complete accordance with their home-decor decisions. Amanda, after all, lived as aspirationally as Martin did. In fact, the more the situation filtered into place, the more it made sense. Which, of course, made her feel even worse.

'Are you staying in the place with the stilts or the place with the private beaches?' Jess finally asked.

'Stilts,' Amanda apologetically replied. 'Jess, listen there's something else—'

'No. No, no.' Jess cut in. 'This is enough for now.'

'Yeah, okay.' Amanda's voice was shaky. 'I suppose it is a lot. Nothing happened while you two were together. I swear it. In fact . . . it's only been since November. Black Friday, actually.'

'Ha!' Jess barked. 'Good one.'

'No, I'm serious.'

'Oh.'

'I mean, I've seen him over the past year, obviously, but not in that way.'

Jess made a noise. Fair enough. Somewhere in the part of her that wasn't hurting right now, she knew that neither Martin nor Amanda were skulk-around-behind-your-back types of people. 'And the flat?' She asked, now entirely confident that everything she'd guessed about Martin's news was tied to Amanda's.

'It's in a new development,' Amanda couldn't keep the edge of pride and excitement from her voice. She started gabbling on about how she'd run into Martin in the Black Friday sales and asked him if he would come look at a flat she was eyeballing for the future and he did and they went and had a drink after and one thing led to another and the next thing she knew they were signing a mortgage on a one-bedroomed super-modern take on 'stadium life' with guaranteed box seats for football matches (a dream come true for Martin) and only a three-minute walk to the train station (a requirement for Amanda who, if forced to ride on public transport, refused to walk any sort of length of time to get on it). It wouldn't be ready until the spring, but there were rooftop gardens and leases already being taken out by Waitrose and Lululemon and some juice bar Jess had never heard of, but it sounded trendy and expensive and straight up Amanda's street.

Jess gave a dry, peculiar-sounding laugh. 'Floor-to-ceiling windows?'

'Yup. Underfloor heating, wet room. The kitchen even has boiling hot water on—' Amanda stopped herself. 'Do you really want to hear any of this? I mean, it's a bit weird, innit?'

Despite working at the poshest of posh schools, Amanda had never bothered smoothing the edges of her vernacular. It was what had drawn Jess to her in the first place. The refusal to erase where she'd come from despite her raw, hungry ache to be part of a different scene. Or, it suddenly occurred to Jess, maybe Amanda simply liked being trendy. Perhaps it was as simple as that. There were no airs or graces about her. No obvious social climbing. So she liked a good thread count, posh restaurants and a lavishing of swish holidays. It didn't make her a bad person. And it was hardly a reason to hate someone. Then again, there was the fact she was enjoying all of these things with Jess's ex-boyfriend.

'Jess. Say something. Please.'

Nope.

She wasn't there on the wishing-them-both-well front.

'I've got to go.'

'Jess, no. We should talk.'

'No,' Jess countered. 'We shouldn't.' And then she hung up the phone and stuffed it under the sofa cushion. Out of sight, out of mind.

Two hours later, Jess wasn't entirely sure her usual cure-all of comfort telly and a pint of chocolate chip cookie dough ice cream had worked. Maybe watching the 'ordinary girl becomes a princess at Christmas' film hadn't been the best of choices. That and now her stomach was over-full so she felt like a big bloated self-pitying blob of unresolved issues, just as she had when she and Martin had called it quits, St Benny's had asked her to 'quietly step away from the conflict', and she had burrowed under her unicorn duvet for weeks on end.

Jessica tends to withdraw in times of stress when...

This was ridiculous. She couldn't let the fact that Amanda was getting sunburnt and moving in with her ex-boyfriend destroy her.

Did it sting?

Definitely.

Did it make her feel as if the rest of the world had been progressing while she'd been grasping at minuscule finger holds, digging herself out of a pit of woe she'd all but swan-dived into when things had gone so horribly wrong?

Yes.

But...

Was the path Amanda and Martin were on the same one she wanted to be on?

Teaching horrid children like Crispin Anand-Haight, boys who punched teachers and scratched their own faces to get someone who actually needed the income and loved their job fired just because they could? Dating someone who clearly wanted different things from life?

Had she, in fact, chosen the life she genuinely wanted, right here on Christmas Street?

Her eyes landed on the painted Christmas tree, the ornaments evidence of how far she had come since those dark days last year.

When she unearthed her phone from under the sofa cushion she saw there were no less than twenty-seven missed calls from Amanda.

It was late. And, a quick Google search showed, very early morning in the Maldives. The last call had been ten minutes ago.

'Hey,' Jess said.

'I'm so, so, so, so, sorry,' Amanda snuffled tearfully. She sounded genuinely upset. 'Jess, honestly, I never would have, in a million years—'

'I know.' Jess said. 'It sounds as if you're happy.'

There was a pause and a rustle while Amanda put her hand over the phone and whispered *It's all right, babes, I'm just going out to the deck.* When she came back on the line Jess could hear waves. 'I am happy. *We're* happy. The only thing we wanted so that we could be – you know – perfectly happy, was to make sure it was all right with you.'

Jess winced. They wanted her blessing?

She thought of the life she'd lived in London and how, despite the eight years she'd lived there, she'd never entirely found her niche. Maybe a different school, a different flat, and a different boyfriend might've rendered a more pleasing tableau, but something about living in London inherently made striving for better, bigger, and more of everything part of the whole experience. Bigger, better and more weren't really who she was. It was, however, exactly who Amanda and Martin were. 'I am happy for you. For you both.'

'Aww, babes,' Amanda hiccoughed-cried. 'Thank you. Look. I really want to talk about this more, but hashtag can't afford the phone bill now that I've got a mortgage.'

'No problem,' Jess said through a weird laugh-sob of her own. One she hadn't realised had been building in her chest. It wasn't like they needed to make a date to, in Drea's words, plait one another's hair. No. There really wasn't anything else to say apart from have fun, wear factor 50 and, if you swim with turtles please don't tell me about it, because . . . well . . .

It had been her dream.

'Happy Christmas, Amanda.'

'Happy Christmas to you, Jess. I hope you get everything you want up there, in your new life.'

'Yeah,' she whispered. 'Me, too.'

When she pressed the red hang-up icon it felt as if a thread had been snipped between her old life and the new one. It felt strangely freeing. That part of her life, she realised, was done and dusted.

When she climbed the stairs and flopped down onto the still-unmade bed, she tried not to let the blues swarm into the newly created space in her heart. There were plenty of new, happy things to put there. Whether or not her email had played a role in it, Drea was getting her dream Christmas. Mr Winters looked on course to receive the best Christmas present ever, a grandson. She had a ready meal for one to buy, yet another invitation to join Martha for a drop of sherry during the Queen's speech and, if Will's promises were anything to go by, some cooking lessons to look forward to. And school. She could actually drum up some genuine excitement about that now. Boughton Primary Academy wasn't a stopgap. Or a Band-Aid to put over the wound leaving St Benedict's had created. It was a new beginning. Just like living here was.

Yes, she thought, pulling her duvet up and around her shoulders. Her life here *was* the life she wanted. Now all she had to do was make sure everything stayed on track until Christmas Eve when, hopefully, everyone's holiday dreams would come true. She would have to wait a bit longer for the same thing to happen to her, but something told her, as sleep began to tease away any tension, that she wouldn't have to wait long. She was in the right place, at the right time, with hope in her heart. And you couldn't ask for much more than that. Apart from someone to bring you a hot-water bottle.

22 December

22 December
02:27
To: JessGreen2000@gmail.com
From: Spencer.Zamboni@BaldwinHaveyWilkinson.com
Subject: Drea Zamboni UK Visit

Dear Jessica,
Thank you for your email which I have only just found in my junk folder. As you can appreciate, this is a family matter which I would prefer not to go into my work email. It was a kind gesture to reach out, but if you could leave it with me, I'd be grateful.

Regards,
Spencer Zamboni
Attorney-at-Law
Baldwin, Havey & Wilkinson

22 December
04:59
To: JessGreen2000@gmail.com
From: WillWinters@TheMerryVictualler.co.uk
Subject: RE: PIES!!!!

Hey Jess(ica) –
Sorry for short note. Insanely busy and yes, that was me
in the van. Didn't have time to stop and, yeah, I'm going to
admit, I'm a bit nervous to meet you. Almost as much as I
am to meet Arnold (Grandad) which is probably why, when
he didn't answer the door straight away, I scarpered. The
act of a grown man? Not really.

The act of a grandson whose heart practically broke in
two when he found out why his father hadn't spoken to his
grandfather in thirty-five years? Pretty much. Your email put
a lot of things into perspective and I feel I ought to talk to
my own father before I meet Arnold in real life. My heart
aches for the man. Seriously. It's the sort of cruel blow that
could knock anyone off their stride, let alone cast a shadow
over, well, everything.

Your email was quite the information overload and I think
I might need more time to unravel things now that, well,
now that there are actual facts and actual pain and genuine
reasons for what I had decided was a silly disagreement
between father and son.

You see, the truth is ... I live down here in England
because of a similarly 'silly' disagreement. My dad and I
still talk and all, but it's not easy and most of what we tell
one another is filtered through my mother. Which, of course,
can't be easy for her. The truth is, I wasn't ever meant to be
in catering. I studied engineering and after I graduated, set

up an engineering business with my brother and my dad. Winters & Sons. It was my dad's dream. It makes even more sense now knowing how badly things had gone between him and his own dad. So, like any good son, I tried to make my dad's dream come true, in between staying up way too late figuring out how to make a tuile that wouldn't crack, a vol-au-vent that didn't scream 1970s, and the perfect deconstructed omelette. (Joke. That was definitely a joke.) I wasn't great at being an engineer. It was never my jam. My brother hated the business too, but never had the heart to say anything. He loved engineering, but had always wanted to work on those mega-high-rises out in the Middle East and Asia. The type Tom Cruise does stunts on. But we knew it was my dad's dream that we all work together, so we ploughed on. He ended up being constantly frustrated by me when the business didn't flourish. He kept saying families who worked together, stuck together. That we could travel the world together if I got properly stuck in, but the furthest we got was Glasgow. He kept heaping more and more pressure on me to take on bigger and bigger pitches (I was the pitch man), until, eventually, one day, when I knew my kid brother couldn't take it anymore, I was giving a make-or-break pitch to BP – Dad's former employer – and cocked the whole thing up. On purpose. Winters & Sons quickly went down the drain, my brother promptly took a job in Seoul and Dad pretty much had a breakdown, though his doctors are calling it a depressive episode. That's actually why he's out on a remote Scottish island filling up stone dykes and counting sheep. It's good for him. He's always worked hard and my mother often said she never saw enough of him, so in the end, my act of sabotage ended up strengthening their marriage. It sent me running south to try and prove my self-worth by setting up The (not so) Merry Victualler. Doing so, as you know, culminated in me losing everything to my girlfriend. I mean, I gave it willingly, but the feverish working my socks off to pay for the catering/deli space is actually to pay for the flat above it so that I have somewhere to live. NB: Illegal camping in one's office isn't strongly recommended.

As you can see, there's a lot to untangle from all of this new information and right now I've got to make about four hundred mini chocolate-and-coconut puds in the shape of snowmen, so...

I'm really chuffed you liked the mince pies and though I know I'm being vague about our meeting up I want to thank you. Seriously. I literally clutched my heart when I read that Grandad shared them round the street. That's a special memory. One I hope happens again and that, with any luck, I'll get to see first hand.

Best xW

22 December
02:27
To: Spencer.Zamboni@BaldwinHaveyWilkinson.com
From: JessGreen2000@gmail.com
Subject: RE: Drea Zamboni UK Visit

Dear Spencer –
I am so, so sorry. Shit. I can't send this can I? Because then I'd be sending yet more personal stuff to your work email and you literally asked me not to do that. Fuck. Your mum really, really, wants you to come. You told her you'd come. I hope that's true. Please come.

Yours sincerely

Delete delete delete

22 December
07:07
To: WillWinters@TheMerryVictualler.co.uk
From: JessGreen2000@gmail.com
Subject: RE: RE: PIES!!!!!!

Dear Will,
Jess(ica) here!!!
    Sugar crumb fairies. You're not the only one reeling from new information. Gosh. I'm so sorry you have had such an awfulmiserablerotten time. It's like we're kindred spirits in the misery

Delete delete delete

Hey Will
Jessica here. (Obviously) *big hugs!!!!*

Delete delete delete

Dear Will,
Even though this may seem a bit *You've Got Mail*, I think I'm falling for you.

Delete delete delete

Computer will power down in 3 . . . . 2 . . . . 1 . . . .

'What if you kept it simple? Maybe . . . ordered a few dozen mince pies from The Merry Victualler—'

Mr Winters' gaze sharpened.

Jess hadn't been quite as subtle as she'd planned. The combination of snipping a big chunk of her old life adrift, absorbing the contents of Will's email, then completely and utterly failing to offer any sort of cognisant response meant she was in a bit of a tizz. (Falling for him? What was that about?) So she'd bundled up her hot mess of mixed emotions and poured it into her mission to make Christmas Eve magic at Mr Winters'.

Mr Winters, however, was not playing ball.

'Okay ... so maybe not mince pies, then. How about ...' Jess tapped her pencil, complete with felted Christmas tree covered in jingle bells, against her notebook. 'How about ...'

'How about you give up the ghost, duck?' he said, not unkindly. 'I know how folk are and how high expectations will be, what with the snow machines and wreath-making and Broadway concerts.'

Jess smiled. That was sweet that he thought of Martha as a Broadway star.

'But the truth is,' he continued, 'I don't want people traipsing about the place expecting hospitality I don't feel comfortable giving.'

Ah.

'I already have a reputation as a Scrooge, so I think, for now, it might be best if I live up to their expectation.'

He tacked on a forlorn *bah humbug* that was so fragile-sounding she felt as though she'd been pierced through the heart.

He couldn't give up now! Just last night he'd been upbeat (for him anyway) and tapping a finger to the side of his nose and, dare she say it, walking with an octo-genarian lilt to his gait.

'You're not a bah humbugger!' Jess protested, point-ing at the cup of hot chocolate he'd made her. 'Ebenezer Scrooge would not go to the shops to buy something he doesn't like so that he can make it for a guest who he knows does.' She nodded at his own, untouched mug as proof of his generosity of spirit.

'I don't—' He began, then stared at his hot chocolate mug for a bit before looking up at her with those lovely, kind blue eyes of his and saying, 'I'm out of practice is what I am.'

'I'll help you,' Jess said in as measured a tone as she was capable of. Pouncing on the possibility that he might like to practise needed to be treated with caution. They did, after all, only have seventy-odd hours to figure out how to defy the entire neighbourhood's expectations. 'I mean, if people do think those mean things, which they shouldn't, it means the bar's pretty low, right? So . . . I don't think we have to do, like, a fireworks display or anything.'

He shook his head, clearly uninterested in exploring his options.

'Mr Winters . . . Arnold. Is there something that hap-pened between last night and today that's made you change your mind?'

'I'd never made up my mind in the first place, young lady,' he intoned.

Okay. Fair enough, but . . .

A shot of fear lanced through her. Maybe, as Will's email to her had been written in the early hours of the morning, he'd dropped a note by to say reaching out was probably a bad idea and that he'd made a mistake.

She glanced round the warm, cosy kitchen. Nothing. She hadn't recalled seeing anything in the entry hall, but it wasn't exactly like one put out an 'I don't want to see you any more' card in pride of place, was it?

She forced herself to can the fear. The Will she absolutely, definitely, wasn't falling for wouldn't do something that harsh. Even if he was stinging from the cruel hand of history repeating itself. No. Will struck her as someone who, when hurting, needed a bit of time and space, but after that? He wanted resolution to the conflict with his own father, and a relationship with the grandfather he'd never known. Shame he hadn't reached out months ago. This house was so roomy, there had to be loads of spare rooms upstairs, unless Mr Winters changed rooms every night. Her heart cinched tight. It must be lonely, living in this big house all on his own, which did beg the question . . . why had he never married again? Or, at the very least, begun a friendship with someone?

She thought back through the previous night's events trying to divine something, anything, that might have made him retreat back into his shell. It hadn't been so awful that he was shutting her out of his life, so it must be something . . .

She replayed the moment when he'd waved to Martha and tapped his finger to the side of his nose.

Had that . . . had he . . . had Arnold been *flirting*? Maybe that was it. He'd accidentally flirted then felt off-footed by it so, like any out-of-practice widower, retreated to the turf he knew best? His own.

'What if . . .' Jess tapped her chin trying to look as if her sole interest in the Christmas Eve event was to keep the neighbourhood holiday spirit humming along rather than doubling it up as a match-making evening. 'What if you had a carols night?'

Mr Winters frowned. 'I don't sing.'

'No, but Martha does and Tyler does and, apparently the children have all been practising for a carol service at church, so, maybe they could have a dry run at yours? Or... an encore, depending upon what time you want to host it?'

'I told you, I don't want to host anything.'

'What are you afraid will happen if you do?'

The question caught him off guard. Jess, too, to be fair. Was she able to pinpoint exactly what it was that terrified her most?

Right now it was screwing up Christmas. Something that seemed pretty guaranteed to happen, judging by this morning's emails and the lack of progress she and Mr Winters were making.

'Ach.' He waved his big old hand between the pair of them. 'Folk don't want to come to mine. You know they don't, Jessica. They want to celebrate with their families and friends. People they care about. I won't be held responsible for ruining everyone's Christmas Eve by pretending I know the first thing about showing someone a good time.'

And there it was. His biggest fear. Being unlovable. This in the ever-growing wake of grief and guilt that had trailed him since his wife had died and son had left never to return. Jess's throat went all scratchy. She excused herself to the cloakroom so she could swallow back the tears that were itching to fall. Part of her wanted to ring Will and demand that he come over and tell his grandfather just how excited he was to meet him and how deeply

Robert felt the loss of not having Arnold in his life. How he, from the sounds of it, had bullied his own sons into a mandatory relationship so that they would never suffer the years-long separation he and Arnold had endured. The other part of her, the part that was still trying to figure out how to interpret Spencer Zamboni's email, told her to cool her jets.

When she returned to the kitchen she came armed with an idea. 'I know this sounds a bit left-field and I need to check with Kai and Rex that they have some left in stock, but I was thinking as the weather's been so horrible and, as you say, everyone usually has something they regularly do on Christmas Eve, how about you do something to make their day "merry and bright".'

Mr Winters shot her a hooded look with a hint of *Go on. I'm listening*.

'Kai and Rex had these great little sparklers down at their shop in the shape of Christmas Trees. What if your 'event' was handing one out to everyone to use in their gardens as a signal to Santa before they went to bed?'

'And . . . ?' Mr Winters asked.

'And that's it.' Jess said. 'Like you said, why put more pressure on people than they're already feeling?'

He took a distracted sip of his hot chocolate and then stared at the mug as if surprised at what he'd just swallowed.

'You make a mean cup of chocolate.' Jess said, meaning it.

'It's my wife's recipe,' Arnold said. 'Her technique, anyway. She never threw the powder in on top of the milk like most people do. Always did a bit in a mug to make up a paste before the milk. Said the extra TLC was what made it taste so good. It's science, of course, what makes it taste so good. Chemistry, but...' He stopped and looked out the window with such a hopeful look in his eye it was almost as if he was expecting to see her there. His Anne. 'I'll take your idea on board, lass. If you'll have a word with the two lads about these sparkler things, I'd be grateful.'

'Consider it done,' Jess beamed, barely able to sit still long enough to finish her hot chocolate before bounding down the street, into her car and down to Berry's Blooms before they shut for the day.

Hours later, in the company of an utterly glowing Drea, Jess was impatiently waiting for the festivities at number 22 to wrap up. She glanced at her watch. They'd already done four rounds. One more to go, then a winner would be announced and she could go home to delve further into the Mr Winters Sr and Jr problem.

'Left foot on a green sprout.'

'Why does Martha get to be the referee?' Someone complained.

Martha answered before anyone else could, 'Because Martha is the oldest and the ricketiest and isn't, for one blessed second, going to play this accursed so-called game.'

'It's not that bad, is it?' Emma, or possibly Gemma, asked.

Everyone looked down at the large bedsheet spread out in the emptied conservatory, the corners pinned down with an assortment of children's toys. It had been mocked up into a huge Christmas Twister. The Gem'n'Emm had clearly spent a better portion of the day sewing on the green sprouts, red reindeer noses, brown Christmas puddings and gold Christmas stars. They were now coming off, gone skew-wiff or, in the case of one gold star, being worn as a hat by a three-year-old. She looked exhausted.

Everyone told her it was wonderful.

Jess spun the dial.

'Right hand on red nose,' Martha announced.

Oh, God.

With a left food already on a gold star, this meant she was going to have to somehow manoeuvre her body between Chantal and Josh, who had been giggling away like a couple of schoolchildren as they bent and twisted round one another's limbs. Eli was standing on one mismatched sock foot on a Christmas pudding, looking so far away it was as if he'd actually teleported himself elsewhere.

Jess looked down at the free red noses. The only one available was directly by Josh's rather lovely left hand, which was disturbingly close to his Christmas-sweater-clad chest and his perfectly formed face (freckles included) . . . *sigh*.

Did she really fancy him? She was well and truly dumped now that Amanda was shacked up with her ex. It would mean crossing the parent–teacher line. She caught Drea staring at her. A pointed reminder that chasing Josh when she didn't really know if her heart was in it was one of those moves that could instantly alienate her from all of her new friends and neighbours when things inevitably went wrong.

And then, there was the weird email she'd written and deleted to Will who was, she'd possibly erroneously thought, much younger than her. Either he'd been a boy genius or he was more around her age. But there were flies in that ointment, too. He was working his socks off and trying to sort out his own emotional baggage, which involved Mr Winters, who would definitely never speak to her again if she hurt Will. And he was stranger, really. Could you fall for someone you'd never met?

Conversation swirled round her like glitter in a snow globe as Jess tried and failed to find the right place to position herself.

'C'mon already! Let's get this game over and done with.'

'Is anyone else struggling to get all of their food shopping into their refrigerator?'

'I've had to leave some things in the garage. I'm just praying it doesn't go off.'

'My deep freezer out in the shed decided to pack up last night.'

'Oh, well, now that is an actual disaster.'

'Any chance of getting a new one?'

'There's probably room for a bit of something in ours. Something small. We've bought enough food for an army!'

'Caitlyn! Leave Violet alone, please. She doesn't want your fingers in her mouth. Sorry. Too much sugar this week.'

'Just put your hand on the red nose already, Jess. It's not the Olympics.'

'There is a prize. There's a prize right, Gemma? Sorry. Emma.'

Jess looked at Josh again. He winked and said, 'C'mon. I believe in you.'

A whorl of gratitude warmed her chest.

It was nice to be believed in. It was also nice to not rely on another person's opinion to feel good about herself.

Particularly the day after she'd found out her ex had shacked up with her London bestie. Her feelings weren't reliable right now. That was the one fact she could rely on.

Pushing all of her do-I-don't-I-fancy-him thoughts to the side, Jess got on with it. She went up on tiptoe, apologising to Chantal as her sock foot slipped off the gold star and onto her sprout as she reached across Josh towards the red nose, only to bring the three of them down in a jumble of limbs and giggles. When she fell, she was nose to nose with Josh. Their eyes met and locked, that semi-uncomfortable zing of electricity whizzing up her spine. He smelt of oranges and gingerbread tonight and was close enough to find out if he tasted the same. Would a holiday snog hurt anyone?

'Right!' A familiar voice called out. 'Give us your hand, Jess. Let's get you up and out of that mess.'

Jess took Drea's hand and, though she was looking cheery as ever, Jess could see impatience creasing her features. She hoped Spencer hadn't changed his mind. That he was still coming. Drea would've told her, right? Or had she, as Spencer had intimated, crossed into territory that wasn't hers to venture into? 'Only forty-eight more hours.' Jess said with a bright smile.

'Tick tock,' Drea replied with a tap on her wrist. 'Tick tock.'

23 December

'Christ Almighty, woman!' Drea blew into Jess's hall-way with a huge gust of wintry wind. She went into the lounge, stopping so quickly Jess almost ran into her. 'I thought you said you were going to wait to open your parents' presents.'

Jess looked round the lounge at all of the open boxes. 'I thought it was time to unpack.' That, and she was buzzing with nervous energy. She was planning on paying a visit to Mr Winters later, but had wanted to formulate a game plan before she did so. The storm had given her the perfect excuse to buy some more thinking time.

'It's blowing a proper gale out there,' Drea glowered as another round of icy rain lashed against Jess's front windows. 'Unpacking, eh?' She fixed Jess with a stern look. 'Does that mean you're going to take that bloody For Sale sign down?'

Jess nodded. She was. Not today because it was revolting, and the only place she could put it was her back garden and the only way there was through the house; but it was definitely time. Mr Winters had lived here over half his life. In good times and in bad times. Mostly the latter, but his house stood for so much more than maybe even he recognised. It was a homing beacon. For his son, hopefully. But more pressingly, his grandson, who Jess was crossing absolutely everything would find the time/compassion/strength to visit his lovely grandad. She wanted her house to be the same. With her parents' house gone and the first Christmas without them looming, she realised she wasn't just untethered from her life in London, she wasn't connected to any of it. No more childhood bedroom to lock herself away in. No unicorn duvet to hide under. No more access to Mum's larder, where she could comfort eat the secret stash of iced-ring biscuits or, even better, Wagon Wheels. It was time to make her own foundation now. Her own traditions that might, in a reversal of the parent–child relationship, lure her parents to her every now and again while Jess made her imprint here on Christmas Street.

'Coffee.' Drea demanded.

'Want some hot chocolate in it as well?'

Drea pulled a face.

'It's Christmas time,' Jess sang à la Cliff Richards, adding. 'Chocolate is totally keto.'

Drea fuzzed her lips. 'What do you know about keto?'

'Next to nothing,' Jess grinned, holding up a finger. 'But the last time I read *Heat* magazine I got the impression putting a pat of butter or cocoa nibs into whatever it was you wanted to eat made it keto.'

'Yeah, that's about right.' Drea said distractedly, instantly making Jess panic that Spencer had told her about Jess's email, said he wasn't coming after all, pointing the finger of blame soundly at Jess. But Drea wouldn't be bothering with coffee if that was the case. She'd be trying to kill Jess.

Jess put the kettle on, taking discreet glances as Drea

nosed through the office supplies box and pocketed some Post-It notes shaped like baby chicks. Not really murdery behaviour. Not yet anyway. Death by paper cuts?

'Why'd you come over?' Jess eventually managed to ask, handing Drea a fifty-fifty mix of thick hot chocolate (the way Mrs Winters made it) and coffee.

Drea looked at her funny. 'Do I need a reason?'

'No,' Jess laughed, quietly relieved Drea wasn't here to blow the whistle on interfering friends.

'Good,' Drea said taking a sip of her coffee. 'That's tasty. Now. What's happening with Mr Winters?'

The doorbell went.

It was Josh. She ushered him into the kitchen after he, too, decided a mocha would take the edge off the winter weather. 'Sorry to break up your coffee morning.'

'This isn't idle girlie chit-chat, Joshua,' Drea coolly informed him. 'This is a serious meeting.' She tipped her head towards Mr Winters' end of the street. 'Jess has been doing some detective work.'

Jess tried to find a tactful way to explain that while, yes, she had made some progress on the Christmas Eve front, she hadn't strictly received the actual thumbs up.

The doorbell rang.

It was a delivery man and Martha. She was signing for a big square parcel and handing the man a shiny pound coin. 'Always nice to acknowledge a job well done at Christmas time dear, isn't it?' Martha said, handing Jess the box and letting herself in. 'You wouldn't happen to have the kettle on, would you?'

Once they were all sitting round her small table with a steaming mocha or, in Martha's case, 'a proper cup of builder's', Jess eventually deduced that the stream of

unexpected visitors were all trying to nail down exactly
what it was Mr Winters was going to do for his evening
and when.

'Why does it matter?' Jess asked.

They all looked at her, wide-eyed with disbelief.

'Uhh, doll face. Some of us have a full day ahead.
Particularly those of us with family arriving from 'Stralia?'
Drea pointed at herself then held out her seasonally manicured nails and began ticking off questions Jess needed to
answer. 'We need to know timings, whether it's indoors or
out. If he's in the right temper. And, most importantly, is
it going to be appropriately – you know . . .' she held out
her hands and gave Jess an intense stare. 'Impressive. It's
got to be impressive.'

'Why?'

'Because my son's going to be here, that's why!' Drea
leaned forward as though she was going to flick Jess on the
forehead then thought better of it when she remembered
Josh and Martha were there. 'And, *obviously*, because the
advent events bring Christmas cheer for everyone here on
the street. The pet parade was to die for, Joshua. And your
night, Martha? Class in a glass. Your voice is an absolute
ripper. Total revelation. I can't believe you aren't still out
there dazzling them on the circuit. What happened there?'

Martha nearly spat out her tea.

Jess cringed.

Josh became very interested in his mug.

Martha cleared her throat and put down her cup. 'I
think that's a story for another day.'

'We have time,' Drea said for all of them.

Josh took a quick glance at his watch then gave an *if
you're willing* nod. Jess's only plans were to put together

her bed and as she'd had a weird dream about Josh, or possibly Kit Harington, doing a Christmas-themed strip-tease last night that felt weird, so . . . yup. She had time, too.

Martha pursed her lips at them then, surprisingly, began to explain. 'Well, you all must know there was a man behind the fur coat and the boas.'

They all nodded.

'Details please, Marti.' Drea said, licking a bit of choc-olate off the rim of her mug.

Martha's lips thinned.

'You'd be helping me,' Drea almost pleaded. 'I'm going out of my head until my boy gets here. He's on the plane on his way to Singapore as we speak. I've got twenty-four more hours of distraction to find, so please, please tell us your story.'

Martha shot them all looks as if trying to ascertain their reliability then, after another sip of tea, continued. 'His name was Augustin Cuvier.'

Jess and Josh shared a look. Martha had an excellent French accent.

'He'd heard me sing in one of the clubs down there in Soho and said he liked my voice.'

Drea glanced at Martha's raindrop dappled fur coat, hanging on the back of her chair. 'I'm guessing he more than liked it, Martha. He liked everything that came with it.'

'Yes, well . . .' Martha arched an eyebrow and took a prim sip of tea, but Jess could see a slight tremor in her hands as the memories flooded back. 'He showered me with gifts. Furs. Boas. The softest leather gloves I'd ever had. Fineries I'd never dreamt of. I'd grown up round here, you see. Practical parents. Practical plans. Nothing so mad as running away to London to become a singer. In fact, I was meant to marry the greengrocer's boy. Harold.'

'But you did it anyway? Ran away to London?' Jess asked in a whisper. It was sort of what she'd done. Sought the so-called glamorous end of being a primary school-teacher for the rich and famous, only to discover that kind of life meant living by a set of rules that didn't seem to include a moral compass.

Martha nodded. 'Broke my parents' hearts, I did. By leaving. But I was young and foolish and what young woman doesn't believe a handsome man with an accent when he tells them he wants to make her a star?'

Josh started to say something, but Drea and Jess shushed him. The question had clearly been rhetorical.

'He wanted me to move to Paris with him.' Martha's features softened at the memory. 'Said that's where all of the "proper" jazz and blues singers lived. Of course, I'd only been a little girl when the true greats were there, but it didn't stop me from thinking Paris was the only destination for a singer who wanted to make it big.'

They all nodded as if they had known that, but a few shared looks made Jess realise Drea and Josh's knowledge of the jazz greats and their residency in Paris was as scant as her own.

'Anyway,' Martha briskly continued, 'like a fool, I believed him. Let myself think I was in love with him and that I would grace multiple album covers and spend the rest of my days wearing sequinned dresses and singing my heart out atop a baby grand piano.' She took another sip of tea, then stared into the cup as if hoping the rest of her story might twist up and out of it along with the steam and tell itself.

Jess wrestled to picture the sweet old lady in front of her in a sequinned dress vampishly crawling across a baby grand piano. If she squinted maybe...?

'And...' Drea eventually prompted.

'And it turned out all he wanted was a mistress,' Martha's voice had an edge to it that meant question time was over.

'Well, for what it's worth,' Jess said, 'we were all absolutely bowled over by your beautiful voice. Augustin lost himself a surefire winner.'

'He also lost himself a wife, his fortune and, if the rumour mill was to be believed, a handful of other mistresses dotted along the Mediterranean. A siren in every port, apparently.'

'And did you marry him in the end?' Josh asked. 'The greengrocer's son?'

'Yes, I did,' Martha said, surprised Josh had found his way to the next phase of her life so easily. 'Kindest, most loving man I'd ever met. We could never have children and never owned a mansion, but it turned out we were so happy together, we didn't need any of those things. The trappings. And it taught me that the love of your life doesn't have to appear with a fanfare and spotlights. Sometimes they're right under your nose, wrapped in plain brown paper, just waiting to be seen.'

Drea scraped her chair leg abrasively across the floor.

Jess involuntarily glanced at Josh, her subconscious clearly seeking that same warm glow, but, much to her surprise, she felt nothing. Friendship, sure, but, no tingles. No butterflies. He ticked so many boxes and those freckles were completely to die for, but . . . Huh. She didn't hunger to be with him the way Martha so clearly ached for those happy years she'd shared with her Harold. What a relief. No messy crush on the gorgeous widower to worry about. Jess returned her attention to Martha.

'I lost him quite a few years back now, to a heart attack, but he gave me the best years of his life, he did. Absolutely loved Christmas time.' She laughed. 'He used to make wreaths out of bunches of carrots and onions and such every Christmas. They were awful. Nothing like Kai and Rex's artworks, but they were made with love. Devoted to me he was, my Harold. Dreadful surname, but you can't have everything, now can you?'

They all shook their heads. No, you couldn't. But it was food for thought. Knowing what was important in a relationship. Fidelity or a glamorous surname. Proximity or . . . well . . . whatever the flip side of proximity was.

'Martha?' Jess asked as they all finished up their drinks. 'Why did you come over?'

'Oh, yes . . . that.' She looked distracted for a minute then said, 'I was wondering if you knew what Mr Winters was up to for Christmas Eve. Tyler mentioned wanting to have a few friends over and as the poor boy doesn't have a home of his own to go to, I thought it might be nice for him if I disappeared for a few hours and he could jam, or raid the drinks trolley or whatever it is they do.'

'Tyler doesn't have parents?'

Martha looked surprised Jess didn't know. 'He was in the foster-care system, dear. Most of his life. This is the longest he's lived anywhere. Not a surprise given the ruckus the lad makes, but . . .'

Jess smiled. There was a world of love in that pause.

'I'm sure whatever it is Mr Winters does will take up enough time for Tyler to have a party. And if it doesn't?' she hastily added – because she was pretty sure if he did anything, he wanted people in and out as quickly as possible – 'you are more than welcome to spend the evening with me. It's my family's tradition to watch *It's a Wonderful Life*, so if you care to join me...?'

Martha clasped her hands together and pressed them to her lips. 'Oh, I'd love that. Shall we make popcorn? Dreadful for the teeth, but I do love a big bowl of popcorn and a bit of Jimmy Stewart. *Thank you*, dear. I accept.'

'Pleasure.' Jess grinned, already feeling a nice buzz of excitement for a lovely Christmas Eve with Martha. It would be fun to see the classic film with someone new. She wondered how Martha felt about chocolate oranges...

'The kids and I are geared up for a movie night, too,' Josh volunteered.

'Oh?' Drea asked. 'What do you watch?'

'It's a proper film fest. We eat early because, you know, Santa. So while we're cooking it's *Frozen* – Zoe's choice. Then during dinner it's *Shrek* – Eli's call – and then after it's *Miracle on 34th Street* on the sofa. The new one. Well. Old one to the kids, but new one to old has-beens like me.'

Drea bridled. 'We're the same age, Joshua. You're hardly a has-been.'

Josh, much to Jess's surprise, flushed. 'Sorry, Yup. Wasn't thinking. Anyway!' He slapped his hands on his thighs and pushed himself up to standing. 'I better push off. Do you know if tonight's on?'

Drea stood up, too. 'I haven't heard otherwise. The

Bartleets will do something. They're always in of an evening.'

Jess shot her a questioning look.

'I see all of the cars come and go at the end of the street, don't I?'

It suddenly occurred to Jess how many Christmas Eves Drea must have spent on her own. She was not a solitary creature, Drea. No wonder she was so wound up, still fretting that her son might not be here to share it with her. She forced her own concerns into the back of her mind and asked, 'Do you and Spencer have any traditions?'

Drea's sunny expression clouded a minute and then said, 'None that would work here. Beaches aren't exactly user-friendly this time of year. No, we'll make some new ones, Spence and I. Maybe pop some fizz and catch up after...' she gave Jess one of her *this is on you* looks, '...we have all enjoyed something spectacular at Number Twenty-Four.'

Jess gulped. She'd willingly taken on the task of encouraging Mr Winters out of his shell and into the neighbourhood celebrations. Sure, Christmas Eve was important, but she knew deep down that if things went well for him tomorrow, he'd be changing his life forever. And she'd do everything in her power to ensure he was changing it for the better.

Mr Winters slid a mug of steaming hot chocolate onto the table in front of Jess. She was already wired from the two mochas she'd had at home, but refusing it wouldn't have been polite and she was pulling out all of the stops today. Not that any of them were working.

'Aye,' Mr Winters said when Jess suggested the sparklers

again. 'We could hold it outside, but I'll no doubt get the blame if the weather stays poor.'

'No one will blame you for the weather being awful.'

He tipped his head back and forth, unconvinced. 'There'd be something. There's always something.'

Before she could stop herself she blurted out, 'Not with everyone. Will doesn't blame you for what happened with your wife. That's why he brought the pies round. As a peace offering.'

The air between them froze.

Jess tried to swallow and couldn't.

She'd stepped onto the very thinnest of ice, unleashing a skein of fissures across their fragile friendship.

After the clock literally ticked a full round, Arnold asked, 'And how do you know this? He flicked his finger towards the street. 'You told him on your screen, I suppose.' He moved his mouth as if he was chewing over some words to decide whether or not they were worth spitting out and opted for silence instead.

Oh, crumbs. That bad.

'I did tell him.' Jess confessed. 'It was a mistake and I regretted it, but even though he found the news a bit full on, he's doesn't blame you.'

'He's not exactly knocking at the front door introducing himself though, is he, lass?'

'Well, no, but he's so busy with his catering company.' She stopped and started over. 'He said he waited for a bit when he dropped the pies by but—'

Mr Winters waved at her to stop talking. He didn't need to be told he was a slowpoke on top of everything else. That it was his fault, again, for things not turning out the way they were meant to.

She felt awful. The kind of awful she'd felt when Ethan's parents had told her they were withdrawing him from St Benedict's because it clearly wasn't a safe environment. The kind of awful that had burrowed deep inside her when the Head Teacher had said she thought she'd made it clear St Benedict's teachers were never, ever, to use corporal punishment; even though Jess had told her a thousand times she'd not, for one tiny second, meant to hurt Crispin, and she certainly hadn't scratched him. The wretched form of awful that had crawled under her skin when Martin had suggested she take the blame and plead with the Anand-Haights for her job back. Being at St Benny's had meant being a somebody and when you were a somebody, even a somebody wearing tar and feathers...

And then she got what Mr Winters meant. It didn't matter what she'd said or how many apologies she'd made or how many times she'd explained what really happened, people wanted someone to blame for things that had gone wrong. And the Cheese Sandwich Incident had needed a villain. Jess, somehow, had become that villain, just as Mr Winters had become the villain in his own, blameless life.

'Do you want to wallow in self-pity then?' She was shocked to hear herself ask.

'What? No. That's not—'

'Well it certainly sounds like it to me. Do you think your wife would've liked this? Watching you sit here in this big house waiting, wondering if one day your son or grandson might come to you?'

Jess didn't wait for him to answer. 'Well they're not. And they won't. Not if you accept the blame everyone's heaped upon you. You're innocent. You didn't do anything. You shouldn't sit here waiting for life to happen to you. I did that for an entire year and all it did was make me more afraid. Did you know that I've owned my house for twenty-three amazing days? Days in which I've been shown nothing but kindness, but I still haven't taken the For Sale sign down.'

He shook his head, clearly confused.

Unexpected tears began trickling down her cheeks as she continued, 'I left it up because I was afraid if I took it down and got used to the idea of being here – being happy here – that something bad might happen and I would be blamed for it and then I'd have to run away again, only this time my parents aren't here to run away to. And that's no way to solve problems, is it? I mean, look at Drea. She's finally got her son coming to see her, and that took years of sending along insanely expensive airplane tickets. And Josh. Living in the same house his wife died in. That had to be next to impossible at the beginning, but he stuck to it. And Martha. Moving back to Boughton after her dreams of becoming a professional singer had been dashed, only to live a genuinely happy life. I mean, if mistakes were reasons for running for the hills, I'll probably end up moving quite a lot, won't I? If I want to stay here, and I do, I'm going to have to learn that trusting my gut is no bad thing. And you're going to have to learn that what happened thirty-five years ago wasn't your fault. It was an awful, horrible, life-changing mistake, but you were not to blame.'

Mr Winters frowned at her, then pulled open a drawer and handed her a freshly ironed handkerchief.

'Thank you,' she sniffled. 'Sorry. I didn't mean to make this about me, or get all preachy; it's just . . . I think you're great and I would hate to think of you mouldering away here for the rest of your life being sad.'

'Mouldering, eh?' Mr Winters said.

Jess pulled an apologetic face. 'Sorry.'

'Quit with your sorries. I know what you're saying. I just . . .' He held up both of his big, capable, Clint Eastwood hands. 'Leave it with me, lass.'

Jess wiped her tears and scrunched her forehead. 'No. I feel bad now. I don't want you to feel pressured into doing something if you genuinely don't want to. I can make cookies or something. Buy some. Whatever.'

'I think you know well enough that I won't be cornered into doing anything I don't want to do.'

Jess smiled. Yeah. She was pretty sure Arnold Winters was his own man, bossy neighbours notwithstanding.

'So . . . can I tell everyone you'll do something?'

He hesitated before answering. 'Tell everyone to make their plans and live their lives, but that at six o'clock tomorrow evening, this mouldering old man will try and find enough life in him to pull something out of the bag. It won't be hours of entertainment, I can tell you that now—'

Jess couldn't help herself. She threw her arms around him and give him a huge hug. He awkwardly patted her shoulders then extracted himself, saying she'd best leave her gratitude until tomorrow. He wasn't making a promise. Nor was it a cast-in-stone commitment to dazzle the residents of Christmas Street from now until the end of time, but . . . it wasn't a no.

As Jess made her way down the street towards her house, she barely registered how miserable the weather was because life had taken a turn for the better. Not only would Mr Winters hold a wonderfully magical Christmas Eve, he'd win everyone over. Forever. Including Drea's son, who would be so thrilled by his initial impression of life here on Christmas Street, he'd chuck in his job and move here and then . . . Jess actually did a little happy dance. Will. Yes. Will would arrive in his little green van at precisely the moment the entire neighbourhood put their hands together to applaud and cheer their shared delight in the best Christmas Eve any of them had ever had. It would, in short, be perfectly perfect. Just as Christmas was meant to be.

24 December

Jess woke up half anxious, half excited. She was feeling jittery about tonight, so probably didn't need her morning cup of coffee, but there was something about spooning the hot chocolate into a mug while the kettle boiled and turning it into a thick, richly scented paste that felt therapeutic. There were other things that were good, too. It had stopped raining. A sign, hopefully, that the day would turn out well. No word from Mr Winters yet, but it was early.

There were three loud pounds on her front door. 'Jess! It's me.'

No *coooeee*! No long-lashed peepers peering through the letter box. This was very un-Drea like.

Jess opened the door and saw her friend clutching her large puffy ankle-length jacket round her. She looked frail and tear-streaked and utterly bereft of the confidence that normally glowed round her with supernatural wattage.

It was absolutely freezing. Where the rain had stopped, Jack Frost had clearly stepped in. Or his evil older brother Ichabod Icicle. Puddles had turned to miniature ice rinks. The wind felt as if it literally cut through you. Clouds hung in leaden, weighted clumps, like portents of doom waiting to unleash untold horrors upon the poor unsuspecting citizens of Whoville. Or, in this case, Boughton.

It didn't bode well.

After Jess had ushered her in, deposited her on the sofa, run upstairs to get her duvet to wrap round her, made a hot chocolate (minus the coffee), and located a box of tissues, Drea numbly began to explain why she wasn't in her house whipping up a massive pile of blueberry pancakes for her son.

'He wasn't on the plane,' Drea said, not sounding at all like Drea.

'And you couldn't have mistaken the flight?'

Drea shook her head. 'Right airline, right airport, right time, no son. Looks like he was pranking me.'

Jess frowned. 'That doesn't sound like Spencer.'

Jess clapped her hand over her mouth.

'What?' Drea flared angrily.

'I – umm . . . I might have sent him an email.'

'You what?' Her expression twisted into something derisive and cruel. 'You can't help yourself, can you? Sticking your little fingers in everyone else's pies.'

'No, that wasn't what I—'

She forced herself to stop. It had been exactly what she'd done.

'Well, you listen to me and you listen real good. You'd be better putting your energy into dealing with your own problems before you try and fix everyone else's, yeah? Because from where I'm sitting, you've got a mess of growing up to do, Jessica Green. This isn't playschool. This is real life and you went too far this time. Well out of bounds.'

A slap on the face would've hurt less.

'No, that wasn't what I—' Jess stumbled over her words trying to explain, but Drea didn't want to hear it. She wanted to punish Jess for meddling in something that wasn't her business.

'Did you talk about the women's refuges as well? Promise him I'd put my name on them? Talk about my failings, did you? Weak Drea. Pathetic Drea. Snivelling, bloody, broken Drea not strong enough to look after her son or stand up to a man, or brave enough to admit her life is a bloody shambles.'

'Your life isn't a shambles,' Jess bridled.

'Aww, Jess,' Drea shook her head, tears skidding down her cheeks so rapidly, she didn't bother to wipe them away. 'You poor, pathetic, naive girl.'

'I'm not pathetic!'

'Right.' Drea was riding her mean streak to its apex. 'That's why your house is perfect. The For Sale sign is gone and you've got cards on the mantel from all of the little kiddies you're going to be teaching next term. I bet you've not even put that bed of yours together yet. What are you waiting for? A big strong man to come and do it for you? Someone, anyone to swoop in and fix life for you because it's too hard to do it yourself like the rest of us have to?'

Jess bit down on the inside of her cheek. She was glad she and Drea weren't having an actual, physical fight. Drea would crush her.

'I think maybe we should drink our hot chocolate and regroup,' Jess began. 'You were up early. Maybe you should have a little rest or something.'

'Why? So you can run off to call your mummy and daddy and tell them the mean lady from up the street's been a right royal bitch because her heart's just been ripped from her chest?' And then Drea really began to cry.

Strong, indefatigable, resilient Drea wept with such a depth of sorrow, Jess could hardly bear it. She did want to run away. She did want to call her mum and dad. But it wasn't an option and it shouldn't be. Not for this. So she put her hurt feelings to the side and crawled onto the sofa with Drea, put her arms around her and held her until she was all cried out.

Eventually, she fell asleep. With her make-up long since washed away by tears, Jess had a glimpse of what Drea must've looked like years back before she'd built the strong, impenetrable mask of strength she wore every day like armour. It was a vulnerable beauty. Open. Honest. Drea's public aesthetic, Jess realised, was what she used to hold people at arm's length. A power she wielded to control men who might think they stood a chance. Here's what you're not getting, it said. Or, if you do, it'll be on my terms.

Jess wished Spencer could see her. Bear witness to how heartbroken his mother was. It had been cruel to get her hopes up like this, then crush them by not appearing at the airport. Her stomach churned at the thought that this could just as easily be her fault. This was no *Love Actually* full of happy, ridiculous, legs-around-the-waist hugs at the airport. It was more... Life Actually. Real life. Full of ups and downs and moments you thought you'd never survive but somehow had to find the strength to soldier through. So... a bit like *Love Actually*.

Jess resolved to put a smile back on Drea's face. No matter what it took. She'd plumb the very depths of her resilience, determined to prove to her friend she'd only ever meant to bring her joy.

Jess pulled the zip of her coat straight up to her chin. Though it was only just past lunchtime, the street had a darkness hanging about it despite most of the houses having some form of Christmas lights twinkling away in or outside. There were a handful of people, like the hippies and the Nishios, who only lit real candles, but for the most part, it was a street that had hit the garden centres hard for holiday decor. Today, however, the flashing icicle lights struck a discordant note, giving the street an end-of-a-long-dreary-day sort of feeling that made taking each carefully placed footstep along the icy pavement that much more difficult. As if to confirm the strange feeling of foreboding that had dug under Jess's coat, the street lamps flickered on, then off, then on again, unable to decide if they felt up to spilling their warm pools of light on the street below.

A car pulled onto the street and slowly made its way down. It stopped beside her, dark windows lowered to reveal Kai and Rex. 'Hey, Jess. You ready for the big day?'

They both looked tired. Not remotely as excited as they tried to sound.

She half shrugged. She'd saved going to the shop to buy her seasonal ready meal for today to see if she could pick up some festive buzz before going home to celebrate her first Christmas on her own. Maybe, now that Drea was tucked up on the sofa watching *A Bad Moms Christmas*, she would have to buy two.

'Are you two coming along tonight?' she asked.

They both looked a bit blank for a minute, then Rex threw a glance at number 24. 'You think he's going to do something?'

'We were kind of thinking we might have a quiet one,' Kai said semi-apologetically. The look on his face explained it all. They were missing their dog. Just like Drea, they were finding it difficult to celebrate when their loved one wouldn't be there. Mr Winters had endured that level of grief for thirty-five long years.

'Arnold told me he was going to do something,' she said a bit more confidently than she felt. 'I doubt it would last long. Please say you'll come.'

A weird rumbling pulled their attention to the end of the street. The gritting truck. It stopped at the end of the street. Jess waved at him. The driver tilted his head to the side then slowly pulled off.

'Did you see that?' Jess asked.

'We've been onto the council for yonks,' Rex rolled his eyes. 'It's a bloody ice rink out here.'

Kai tsked. 'What do they think? That we love skidding around on this ice? It's dangerous is what it is.'

Mr Winters and his advent-calendar offering forgotten, Kai and Rex blew her a couple of non-committal kisses, Rex making a show of finding the button to roll up the windows for Kai who was, quite clearly, shivering from the cold.

Jess tried not to take Rex and Kai's wavering as a sign that other people might follow suit, presume Arnold wouldn't do anything and not bother coming. A blanket set of no-shows would be the worst possible result, particularly considering how high Drea's expectations had been that doing the advent calendar would draw the neighbours closer together. It had. It really had. Not just for her, the newbie on the street, but for the long-term residents as well. The nightly gatherings had clearly strengthened friendships that already existed, and had also created new ones. As eclectic as they were, the residents of Christmas Street formed a sort of second family. If one person didn't have a spare cup of milk or sugar, surely another would. A desperation seized her to make this night a truly fabulous cherry atop a wondrously festive cake.

Jess opened up the picket fence, nearly losing her balance not once, but twice as she climbed Mr Winters' steps.

When she went out, she'd hunt down an industrial-sized bag of salt to pour on them. They wouldn't be adding a law suit to Mr Winters' woes. Not tonight.

Just as she was about to knock there was a distant sound of car tyres squealing, a couple of horns honking, a huge bang and then an unnatural, eerie silence.

The street lights went off.

The light that had been on in Mr Winters' front window went off.

When she turned round, there wasn't a single blinking icicle in sight.

Oh, crumbs.

'Honey?' she heard Rex call to Kai. 'The alarm thingy isn't working.'

As if she'd entered one of those slow-motion movie moments, Jess's eyes inched along the street. All of the lights that had been glittering and blinking away were now dark, their absence absorbing even more of the scant light filtering through the grey cloudscape.

Kev came out of his front door in a pair of coveralls, clocked Jess and shouted. 'Power's out.'

As if everyone had heard his call, a few more doors

347

opened. Dads shuffling out in slippers, looking up at their eaves or out to their reindeer lit with fairy lights to confirm that, yes, the power had gone out outside as well as inside and no, they were pretty sure it wasn't just a fuse.

Jess left Mr Winters' to gather more information. She'd go back in a minute to make sure he was all right, but she needed to know everything she could before she spoke with him. Mr Winters would not and could not give up on Christmas. Not at this juncture.

Kai held up his phone. 'Apparently there's been a "major incident".'

She walked on, feeling like Jimmy Stewart stumbling around Pottersville when everything was going horrifically, awfully wrong. Unseen. Unheard. Unable to help when sharp-tongued conversations broke out over whether or not a turkey would go off with the power out, or, more importantly, how they'd cook the damn thing given the fact that *someone* had failed to refill the fuel tank for the barbecue and *someone else* had refused an invitation to go to her parents even though it meant less work, no washing up and a decent bottle of wine. No, it was too late to accept the invitation now. The Whitmores and their children had flown in all the way from Canada because they *appreciated* family. Martha was outside tapping a fork against a tin of cat food calling out 'Billie! Billie! Billie!' Josh and the Nishios were having a quiet, serious-looking discussion about whether or not there were any moral implications involved in using their staff keys to 'break into' the university and use one of the residence kitchens to make their dinners.

Josh looked up to give her a quick wave and said, 'Did you get the text?'

She shook her head no.

He held out his phone. 'It's from the power company. Apparently a massive lorry took out two power lines a couple of streets over. Black ice. Power's going to be out until tomorrow, at the earliest.'

'Ah,' she said, in a weird, bright voice. 'Thanks.'

One of the Gem'n'Emms was standing in the centre of her front window, tears trickling down her cheeks.

When Jess got back to her own house, fingers numb with cold, Drea was glowering at her phone. She didn't even look up when Jess entered, just muttered something about hardly any battery power left and going back to sleep being the best option.

After checking and confirming that her own phone battery was woefully low, Jess made her way back down to Mr Winters' house. The street had become properly murky and eerily still now. With no Christmas lights or street lamps to illuminate it, the journey was doubly trepidatious as any black ice that had managed to melt was forming again. There was the smell of smoke in the air which, intellectually, Jess knew had to be cosy fires, but after that huge bang had reverberated round the neighbourhood, she couldn't help but imagine an enormous hole in the earth, with the smouldering remains of Santa's sleigh and the millions of presents he had yet to deliver.

She knocked on Arnold's door.

He quickly ushered her in saying, 'The cold, the cold, the cold.'

He was wearing his usual ensemble of a shirt and sweater vest, but with an extra addition of a button-up cardigan. When they went into the lounge she felt strangely comforted, then realised there was a big jolly fire crackling away in the wood stove keeping the room cosy and warm. He had a couple of battery-powered camping lanterns tactically placed in front of mirrors he must've carried in from other rooms, as they were balanced in unusual locations.

There was no tree, but on one of the side tables there was a tiny brass carousel circling the silhouettes of angels round and round the firelit room.

'So,' he said, opening a hand to indicate a second chair that was already drawn up to the fireplace, fringed cushion plumped, as if he had been expecting her.

'So,' she repeated, letting the chair accept her weight.

'Looks like there's a *Mrs* Scrooge out there, today.'

Jess quirked her head to the side.

'My feeble attempt at a joke,' he said. 'I was talking about Mother Nature. The ice,' he explained. 'Ice on the road made the lorry skid. I heard it on the radio. Quite a nasty accident. It's lucky there was no one hurt. It'd be a tragedy on any day, but . . .' He left the sentence dangling as there was no need to fill it in. Everything felt more potent on Christmas Eve. More visceral. As if a year's worth of expectations were heaped upon this one magical set of twenty-four hours when kindness and beauty and joy reigned.

'Do you have food in?' Jess asked. 'I'm happy to go to the shops for you if you need anything.'

'No, lass. I wouldn't ask you to go out driving. Not in weather like this.'

'I bet Kev has some salt hidden away in his garage.' She didn't have a clue if he did or didn't, but Kev seemed practical like that. Mr Nishio hadn't stopped singing his praises since he had serviced their car. 'It wouldn't be a problem. Honestly,' she said, a bit desperate now to do something, anything helpful.

'Please.' Mr Winters pressed his hands down as if trying to calm the air around her then leant forward and patted her knee. 'I'm fine as I am. I think the real question is, are you going to be all right?'

A sharp sting of emotion hit the back of Jess's throat. She wasn't sure, but that's how life worked sometimes, wasn't it? Taking the sucker punches life threw at you then getting up and carrying on. Besides, it wasn't like she could abandon Drea and curl up here in front of Mr Winters' fire with one of the lovely tartan blankets she'd spied in the corner. Nor would she.

No. She was going to get up and walk back down the street into her little house and help her friend whose Christmas she had very possibly destroyed. She would find something for them to eat and maybe, if she could convince Drea, they'd play a board game by candlelight. She was sure her Bananagrams was somewhere.

That'd be fun.

They could get a takeaway. Have a good sleep. Christmas would be a bit shit, but it might also be funny. The funny-later sort of funny, but one day she hoped tears of laughter would roll down their cheeks as they recalled this Christmas. And that was the thing about life, wasn't it? No matter what happened, you had to look forward. You had to keep on climbing.

After ensuring Mr Winters knew he could ring her at any time if he needed anything, Jess stepped out onto the street, her newfound optimism evaporating as quickly as it appeared.

It was dark. Several couples were out having quiet and not-so-quiet discussions about how on earth they were going to salvage even a smidgen of Christmas cheer. Words shot out at her like bullets. *Ruined. Disaster. Worst ever.*

The happy bonhomie everyone had shared with all of the advent events seemed to have evaporated, too. There wasn't any talk of sharing or helping or joining forces.

Jess's skin prickled more from discomfort than cold as she slipped back into her house. Maybe this wouldn't be funny later. Maybe it would be the Christmas No One Ever Mentioned. Maybe it really was the worst ever Christmas everyone on Christmas Street would ever have.

25 December

'Ho! Ho! Ho!'
Jess peered through Drea's mail flap. Nothing. Maybe she was still asleep. Or had frozen to death. It was really, really cold. Jess called out again, trying to keep her voice Christmas-morning cheery. She'd woken up, not warm and cosy exactly, but with an unexpected surge of positive determination. The type of energy burst she used to get when one of her classes, for whatever reason, was in a collective strop. She always managed to turn things around. Even if it was in the last minute of class, she had them laughing and smiling, and she was determined to do the same again today.

After a couple of more minutes Drea yanked open the door. She was wearing a quilted onesie, a knitted cap, mittens and an ultra-cosy pair of Uggs. She glared at Jess then shifted her frown into a sort of smile/smirk. Putting the blinking antlers and ridiculous jumper on had been worth it.

'Happy Christmas.'

'Happy Christmas to you, doll face,' Drea reached out and gave Jess's Rudolph nose a honk.

'Want to come over and open presents with me?'

'Not unless one is a generator and the other is my son.' Drea's chin betrayed the tiniest of quivers.

Jess gave her mittened hand a squeeze. 'Maybe we got it wrong. Maybe he just missed the flight.'

'Spencer doesn't miss flights.' Drea's tone made it clear she was the only one allowed to speculate on her son's actions and, as such, the subject was over.

After some rather epic pleading, Jess eventually convinced her to come over for Christmas lunch, only to realise, as she rustled round in the kitchen with a tiny Swiss army torch, that half a packet of vegetable crisps and a mini variety cereal pack did not a Christmas lunch make.

'How do you feel about Coco Pops and out-of-date mince-pie yoghurt?

Drea's pursed lips did the talking for her. Then, when her stomach audibly growled, she pulled her coat closer round and huffed out a vaguely conciliatory, 'Surely there's at least one restaurant open today.'

Jess stopped herself short of saying that even if there was somewhere open, they'd probably been booked out last night when the power was cut. This was a day to look at what was possible, not what wasn't.

She quickly made them mugs of chocolate milk, made a big show of giving Drea her last Wagon Wheel, took a fortifying swig then clapped her hands together. The wall clock she'd taken from her parents' kitchen – bearing a large molar and the motto 'There's Always Time To Brush Your Teeth' – drew her attention. It was just past ten.

Okay. Good. She had three hours to magic up a Christmas lunch. She could do this.

She pulled open the 'everything' drawer to see if any of

the takeaway menus she'd acquired over the past month might surprise her with Christmas hours.

Her heart jammed in her throat.

There, unopened, sat the large envelope from St Benedict's.

Jess frowned at the letter then made a decision.

She read silently for a few moments, her eyes racing over the letter at first then, more slowly a second and third time.

'What?' Drea finally demanded. 'Tell me.'

'It's . . .' Jess shook her head hardly believing it. 'It's a formal apology and an invitation to come back and teach at St Benedict's if I want to.'

Drea's frown deepened then shifted to a half smile as she lifted up her chocolate milk in a toast. 'Well done you. Has the little blighter ended up in juvey?'

Jess pulled a face. 'Sort of?'

Drea blinked her surprise. 'Seriously?'

'Military academy,' Jess explained then handed her the letter and the mini torch she didn't really need now because actual genuine sunlight was flooding into the room.

In fact, for all of the misery the heavens had unleashed on them yesterday, today seemed . . . pleasant. The calm after the storm. She pulled on some socks and practically skipped over to the window while Drea read. The sky was a sharp, bright blue and while the window was cold to the touch, the day seemed invigorating, inviting even. A day full of promise.

'Well,' Drea said when she had finished reading the letter. 'Looks like someone who actually deserved to be disciplined finally was.'

Without offering the full 'set of circumstances under which Crispin's behaviour came to light', the Head Teacher of St Benedict's Preparatory School had made it clear that, after some 'careful consideration and considerable evidence', he was compelled to acknowledge that Jessica's version of the story had, in fact, been true.

'One of his buddies must've filmed him bragging. I bet it's on YouTube,' Drea said, as if she'd spent a lifetime getting to the bottom of these types of mysteries.

Jess didn't really care. She felt light and unburdened in a way she couldn't have imagined possible. Another thread tying her to a past she no longer wanted, snipped. She was a good teacher again. A good person. She'd known somewhere in her heart that it had to be true, but having one of the most prestigious schools in the country take a spoilt child's word over hers had felt akin to a dictator announcing they'd won a 'free and fair' election.

The doorbell went.

Drea and Jess looked at one another, then, fortified by Jess's news, raced to open it.

'Two-pence pieces?' Jess repeated.

Mr Winters nodded. 'I tried to replace the mechanism with something that would accept chocolate coins, but...' He stopped himself.

'Mr Winters?' Jess asked carefully. 'Are you all right? You didn't slip and fall or anything last night, did you?'

Arnold laughed. A genuine, shoulder-shaking, see-your-tonsils type of laugh.

'No, I'm fine, duck. I wanted the whole thing to be a surprise, but with the shops closed and my reputation on the street being what it is – you know...' he shifted his weight then looked her in the eye again. 'I'm not in the habit of asking for favours—' Jess opened her mouth to say he was welcome to ask whatever favour he wanted but he shook his head, *no please, that's not what this is about*, and continued, 'The long and short of it is, I wanted to get things set up before I invited everyone over.'

'Set what up?' Drea asked

'Ah,' said Mr Winters, his blue eyes glinting with mischief. 'Now that would be telling.'

After assuring Mr Winters they'd scrabble together as many two-pence pieces as they could then meet him at his, Drea went home and Jess hastily pulled on three pairs of tights and a thick corduroy skirt done up with a centre line of colourful, mismatched buttons. She tugged on two jumpers then dove into an as-yet-unpacked box and unearthed the silliest Christmas jumper she owned, a sparkly elf body with the classic elf neckline complete with jingle bells running along a mock turtleneck. She raced over to number 1 where Drea had, surprise sur-prise, pulled on a winter ensemble more suited to Bond Street than Christmas Street, an hilarious contrast to her pleasure in showing Jess her startlingly large collection of two-pence pieces. Drea explained that, back in the day when money hadn't been quite so plentiful, Spencer used to love building up stacks of coins into little towers until there were enough towers to afford a night at the movies. Precious nights when it had been just the two of them. Popcorn, sweeties from the concessions. The lot. She'd been saving her two-pence pieces ever since she'd begun sending him airline tickets, hoping to recreate the adventure.

'Are you sure you're happy to use them?'

Drea's jaw did one of those back and forth wiggles that meant she was fighting off a surge of emotion. 'It's Christmas, doll. I've got to try and celebrate what I do have. Not what I don't.'

After a quick hug and a mascara touch-up for Drea, the pair of them practically jogged down the street towards Mr Winters, delighted to note the gritting machine had, at long last, made the turn down their little cul-de-sac.

When Jess and Drea arrived at number 24, Jess felt the breath knocked out of her.

In place of Mr Winters' reliable old Volvo was a food truck. A familiar-looking logo was painted on the side.

The Merry Victualler.

Jess's stomach did a flip.

Will. Will was here.

The window on the truck wasn't open yet but the scents wafting from it immediately made Jess's mouth water.

It was stupid to be as excited as she was, because of course she couldn't fancy someone she'd never met, not to mention the fact he was very likely younger than—

Ohhh... no, he wasn't.

A dark-haired, thirty-something man – tallish, lanky, a face wreathed in kindness and, yes, rather striking good looks Jess had seen hints of in Mr Winters – climbed out of the food truck, eyes darting between her and Drea. His eyes were the same sparkling blue that his grandfather had. He also had a ridiculously lovely set of teeth. No periodontitis in this guy.

'Jess?' He said, eyes hopping from one to the other.

Drea pushed her forward. 'This is Jess.'

'H-hello.'

Will bounded towards her and took both of her hands in his. 'I can't thank you enough.'

'Me? What? Why would you—'

Mr Winters appeared from round the corner wheeling a hand trolley. 'William? Would you mind giving your grandad a hand with – oh! Jess. Lovely. You've met my grandson, I see.'

Jess beamed at Mr Winters. Then at Will. Then, after a nudge in the back, at Drea. 'Yes. We have. Ummm – what is all this? It looks like you're . . .' She floundered for the right words.

'Well,' Mr Winters said, clapping a hand on his grandson's shoulder. 'As Old Man Winter stole the celebrations from everyone last night, my grandson and I thought we'd show him what the Winters family could do when they put their minds to it. Thought we'd bring a bit of Christmas to Christmas Street, didn't we, William?'

Jess's heart skipped a beat. There was such a depth of affection in Mr Winters' voice in that one, lovely word: grandson.

Drea covered a small sob with a cough. Jess grabbed her hand and gave it a squeeze. It would be a tough day for Drea, but they'd get through it together.

'How?' Jess gestured at the two Winters men, the house, the food truck, still not entirely able to capture her powers of speech.

'No time for that, lass. We'll work and talk at the same time if it suits you.'

After demanding use of Will's generator to charge her phone, Drea dispatched herself round the street to spread the news that Christmas dinner would be served in three hours. She also had a list of things to collect from the

359

neighbours as she did. Chantal's tables. The Gem'n'Emms' outdoor heaters. Everyone's folding chairs. The list went on.

Will, it turned out, had been up half the night prepping loads of food and roasting several turkeys, as his catering facility in Greenleigh had power; but there was still a lot to do.

Jess was sent into the food truck to peel a mountain of potatoes, humming along to the radio which was, of course, playing a non-stop stream of Christmas songs.

When Will and Arnold reappeared from round the back of the house they called for her to join them. 'Where do you think we should put this?' Arnold asked her.

Jess's jaw literally dropped.

Will was edging a mini-pallet down the drive and onto the street. Balanced on it was the most beautiful, vintage vending machine Jess had ever seen. It was cherry red. There were feathery little snowflake whorls painted round a classic 1950s-style Santa who, between his mittened hands, was holding a freshly painted sign that read 'Merry Christmas'. The machine had four windows showing a magical display of chocolate coins, miniature chocolate oranges, tiny bottles of bubbles and – she actually gasped at this one – dozens of small packets of Christmas tree-shaped sparklers. The price? Two pence.

'Was this what you were going to do last night?' Jess asked, her hands clasped one atop the other over her pounding heart.

Mr Winters nodded. 'It didn't seem right. The timing,' he said.

'But . . .' she looked round the back of the machine. No. There was no plug. No electricity. It was run on good old-fashioned clockwork mechanisms. She shook her head, trying to get everything to make sense and then, seeing Mr Winters look at Will with such a glow of pride, she realised he was right. It was all about timing, wasn't it? If she had opened that letter from St Benny's back when she'd received it, she might have accepted the job offer and headed back to London only to discover that her life had moved on without her.

Drea reappeared in full troop-commander mode, demanding menu details before she carried on having just been to the hippies' who, while delighted, wanted to know about vegan, gluten-free, sugar-free, and soy-free options. They would, it was announced, 'make an exception for turkey', seeing as it was Christmas. And they also had plenty of homemade elderflower champagne to bring if anyone was interested. Drea had already accepted that offer.

Will gave her a printed-out list as if he'd been expecting the barrage of requests.

Drea scanned it then began doling out instructions. Even though it wasn't her event to set up, Will and Mr Winters agreed with Jess that it was probably best to let her helm the 'command centre', as she'd taken to calling the large turning circle at the end of the cul-de-sac where they would set up the outdoors feast. Her way, Jess supposed, of coping with the fact that, unlike Mr Winters, she would not be spending Christmas with family.

Some three hours later, nearly everyone on the street, bundled up in new Christmas jumpers and scarves and bobbly hats, was merrily chatting away, exchanging 'war stories' of the worst Christmas Eve ever as they collectively set out Will's recyclable (applause from the hippies) plates and cutlery with a motley collection of serviettes people had brought along when it turned out Will had forgotten to bring some. They'd also brought wine and soft drinks. Anyone who had a camp stove had brought it along so hot pots of tea and a lovely cinnamon-scented apple drink could be kept warm on little tables near the food truck. Kai and Rex had run into town and handed out piles of sheepskin rugs and baskets of woollen blankets – and, Jess was thrilled to see, did it all with their brand-new puppy, Ickle Pickle. Kai was carrying him in a baby sling, explaining to anyone who would listen that it was important for the puppy to hear his heart beat for *bonding* purposes. Martha said something about trying to do that with a cat and see where it landed him, but Kai was too over the moon to take any notice. Tyler, Jess was amused to note, had pulled him aside and volunteered to dog-sit.

A few people had brought out their Christmas trees. Those who hadn't already added their wreaths to the picket fence so each family was represented.

Will had, in the course of mashing an enormous stockpot full of potatoes, asked if the wreaths were the ones Jess had put up when she'd been in a huff with his grandfather.

She nodded sheepishly, trying to hide the fact she'd been staring at his arm muscles as he turned the vat of boiled potatoes into a fluffy, buttery pile of steamy mash.

Their eyes met and cinched. A deep, lovely, flicker of heat lit up Jess's belly then chest, setting her heart off on an erratic pitter-patter that was usually reserved for cartoon characters when their hearts came bouncing out of their chests and a swirl of robins twirled round their heads. As if the intensity was too much to handle they both looked out at the wreaths then back at one another, a bit more shyly this time.

'They look nice,' Will said, scanning the wreaths lining the family home he'd never known. She watched him absorb it, trying to fill in the 'what ifs' and then, as if he'd made peace with the fact his best bet was to focus on the future, his eyes dropped to hers, then to her mouth, then back up to her eyes again. 'Very nice.'

Jess instantly turned crimson and busied herself piling a thousand chipolatas onto a platter. Her heartbeat was still erratic as, in such close quarters, their arms kept brushing, but they were mercifully busy filling tray after tray with juicy slices of turkey, piles of roast potatoes, chargrilled Brussel sprouts with (and without) bacon, roasted carrots with cardamom, pitchers of gravy and, of course, a mountain of mashed potato. 'There's never enough potato,' Will said with a cheeky grin as he daubed a mouthful onto a spoon then lifted it up to Jess's lips for her to try.

When Mr Winters rang a dinner bell he'd found and which, with Will's permission, he'd attached to the outside of the food truck, the neighbours fell upon the piles of delicious food as if they hadn't eaten for a month.

'May I have the pleasure of offering mademoiselle her Christmas dinner?' Will asked, handing her a plate laden with a bit of everything then pointing towards a pair of empty chairs not too far from the truck.

She nodded and, before she could ask where his own food was, he produced another plate then held his arm out for her to lead the way to the chairs.

They sat and ate, occasionally joining in the happy, sometimes silly, sometimes sentimental conversations swirling round them. But mostly they enjoyed forkful after forkful of delicious food, sharing grins, enjoying the different little scenes that popped up around them, and, in Jess's case, the odd hit of frisson when their hands brushed as they passed the gravy and traded toys from their Christmas crackers (Drea had made sure they got some of hers). Mr Winters was sandwiched between Martha and Tyler, who were sitting across from the Nishios. They cajoled him into explaining how he'd managed to find and fill the beautiful vending machine with the last-minute delights. Twenty-four-hour supermarkets, apparently. And a need to see if he could put some good back in the world.

Some of the children had unearthed the Christmas-themed Twister and were playing it with Audrey lying in the middle of the sheet as ballast. One of the dads had prised the Jenga set apart and had set it up on the end of one of the camping tables, shouting *whoooaaa, easy* every time someone at the other end of the table got up for second helpings.

Josh was sitting with Drea and one of the Rob'n'Bobs, the three of them involved in a lively conversation about intellectual copyrights, while Eli leant against his father reading the first pages of what must be a Christmas present. Josh, she realised, looked as though he was lit from within as he watched Drea speak. He laughed a bit more loudly at her jokes. Noticed when her wine glass wasn't full. Got up to snag the remains of the cardamom carrots for her after she'd announced a passion for them. At one point, Jess caught him reaching out to brush an invisible crumb from Drea's cheek, his fingertips lingering just long enough for Jess to realise it was Drea and Josh who had been mad for one another all along. Yes, Jess had sat next to him at cookie-decorating day, but Drea had sat across from him, keeping track of the conversation, his children, Jess. Dinner at his house hadn't been for Jess's benefit; it had been for Drea's, Jess serving as the buffer for an attraction the two of them were perhaps a bit frightened to pursue. Neither of them looked frightened now. Zoe ran up to Drea and whispered something in her ear. Drea grinned, pushed back her chair, unzipped her enormous fluffy duvet of a winter coat and pulled Zoe up onto her lap, snuggling the coat around the pair of them, Drea's chin rested on the little girl's head as her eyes happily pinged from Rob'n'Bob to Josh. Perhaps the family she'd needed had been here all along.

'You look happy,' Will said the next time their eyes met.

'I am ridiculously happy,' Jess said, realising as she spoke how much she meant it.

This was what she'd been seeking. What she'd been hoping for. Being part of a community. Part of something bigger than herself. The only thing that was missing was her parents.

She, too, had plugged her phone into Will's truck. 'I might go check on the puddings,' she said. Somehow Will divined that she needed a few minutes of alone time and thanked her, saying he was going to check in on his grandad.

She turned her phone on and grinned when a notice came up that she'd received a video message from her parents. Tanned, a tiny bit slurry and very jolly, they blew her kisses and wished her the happiest of Christmases then switched the phone round so that she could see how they'd decorated their banana tree in the absence of a pine tree. They'd taken pictures of all of their patients with their new Instamatic camera. Not their faces. Just their smiles. It was a smile-covered banana tree. She didn't realise tears were skidding down her cheeks until one landed on her phone.

'Everything all right?' Will climbed into the truck and, by way of explaining his presence, said, 'It's pudding o'clock.'

Jess swiped at her tears and gave him a watery smile. 'Just missing my parents a bit. It's our first Christmas apart.'

Will clutched a hand to his heart. 'Are you all right? Anything I can do to help?'

She gave a wobbly nod. Yes. She was all right and then, no. He couldn't make that particular ache better, but showing up and doing all of this had brought a world of happiness, not just to her, but to everyone here on Christmas Street.

'I've got an excellent cure for homesickness,' Will said, pulling a couple of mugs out of a high cupboard, then brandished a container of hot chocolate. He spooned a couple of heaping teaspoons of the dark powder into a mug then poured in a bit of milk. 'My dad always said you have to mix some milk in with the powder before adding it to the hot milk. Makes it more chocolatey.'

When he'd made the two mugs and added a splash of peppermint schnapps, they clinked mugs and, side by side, looked out onto the scene that just twenty-four hours earlier Jess would've thought utterly unimaginable.

25 December: Later

'Speech!' Someone shouted.

'Toast!' Another called.

'To Mr Winters!' A few voices cheerily called out.

Cutlery was clinked on glasses as calls grew for Mr Winters and Drea to receive a round of applause. Mr Winters batted it away, but you could see, as he lowered himself back down to his chair insisting it was more his grandson's doing than his own, that he was pleased. Drea curtsied and, with a catch in her voice, said that seeing everyone come together in the way they had made her feel that Christmas was a spirit that lived within each and every one of them and, as such, this year had been much more special than she could have ever imagined. Jess blew her a kiss, knowing Drea was covering some very real heartache. Drea blew one back, shouting out that she couldn't have pulled it off without her little elf Jessica by her side. A chorus of *awww*s and *that's sweet*s circled round, along with a fresh cry for Martha to do a reprise of her mini-concert with Tyler. Martha pursed her lips and told everyone not to be ridiculous, but Tyler was already legging it down the street to get his guitar.

When he returned, Jess noticed that the bright,

invigorating daylight was beginning to disappear, the distinct details of the street fading into the twilight.

Tyler propped himself up on the edge of a wooden picnic table someone had dragged out onto the street, pulled his acoustic guitar onto his knee and beckoned Martha to join him.

She protested but rose, pulled her fur coat closer round her neck and coyly shifted through to crowd to join him. After a moment's thought, she announced, 'I won't be doing a reprise of "Silent Night".'

There were a few *No*s and *Please*s, but she held up a finger, her body language transfigured by the performer who so clearly still lived within her. The street fell silent as she said something to Tyler about following her lead. Unaccompanied, she began to sing the opening notes of 'Have Yourself a Merry Little Christmas'. Tyler, with unerring skill, backed her up with his acoustic guitar. Families gathered in closer. Couples snuggled a bit tighter. Jess even caught Mr Winters tugging out one of his pressed hankies when emotion fleetingly got the better of him.

As Martha continued to sing, Jess noticed a man walking down the street dragging a wheelie suitcase. He looked about her age. A bit younger? Drea suddenly sat straight up, her eyes locked on the young man. Then, in an instant, she was running down the street and pulling him into her arms, saying over and over, 'My boy, my boy. My beautiful boy.' They tipped their foreheads together, explanations as to what had happened bandied back and forth in low voices.

As if by silent agreement, the reunion remained private, with only the sound of Martha's beautiful singing as accompaniment. When, at last, she drew the song to a close, Drea re-entered the crowd, hand in hand with her son.

The crowd burst into rapturous applause. Then, as if set off by the undiluted holiday cheer, the lights began to flicker to life in everyone's homes. For some reason, the street lights failed to come on, but there were enough houses bedecked in twinkly fairy lights to add a festive glow. No one raced back to their house. No one mentioned running in to catch the Queen's speech. No one, in fact, apart from Martha, who was still swaying to the music Tyler was no longer playing, was moving at all.

After a few moments of exquisite silence, the spell broke when one of the children loudly announced a need for a wee. Tyler began playing 'Rockin' Around the Christmas Tree', a queue formed at Mr Winters' vending machine and soon the street was filled with children dancing round with tree-shaped sparklers, blowing bubbles and unwrapping chocolate coins.

Drea was introducing her handsome and utterly charming son to absolutely everyone whose path she crossed, explaining that, while incredibly intelligent, the boy couldn't read an airline ticket to save his life – proud mother bragging rights clearly trumping her upset over the misread date. Above the hubbub, Jess could hear snippets of praise being lavished upon him. 'Melbourne's hottest legal eagle', 'precociously intelligent' and, more endearing, 'my darling boy'.

Kai had an orderly queue comprised of little girls and Tyler waiting to hold Ickle Pickle; and Martha, much to Jess's delight, was tucking a blanket over Mr Winters' knees as the two of them settled in for a chat with Kev and his wife beneath the glow of a heat lamp.

It was, in short, utterly magical.

Later, as the crowd began to thin, Drea appeared by Jess's side and whacked an arm round Jess's shoulders. 'Thanks, doll face.'

'For what?'

'Your email. The one you sent to Spence.'

Jess pulled a face. 'Don't thank me for that.'

'Why not? He said it tipped the balance. He'd been dithering and then when he received your email, said he thought his old mum must've changed.'

'How did he get that from my email?'

'You went to bat for me with no thought for yourself and he liked it.'

Jess scuffed her foot on the floor, a combination of really pleased and stupidly embarrassed.

'Do you think it will always be like this?' Drea drew her attention back to the crowd, now just a few clusters of families gathering up the final bits and bobs before heading home for the night.

'No,' Jess laughed. 'But whatever it'll be, it'll be better because of this.'

'You don't think everyone has secret voodoo dolls of me hidden away in their houses, do you?'

Jess shook her head. 'Not in the slightest. You are a bossy little moo, but you're utterly gorgeous.' She slipped her arm round Drea's waist and gave her a squeeze. She'd only known her a few weeks and already felt as close to her as she imagined sisters might feel after a lifetime of knowing one another's quirks and foibles but loving them all the same.

'Are you and Spencer going to stay up and plait one another's hair tonight?' Jess gave her a gentle nudge with her shoulder.

Drea gave a dry, ha-ha then softened, her eyes lighting on Josh. 'We've been invited over for a movie blitz at Josh's and as Spence is so jet-lagged, I thought it'd be a nice way to end a long day.'

'Oh?' Jess tried to look innocent. 'At Josh's?'

Drea bashed Jess with her shoulder. 'Shut up.'

'No, you shut up.' Jess grinned. 'Happy Christmas, Drea.'

'Happy Christmas, doll face.'

They hugged and parted, sharing a smile that said they both knew they would be in and out of each other's lives from here on out.

Jess made her way through the lightly thinning crowd to Mr Winters.

'All right, lass?' He was standing in front of the gate to his picket fence wearing a serene expression.

'Very well. You?'

He nodded. 'I was thinking of mentioning to William here about the spare rooms in the house.'

'Oh?' Her tummy fluttered when, as if cued by an invisible director, Will appeared in the window of his food truck, waved, then pulled the shutter down.

'Aye. He says he's more than happy living in the office above his premises, but a man needs a break from his work now and again, don't you think? He doesn't need to set up here as a permanent residence or anything, but... it'd be nice to see a bit more of the lad.'

Jess shook her head yes. She thought so, too. She also agreed that a break from everyday life was sometimes necessary to separate the Day-Glo kitschy Santas from the truly wonderful vintage Father Christmases. She'd had her eyes on the wrong prize back in her St Benedict's days. It took losing her job, her boyfriend and her sense of self to find who she really was again. Had it been one of the most difficult years of her life? Absolutely. Had it been ultimately rewarding? Very much so.

Will bounded up to them, hot chocolate container in hand. 'Either of you fancy a warming cup of chocolate?'

'If I eat one more thing I'll explode, lad,' Mr Winters said, patting him on the shoulder. 'Now, if you two'll excuse me, I'm afraid I need to take this sack of bones inside to sit by the fire for a bit.'

When he'd left, Jess realised she was twisting back and forth like a love-struck schoolgirl.

'How 'bout you? Full to the brim or a bit of room for some more?'

Jess patted her stomach and feigned a groan of despair. 'I'm so full right now. Could I take a rain check?'

As their eyes met, the energy between them escalated to something heated and life-affirming.

'Absolutely,' Will said. 'Brunch maybe?'

'That'd be great.'

'And then lunch?'

Jess giggled. 'That'd be nice, too.'

'And maybe supper after that? I make a mean espresso martini which could easily keep you up for a midnight snack. You've not lived until you've tried one of my one a.m. bacon butties.'

She laughed and flushed. So he'd felt it, too. The connection.

'That all sounds wonderful – but tonight, I've got something I need to do.'

Will lifted his chin, clearly aware she wasn't blowing him off. 'It was nice to meet you, Jessica Green.'

'It was nice to meet you, Will Winters.'

'Happy Christmas.'

She went up on tiptoe and gave him a kiss on his lightly stubbled cheek. 'Happy Christmas to you. And thank you.'

When she pulled back, his hands lightly resting on her waist, her hands on his arms, their breath meeting in tiny clouds, the air between them crackled with magnetic tingles of electricity. 'See you later then, Merry Victualler.'

'See you later, Miss Green.' He leant forward and gave her another kiss on the cheek, slower this time, more lingering, then pulled back, hopping from foot to foot, mumbling something about it being cold and the pair of them needing to make tracks before they turned into snowmen. He waved and watched as, still smiling, Jess headed down the street, turned left onto the little stone path that led to her house and before she got to the door, took down the For Sale sign. She was here now. She was home.

Acknowledgements

I would like to double up on the gratitude and thanks for the team at Orion, in particular my editor Olivia Barber who has been an absolute dreamcake to work with. Thanks are also due to my friend and long-suffering 'first draft reader' Jackie N, who is a genuine Christmas angel. Thanks as well, for reading and supporting and all round wonderfulness go to Pam Brooks, Christine Brookes, Nicolette Heaton-Harris, and Sophia Bartleet. Thanks to everyone who let me steal their names and, of course, to the Morgan family for loaning me use of the fabulous and real life Martha Snodgrass's name – a fiery woman, sadly no longer with us, but who had me as a boarder way back in the day (minus the electric guitars). Gratitude to the queen of Christmas, Debbie M who not only inspires on a regular basis, but gave me some ridiculously tasty Christmas themed chocolate (if you can get your mitts on candy cane crunch, I strongly recommend it). And thanks, of course, to my gorgeous hub-a-roo for not only proof-reading the first draft but not even questioning the "household decision" to leave up the Christmas decorations well into the year as writing commenced. You are Christmas. You are joy. xoxoxo

Credits

Annie O'Neil and Orion Fiction would like to thank everyone at Orion who worked on the publication of *Miracle on Christmas Street* in the UK.

Editorial
Olivia Barber

Copy Editor
Justine Taylor

Proof Reader
John Garth

Audio
Paul Stark
Amber Bates

Design
Rachel Lancaster
Joanna Ridley
Nick May

Editorial Management
Charlie Panayiotou
Jane Hughes
Alice Davis

Production
Ruth Sharvell

Marketing
Tanjiah Islam

Publicity
Ellen Turner

Finance
Jasdip Nandra
Afeera Ahmed
Elizabeth Beaumont
Sue Baker

Rights
Susan Howe
Krystyna Kujawinska
Jessica Purdue
Richard King
Louise Henderson

Contracts
Anne Goddard
Paul Bulos
Jake Alderson

Operations
Jo Jacobs
Sharon Willis
Lisa Pryde
Lucy Brem

Sales
Jen Wilson
Esther Waters
Victoria Laws
Rachael Hum
Ellie Kyrke-Smith
Frances Doyle
Georgina Cutler